Tales of Horror and the Supernatural

Arthur Conan Doyle

ALMA CLASSICS

ALMA CLASSICS
an imprint of

ALMA BOOKS LTD
60 High Street
Wimbledon Village
London SW19 5EE
United Kingdom
www.almaclassics.com

Represented by:
Authorised Rep Compliance Ltd
Ground Floor
71 Lower Baggot Street
Dublin, D02 P593
Ireland
www.arccompliance.com

Tales of Twilight and the Unseen first published in 1922
First published by Alma Classics in 2013

Tales of Terror and Mystery first published in 1922
First published by Alma Classics in 2014

This collection, with revised texts and additional notes, first published by Alma Classics in 2026

Cover: David Wardle

Printed in Great Britain by CPI Group (UK) Ltd, Croydon CR0 4YY

FSC
www.fsc.org
MIX
Paper | Supporting responsible forestry
FSC® C013604

ISBN: 978-1-84749-947-9

Contents

Tales of Horror and the Supernatural

TALES OF TWILIGHT AND THE UNSEEN

The Brown Hand

Everyone knows that Sir Dominick Holden, the famous Indian surgeon, made me his heir, and that his death changed me in an hour from a hard-working and impecunious medical man to a well-to-do landed proprietor. Many know also that there were at least five people between the inheritance and me, and that Sir Dominick's selection appeared to be altogether arbitrary and whimsical. I can assure them, however, that they are quite mistaken, and that, although I only knew Sir Dominick in the closing years of his life, there were nonetheless very real reasons why he should show his goodwill towards me. As a matter of fact, though I say it myself, no man ever did more for another than I did for my Indian uncle. I cannot expect the story to be believed, but it is so singular that I should feel that it was a breach of duty if I did not put it upon record – so here it is, and your belief or incredulity is your own affair.

Sir Dominick Holden, CB, KCSI,* and I don't know what besides, was the most distinguished Indian surgeon of his day. In the army originally, he afterwards settled down into civil practice in Bombay, and visited as a consultant every part of India. His name is best remembered in connection with the Oriental Hospital, which he founded and supported. The time came, however, when his iron constitution began to show signs of the long strain to which he had subjected it, and his brother practitioners (who were not, perhaps, entirely disinterested upon the point) were unanimous in recommending him to return to England. He held on so long as he could, but at last he developed nervous symptoms of a very pronounced character, and so came back, a broken man, to his native county of Wiltshire. He bought a considerable estate with an ancient manor house upon the edge of Salisbury Plain, and devoted his old age to the study of comparative pathology, which had been his learned hobby all his life, and in which he was a foremost authority.

We of the family were, as may be imagined, much excited by the news of the return of this rich and childless uncle to England. On his part, although by no means exuberant in his hospitality, he showed some sense of his duty to his relations, and each of us in turn had an invitation to visit him. From the accounts of my cousins it appeared to be a melancholy business, and it was with mixed feelings that I at last received my own summons to appear at Rodenhurst. My wife was so carefully excluded in the invitation that my first impulse was to refuse it, but the interests of the children had to be considered, and so, with her consent, I set out one October afternoon upon my visit to Wiltshire, with little thought of what that visit was to entail.

My uncle's estate was situated where the arable land of the plains begins to swell upwards into the rounded chalk hills which are characteristic of the county. As I drove from Dinton station in the waning light of that autumn day, I was impressed by the weird nature of the scenery. The few scattered cottages of the peasants were so dwarfed by the huge evidences of prehistoric life that the present appeared to be a dream and the past to be the obtrusive and masterful reality. The road wound through the valleys, formed by a succession of grassy hills, and the summit of each was cut and carved into the most elaborate fortifications, some circular, and some square, but all on a scale which has defied the winds and the rains of many centuries. Some call them Roman and some British, but their true origin and the reasons for this particular tract of country being so interlaced with entrenchments have never been finally made clear. Here and there on the long, smooth, olive-coloured slopes there rose small rounded barrows or tumuli. Beneath them lie the cremated ashes of the race which cut so deeply into the hills, but their graves tell us nothing save that a jar full of dust represents the man who once laboured under the sun.

It was through this weird country that I approached my uncle's residence of Rodenhurst, and the house was, as I found, in due keeping with its surroundings. Two broken and weather-stained pillars, each surmounted by a mutilated heraldic emblem, flanked the entrance to a neglected drive. A cold wind whistled through the elms which lined it, and the air was full of the drifting leaves. At the far end, under the gloomy arch of trees, a single yellow lamp burned steadily. In the dim half-light of the coming night I saw a long, low building stretching out two irregular wings, with deep eaves, a sloping gambrel roof, and walls which were criss-crossed with timber baulks in the fashion of the Tudors. The cheery light of a fire flickered in the broad, latticed window to the left of the low-porched door, and this, as it proved, marked the study of my uncle, for it was thither that I was led by his butler in order to make my host's acquaintance.

He was cowering over his fire, for the moist chill of an English autumn had set him shivering. His lamp was unlit, and I only saw the red glow of the embers beating upon a huge, craggy face, with a Red Indian nose and cheek, and deep furrows and seams from eye to chin, the sinister marks of hidden volcanic fires. He sprang up at my entrance with something of an old-world courtesy and welcomed me warmly to Rodenhurst. At the same time I was conscious, as the lamp was carried in, that it was a very critical pair of light-blue eyes which looked out at me from under shaggy eyebrows, like scouts beneath a bush, and that this outlandish uncle of mine was carefully reading off my character with all the ease of a practised observer and an experienced man of the world.

For my part I looked at him, and looked again, for I had never seen a man whose appearance was more fitted to hold one's attention. His figure was the framework of a giant, but he had fallen away until his coat dangled straight down in a shocking fashion from a pair of broad and bony shoulders. All his limbs were huge and yet emaciated, and I could not take my gaze from his knobby wrists and long, gnarled hands. But his eyes – those peering light-blue eyes – they were the most arrestive of any of his peculiarities. It was not their colour alone, nor was it the ambush of hair in which they lurked; but it was the expression which I read in them. For the appearance and bearing of the man were masterful, and one expected a certain corresponding arrogance in his eyes, but instead of that I read the look which tells of a spirit cowed and crushed, the furtive, expectant look of the dog whose master has taken the whip from the rack. I formed my own medical diagnosis upon one glance at those critical and yet appealing eyes. I believed that he was stricken with some mortal ailment, that he knew himself to be exposed to sudden death, and that he lived in terror of it. Such was my judgement – a false one, as the event showed; but I mention it that it may help you to realize the look which I read in his eyes.

My uncle's welcome was, as I have said, a courteous one, and in an hour or so I found myself seated between him and his wife at a comfortable dinner, with curious pungent delicacies upon the table, and a stealthy, quick-eyed oriental waiter behind his chair. The old couple had come round to that tragic imitation of the dawn of life when husband and wife, having lost or scattered all those who were their intimates, find themselves face to face and alone once more, their work done, and the end nearing fast. Those who have reached that stage in sweetness and love, who can change their winter into a gentle Indian summer, have come as victors through the ordeal of life. Lady Holden was a small, alert woman with a kindly eye, and her expression as she glanced at him was a certificate of character to her husband. And yet, though I read a mutual love in their glances, I read also mutual horror, and recognized in her face some reflection of that stealthy fear which I had detected in his. Their talk was sometimes merry and sometimes sad, but there was a forced note in their merriment and a naturalness in their sadness which told me that a heavy heart beat upon either side of me.

We were sitting over our first glass of wine, and the servants had left the room, when the conversation took a turn which produced a remarkable effect upon my host and hostess. I cannot recall what it was which started the topic of the supernatural, but it ended in my showing them that the abnormal in psychical experiences was a subject to which I had, like many neurologists, devoted a great deal of attention. I concluded by narrating my experiences when, as a member of the Psychical Research Society, I had formed one of a committee of three who spent the night in a haunted house. Our adventures were neither exciting nor convincing, but, such as it was, the story appeared to interest my auditors in a remarkable degree. They listened with an eager silence, and I caught a look of intelligence between them which I could not understand. Lady Holden immediately afterwards rose and left the room.

Sir Dominick pushed the cigar box over to me, and we smoked for some little time in silence. That huge bony hand of his was twitching as he raised it with his cheroot to his lips, and I felt that the man's nerves were vibrating like fiddle strings. My instincts told me that he was on the verge of some intimate confidence, and I feared to speak lest I should interrupt it. At last he turned towards me with a spasmodic gesture like a man who throws his last scruple to the winds.

"From the little that I have seen of you it appears to me, Dr Hardacre," said he, "that you are the very man I have wanted to meet."

"I am delighted to hear it, sir."

"Your head seems to be cool and steady. You will acquit me of any desire to flatter you, for the circumstances are too serious to permit of insincerities. You have some special knowledge upon these subjects, and you evidently view them from that philosophical standpoint which robs them of all vulgar terror. I presume that the sight of an apparition would not seriously discompose you?"

"I think not, sir."

"Would even interest you, perhaps?"

"Most intensely."

"As a psychical observer, you would probably investigate it in as impersonal a fashion as an astronomer investigates a wandering comet?"

"Precisely."

He gave a heavy sigh.

"Believe me, Dr Hardacre, there was a time when I could have spoken as you do now. My nerve was a byword in India. Even the Mutiny* never shook it for an instant. And yet you see what I am reduced to – the most timorous man, perhaps, in all this county of Wiltshire. Do not speak too bravely upon this subject, or you may find yourself subjected to as long-drawn a test as I am – a test which can only end in the madhouse or the grave."

I waited patiently until he should see fit to go further in his confidence. His preamble had, I need not say, filled me with interest and expectation.

"For some years, Dr Hardacre," he continued, "my life and that of my wife have been made miserable by a cause which is so grotesque that it borders upon the ludicrous. And yet familiarity has never made it more easy to bear – on the contrary, as time passes my nerves become more worn and shattered by the constant attrition. If you have no physical fears, Dr Hardacre, I should very much value your opinion upon this phenomenon which troubles us so."

"For what it is worth my opinion is entirely at your service. May I ask the nature of the phenomenon?"

"I think that your experiences will have a higher evidential value if you are not told in advance what you may expect to encounter. You are yourself aware of the quibbles of unconscious cerebration and subjective impressions with which a scientific sceptic may throw a doubt upon your statement. It would be as well to guard against them in advance."

"What shall I do, then?"

"I will tell you. Would you mind following me this way?" He led me out of the dining room and down a long passage until we came to a terminal door. Inside there was a large bare room fitted as a laboratory, with numerous scientific instruments and bottles. A shelf ran along one side, upon which there stood a long line of glass jars containing pathological and anatomical specimens.

"You see that I still dabble in some of my old studies," said Sir Dominick. "These jars are the remains of what was once a most excellent collection, but unfortunately I lost the greater part of them when my house was burnt down in Bombay in '92. It was a most unfortunate affair for me – in more ways than one. I had examples of many rare conditions, and my splenic collection was probably unique. These are the survivors."

I glanced over them, and saw that they really were of a very great value and rarity from a pathological point of view: bloated organs, gaping cysts, distorted bones, odious parasites – a singular exhibition of the products of India.

"There is, as you see, a small settee here," said my host. "It was far from our intention to offer a guest so meagre an accommodation, but since affairs have taken this turn, it would be a great kindness upon your part if you would consent to spend the night in this apartment. I beg that you will not hesitate to let me know if the idea should be at all repugnant to you."

"On the contrary," I said, "it is most acceptable."

"My own room is the second on the left, so that if you should feel that you are in need of company a call would always bring me to your side."

"I trust that I shall not be compelled to disturb you."

"It is unlikely that I shall be asleep. I do not sleep much. Do not hesitate to summon me."

And so with this agreement we joined Lady Holden in the drawing room and talked of lighter things.

It was no affectation upon my part to say that the prospect of my night's adventure was an agreeable one. I have no pretence to greater physical courage than my neighbours, but familiarity with a subject robs it of those vague and undefined terrors which are the most appalling to the imaginative mind. The human brain is capable of only one strong emotion at a time and, if it be filled with curiosity or scientific enthusiasm, there is no room for fear. It is true that I had my uncle's assurance that he had himself originally taken this point of view, but I reflected that the breakdown of his nervous system might be due to his forty years in India as much as to any psychical experiences which had befallen him. I at least was sound in nerve and brain, and it was with something of the pleasurable thrill of anticipation with which the sportsman takes his position beside the haunt of his game that I shut the laboratory door behind me and, partially undressing, lay down upon the rug-covered settee.

It was not an ideal atmosphere for a bedroom. The air was heavy with many chemical odours, that of methylated spirit predominating. Nor were the decorations of my chamber very sedative. The odious line of glass jars with their relics of disease and suffering stretched in front of my very eyes. There was no blind to the window, and a three-quarter moon streamed its white light into the room, tracing a silver square with filigree lattices upon the opposite wall. When I had extinguished my candle this one bright patch in the midst of the general gloom had certainly an eerie and discomposing aspect. A rigid and absolute silence reigned throughout the old house, so that the low swish of the branches in the garden came softly and smoothly to my ears. It may have been the hypnotic lullaby of this gentle susurrus, or it may have been the result of my tiring day, but after many dozings and many efforts to regain my clearness of perception, I fell at last into a deep and dreamless sleep.

I was awakened by some sound in the room, and I instantly raised myself upon my elbow on the couch. Some hours had passed, for the square patch upon the wall had slid downwards and sideways until it lay obliquely at the end of my bed. The rest of the room was in deep shadow. At first I could see nothing; presently, as my eyes became accustomed to the faint light, I was aware, with a thrill which all my scientific absorption could not entirely prevent, that something was moving slowly along the line of the wall. A gentle, shuffling sound, as of soft slippers, came to my ears, and I dimly discerned a human figure walking stealthily from the direction of the door. As it emerged into the patch of moonlight I saw very clearly what it was and how it was employed. It was a man, short and squat, dressed in some sort of dark-grey gown, which hung straight from his shoulders to his feet. The moon shone upon the side of his face, and I saw that it was chocolate-brown in colour, with a ball of black hair like a woman's at the back of his head. He walked slowly, and his eyes were cast upwards towards the line of bottles which contained those gruesome remnants of humanity. He seemed to examine each jar with attention, and then to pass on to the next. When he had come to the end of the line, immediately opposite my bed, he stopped, faced me, threw up his hands with a gesture of despair, and vanished from my sight.

I have said that he threw up his hands, but I should have said his arms, for as he assumed that attitude of despair I observed a singular peculiarity about his appearance. He had only one hand! As the sleeves drooped down from the upflung arms I saw the left plainly, but the right ended in a knobby and unsightly stump. In every other way his appearance was so natural, and I had both seen and heard him so clearly, that I could easily have believed that he was an Indian servant of Sir Dominick's who had come into my room in search of something. It was only his sudden disappearance which suggested anything more sinister to me. As it was I sprang from my couch, lit a candle and examined the whole room carefully. There were no signs of my visitor, and I was forced to conclude that there had really been something outside the normal laws of nature in his appearance. I lay awake for the remainder of the night, but nothing else occurred to disturb me.

I am an early riser, but my uncle was an even earlier one, for I found him pacing up and down the lawn at the side of the house. He ran towards me in his eagerness when he saw me come out from the door.

"Well, well!" he cried. "Did you see him?"

"An Indian with one hand?"

"Precisely."

"Yes, I saw him" – and I told him all that occurred. When I had finished, he led the way into his study.

"We have a little time before breakfast," said he. "It will suffice to give you an explanation of this extraordinary affair – so far as I can explain that which is essentially inexplicable. In the first place, when I tell you that for four years I have never passed one single night, either in Bombay, aboard ship or here in England, without my sleep being broken by this fellow, you will understand why it is that I am a wreck of my former self. His programme is always the same. He appears by my bedside, shakes me roughly by the shoulder, passes from my room into the laboratory, walks slowly along the line of my bottles, and then vanishes. For more than a thousand times he has gone through the same routine."

"What does he want?"

"He wants his hand."

"His hand?"

"Yes, it came about in this way. I was summoned to Peshawur* for a consultation some ten years ago, and while there I was asked to look at the hand of a native who was passing through with an Afghan caravan. The fellow came from some mountain tribe living away at the back of beyond somewhere on the other side of Kaffiristan.* He talked a bastard Pushtoo,* and it was all I could do to understand him. He was suffering from a soft sarcomatous swelling of one of the metacarpal joints, and I made him realize that it was only by losing his hand that he could hope to save his life. After much persuasion he consented to the operation, and he asked me, when it was over, what fee I demanded. The poor fellow was almost a beggar, so that the idea of a fee was absurd, but I answered in jest that my fee should be his hand, and that I proposed to add it to my pathological collection.

"To my surprise he demurred very much to the suggestion, and he explained that according to his religion it was an all-important matter that the body should be reunited after death, and so make a perfect dwelling for the spirit. The belief is, of course, an old one, and the mummies of the Egyptians arose from an analogous superstition. I answered him that his hand was already off, and asked him how he intended to preserve it. He replied that he would pickle it in salt and carry it about with him. I suggested that it might be safer in my keeping than his, and that I had better means than salt for preserving it. On realizing that I really intended to carefully keep it, his opposition vanished instantly. 'But remember, sahib,' said he, 'I shall want it back when I am dead.' I laughed at the remark, and so the matter ended. I returned to my practice, and he no doubt in the course of time was able to continue his journey to Afghanistan.

"Well, as I told you last night, I had a bad fire in my house at Bombay. Half of it was burnt down and, among other things, my pathological collection was largely destroyed. What you see are the poor remains of it. The hand of the hillman went with the rest, but I gave the matter no particular thought at the time. That was six years ago.

"Four years ago – two years after the fire – I was awakened one night by a furious tugging at my sleeve. I sat up under the impression that my favourite mastiff was trying to arouse me. Instead of this, I saw my Indian patient of long ago, dressed in the long grey gown which was the badge of his people. He was holding up his stump and looking reproachfully at me. He then went over to my bottles, which at that time I kept in my room, and he examined them carefully, after which he gave a gesture of anger and vanished. I realized that he had just died, and that he had come to claim my promise that I should keep his limb in safety for him.

"Well, there you have it all, Dr Hardacre. Every night at the same hour for four years this performance has been repeated. It is a simple thing in itself, but it has worn me out like water dropping on a stone. It has brought a vile insomnia with it, for I cannot sleep now for the expectation of his coming. It has poisoned my old age and that of my wife, who has been the sharer in this great trouble. But there is the breakfast gong, and she will be waiting impatiently to know how it fared with you last night. We are both much indebted to you for your gallantry, for it takes something from the weight of our misfortune when we share it, even for a single night, with a friend, and it reassures us to our sanity, which we are sometimes driven to question."

This was the curious narrative which Sir Dominick confided to me – a story which to many would have appeared to be a grotesque impossibility, but which, after my experience of the night before, and my previous knowledge of such things, I was prepared to accept as an absolute fact. I thought deeply over the matter, and brought the whole range of my reading and experience to bear upon it. After breakfast, I surprised my host and hostess by announcing that I was returning to London by the next train.

"My dear doctor," cried Sir Dominick in great distress, "you make me feel that I have been guilty of a gross breach of hospitality in intruding this unfortunate matter upon you. I should have borne my own burden."

"It is, indeed, that matter which is taking me to London," I answered, "but you are mistaken, I assure you, if you think that my experience of last night was an unpleasant one to me. On the contrary, I am about to ask your permission to return in the evening and spend one more night in your laboratory. I am very eager to see this visitor once again."

My uncle was exceedingly anxious to know what I was about to do, but my fears of raising false hopes prevented me from telling him. I was back in my own consulting room a little after luncheon, and was confirming my memory of a passage in a recent book upon occultism which had arrested my attention when I read it.

> In the case of earth-bound spirits – said my authority – some one dominant idea obsessing them at the hour of death is sufficient to hold them in this material world. They are the amphibia of this life and of the next, capable of passing from one to the other as the turtle passes from land to water. The causes which may bind a soul so strongly to a life which its body has abandoned are any violent emotion. Avarice, revenge, anxiety, love and pity have all been known to have this effect. As a rule it springs from some unfulfilled wish, and when the wish has been fulfilled the material bond relaxes. There are many cases upon record which show the singular persistence of these visitors, and also their disappearance when their wishes have been fulfilled, or in some cases when a reasonable compromise has been effected.

A reasonable compromise effected – those were the words which I had brooded over all the morning, and which I now verified in the original. No actual atonement could be made here – but a reasonable compromise! I made my way as fast as a train could take me to the Shadwell Seamen's Hospital, where my old friend Jack Hewett was house surgeon. Without explaining the situation I made him understand what it was that I wanted.

"A brown man's hand!" said he in amazement. "What in the world do you want that for?"

"Never mind. I'll tell you some day. I know that your wards are full of Indians."

"I should think so. But a hand…" He thought a little and then struck a bell.

"Travers," said he to a student dresser, "what became of the hands of the lascar which we took off yesterday? I mean the fellow from the East India Dock who got caught in the steam winch."

"They are in the post-mortem room, sir."

"Just pack one of them in antiseptics and give it to Dr Hardacre."

And so I found myself back at Rodenhurst before dinner with this curious outcome of my day in town. I still said nothing to Sir Dominick, but I slept that night in the laboratory, and I placed the lascar's hand in one of the glass jars at the end of my couch.

So interested was I in the result of my experiment that sleep was out of the question. I sat with a shaded lamp beside me and waited patiently for my visitor. This time I saw him clearly from the first. He appeared beside the door, nebulous for an instant, and then hardening into as distinct an outline as any living man. The slippers beneath his grey gown were red and heelless, which accounted for the low, shuffling sound which he made as he walked. As on the previous night he passed slowly along the line of bottles until he paused before that which contained the hand. He reached up to it, his whole figure quivering with expectation, took it down, examined it eagerly, and then, with a face which was convulsed with fury and disappointment, he hurled it down on the floor. There was a crash which resounded through the house, and when I looked up the mutilated Indian had disappeared. A moment later my door flew open and Sir Dominick rushed in.

"You are not hurt?" he cried.

"No – but deeply disappointed."

He looked in astonishment at the splinters of glass, and the brown hand lying upon the floor.

"Good God!" he cried. "What is this?"

I told him my idea and its wretched sequel. He listened intently, but shook his head.

"It was well thought of," said he, "but I fear that there is no such easy end to my sufferings. But one thing I now insist upon. It is that you shall never again upon any pretext occupy this room. My fears that something might have happened to you – when I heard that crash – have been the most acute of all the agonies which I have undergone. I will not expose myself to a repetition of it."

He allowed me, however, to spend the remainder of that night where I was, and I lay there worrying over the problem and lamenting my own failure. With the first light of morning there was the lascar's hand still lying upon the floor to remind me of my fiasco. I lay looking at it – and as I lay suddenly an idea flew like a bullet through my head and brought me quivering with excitement out of my couch. I raised the grim relic from where it had fallen. Yes, it was indeed so. The hand was the *left* hand of the lascar.

By the first train I was on my way to town, and hurried at once to the Seamen's Hospital. I remembered that both hands of the lascar had been amputated, but I was terrified lest the precious organ which I was in search of might have been already consumed in the crematory. My suspense was soon ended. It had still been preserved in the post-mortem room. And so I returned to Rodenhurst in the evening with my mission accomplished and the material for a fresh experiment.

But Sir Dominick Holden would not hear of my occupying the laboratory again. To all my entreaties he turned a deaf ear. It offended his sense of hospitality, and he could no longer permit it. I left the hand, therefore, as I had done its fellow the night before, and I occupied a comfortable bedroom in another portion of the house, some distance from the scene of my adventures.

But in spite of that my sleep was not destined to be uninterrupted. In the dead of night my host burst into my room, a lamp in his hand. His huge gaunt figure was enveloped in a loose dressing gown, and his whole appearance might certainly have seemed more formidable to a weak-nerved man than that of the Indian of the night before. But it was not his entrance so much as his expression which amazed me. He had turned suddenly younger by twenty years at the least. His eyes were shining, his features radiant, and he waved one hand in triumph over his head. I sat up astounded, staring sleepily at this extraordinary visitor. But his words soon drove the sleep from my eyes.

"We have done it! We have succeeded!" he shouted. "My dear Hardacre, how can I ever in this world repay you?"

"You don't mean to say that it is all right?"

"Indeed I do. I was sure that you would not mind being awakened to hear such blessed news."

"Mind! I should think not indeed. But is it really certain?"

"I have no doubt whatever upon the point. I owe you such a debt, my dear nephew, as I have never owed a man before, and never expected to. What can I possibly do for you that is commensurate? Providence must have sent you to my rescue. You have saved both my reason and my life, for another six months of this must have seen me either in a cell or a coffin.

And my wife – it was wearing her out before my eyes. Never could I have believed that any human being could have lifted this burden off me." He seized my hand and wrung it in his bony grip.

"It was only an experiment – a forlorn hope – but I am delighted from my heart that it has succeeded. But how do you know that it is all right? Have you seen something?"

He seated himself at the foot of my bed.

"I have seen enough," said he. "It satisfies me that I shall be troubled no more. What has passed is easily told. You know that at a certain hour this creature always comes to me. Tonight he arrived at the usual time, and aroused me with even more violence than is his custom. I can only surmise that his disappointment of last night increased the bitterness of his anger against me. He looked angrily at me, and then went on his usual round. But in a few minutes I saw him, for the first time since this persecution began, return to my chamber. He was smiling. I saw the gleam of his white teeth through the dim light. He stood facing me at the end of my bed, and three times he made the low Eastern salaam which is their solemn leave-taking. And the third time that he bowed he raised his arms over his head, and I saw his *two* hands outstretched in the air. So he vanished, and, as I believe, for ever."

So that is the curious experience which won me the affection and the gratitude of my celebrated uncle, the famous Indian surgeon. His anticipations were realized, and never again was he disturbed by the visits of the restless hillman in search of his lost member. Sir Dominick and Lady Holden spent a very happy old age, unclouded, so far as I know, by any trouble, and they finally died during the great influenza epidemic within a few weeks of each other. In his lifetime he always turned to me for advice in everything which concerned that English life of which he knew so little; and I aided him also in the purchase and development of his estates. It was no great surprise to me, therefore, that I found myself eventually promoted over the heads of five exasperated cousins, and changed in a single day from a hard-working country doctor into the head of an important Wiltshire family. I at least have reason to bless the memory of the man with the brown hand, and the day when I was fortunate enough to relieve Rodenhurst of his unwelcome presence.

The Usher of Lea House School

Mr Lumsden, the senior partner of Lumsden and Westmacott, the well-known scholastic and clerical agents, was a small, dapper man, with a sharp, abrupt manner, a critical eye and an incisive way of speaking.

"Your name, sir?" said he, sitting pen in hand with his long, red-lined folio in front of him.

"Harold Weld."

"Oxford or Cambridge?"

"Cambridge."

"Honours?"

"No, sir."

"Athlete?"

"Nothing remarkable, I am afraid."

"Not a blue?"

"Oh no."

Mr Lumsden shook his head despondently and shrugged his shoulders in a way which sent my hopes down to zero. "There is a very keen competition for masterships, Mr Weld," said he. "The vacancies are few and the applicants innumerable. A first-class athlete, oar or cricketer, or a man who has passed very high in his examinations, can usually find a vacancy – I might say always in the case of the cricketer. But the average man – if you will excuse the description, Mr Weld – has a very great difficulty, almost an insurmountable difficulty. We have already more than a hundred such names upon our lists, and if you think it worthwhile our adding yours, I dare say that in the course of some years we may possibly be able to find you some opening which…"

He paused on account of a knock at the door. It was a clerk with a note. Mr Lumsden broke the seal and read it.

"Why, Mr Weld," said he, "this is really rather an interesting coincidence. I understand you to say that Latin and English are your subjects, and that you would prefer for a time to accept a place in an elementary establishment, where you would have time for private study?"

"Quite so."

"This note contains a request from an old client of ours, Dr Phelps McCarthy, of Willow Lea House Academy, West Hampstead, that I should at once send him a young man who should be qualified to teach Latin and English to a small class of boys under fourteen years of age. His vacancy appears to be the very one which you are looking for. The terms are not munificent – sixty pounds, board, lodging and washing – but the work is not onerous, and you would have the evenings to yourself."

"That would do," I cried, with all the eagerness of the man who sees work at last after weary months of seeking.

"I don't know that it is quite fair to these gentlemen whose names have been so long upon our list," said Mr Lumsden, glancing down at his open ledger. "But the coincidence is so striking that I feel we must really give you the refusal of it."

"Then I accept it, sir, and I am much obliged to you."

"There is one small provision in Dr McCarthy's letter. He stipulates that the applicant must be a man with an imperturbably good temper."

"I am the very man," said I, with conviction.

"Well," said Mr Lumsden, with some hesitation, "I hope that your temper is really as good as you say, for I rather fancy that you may need it."

"I presume that every elementary schoolmaster does."

"Yes, sir, but it is only fair to you to warn you that there may be some especially trying circumstances in this particular situation. Dr Phelps McCarthy does not make such a condition without some very good and pressing reason."

There was a certain solemnity in his speech which struck a chill in the delight with which I had welcomed this providential vacancy.

"May I ask the nature of these circumstances?" I asked.

"We endeavour to hold the balance equally between our clients, and to be perfectly frank with all of them. If I knew of objections to you I should certainly communicate them to Dr McCarthy, and so I have no hesitation in doing as much for you. I find," he continued, glancing over the pages of his ledger, "that within the last twelve months we have supplied no fewer than seven Latin masters to Willow Lea House Academy, four of them having left so abruptly as to forfeit their month's salary, and none of them having stayed more than eight weeks."

"And the other masters? Have they stayed?"

"There is only one other residential master, and he appears to be unchanged. You can understand, Mr Weld," continued the agent, closing both the ledger and the interview, "that such rapid changes are not desirable from a master's point of view, whatever may be said for them by an agent working on commission. I have no idea why these gentlemen have resigned their situations so early. I can only give you the facts, and advise you to see Dr McCarthy at once and to form your own conclusions."

Great is the power of the man who has nothing to lose, and it was therefore with perfect serenity, but with a good deal of curiosity, that I rang early that afternoon the heavy wrought-iron bell of the Willow Lea House Academy. The building was a massive pile, square and ugly, standing in its own extensive grounds, with a broad carriage sweep curving up to it from the road. It stood high, and commanded a view on the one side of the grey roofs and bristling spires of northern London, and on the other of the well-wooded and beautiful country which fringes the great city. The door was opened by a boy in buttons, and I was shown into a well-appointed study, where the principal of the academy presently joined me.

The warnings and insinuations of the agent had prepared me to meet a choleric and overbearing person – one whose manner was an insupportable provocation to those who worked under him. Anything further from the reality cannot be imagined. He was a frail, gentle creature, clean-shaven and round-shouldered, with a bearing which was so courteous that it became almost deprecating. His bushy hair was thickly shot with grey, and his age I should imagine to verge upon sixty. His voice was low and suave, and he walked with a certain mincing delicacy of manner. His whole appearance was that of a kindly scholar, who was more at home among his books than in the practical affairs of the world.

"I am sure that we shall be very happy to have your assistance, Mr Weld," said he, after a few professional questions. "Mr Percival Manners left me yesterday, and I should be glad if you could take over his duties tomorrow."

"May I ask if that is Mr Percival Manners of Selwyn?"* I asked.

"Precisely. Did you know him?"

"Yes, he is a friend of mine."

"An excellent teacher, but a little hasty in his disposition. It was his only fault. Now, in your case, Mr Weld, is your own temper under good control? Supposing for argument's sake that I were to so far forget myself as to be rude to you or to speak roughly or to jar your feelings in any way, could you rely upon yourself to control your emotions?"

I smiled at the idea of this courteous, little, mincing creature ruffling my nerves.

"I think that I could answer for it, sir," said I.

"Quarrels are very painful to me," said he. "I wish everyone to live in harmony under my roof. I will not deny Mr Percival Manners had provocation, but I wish to find a man who can raise himself above provocation, and sacrifice his own feelings for the sake of peace and concord."

"I will do my best, sir."

"You cannot say more, Mr Weld. In that case I shall expect you tonight, if you can get your things ready so soon."

I not only succeeded in getting my things ready, but I found time to call at the Benedict Club in Piccadilly, where I knew that I should find Manners if he were still in town. There he was, sure enough, in the smoking room, and I questioned him, over a cigarette, as to his reasons for throwing up his recent situation.

"You don't tell me that you are going to Dr Phelps McCarthy's academy?" he cried, staring at me in surprise. "My dear chap, it's no use. You can't possibly remain there."

"But I saw him, and he seemed the most courtly, inoffensive fellow. I never met a man with more gentle manners."

"He! Oh, he's all right. There's no vice in him. Have you seen Theophilus St James?"

"I have never heard the name. Who is he?"

"Your colleague. The other master."

"No, I have not seen him."

"*He's* the terror. If you can stand him, you have either the spirit of a perfect Christian or else you have no spirit at all. A more perfect bounder never bounded."

"But why does McCarthy stand it?"

My friend looked at me significantly through his cigarette smoke, and shrugged his shoulders.

"You will form your own conclusions about that. Mine were formed very soon, and I never found occasion to alter them."

"It would help me very much if you would tell me them."

"When you see a man in his own house allowing his business to be ruined, his comfort destroyed and his authority defied by another man in a subordinate position, and calmly submitting to it without so much as a word of protest, what conclusion do you come to?"

"That the one has a hold over the other."

Percival Manners nodded his head.

"There you are! You've hit it first barrel. It seems to me that there's no other explanation which will cover the facts. At some period in his life the little doctor has gone astray. *Humanum est errare.** I have even done it myself. But this was something serious, and the other man got a hold of it and has never let go. That's the truth. Blackmail is at the bottom of it. But he had no hold over me, and there was no reason why *I* should stand his insolence, so I came away – and I very much expect to see you do the same."

For some time he talked over the matter, but he always came to the same conclusion – that I should not retain my new situation very long.

It was with no very pleasant feelings after this preparation that I found myself face to face with the very man of whom I had received so evil an account. Dr McCarthy introduced us to each other in his study on the evening of that same day immediately after my arrival at the school.

"This is your new colleague, Mr St James," said he, in his genial, courteous fashion. "I trust that you will mutually agree, and that I shall find nothing but good feeling and sympathy beneath this roof."

I shared the good doctor's hope, but my expectations of it were not increased by the appearance of my confrère. He was a young, bull-necked fellow about thirty years of age, dark-eyed and black-haired, with an exceedingly vigorous physique. I have never seen a more strongly built man, though he tended to run to fat in a way which showed that he was in the worst of training. His face was coarse, swollen and brutal, with a pair of small black eyes deeply sunken in his head. His heavy jowl, his projecting ears and his thick bandy legs all went to make up a personality which was as formidable as it was repellent.

"I hear you've never been out before," said he, in a rude, brusque fashion. "Well, it's a poor life: hard work and starvation pay, as you'll find out for yourself."

"But it has some compensations," said the principal. "Surely you will allow that, Mr St James?"

"Has it? I never could find them. What do you call compensations?"

"Even to be in the continual presence of youth is a privilege. It has the effect of keeping youth in one's own soul, for one reflects something of their high spirits and their keen enjoyment of life."

"Little beasts!" cried my colleague.

"Come, come, Mr St James, you are too hard upon them."

"I hate the sight of them! If I could put them and their blessed copybooks and lexicons and slates into one bonfire I'd do it tonight."

"This is Mr St James's way of talking," said the principal, smiling nervously as he glanced at me. "You must not take him too seriously. Now,

Mr Weld, you know where your room is, and no doubt you have your own little arrangements to make. The sooner you make them the sooner you will feel yourself at home."

It seemed to me that he was only too anxious to remove me at once from the influence of this extraordinary colleague, and I was glad to go, for the conversation had become embarrassing.

And so began an epoch which always seems to me as I look back to it to be the most singular in all my experience. The school was in many ways an excellent one. Dr Phelps McCarthy was an ideal principal. His methods were modern and rational. The management was all that could be desired. And yet in the middle of this well-ordered machine there intruded the incongruous and impossible Mr St James, throwing everything into confusion. His duties were to teach English and mathematics, and how he acquitted himself of them I do not know, as our classes were held in separate rooms. I can answer for it, however, that the boys feared him and loathed him, and I know that they had good reason to do so, for frequently my own teaching was interrupted by his bellowings of anger, and even by the sound of his blows. Dr McCarthy spent most of his time in his class, but it was, I suspect, to watch over the master rather than the boys, and to try to moderate his ferocious temper when it threatened to become dangerous.

It was in his bearing to the headmaster, however, that my colleague's conduct was most outrageous. The first conversation which I have recorded proved to be typical of their intercourse. He domineered over him openly and brutally. I have heard him contradict him roughly before the whole school. At no time would he show him any mark of respect, and my temper often rose within me when I saw the quiet acquiescence of the old doctor, and his patient tolerance of this monstrous treatment. And yet the sight of it surrounded the principal also with a certain vague horror in my mind, for supposing my friend's theory to be correct – and I could devise no better one – how black must have been the story which could be held over his head by this man and, by fear of its publicity, force him to undergo such humiliations. This quiet, gentle doctor might be a profound hypocrite, a criminal, a forger possibly, or a poisoner. Only such a secret as this could account for the complete power which the young man held over him. Why else should he admit so hateful a presence into his house and so harmful an influence into his school? Why should he submit to degradations which could not be witnessed, far less endured, without indignation?

And yet, if it were so, I was forced to confess that my principal carried it off with extraordinary duplicity. Never by word or sign did he show that the young man's presence was distasteful to him. I have seen him look pained, it is true, after some peculiarly outrageous exhibition, but he gave me the impression that it was always on account of the scholars or of me, never on account of himself. He spoke to and of St James in an indulgent fashion, smiling gently at what made my blood boil within me. In his way of looking at him and addressing him, one could see no trace of resentment, but rather a sort of timid and deprecating goodwill. His company he certainly courted, and they spent many hours together in the study and the garden.

As to my own relations with Theophilus St James, I made up my mind from the beginning that I should keep my temper with him, and to that resolution I steadfastly adhered. If Dr McCarthy chose to permit this disrespect, and to condone these outrages, it was his affair and not mine. It was evident that his one wish was that there should be peace between us, and I felt that I could help him best by respecting this desire. My easiest way to do so was to avoid my colleague, and this I did to the best of my ability. When we were thrown together I was quiet, polite and reserved. He, on his part, showed me no ill will, but met me rather with a coarse joviality and a rough familiarity which he meant to be ingratiating. He was insistent in his attempts to get me into his room at night, for the purpose of playing euchre* and of drinking.

"Old McCarthy doesn't mind," said he. "Don't you be afraid of him. We'll do what we like, and I'll answer for it that he won't object." Once only I went, and when I left, after a dull and gross evening, my host was stretched dead drunk upon the sofa. After that I gave the excuse of a course of study, and spent my spare hours alone in my own room.

One point upon which I was anxious to gain information was as to how long these proceedings had been going on. When did St James assert his hold over Dr McCarthy? From neither of them could I learn how long my colleague had been in his present situation. One or two leading questions upon my part were eluded or ignored in a manner so marked that it was easy to see that they were both of them as eager to conceal the point as I was to know it. But at last one evening I had the chance of a chat with Mrs Carter, the matron – for the doctor was a widower – and from her I got the information which I wanted. It needed no questioning to get at her knowledge, for she was so full of indignation that she shook with passion as she spoke of it, and raised her hands into the air in the earnestness of her denunciation, as she described the grievances which she had against my colleague.

"It was three years ago, Mr Weld, that he first darkened this doorstep," she cried. "Three bitter years they have been to me. The school had fifty boys then. Now it has twenty-two. That's what he has done for us in three years. In another three there won't be one. And the doctor, that angel of patience, you see how he treats him, though he is not fit to lace his boots for him. If it wasn't for the doctor, you may be sure that I wouldn't stay an hour under the same roof with such a man, and so I told him to his own face, Mr Weld. If the doctor would only pack him about his business – but I know that I am saying more than I should!" She stopped herself with an effort, and spoke no more upon the subject. She had remembered that I was almost a stranger in the school, and she feared that she had been indiscreet.

There were one or two very singular points about my colleague. The chief one was that he rarely took any exercise. There was a playing field within the college grounds, and that was his farthest point. If the boys went out, it was I or Dr McCarthy who accompanied them. St James gave as a reason for this that he had injured his knee some years before and that walking was painful to him. For my own part I put it down to pure laziness upon his part, for he was of an obese, heavy temperament. Twice, however, I saw him from my window stealing out of the grounds late at night, and the second time I watched him return in the grey of the morning and slink in through an open window. These furtive excursions were never alluded to, but they exposed the hollowness of his story about his knee, and they increased the dislike and distrust which I had of the man. His nature seemed to be vicious to the core.

Another point, small but suggestive, was that he hardly ever during the months that I was at Willow Lea House received any letters, and on those few occasions they were obviously tradesmen's bills. I am an early riser, and used every morning to pick my own correspondence out of the bundle upon the hall table. I could judge therefore how few were ever there for Mr Theophilus St James. There seemed to me to be something peculiarly ominous in this. What sort of a man could he be who during thirty years of life had never made a single friend, high or low, who cared to continue to keep in touch with him? And yet the sinister fact remained that the headmaster not only tolerated, but was even intimate with him. More than once on entering a room I had found them talking confidentially together, and they would walk arm in arm in deep conversation up and down the garden paths. So curious did I become to know what the tie was which bound them, that I found it gradually push out my other interests and become the main purpose of my life. In school and out of school, at meals and at play, I was perpetually engaged in watching Dr Phelps McCarthy and Mr Theophilus St James, and in endeavouring to solve the mystery which surrounded them.

But, unfortunately, my curiosity was a little too open. I had not the art to conceal the suspicions which I felt about the relations which existed between these two men and the nature of the hold which the one appeared to have over the other. It may have been my manner of watching them, it may have been some indiscreet question, but it is certain that I showed too clearly what I felt. One night I was conscious that the eyes of Theophilus St James were fixed upon me in a surly and menacing stare. I had a foreboding of evil, and I was not surprised when Dr McCarthy called me next morning into his study.

"I am very sorry, Mr Weld," said he, "but I am afraid that I shall be compelled to dispense with your services."

"Perhaps you would give me some reason for dismissing me," I answered, for I was conscious of having done my duties to the best of my power, and knew well that only one reason could be given.

"I have no fault to find with you," said he, and the colour came to his cheeks.

"You send me away at the suggestion of my colleague."

His eyes turned away from mine.

"We will not discuss the question, Mr Weld. It is impossible for me to discuss it. In justice to you, I will give you the strongest recommendation for your next situation. I can say no more. I hope that you will continue your duties here until you have found a place elsewhere."

My whole soul rose against the injustice of it, and yet I had no appeal and no redress. I could only bow and leave the room, with a bitter sense of ill usage at my heart.

My first instinct was to pack my boxes and leave the house. But the headmaster had given me permission to remain until I had found another situation. I was sure that St James desired me to go, and that was a strong reason why I should stay. If my presence annoyed him, I should give him as much of it as I could. I had begun to hate him and to long to have my revenge upon him. If he had a hold over our principal, might not I in turn obtain one over him? It was a sign of weakness that he should be so afraid of my curiosity. He would not resent it so much if he had not something to fear from it. I entered my name once more upon the books of the agents, but meanwhile I continued to fulfil my duties at Willow Lea

House, and so it came about that I was present at the denouement of this singular situation.

During that week – for it was only a week before the crisis came – I was in the habit of going down each evening, after the work of the day was done, to enquire about my new arrangements. One night, it was a cold and windy evening in March, I had just stepped out from the hall door when a strange sight met my eyes. A man was crouching before one of the windows of the house. His knees were bent and his eyes were fixed upon the small line of light between the curtain and the sash. The window threw a square of brightness in front of it, and in the middle of this the dark shadow of this ominous visitor showed clear and hard. It was but for an instant that I saw him, for he glanced up and was off in a moment through the shrubbery. I could hear the patter of his feet as he ran down the road, until it died away in the distance.

It was evidently my duty to turn back and to tell Dr McCarthy what I had seen. I found him in his study. I had expected him to be disturbed at such an incident, but I was not prepared for the state of panic into which he fell. He leant back in his chair, white and gasping, like one who has received a mortal blow.

"Which window, Mr Weld?" he asked, wiping his forehead. "Which window was it?"

"The next to the dining room – Mr St James's window."

"Dear me! Dear me! This is, indeed, unfortunate! A man looking through Mr St James's window!" He wrung his hands like a man who is at his wits' end what to do.

"I shall be passing the police station, sir. Would you wish me to mention the matter?"

"No, no," he cried, suddenly, mastering his extreme agitation. "I have no doubt that it was some poor tramp who intended to beg. I attach no importance to the incident – none at all. Don't let me detain you, Mr Weld, if you wish to go out."

I left him sitting in his study with reassuring words upon his lips, but with horror upon his face. My heart was heavy for my little employer as I started off once more for town. As I looked back from the gate at the square of light which marked the window of my colleague, I suddenly saw the black outline of Dr McCarthy's figure passing against the lamp. He had hastened from his study then to tell St James what he had heard. What was the meaning of it all, this atmosphere of mystery, this inexplicable terror, these confidences between two such dissimilar men? I thought and thought as I walked, but do what I would I could not hit upon any adequate conclusion. I little knew how near I was to the solution of the problem.

It was very late – nearly twelve o'clock – when I returned, and the lights were all out save one in the doctor's study. The black, gloomy house loomed before me as I walked up the drive, its sombre bulk broken only by the one glimmering point of brightness. I let myself in with my latchkey, and was about to enter my own room when my attention was arrested by a short, sharp cry like that of a man in pain. I stood and listened, my hand upon the handle of my door.

All was silent in the house save for a distant murmur of voices which came, I knew, from the doctor's room. I stole quietly down the corridor in that direction. The sound resolved itself now into two voices, the rough bullying tones of St James and the lower tone of the doctor, the one apparently insisting and the other arguing and pleading. Four thin lines of light in the blackness showed me the door of the doctor's room, and step by step I drew nearer to it in the darkness. St James's voice within rose louder and louder, and his words now came plainly to my ear.

"I'll have every pound of it. If you won't give it me I'll take it. Do you hear?"

Dr McCarthy's reply was inaudible, but the angry voice broke in again.

"Leave you destitute! I leave you this little gold mine of a school, and that's enough for one old man, is it not? How am I to set up in Australia without money? Answer me that!"

Again the doctor said something in a soothing voice, but his answer only roused his companion to a higher pitch of fury.

"Done for me! What have you ever done for me except what you couldn't help doing? It was for your good name, not for my safety, that you cared. But enough cackle! I must get on my way before morning. Will you open your safe or will you not?"

"Oh, James, how can you use me so?" cried a wailing voice, and then there came a sudden little scream of pain. At the sound of that helpless appeal from brutal violence I lost for once that temper upon which I had prided myself. Every bit of manhood in me cried out against any further neutrality. With my walking cane in my hand I rushed into the study. As I did so I was conscious that the hall doorbell was violently ringing.

"You villain!" I cried. "Let him go!"

The two men were standing in front of a small safe, which stood against one wall of the doctor's room. St James held the old man by the wrist, and he had twisted his arm round in order to force him to produce the key.

My little headmaster, white but resolute, was struggling furiously in the grip of the burly athlete. The bully glared over his shoulder at me with a mixture of fury and terror upon his brutal features. Then, realizing that I was alone, he dropped his victim and made for me with a horrible curse.

"You infernal spy!" he cried. "I'll do for you anyhow before I leave."

I am not a very strong man, and I realized that I was helpless if once at close quarters. Twice I cut at him with my stick, but he rushed in at me with a murderous growl, and seized me by the throat with both his muscular hands. I fell backwards and he on the top of me, with a grip which was squeezing the life from me. I was conscious of his malignant yellow-tinged eyes within a few inches of my own, and then, with a beating of pulses in my head and a singing in my ears, my senses slipped away from me. But even in that supreme moment I was aware that the doorbell was still violently ringing.

When I came to myself, I was lying upon the sofa in Dr McCarthy's study, and the doctor himself was seated beside me. He appeared to be watching me intently and anxiously, for as I opened my eyes and looked about me he gave a great cry of relief. "Thank God!" he cried. "Thank God!"

"Where is he?" I asked, looking round the room. As I did so, I became aware that the furniture was scattered in every direction, and that there were traces of an even more violent struggle than that in which I had been engaged.

The doctor sank his face between his hands.

"They have him," he groaned. "After these years of trial they have him again. But how thankful I am that he has not for a second time stained his hands in blood."

As the doctor spoke I became aware that a man in the braided jacket of an inspector of police was standing in the doorway.

"Yes, sir," he remarked, "you have had a pretty narrow escape. If we had not got in when we did, you would not be here to tell the tale. I don't know that I ever saw anyone much nearer to the undertaker."

I sat up with my hands to my throbbing head.

"Dr McCarthy," said I, "this is all a mystery to me. I should be glad if you could explain to me who this man is, and why you have tolerated him so long in your house."

"I owe you an explanation, Mr Weld – and the more so since you have, in so chivalrous a fashion, almost sacrificed your life in my defence. There is no reason now for secrecy. In a word, Mr Weld, this unhappy man's real name is James McCarthy, and he is my only son."

"Your son?"

"Alas, yes. What sin have I ever committed that I should have such a punishment? He has made my whole life a misery from the first years of his boyhood. Violent, headstrong, selfish, unprincipled, he has always been the same. At eighteen he was a criminal. At twenty, in a paroxysm of passion, he took the life of a boon companion and was tried for murder. He only just escaped the gallows, and he was condemned to penal servitude. Three years ago he succeeded in escaping, and managed, in face of a thousand obstacles, to reach my house in London. My wife's heart had been broken by his condemnation, and as he had succeeded in getting a suit of ordinary clothes, there was no one here to recognize him. For months he lay concealed in the attics until the first search of the police should be over. Then I gave him employment here, as you have seen, though by his rough and overbearing manners he made my own life miserable, and that of his fellow masters unbearable. You have been with us for four months, Mr Weld, but no other master endured him so long. I apologize now for all you have had to submit to, but I ask you what else could I do? For his dead mother's sake I could not let harm come to him as long as it was in my power to fend it off. Only under my roof could he find a refuge – the only spot in all the world – and how could I keep him here without its exciting remark unless I gave him some occupation? I made him English master therefore, and in that capacity I have protected him here for three years. You have no doubt observed that he never during the daytime went beyond the college grounds. You now understand the reason. But when tonight you came to me with your report of a man who was looking through his window, I understood that his retreat was at last discovered. I besought him to fly at once, but he had been drinking, the unhappy fellow, and my words fell upon deaf ears. When at last he made up his mind to go he wished to take from me in his flight every shilling which I possessed. It was your entrance which saved me from him, while the police in turn arrived only just in time to rescue you. I have made myself amenable to the law by harbouring an escaped prisoner, and remain here in the custody of the inspector, but a prison has no terrors for me after what I have endured in this house during the last three years."

"It seems to me, doctor," said the inspector, "that, if you have broken the law, you have had quite enough punishment already."

"God knows I have!" cried Dr McCarthy, and sank his haggard face upon his hands.

B. 24

I told my story when I was taken, and no one would listen to me. Then I told it again at the trial – the whole thing absolutely as it happened, without so much as a word added. I set it all out truly, so help me God, all that Lady Mannering said and did, and then all that I had said and done, just as it occurred. And what did I get for it? "The prisoner put forward a rambling and inconsequential statement, incredible in its details, and unsupported by any shred of corroborative evidence." That was what one of the London papers said, and others let it pass as if I had made no defence at all. And yet, with my own eyes I saw Lord Mannering murdered, and I am as guiltless of it as any man on the jury that tried me.

Now, sir, you are there to receive the petitions of prisoners. It all lies with you. All I ask is that you read it – just read it – and then that you make an enquiry or two about the private character of this "lady" Mannering, if she still keeps the name that she had three years ago, when to my sorrow and ruin I came to meet her. You could use a private-inquiry agent or a good lawyer, and you would soon learn enough to show you that my story is the true one. Think of the glory it would be to you to have all the papers saying that there would have been a shocking miscarriage of justice if it had not been for your perseverance and intelligence! That must be your reward, since I am a poor man and can offer you nothing. But if you don't do it, may you never lie easy in your bed again! May no night pass that you are not haunted by the thought of the man who rots in jail because you have not done the duty which you are paid to do! But you will do it, sir, I know. Just make one or two enquiries, and you will soon find which way the wind blows. Remember, also, that the only person who profited by the crime was herself, since it changed her from an unhappy wife to a rich young widow. There's the end of the string in your hand, and you only have to follow it up and see where it leads to.

Mind you, sir, I make no complaint as far as the burglary goes. I don't whine about what I have deserved, and so far I have had no more than I have deserved. Burglary it was, right enough, and my three years have gone to pay for it. It was shown at the trial that I had had a hand in the

Merton Cross business, and did a year for that, so my story had the less attention on that account. A man with a previous conviction never gets a really fair trial. I own to the burglary, but when it comes to the murder which brought me a lifer – any judge but Sir James might have given me the gallows – then I tell you that I had nothing to do with it, and that I am an innocent man. And now I'll take that night, the 13th of September 1894, and I'll give you just exactly what occurred, and may God's hand strike me down if I go one inch over the truth.

I had been at Bristol in the summer looking for work, and then I had a notion that I might get something at Portsmouth, for I was trained as a skilled mechanic, so I came tramping my way across the south of England, and doing odd jobs as I went. I was trying all I knew to keep off the cross, for I had done a year in Exeter jail, and I had had enough of visiting Queen Victoria. But it's cruel hard to get work when once the black mark is against your name, and it was all I could do to keep soul and body together. At last, after ten days of wood-cutting and stone-breaking on starvation pay, I found myself near Salisbury with a couple of shillings in my pocket, and my boots and my patience clean wore out. There's an alehouse called the Willing Mind, which stands on the road between Blandford and Salisbury, and it was there that night I engaged a bed. I was sitting alone in the taproom just about closing time, when the innkeeper – Allen his name was – came beside me and began yarning about the neighbours. He was a man that liked to talk and to have someone to listen to his talk, so I sat there smoking and drinking a mug of ale which he had stood me; and I took no great interest in what he said until he began to talk (as the Devil would have it) about the riches of Mannering Hall.

"Meaning the large house on the right before I came to the village?" said I. "The one that stands in its own park?"

"Exactly," said he – and I am giving all our talk so that you may know that I am telling you the truth and hiding nothing. "The long white house with the pillars," said he. "At the side of the Blandford Road."

Now I had looked at it as I passed, and it had crossed my mind, as such thoughts will, that it was a very easy house to get into with that great row of grand windows and glass doors. I had put the thought away from me, and now here was this landlord bringing it back with his talk about the riches within. I said nothing, but I listened, and as luck would have it, he would always come back to this one subject.

"He was a miser young, so you can think what he is now in his age," said he. "Well, he's had some good out of his money."

"What good can he have had if he does not spend it?" said I.

"Well, it bought him the prettiest wife in England, and that was some good that he got out of it. She thought she would have the spending of it, but she knows the difference now."

"Who was she then?" I asked, just for the sake of something to say.

"She was nobody at all until the old lord made her his lady," said he. "She came from up London way, and some said that she had been on the stage there, but nobody knew. The old lord was away for a year, and when he came home he brought a young wife back with him, and there she has been ever since. Stephens, the butler, did tell me once that she was the light of the house when fust she came, but what with her husband's mean and aggravatin' way, and what with her loneliness – for he hates to see a visitor within his doors; and what with his bitter words – for he has a tongue like a hornet's sting, her life all went out of her, and she became a white, silent creature, moping about the country lanes. Some say that she loved another man, and that it was just the riches of the old lord which tempted her to be false to her lover, and that now she is eating her heart out because she has lost the one without being any nearer to the other, for she might be the poorest woman in the parish for all the money that she has the handling of."

Well, sir, you can imagine that it did not interest me very much to hear about the quarrels between a lord and a lady. What did it matter to me if she hated the sound of his voice, or if he put every indignity upon her in the hope of breaking her spirit, and spoke to her as he would never have dared to speak to one of his servants? The landlord told me of these things, and of many more like them, but they passed out of my mind, for they were no concern of mine. But what I did want to hear was the form in which Lord Mannering kept his riches. Title deeds and stock certificates are but paper, and more danger than profit to the man who takes them. But metal and stones are worth a risk. And then, as if he were answering my very thoughts, the landlord told me of Lord Mannering's great collection of gold medals, that it was the most valuable in the world, and that it was reckoned that if they were put into a sack the strongest man in the parish would not be able to raise them. Then his wife called him, and he and I went to our beds.

I am not arguing to make out a case for myself, but I beg you, sir, to bear all the facts in your mind, and to ask yourself whether a man could be more sorely tempted than I was. I make bold to say that there are few who could have held out against it. There I lay on my bed that night, a desperate man without hope or work, and with my last shilling in my pocket. I had tried to be honest, and honest folk had turned their backs upon me. They taunted me for theft, and yet they pushed me towards it. I was caught in the stream and could not get out. And then it was such a chance: the great house all lined with windows, the golden medals which could so easily be melted down. It was like putting a loaf before a starving man and expecting him not to eat it. I fought against it for a time, but it was no use. At last I sat up on the side of my bed, and I swore that that night I should either be a rich man and able to give up crime for ever, or that the irons should be on my wrists once more. Then I slipped on my clothes and, having put a shilling on the table – for the landlord had treated me well, and I did not wish to cheat him – I passed out through the window into the garden of the inn.

There was a high wall round this garden, and I had a job to get over it, but once on the other side it was all plain sailing. I did not meet a soul upon the road, and the iron gate of the avenue was open. No one was moving at the lodge. The moon was shining, and I could see the great house glimmering white through an archway of trees. I walked up it for a quarter of a mile or so, until I was at the edge of the drive, where it ended in a broad, gravelled space before the main door. There I stood in the shadow and looked at the long building, with a full moon shining in every window and silvering the high stone front. I crouched there for some time, and I wondered where I should find the easiest entrance. The corner window of the side seemed to be the one which was least overlooked, and a screen of ivy hung heavily over it. My best chance was evidently there. I worked my way under the trees to the back of the house, and then crept along in the black shadow of the building. A dog barked and rattled his chain, but I stood waiting until he was quiet, and then I stole on once more until I came to the window which I had chosen.

It is astonishing how careless they are in the country, in places far removed from large towns, where the thought of burglars never enters their heads. I call it setting temptation in a poor man's way when he puts his hand, meaning no harm, upon a door, and finds it swing open before him. In this case it was not so bad as that, but the window was merely fastened with the ordinary catch, which I opened with a push from the blade of my knife. I pulled up the window as quickly as possible, then I thrust the knife through the slit in the shutter and prised it open. They were folding shutters, and I shoved them before me and walked into the room.

"Good evening, sir! You are very welcome!" said a voice.

I've had some starts in my life, but never one to come up to that one. There, in the opening of the shutters, within reach of my arm, was standing a woman with a small coil of wax taper burning in her hand. She was tall and straight and slender, with a beautiful white face that might have been cut out of clear marble, but her hair and eyes were as black as night. She was dressed in some sort of white dressing gown which flowed down to her feet, and what with this robe and what with her face, it seemed as if a spirit from above was standing in front of me. My knees knocked together, and I held on to the shutter with one hand to give me support. I should have turned and run away if I had had the strength, but I could only just stand and stare at her.

She soon brought me back to myself once more.

"Don't be frightened!" said she, and they were strange words for the mistress of a house to have to use to a burglar. "I saw you out of my bedroom window when you were hiding under those trees, so I slipped downstairs, and then I heard you at the window. I should have opened it for you if you had waited, but you managed it yourself just as I came up."

I still held in my hand the long clasp knife with which I had opened the shutter. I was unshaven and grimed from a week on the roads. Altogether, there are few people who would have cared to face me alone at one in the morning; but this woman, if I had been her lover meeting her by appointment, could not have looked upon me with a more welcoming eye. She laid her hand upon my sleeve and drew me into the room.

"What's the meaning of this, ma'am? Don't get trying any little games upon me," said I, in my roughest way – and I can put it on rough when I like. "It'll be the worse for you if you play me any trick," I added, showing her my knife.

"I will play you no trick," said she. "On the contrary, I am your friend, and I wish to help you."

"Excuse me, ma'am, but I find it hard to believe that," said I. "Why should you wish to help me?"

"I have my own reasons," said she; and then suddenly, with those black eyes blazing out of her white face: "It's because I hate him, hate him, hate him! Now you understand."

I remembered what the landlord had told me, and I did understand. I looked at Her Ladyship's face, and I knew that I could trust her. She wanted to revenge herself upon her husband. She wanted to hit him where it would hurt him most – upon the pocket. She hated him so that she would even lower her pride to take such a man as me into her confidence if she could gain her end by doing so. I've hated some folk in my time, but I don't think I ever understood what hate was until I saw that woman's face in the light of the taper.

"You'll trust me now?" said she, with another coaxing touch upon my sleeve.

"Yes, Your Ladyship."

"You know me, then?"

"I can guess who you are."

"I dare say my wrongs are the talk of the county. But what does he care for that? He only cares for one thing in the whole world, and that you can take from him this night. Have you a bag?"

"No, Your Ladyship."

"Shut the shutter behind you. Then no one can see the light. You are quite safe. The servants all sleep in the other wing. I can show you where all the most valuable things are. You cannot carry them all, so we must pick the best."

The room in which I found myself was long and low, with many rugs and skins scattered about on a polished wood floor. Small cases stood here and there, and the walls were decorated with spears and swords and paddles, and other things which find their way into museums. There were some queer clothes, too, which had been brought from savage countries, and the lady took down a large leather sack bag from among them.

"This sleeping sack will do," said she. "Now come with me and I will show you where the medals are."

It was like a dream to me to think that this tall, white woman was the lady of the house, and that she was lending me a hand to rob her own home. I could have burst out laughing at the thought of it, and yet there was something in that pale face of hers which stopped my laughter and turned me cold and serious. She swept on in front of me like a spirit, with the green taper in her hand, and I walked behind with my sack until we came to a door at the end of this museum. It was locked, but the key was in it, and she led me through.

The room beyond was a small one, hung all round with curtains which had pictures on them. It was the hunting of a deer that was painted on it, as I remember, and in the flicker of that light you'd have sworn that the dogs and the horses were streaming round the walls. The only other thing in the room was a row of cases made of walnut, with brass ornaments. They had glass tops, and beneath this glass I saw the long lines of those gold medals, some of them as big as a plate and half an inch thick, all resting upon red velvet and glowing and gleaming in the darkness. My fingers were just itching to be at them, and I slipped my knife under the lock of one of the cases to wrench it open.

"Wait a moment," said she, laying her hand upon my arm. "You might do better than this."

"I am very well satisfied, ma'am," said I, "and much obliged to Your Ladyship for kind assistance."

"You can do better," she repeated. "Would not golden sovereigns be worth more to you than these things?"

"Why, yes," said I. "That's best of all."

"Well," said she. "He sleeps just above our head. It is but one short staircase. There is a tin box with money enough to fill this bag under his bed."

"How can I get it without waking him?"

"What matter if he does wake?" She looked very hard at me as she spoke. "You could keep him from calling out."

"No, no, ma'am, I'll have none of that."

"Just as you like," said she. "I thought that you were a stout-hearted sort of man by your appearance, but I see that I made a mistake. If you are afraid to run the risk of one old man, then of course you cannot have the gold which is under his bed. You are the best judge of your own business, but I should think that you would do better at some other trade."

"I'll not have murder on my conscience."

"You could overpower him without harming him. I never said anything about murder. The money lies under the bed. But if you are faint-hearted, it is better that you should not attempt it."

She worked upon me so, partly with her scorn and partly with this money that she held before my eyes, that I believe I should have yielded and taken my chances upstairs, had it not been that I saw her eyes following the struggle within me in such a crafty, malignant fashion that it was evident she was bent upon making me the tool of her revenge, and that she would leave me no choice but to do the old man an injury or to be captured by him. She felt suddenly that she was giving herself away, and she changed her face to a kindly, friendly smile; but it was too late, for I had had my warning.

"I will not go upstairs," said I. "I have all I want here."

She looked her contempt at me, and there never was a face which could look it plainer.

"Very good. You can take these medals. I should be glad if you would begin at this end. I suppose they will all be the same value when melted down, but these are the ones which are the rarest, and, therefore, the most precious to him. It is not necessary to break the locks. If you press that brass knob you will find that there is a secret spring. So! Take that small one first – it is the very apple of his eye."

She had opened one of the cases, and the beautiful things all lay exposed before me. I had my hand upon the one which she had pointed out, when suddenly a change came over her face, and she held up one finger as a warning. "Hist!" she whispered. "What is that?"

Far away in the silence of the house we heard a low, dragging, shuffling sound, and the distant tread of feet. She closed and fastened the case in an instant.

"It's my husband!" she whispered. "All right. Don't be alarmed. I'll arrange it. Here! Quick, behind the tapestry!"

She pushed me behind the painted curtains upon the wall, my empty leather bag still in my hand. Then she took her taper and walked quickly into the room from which we had come. From where I stood I could see her through the open door.

"Is that you, Robert?" she cried.

The light of a candle shone through the door of the museum, and the shuffling steps came nearer and nearer. Then I saw a face in the doorway, a great, heavy face, all lines and creases, with a huge curving nose and a pair of gold glasses fixed across it. He had to throw his head back to see through the glasses, and that great nose thrust out in front of him like the beak of some sort of fowl. He was a big man, very tall and burly, so that in his loose dressing gown his figure seemed to fill up the whole doorway. He had a pile of grey, curling hair all round his head, but his face was clean-shaven. His mouth was thin and small and prim, hidden away under his long, masterful nose. He stood there, holding the candle in front of him, and looking at his wife with a queer, malicious gleam in his eyes. It only needed that one look to tell me that he was as fond of her as she was of him.

"How's this?" he asked. "Some new tantrum? What do you mean by wandering about the house? Why don't you go to bed?"

"I could not sleep," she answered. She spoke languidly and wearily. If she was an actress once, she had not forgotten her calling.

"Might I suggest," said he, in the same mocking kind of voice, "that a good conscience is an excellent aid to sleep?"

"That cannot be true," she answered, "for you sleep very well."

"I have only one thing in my life to be ashamed of," said he, and his hair bristled up with anger until he looked like an old cockatoo. "You know best what that is. It is a mistake which has brought its own punishment with it."

"To me as well as to you. Remember that!"

"You have very little to whine about. It was I who stooped and you who rose."

"Rose!"

"Yes, rose. I suppose you do not deny that it is a promotion to exchange the music hall for Mannering Hall. Fool that I was ever to take you out of your true sphere!"

"If you think so, why do you not separate?"

"Because private misery is better than public humiliation. Because it is easier to suffer for a mistake than to own to it. Because also I like to keep you in my sight, and to know that you cannot go back to him."

"You villain! You cowardly villain!"

"Yes, yes, My Lady. I know your secret ambition, but it shall never be while I live, and if it happens after my death I will at least take care that you go to him as a beggar. You and dear Edward will never have the satisfaction of squandering my savings, and you may make up your mind to that, My Lady. Why are those shutters and the window open?"

"I found the night very close."

"It is not safe. How do you know that some tramp may not be outside? Are you aware that my collection of medals is worth more than any similar collection in the world? You have left the door open also. What is there to prevent anyone from rifling the cases?"

"I was here."

"I know you were. I heard you moving about in the medal room, and that was why I came down. What were you doing?"

"Looking at the medals. What else should I be doing?"

"This curiosity is something new." He looked suspiciously at her and moved on towards the inner room, she walking beside him.

It was at this moment that I saw something which startled. I had laid my clasp knife open upon the top of one of the cases, and there it lay in full view. She saw it before he did, and with a woman's cunning she held her taper out so that the light of it came between Lord Mannering's eyes and the knife. Then she took it with her left hand and held it against her gown out of his sight. He looked about from case to case – I could have put my hand at one time upon his long nose – but there was nothing to show that the medals had been tampered with, and so, still snarling and grumbling, he shuffled off into the other room once more.

And now I have to speak of what I heard rather than of what I saw, but I swear to you, as I shall stand some day before my Maker, that what I say is the truth.

When they passed into the outer room I saw him lay his candle upon the corner of one of the tables, and he sat himself down, but in such a position that he was just out of my sight. She moved behind him, as I could tell from the fact that the light of her taper threw his long, lumpy shadow upon the floor in front of him. Then he began talking about this man whom he called Edward, and every word that he said was like a blistering drop of vitriol. He spoke low, so that I could not hear it all, but from what I heard I should guess that she would as soon have been lashed with a whip. At first she said some hot words in reply, but then she was silent, and he went on and on in that cold, mocking voice of his, nagging and insulting and tormenting, until I wondered that she could bear to stand there in silence and listen to it. Then suddenly I heard him say in a sharp voice, "Come from behind me! Leave go of my collar! What! Would you dare to strike me!" There was a sound like a blow, just a soft sort of thud, and then I heard him cry out, "My God, it's blood!" He shuffled with his feet as if he was getting up, and then I heard another blow, and he cried out, "Oh, you she-devil!" and was quiet, except for a dripping and splashing upon the floor.

I ran out from behind my curtain at that, and rushed into the other room, shaking all over with the horror of it. The old man had slipped down in the chair, and his dressing gown had rucked up until he looked as if he had a monstrous hump to his back. His head, with the gold glasses still fixed on his nose, was lolling over upon one side, and his little mouth was open just like a dead fish. I could not see where the blood was coming from, but I could still hear it drumming upon the floor. She stood behind him with the candle shining full upon her face. Her lips were pressed together and her eyes shining, and a touch of colour had come into each of her cheeks. It just wanted that to make her the most beautiful woman I had ever seen in my life.

"You've done it now!" said I.

"Yes," said she, in her quiet way, "I've done it now."

"What are you going to do?" I asked. "They'll have you for murder as sure as fate."

"Never fear about me. I have nothing to live for, and it does not matter. Give me a hand to set him straight in the chair. It is horrible to see him like this!"

I did so, though it turned me cold all over to touch him. Some of his blood came on my hand and sickened me.

"Now," said she, "you may as well have the medals as anyone else. Take them and go."

"I don't want them. I only want to get away. I was never mixed up with a business like this before."

"Nonsense!" said she. "You came for the medals, and here they are at your mercy. Why should you not have them? There is no one to prevent you."

I held the bag still in my hand. She opened the case, and between us we threw a hundred or so of the medals into it. They were all from the one case, but I could not bring myself to wait for any more. Then I made for the window, for the very air of this house seemed to poison me after what I had seen and heard. As I looked back, I saw her standing there, tall and graceful, with the light in her hand, just as I had seen her first. She waved goodbye, and I waved back at her and sprang out into the gravel drive.

I thank God that I can lay my hand upon my heart and say that I have never done a murder, but perhaps it would be different if I had been able to read that woman's mind and thoughts. There might have been two bodies in the room instead of one if I could have seen behind that last smile of hers. But I thought of nothing but of getting safely away, and it never entered my head how she might be fixing the rope round my neck. I had not taken five steps out from the window skirting down the shadow of the house in the way that I had come, when I heard a scream that might have raised the parish, and then another and another.

"Murder!" she cried. "Murder! Murder! Help!" and her voice rang out in the quiet of the night-time and sounded over the whole countryside. It went through my head, that dreadful cry. In an instant lights began to move and windows to fly up, not only in the house behind me, but at the lodge and in the stables in front. Like a frightened rabbit I bolted down the drive, but I heard the clang of the gate being shut before I could reach it. Then I hid my bag of medals under some dry faggots, and I tried to get away across the park, but someone saw me in the moonlight, and presently I had half a dozen of them with dogs upon my heels. I crouched down among the brambles, but those dogs were too many for me, and I was glad enough when the men came up and prevented me from being torn into pieces. They seized me, and dragged me back to the room from which I had come.

"Is this the man, Your Ladyship?" asked the oldest of them – the same whom I found out afterwards to be the butler.

She had been bending over the body, with her handkerchief to her eyes, and now she turned upon me with the face of a Fury. Oh, what an actress that woman was!

"Yes, yes, it is the very man," she cried. "Oh, you villain, you cruel villain, to treat an old man so!"

There was a man there who seemed to be a village constable. He laid his hand upon my shoulder.

"What do you say to that?" said he.

"It was she who did it," I cried, pointing at the woman, whose eyes never flinched before mine.

"Come! Come! Try another!" said the constable, and one of the menservants struck at me with his fist.

"I tell you that I saw her do it. She stabbed him twice with a knife. She first helped me to rob him, and then she murdered him."

The footman tried to strike me again, but she held up her hand.

"Do not hurt him," said she. "I think that his punishment may safely be left to the law."

"I'll see to that, Your Ladyship," said the constable. "Your Ladyship actually saw the crime committed, did you not?"

"Yes, yes, I saw it with my own eyes. It was horrible. We heard the noise and we came down. My poor husband was in front. The man had one of the cases open, and was filling a black leather bag which he held in his hand. He rushed past us, and my husband seized him. There was a struggle, and he stabbed him twice. There you can see the blood upon his hands. If I am not mistaken, his knife is still in Lord Mannering's body."

"Look at the blood upon her hands!" I cried.

"She has been holding up His Lordship's head, you lying rascal," said the butler.

"And here's the very sack Her Ladyship spoke of," said the constable, as a groom came in with the one which I had dropped in my flight. "And here are the medals inside it. That's good enough for me. We will keep him safe here tonight, and tomorrow the inspector and I can take him into Salisbury."

"Poor creature," said the woman. "For my own part, I forgive him any injury which he has done me. Who knows what temptation may have driven him to crime? His conscience and the law will give him punishment enough without any reproach of mine rendering it more bitter."

I could not answer – I tell you, sir, I could not answer, so taken aback was I by the assurance of the woman. And so, seeming by my silence to agree to all that she had said, I was dragged away by the butler and the constable into the cellar, in which they locked me for the night.

There, sir, I have told you the whole story of the events which led up to the murder of Lord Mannering by his wife upon the night of September the 13th,* in the year 1894. Perhaps you will put my statement on one side as the constable did at Mannering Towers, or the judge afterwards at the county assizes. Or perhaps you will see that there is the ring of truth in what I say, and you will follow it up, and so make your name for ever as a man who does not grudge personal trouble where justice is to be done. I have only you to look to, sir, and if you will clear my name of this false accusation, then I will worship you as one man never yet worshipped another. But if you fail me, then I give you my solemn promise that I will rope myself up, this day month, to the bar of my window, and from that time on I will come to plague you in your dreams if ever yet one man was able to come back and to haunt another. What I ask you to do is very simple. Make enquiries about this woman, watch her, learn her past history, find out what use she is making of the money which has come to her, and whether there is not a man Edward as I have stated. If from all this you learn anything which shows you her real character, or which seems to you to corroborate the story which I have told you, then I am sure that I can rely upon your goodness of heart to come to the rescue of an innocent man.

The Great Keinplatz Experiment

Of all the sciences which have puzzled the sons of men, none had such an attraction for the learned Professor von Baumgarten as those which relate to psychology and the ill-defined relations between mind and matter. A celebrated anatomist, a profound chemist and one of the first physiologists in Europe, it was a relief for him to turn from these subjects and to bring his varied knowledge to bear upon the study of the soul and the mysterious relationship of spirits. At first, when as a young man he began to dip into the secrets of mesmerism, his mind seemed to be wandering in a strange land where all was chaos and darkness, save that here and there some great unexplainable and disconnected fact loomed out in front of him. As the years passed, however, and as the worthy professor's stock of knowledge increased, for knowledge begets knowledge as money bears interest, much which had seemed strange and unaccountable began to take another shape in his eyes. New trains of reasoning became familiar to him, and he perceived connecting links where all had been incomprehensible and startling. By experiments which extended over twenty years, he obtained a basis of facts upon which it was his ambition to build up a new exact science which should embrace mesmerism, spiritualism and all cognate subjects. In this he was much helped by his intimate knowledge of the more intricate parts of animal physiology which treat of nerve currents and the working of the brain; for Alexis von Baumgarten was Regius Professor of Physiology at the University of Keinplatz, and had all the resources of the laboratory to aid him in his profound researches.

Professor von Baumgarten was tall and thin, with a hatchet face and steel-grey eyes, which were singularly bright and penetrating. Much thought had furrowed his forehead and contracted his heavy eyebrows, so that he appeared to wear a perpetual frown, which often misled people as to his character, for though austere he was tender-hearted. He was popular among the students, who would gather round him after his lectures and listen eagerly to his strange theories. Often he would call for volunteers from amongst them in order to conduct some experiment, so that eventually there was hardly a lad in the class who had not, at one time or another, been thrown into a mesmeric trance by his professor.

Of all these young devotees of science there was none who equalled in enthusiasm Fritz von Hartmann. It had often seemed strange to his fellow students that wild, reckless Fritz, as dashing a young fellow as ever hailed from the Rhinelands, should devote the time and trouble which he did in reading up abstruse works and in assisting the professor in his strange experiments. The fact was, however, that Fritz was a knowing and long-headed fellow. Months before he had lost his heart to young Elise, the blue-eyed, yellow-haired daughter of the lecturer. Although he had succeeded in learning from her lips that she was not indifferent to his suit, he had never dared to announce himself to her family as a formal suitor. Hence he would have found it a difficult matter to see his young lady had he not adopted the expedient of making himself useful to the professor. By this means he frequently was asked to the old man's house, where he willingly submitted to be experimented upon in any way as long as there was a chance of his receiving one bright glance from the eyes of Elise or one touch of her little hand.

Young Fritz von Hartmann was a handsome lad enough. There were broad acres, too, which would descend to him when his father died. To many he would have seemed an eligible suitor, but Madame frowned upon his presence in the house, and lectured the professor at times on his allowing such a wolf to prowl around their lamb. To tell the truth, Fritz had an evil name in Keinplatz. Never was there a riot or a duel, or any other mischief afoot, but the young Rhinelander figured as a ringleader in it. No one used more free and violent language, no one drank more, no one played cards more habitually, no one was more idle, save in the one solitary subject. No wonder, then, that the good Frau Professorin gathered her Fräulein under her wing, and resented the attentions of such a *mauvais sujet*.* As to the worthy lecturer, he was too much engrossed by his strange studies to form an opinion upon the subject one way or the other.

For many years there was one question which had continually obtruded itself upon his thoughts. All his experiments and his theories turned upon a single point. A hundred times a day the professor asked himself whether it was possible for the human spirit to exist apart from the body for a time and then to return to it once again. When the possibility first suggested itself to him his scientific mind had revolted from it. It clashed too violently with preconceived ideas and the prejudices of his early training. Gradually, however, as he proceeded farther and farther along the pathway of original research, his mind shook off its old fetters and became ready to face any conclusion which could reconcile the facts. There were many things which made him believe that it was possible for mind to exist apart from matter. At last it occurred to him that by a daring and original experiment the question might be definitely decided.

> It is evident – he remarked in his celebrated article upon invisible entities, which appeared in the *Keinplatz wöchentliche Medicalschrift** about this time, and which surprised the whole scientific world – it is evident that under certain conditions the soul or mind does separate itself from the body. In the case of a mesmerized person, the body lies in a cataleptic condition, but the spirit has left it. Perhaps you reply that the soul is there, but in a dormant condition. I answer that this is not so, otherwise how can one account for the condition of clairvoyance, which has fallen into disrepute through the knavery of certain scoundrels, but which can easily be shown to be an undoubted fact. I have been able myself, with a sensitive subject, to obtain an accurate description of what was going on in another room or another house. How can such knowledge be accounted for on any hypothesis save that the soul of the subject has left the body and is wandering through space? For a moment it is recalled by the voice of the operator and says what it has seen, and then wings its way once more through the air. Since the spirit is by its very nature invisible, we cannot see these comings and goings, but we see their effect in the body of the subject, now rigid and inert, now struggling to narrate impressions which could never have come to it by natural means. There is only one way which I can see by which the fact can be demonstrated. Although we in the flesh are unable to see these spirits, yet our own spirits, could we separate them from the body, would be conscious of the presence of others. It is my intention, therefore, shortly to mesmerize one of my pupils. I shall then mesmerize myself in a manner which has become easy to me. After that, if my theory holds good, my spirit will have no difficulty in meeting and communing with the spirit of my pupil, both being separated from the body. I hope to be able to communicate the result of this interesting experiment in an early number of the *Keinplatz wöchentliche Medicalschrift*.

When the good professor finally fulfilled his promise, and published an account of what occurred, the narrative was so extraordinary that it was received with general incredulity. The tone of some of the papers was so offensive in their comments upon the matter that the angry savant declared that he would never open his mouth again or refer to the subject in any way – a promise which he has faithfully kept. This narrative has been compiled, however, from the most authentic sources, and the events cited in it may be relied upon as substantially correct.

It happened, then, that shortly after the time when Professor von Baumgarten conceived the idea of the above-mentioned experiment, he was walking thoughtfully homewards after a long day in the laboratory, when he met a crowd of roistering students who had just streamed out from a beer house. At the head of them, half intoxicated and very noisy, was young Fritz von Hartmann. The professor would have passed them, but his pupil ran across and intercepted him.

"Heh! My worthy master," he said, taking the old man by the sleeve, and leading him down the road with him. "There is something that I have to say to you, and it is easier for me to say it now, when the good beer is humming in my head, than at another time."

"What is it, then, Fritz?" the physiologist asked, looking at him in mild surprise.

"I hear, *mein Herr*, that you are about to do some wondrous experiment in which you hope to take a man's soul out of his body, and then to put it back again. Is it not so?"

"It is true, Fritz."

"And have you considered, my dear sir, that you may have some difficulty in finding someone on whom to try this? *Potztausend!** Suppose that the soul went out and would not come back. That would be a bad business. Who is to take the risk?"

"But, Fritz," the professor cried, very much startled by this view of the matter, "I had relied upon your assistance in the attempt. Surely you will not desert me. Consider the honour and glory."

"Consider the fiddlesticks!" the student cried angrily. "Am I to be paid always thus? Did I not stand two hours upon a glass insulator while you poured electricity into my body? Have you not stimulated my phrenic nerves, besides ruining my digestion with a galvanic current round my stomach? Four-and-thirty times you have mesmerized me, and what have I got from all this? Nothing. And now you wish to take my soul out, as you would take the works from a watch. It is more than flesh and blood can stand."

"Dear, dear!" the professor cried in great distress. "That is very true, Fritz. I never thought of it before. If you can but suggest how I can compensate you, you will find me ready and willing."

"Then listen," said Fritz solemnly. "If you will pledge your word that after this experiment I may have the hand of your daughter, then I am willing to assist you; but if not, I shall have nothing to do with it. These are my only terms."

"And what would my daughter say to this?" the professor exclaimed, after a pause of astonishment.

"Elise would welcome it," the young man replied. "We have loved each other long."

"Then she shall be yours," the physiologist said with decision, "for you are a good-hearted young man, and one of the best neurotic subjects that I have ever known – that is when you are not under the influence of alcohol. My experiment is to be performed upon the fourth of next month. You will attend at the physiological laboratory at twelve o'clock. It will be a great occasion, Fritz. Von Gruben is coming from Jena, and Hinterstein from Basle. The chief men of science of all South Germany will be there."

"I shall be punctual," the student said briefly; and so the two parted. The professor plodded homeward, thinking of the great coming event, while the young man staggered along after his noisy companions, with his mind full of the blue-eyed Elise, and of the bargain which he had concluded with her father.

The professor did not exaggerate when he spoke of the widespread interest excited by his novel psychological experiment. Long before the hour had arrived the room was filled by a galaxy of talent. Besides the celebrities whom he had mentioned, there had come from London the great Professor Lurcher, who had just established his reputation by a remarkable treatise upon cerebral centres. Several great lights of the spiritualistic body had also come a long distance to be present, as had a Swedenborgian minister,* who considered that the proceedings might throw some light upon the doctrines of the Rosy Cross.*

There was considerable applause from this eminent assembly upon the appearance of Professor von Baumgarten and his subject upon the platform. The lecturer, in a few well-chosen words, explained what his views were, and how he proposed to test them. "I hold," he said, "that when a person is under the influence of mesmerism, his spirit is for the time released from his body, and I challenge anyone to put forward any other hypothesis which will account for the fact of clairvoyance. I therefore hope that upon mesmerizing my young friend here, and then putting myself into a trance, our spirits may be able to commune together, though our bodies lie still and inert. After a time Nature will resume her sway, our spirits will return into our respective bodies, and all will be as before. With your kind permission, we shall now proceed to attempt the experiment."

The applause was renewed at this speech, and the audience settled down in expectant silence. With a few rapid passes the professor mesmerized the young man, who sank back in his chair, pale and rigid. He then took a bright globe of glass from his pocket, and by concentrating his gaze upon it and making a strong mental effort, he succeeded in throwing himself into the same condition. It was a strange and impressive sight to see the old man and the young sitting together in the same cataleptic condition. Whither, then, had their souls fled? That was the question which presented itself to each and every one of the spectators.

Five minutes passed, and then ten, and then fifteen, and then fifteen more, while the professor and his pupil sat stiff and stark upon the platform. During that time not a sound was heard from the assembled savants, but every eye was bent upon the two pale faces, in search of the first signs of returning consciousness. Nearly an hour had elapsed before the patient watchers were rewarded. A faint flush came back to the cheeks of Professor von Baumgarten. The soul was coming back once more to its earthly tenement. Suddenly he stretched out his long thin arms, as one awaking from sleep, and, rubbing his eyes, stood up from his chair and gazed about him as though he hardly realized where he was. "*Tausend Teufel!*"* he exclaimed, rapping out a tremendous South German oath, to the great astonishment of his audience and to the disgust of the Swedenborgian. "Where the *Henker* am I then,* and what in thunder has occurred? Oh yes, I remember now. One of these nonsensical mesmeric experiments. There is no result this time, for I remember nothing at all since I became unconscious; so you have had all your long journeys for nothing, my learned friends, and a very good joke too"; at which the Regius Professor of Physiology burst into a roar of laughter and slapped his thigh in a highly indecorous fashion. The audience were so enraged at this unseemly behaviour on the part of their host that there might have been a considerable disturbance, had it not been for the judicious interference of young Fritz von Hartmann, who had now recovered from his lethargy. Stepping to the front of the platform, the young man apologized for the conduct of his companion. "I am sorry to say," he said, "that he is a harum-scarum sort of fellow, although he appeared so grave at the commencement of this experiment. He is still suffering from mesmeric reaction, and is hardly accountable for his words. As to the experiment itself, I do not consider it to be a failure. It is very possible that our spirits may have been communing in space during this hour; but, unfortunately, our gross bodily memory is distinct from our spirit, and we cannot recall what has occurred. My energies shall now be devoted to devising some means by which spirits may be able to recollect what occurs to them in their free state, and I trust that when I have worked this out, I may have the pleasure of meeting you all once again in this hall, and demonstrating to you the result." This address, coming from so young a student, caused considerable astonishment among the audience, and some were inclined to be offended, thinking that he assumed rather too much importance. The majority, however, looked upon him as a young man of great promise, and many comparisons were made as they left the hall between his dignified conduct and the levity of his professor, who during the above remarks was laughing heartily in a corner, by no means abashed at the failure of the experiment.

Now although all these learned men were filing out of the lecture room under the impression that they had seen nothing of note, as a matter of fact one of the most wonderful things in the whole history of the world had just occurred before their very eyes. Professor von Baumgarten had been so far correct in his theory that both his spirit and that of his pupil had been for a time absent from the body. But here a strange and unforeseen complication had occurred. In their return the spirit of Fritz von Hartmann had entered into the body of Alexis von Baumgarten, and that of Alexis von Baumgarten had taken up its abode in the frame of Fritz von Hartmann. Hence the slang and scurrility which issued from the lips of the serious professor, and hence also the weighty words and grave statements which fell from the careless student. It was an unprecedented event, yet no one knew of it, least of all those whom it concerned.

The body of the professor, feeling conscious suddenly of a great dryness about the back of the throat, sallied out into the street, still chuckling to himself over the result of the experiment, for the soul of Fritz within was reckless at the thought of the bride whom he had won so easily. His first impulse was to go up to the house and see her, but on second thoughts he came to the conclusion that it would be best to stay away until Madame Baumgarten should be informed by her husband of the agreement which had been made. He therefore made his way down to the Grüner Mann,* which was one of the favourite trysting places of the wilder students, and ran, boisterously waving his cane in the air, into the little parlour, where sat Spiegel and Müller and half a dozen other boon companions.

"Ha, ha! My boys," he shouted. "I knew I should find you here. Drink up, every one of you, and call for what you like, for I'm going to stand treat today."

Had the green man who is depicted upon the signpost of that well-known inn suddenly marched into the room and called for a bottle of wine, the students could not have been more amazed than they were by this unexpected entry of their revered professor. They were so astonished that for a minute or two they glared at him in utter bewilderment without being able to make any reply to his hearty invitation.

"*Donner und Blitzen!*"* shouted the professor angrily. "What the deuce is the matter with you, then? You sit there like a set of stuck pigs staring at me. What is it then?"

"It is the unexpected honour," stammered Spiegel, who was in the chair.

"Honour – rubbish!" said the professor testily. "Do you think that just because I happen to have been exhibiting mesmerism to a parcel of old fossils, I am therefore too proud to associate with dear old friends like you? Come out of that chair, Spiegel, my boy, for I shall preside now. Beer, or wine, or schnapps, my lads – call for what you like, and put it all down to me."

Never was there such an afternoon in the Grüner Mann. The foaming flagons of lager and the green-necked bottles of Rhenish circulated merrily. By degrees the students lost their shyness in the presence of their professor. As for him, he shouted, he sang, he roared, he balanced a long tobacco pipe upon his nose, and offered to run a hundred yards against any member of the company. The *Kellner** and the barmaid whispered to each other outside the door their astonishment at such proceedings on the part of a regius professor of the ancient university of Keinplatz. They had still more to whisper about afterwards, for the learned man cracked the *Kellner*'s crown, and kissed the barmaid behind the kitchen door.

"Gentlemen," said the professor, standing up, albeit somewhat totteringly, at the end of the table, and balancing his high old-fashioned wine glass in his bony hand, "I must now explain to you what is the cause of this festivity."

"Hear! Hear!" roared the students, hammering their beer glasses against the table. "A speech, a speech! Silence for a speech!"

"The fact is, my friends," said the professor, beaming through his spectacles, "I hope very soon to be married."

"Married!" cried a student, bolder than the others. "Is Madame dead, then?"

"Madame who?"

"Why, Madame von Baumgarten, of course."

"Ha, ha!" laughed the professor. "I can see, then, that you know all about my former difficulties. No, she is not dead, but I have reason to believe that she will not oppose my marriage."

"That is very accommodating of her," remarked one of the company.

"In fact," said the professor, "I hope that she will now be induced to aid me in getting a wife. She and I never took to each other very much, but now I hope all that may be ended, and when I marry she will come and stay with me."

"What a happy family!" exclaimed some wag.

"Yes, indeed; and I hope you will come to my wedding, all of you. I won't mention names, but here is to my little bride!" and the professor waved his glass in the air.

"Here's to his little bride!" roared the roisterers, with shouts of laughter. "Here's her health. *Sie soll leben – hoch!*"* And so the fun waxed still more fast and furious, while each young fellow followed the professor's example, and drank a toast to the girl of his heart.

While all this festivity had been going on at the Grüner Mann, a very different scene had been enacted elsewhere. Young Fritz von Hartmann, with a solemn face and a reserved manner, had, after the experiment, consulted and adjusted some mathematical instruments; after which, with a few peremptory words to the janitor, he had walked out into the street and wended his way slowly in the direction of the house of the professor. As he walked he saw von Althaus, the professor of anatomy, in front of him, and quickening his pace he overtook him.

"I say, von Althaus," he exclaimed, tapping him on the sleeve, "you were asking me for some information the other day concerning the middle coat of the cerebral arteries. Now I find—"

"*Donnerwetter!*"* shouted von Althaus, who was a peppery old fellow. "What the deuce do you mean by your impertinence! I'll have you up before the Academical Senate for this, sir" – with which threat he turned on his heel and hurried away. Von Hartmann was much surprised at this reception. "It's on account of this failure of my experiment," he said to himself, and continued moodily on his way.

Fresh surprises were in store for him, however. He was hurrying along when he was overtaken by two students. These youths, instead of raising their caps or showing any other sign of respect, gave a wild whoop of delight the instant that they saw him, and, rushing at him, seized him by each arm and commenced dragging him along with them.

"*Gott in Himmel!*"* roared von Hartmann. "What is the meaning of this unparalleled insult? Where are you taking me?"

"To crack a bottle of wine with us," said the two students. "Come along! That is an invitation which you have never refused."

"I never heard of such insolence in my life!" cried von Hartmann. "Let go my arms! I shall certainly have you rusticated for this. Let me go, I say!" and he kicked furiously at his captors.

"Oh, if you choose to turn ill-tempered, you may go where you like," the students said, releasing him. "We can do very well without you."

"I know you. I'll pay you out," said von Hartmann furiously, and continued in the direction which he imagined to be his own home, much incensed at the two episodes which had occurred to him on the way.

Now, Madame von Baumgarten, who was looking out of the window and wondering why her husband was late for dinner, was considerably astonished to see the young student come stalking down the road. As already remarked, she had a great antipathy to him, and if ever he ventured into the house it was on sufferance, and under the protection of the professor. Still more astonished was she, therefore, when she beheld him undo the wicket gate and stride up the garden path with the air of one who is master of the situation. She could hardly believe her eyes, and hastened to the door with all her maternal instincts up in arms. From the upper windows the fair Elise had also observed this daring move upon the part of her lover, and her heart beat quick with mingled pride and consternation.

"Good day, sir," Madame Baumgarten remarked to the intruder, as she stood in gloomy majesty in the open doorway.

"A very fine day indeed, Martha," returned the other. "Now, don't stand there like a statue of Juno, but bustle about and get the dinner ready, for I am well-nigh starved."

"Martha! Dinner!" ejaculated the lady, falling back in astonishment.

"Yes, dinner, Martha, dinner!" howled von Hartmann, who was becoming irritable. "Is there anything wonderful in that request when a man has been out all day? I'll wait in the dining room. Anything will do. *Schinken*,* and sausage, and prunes – any little thing that happens to be about. There you are, standing staring again. Woman, will you or will you not stir your legs?"

This last address, delivered with a perfect shriek of rage, had the effect of sending good Madame Baumgarten flying along the passage and through the kitchen, where she locked herself up in the scullery and went into violent hysterics. In the meantime von Hartmann strode into the room and threw himself down upon the sofa in the worst of tempers.

"Elise!" he shouted. "Confound the girl! Elise!"

Thus roughly summoned, the young lady came timidly downstairs and into the presence of her lover. "Dearest!" she cried, throwing her arms round him. "I know this is all done for my sake! It is a *ruse* in order to see me."

Von Hartmann's indignation at this fresh attack upon him was so great that he became speechless for a minute from rage, and could only glare and shake his fists, while he struggled in her embrace. When he at last regained his utterance, he indulged in such a bellow of passion that the young lady dropped back, petrified with fear, into an armchair.

"Never have I passed such a day in my life," von Hartmann cried, stamping upon the floor. "My experiment has failed. Von Althaus has insulted me. Two students have dragged me along the public road. My wife nearly faints when I ask her for dinner, and my daughter flies at me and hugs me like a grizzly bear."

"You are ill, dear," the young lady cried. "Your mind is wandering. You have not even kissed me once."

"No, and I don't intend to either," von Hartmann said with decision. "You ought to be ashamed of yourself. Why don't you go and fetch my slippers, and help your mother to dish the dinner?"

"And is it for this," Elise cried, burying her face in her handkerchief, "is it for this that I have loved you passionately for upwards of ten months? Is it for this that I have braved my mother's wrath? Oh, you have broken my heart; I am sure you have!" and she sobbed hysterically.

"I can't stand much more of this," roared von Hartmann furiously. "What the deuce does the girl mean? What did I do ten months ago which inspired you with such a particular affection for me? If you are really so very fond, you would do better to run away down and find the *Schinken* and some bread, instead of talking all this nonsense."

"Oh, my darling!" cried the unhappy maiden, throwing herself into the arms of what she imagined to be her lover. "You do but joke in order to frighten your little Elise."

Now it chanced that at the moment of this unexpected embrace von Hartmann was still leaning back against the end of the sofa, which, like much German furniture, was in a somewhat rickety condition. It also chanced that beneath this end of the sofa there stood a tank full of water in which the physiologist was conducting certain experiments upon the ova of fish, and which he kept in his drawing room in order to ensure an equable temperature. The additional weight of the maiden, combined with the impetus with which she hurled herself upon him, caused the precarious piece of furniture to give way, and the body of the unfortunate student was hurled backwards into the tank, in which his head and shoulders were firmly wedged, while his lower extremities flapped helplessly about in the air. This was the last straw. Extricating himself with some difficulty from his unpleasant position, von Hartmann gave an inarticulate yell of fury and, dashing out of the room, in spite of the entreaties of Elise, he seized his hat and rushed off into the town, all dripping and dishevelled, with the intention of seeking in some inn the food and comfort which he could not find at home.

As the spirit of von Baumgarten encased in the body of von Hartmann strode down the winding pathway which led down to the little town, brooding angrily over his many wrongs, he became aware that an elderly man was approaching him who appeared to be in an advanced state of intoxication. Von Hartmann waited by the side of the road and watched this individual, who came stumbling along, reeling from one side of the road to the other, and singing a student song in a very husky and drunken voice. At first his interest was merely excited by the fact of seeing a man of so venerable an appearance in such a disgraceful condition, but as he approached nearer, he became convinced that he knew the other well, though he could not recall when or where he had met him. This impression became so strong with him that when the stranger came abreast of him he stepped in front of him and took a good look at his features.

"Well, sonny," said the drunken man, surveying von Hartmann and swaying about in front of him, "where the *Henker* have I seen you before? I know you as well as I know myself. Who the deuce are you?"

"I am Professor von Baumgarten," said the student. "May I ask who you are? I am strangely familiar with your features."

"You should never tell lies, young man," said the other. "You're certainly not the professor, for he is an ugly snuffy old chap, and you are a big broad-shouldered young fellow. As to myself, I am Fritz von Hartmann at your service."

"That you certainly are not," exclaimed the body of von Hartmann. "You might very well be his father. But hullo, sir, are you aware that you are wearing my studs and my watch chain?"

"*Donnerwetter!*" hiccuped the other. "If those are not the trousers for which my tailor is about to sue me, may I never taste beer again."

Now as von Hartmann, overwhelmed by the many strange things which had occurred to him that day, passed his hand over his forehead and cast his eyes downwards, he chanced to catch the reflection of his own face in a pool which the rain had left upon the road. To his utter astonishment he perceived that his face was that of a youth, that his dress was that of a fashionable young student, and that in every way he was the antithesis of the grave and scholarly figure in which his mind was wont to dwell. In an instant his active brain ran over the series of events which had occurred and sprang to the conclusion. He fairly reeled under the blow.

"*Himmel!*" he cried. "I see it all. Our souls are in the wrong bodies. I am you and you are I. My theory is proved – but at what an expense! Is the most scholarly mind in Europe to go about with this frivolous exterior? Oh the labours of a lifetime are ruined!" and he smote his breast in his despair.

"I say," remarked the real von Hartmann from the body of the professor, "I quite see the force of your remarks, but don't go knocking my body about like that. You received it in excellent condition, but I perceive that you have wet it and bruised it, and spilt snuff over my ruffled shirt front."

"It matters little," the other said moodily. "Such as we are so must we stay. My theory is triumphantly proved, but the cost is terrible."

"If I thought so," said the spirit of the student, "it would be hard indeed. What could I do with these stiff old limbs, and how could I woo Elise and persuade her that I was not her father? No, thank Heaven, in spite of the beer which has upset me more than ever it could upset my real self, I can see a way out of it."

"How?" gasped the professor.

"Why, by repeating the experiment. Liberate our souls once more, and the chances are that they will find their way back into their respective bodies."

No drowning man could clutch more eagerly at a straw than did von Baumgarten's spirit at this suggestion. In feverish haste he dragged his own frame to the side of the road and threw it into a mesmeric trance; he then extracted the crystal ball from the pocket, and managed to bring himself into the same condition.

Some students and peasants who chanced to pass during the next hour were much astonished to see the worthy professor of physiology and his favourite student both sitting upon a very muddy bank and both completely insensible. Before the hour was up quite a crowd had assembled, and they were discussing the advisability of sending for an ambulance to convey the pair to hospital, when the learned savant opened his eyes and gazed vacantly around him. For an instant he seemed to forget how he had come there, but next moment he astonished his audience by waving his skinny arms above his head and crying out in a voice of rapture, "*Gott sei gedanket!** I am myself again. I feel I am!" Nor was the amazement lessened when the student, springing to his feet, burst into the same cry, and the two performed a sort of *pas de joie** in the middle of the road.

For some time after that people had some suspicion of the sanity of both the actors in this strange episode. When the professor published his experiences in the *Medicalschrift* as he had promised, he was met by an intimation, even from his colleagues, that he would do well to have his mind cared for, and that another such publication would certainly consign him to a madhouse. The student also found by experience that it was wisest to be silent about the matter.

When the worthy lecturer returned home that night he did not receive the cordial welcome which he might have looked for after his strange adventures. On the contrary, he was roundly upbraided by both his female relatives for smelling of drink and tobacco, and also for being absent while a young scapegrace invaded the house and insulted its occupants. It was long before the domestic atmosphere of the lecturer's house resumed its normal quiet, and longer still before the genial face of von Hartmann was seen beneath its roof. Perseverance, however, conquers every obstacle, and the student eventually succeeded in pacifying the enraged ladies and in establishing himself upon the old footing. He has now no longer any cause to fear the enmity of Madame, for he is Hauptmann von Hartmann of the Emperor's own Uhlans,* and his loving wife Elise has already presented him with two little Uhlans as a visible sign and token of her affection.

Cyprian Overbeck Wells

A Literary Mosaic

From my boyhood I have had an intense and overwhelming conviction that my real vocation lay in the direction of literature. I have, however, had a most unaccountable difficulty in getting any responsible person to share my views. It is true that private friends have sometimes, after listening to my effusions, gone the length of remarking, "Really, Smith, that's not half bad!" or, "You take my advice, old boy, and send that to some magazine!" but I have never on these occasions had the moral courage to inform my adviser that the article in question had been sent to well-nigh every publisher in London, and had come back again with a rapidity and precision which spoke well for the efficiency of our postal arrangements.

Had my manuscripts been paper boomerangs they could not have returned with greater accuracy to their unhappy dispatcher. Oh, the vileness and utter degradation of the moment when the stale little cylinder of closely written pages, which seemed so fresh and full of promise a few days ago, is handed in by a remorseless postman! And what moral depravity shines through the editor's ridiculous plea of "want of space"! But the subject is a painful one, and a digression from the plain statement of facts which I originally contemplated.

From the age of seventeen to that of three-and-twenty I was a literary volcano in a constant state of eruption. Poems and tales, articles and reviews, nothing came amiss to my pen. From the great sea serpent to the nebular hypothesis,* I was ready to write on anything or everything, and I can safely say that I seldom handled a subject without throwing new lights upon it. Poetry and romance, however, had always the greatest attractions for me. How I have wept over the pathos of my heroines, and laughed at the comicalities of my buffoons! Alas! I could find no one to join me in my appreciation, and solitary admiration for one's self, however genuine, becomes satiating after a time. My father remonstrated with me too on the score of expense and loss of time, so that I was finally compelled to relinquish my dreams of literary independence and to become a clerk in a wholesale mercantile firm connected with the West African trade.

Even when condemned to the prosaic duties which fell to my lot in the office, I continued faithful to my first love. I have introduced pieces of word-painting into the most commonplace business letters which have, I am told, considerably astonished the recipients. My refined sarcasm has made defaulting creditors writhe and wince. Occasionally, like the great Silas Wegg, I would drop into poetry,* and so raise the whole tone of the correspondence. Thus what could be more elegant than my rendering of the firm's instructions to the captain of one of their vessels? It ran in this way:

From England, Captain, you must steer a
Course directly to Madeira,
Land the casks of salted beef,
Then away to Tenerife.
Pray be careful, cool and wary
With the merchants of Canary.
When you leave them make the most
Of the trade winds to the coast.
Down it you shall sail as far
As the land of Calabar,*
And from there you'll onward go
To Bonny and Fernando Po…*

and so on for four pages. The captain, instead of treasuring up this little gem, called at the office next day, and demanded with quite unnecessary warmth what the thing meant, and I was compelled to translate it all back into prose. On this, as on other similar occasions, my employer took me severely to task – for he was, you see, a man entirely devoid of all pretensions to literary taste!

All this, however, is a mere preamble, and leads up to the fact that after ten years or so of drudgery I inherited a legacy which, though small, was sufficient to satisfy my simple wants. Finding myself independent, I rented a quiet house removed from the uproar and bustle of London, and there I settled down with the intention of producing some great work which should single me out from the family of the Smiths, and render my name immortal. To this end I laid in several quires of foolscap, a box of quill pens and a sixpenny bottle of ink, and, having given my housekeeper injunctions to deny me to all visitors, I proceeded to look round for a suitable subject.

I was looking round for some weeks. At the end of that time I found that I had by constant nibbling devoured a large number of the quills, and had spread the ink out to such advantage, what with blots, spills and abortive commencements, that there appeared to be some everywhere except in the bottle. As to the story itself, however, the facility of my youth had deserted me completely, and my mind remained a complete blank; nor could I, do what I would, excite my sterile imagination to conjure up a single incident or character.

In this strait I determined to devote my leisure to running rapidly through the works of the leading English novelists, from Daniel Defoe to the present day, in the hope of stimulating my latent ideas and of getting a good grasp of the general tendency of literature. For some time past I had avoided opening any work of fiction, because one of the greatest faults of my youth had been that I invariably and unconsciously mimicked the style of the last author whom I had happened to read. Now, however, I made up my mind to seek safety in a multitude, and by consulting *all* the English classics to avoid the danger of imitating any one too closely. I had just accomplished the task of reading through the majority of the standard novels at the time when my narrative commences.

It was, then, about twenty minutes to ten on the night of the fourth of June, eighteen hundred and eighty-six, that, after disposing of a pint of beer and a Welsh rarebit for my supper, I seated myself in my armchair, cocked my feet upon a stool and lit my pipe, as was my custom. Both my pulse and my temperature were, as far as I know, normal at the time. I would give the state of the barometer, but that unlucky instrument had experienced an unprecedented fall of forty-two inches – from a nail to the ground – and was not in a reliable condition. We live in a scientific age, and I flatter myself that I move with the times.

Whilst in that comfortable lethargic condition which accompanies both digestion and poisoning by nicotine, I suddenly became aware of the extraordinary fact that my little drawing room had elongated into a great salon, and that my humble table had increased in proportion. Round this colossal mahogany were seated a great number of people who were talking earnestly together, and the surface in front of them was strewn with books and pamphlets. I could not help observing that these persons were dressed in a most extraordinary mixture of costumes, for those at the end nearest to me wore peruke wigs,* swords and all the fashions of two centuries back; those about the centre had tight knee breeches, high cravats and heavy bunches of seals; while among those at the far side the majority were dressed in the most modern style, and among them I saw, to my surprise, several eminent men of letters whom I had the honour of knowing. There were two or three women in the company. I should have risen to my feet to greet these unexpected guests, but all power of motion appeared to have deserted me, and I could only lie still and listen to their conversation, which I soon perceived to be all about myself.

"Egad!" exclaimed a rough, weather-beaten man, who was smoking a long churchwarden pipe at my end of the table. "My heart softens for him. Why, gossips, we've been in the same straits ourselves. Gadzooks, never did mother feel more concern for her eldest born than I when Rory Random* went out to make his own way in the world."

"Right, Tobias, right!" cried another man, seated at my very elbow. "By my troth, I lost more flesh over poor Robin on his island* than had I the sweating sickness twice told. The tale was well-nigh done when in swaggers my Lord of Rochester* – a merry gallant, and one whose word in matters literary might make or mar. 'How now, Defoe,' quoth he, 'hast a tale on hand?' 'Even so, Your Lordship,' I returned. 'A right merry one, I trust,' quoth he. 'Discourse unto me concerning thy heroine, a comely lass, Dan, or I mistake.' 'Nay,' I replied, 'there is no heroine in the matter.' 'Split not your phrases,' quoth he, 'thou weighest every word like a scald attorney. Speak to me of thy principal female character, be she heroine or no.' 'My Lord,' I answered, 'there is no female character.' 'Then out upon thyself and thy book too!' he cried. 'Thou hadst best burn it!' – and so out in great dudgeon, whilst I fell to mourning over my poor romance, which was thus, as it were, sentenced to death before its birth. Yet there are a thousand now who have heard of Robin and his man Friday to one who has heard of my Lord of Rochester."

"Very true, Defoe," said a genial-looking man in a red waistcoat, who was sitting at the modern end of the table. "But all this won't help our good friend Smith in making a start at his story, which, I believe, was the reason why we assembled."

"The Dickens it is!"* stammered a little man beside him, and everybody laughed, especially the genial man, who cried out, "Charley Lamb, Charley Lamb,* you'll never alter. You would make a pun if you were hanged for it."

"That would be a case of haltering," returned the other, on which everybody laughed again.

By this time I had begun to dimly realize in my confused brain the enormous honour which had been done me. The greatest masters of fiction in every age of English letters had apparently made a rendezvous beneath my roof, in order to assist me in my difficulties. There were many faces at the table whom I was unable to identify; but when I looked hard at others I often found them to be very familiar to me, whether from paintings or from mere description. Thus between the first two speakers, who had betrayed themselves as Defoe and Smollett, there sat a dark, saturnine, corpulent old man, with harsh prominent features, who I was sure could be none other than the famous author of Gulliver.* There were several others of whom I was not so sure, sitting at the other side of the table, but I conjecture that both Fielding and Richardson were among them, and I could swear to the lantern jaws and cadaverous visage of Laurence Sterne.* Higher up I could see among the crowd the high forehead of Sir Walter Scott, the masculine features of George Eliot and the flattened nose of Thackeray;* while amongst the living I recognized James Payn, Walter Besant, the lady known as "Ouida", Robert Louis Stevenson,* and several of lesser note. Never before, probably, had such an assemblage of choice spirits gathered under one roof.

"Well," said Sir Walter Scott, speaking with a very pronounced accent, "ye ken the auld proverb, sirs, 'Ower mony cooks', or as the Border minstrel sang:

"'Black Johnstone wi' his troopers ten
Might mak' the heart turn cauld,
But Johnstone when he's a' alane
Is waur ten thoosand fauld.'

"The Johnstones were one of the Redesdale families, second cousins of the Armstrongs, and connected by marriage to—"

"Perhaps, Sir Walter," interrupted Thackeray, "you would take the responsibility off our hands by yourself dictating the commencement of a story to this young literary aspirant."

"Na, na!" cried Sir Walter. "I'll do my share, but there's Chairlie over there as full o' wut as a Radical's full o' treason. He's the laddie to give a cheery opening to it."

Dickens was shaking his head, and apparently about to refuse the honour, when a voice from among the moderns – I could not see who it was for the crowd – said:

"Suppose we begin at the end of the table and work round, anyone contributing a little as the fancy seizes him?"

"Agreed! Agreed!" cried the whole company, and every eye was turned on Defoe, who seemed very uneasy, and filled his pipe from a great tobacco box in front of him.

"Nay, gossips," he said, "there are others more worthy—" But he was interrupted by loud cries of "No! No!" from the whole table, and Smollett shouted out, "Stand to it, Dan – stand to it! You and I and the Dean* here will make three short tacks just to fetch her out of harbour, and then she may drift where she pleases." Thus encouraged, Defoe cleared his throat, and began in this way, talking between the puffs of his pipe:

"My father was a well-to-do yeoman of Cheshire, named Cyprian Overbeck, but, marrying about the year 1617, he assumed the name of his wife's family, which was Wells; and thus I, their eldest son, was named Cyprian Overbeck Wells. The farm was a very fertile one, and contained some of the best grazing land in those parts, so that my father was enabled to lay by money to the extent of a thousand crowns, which he laid out in an adventure to the Indies with such surprising success that in less than three years it had increased fourfold. Thus encouraged, he bought a part share of the trader and, fitting her out once more with such commodities as were most in demand (viz. old muskets, hangers and axes, besides glasses, needles and the like), he placed me on board as supercargo to look after his interests, and dispatched us upon our voyage.

"We had a fair wind as far as Cape de Verde, and there, getting into the north-west trade winds, made good progress down the African coast. Beyond sighting a Barbary rover* once, whereat our mariners were in sad distress, counting themselves already as little better than slaves, we had good luck until we had come within a hundred leagues of the Cape of Good Hope, when the wind veered round to the southward and blew exceeding hard, while the sea rose to such a height that the end of the mainyard dipped into the water, and I heard the master say that though he had been at sea for five-and-thirty years he had never seen the like of it, and that he had little expectation of riding through it. On this I fell to wringing my hands and bewailing myself until, the mast going by the board with a crash, I thought that the ship had struck, and swooned with terror, falling into the scuppers and lying like one dead, which was the saving of me, as will appear in the sequel. For the mariners, giving up all hope of saving the ship, and being in momentary expectation that she would founder, pushed off in the longboat, whereby I fear that they met the fate which they hoped to avoid, since I have never from that day heard anything of them. For my own part, on recovering from the swoon into which I had fallen, I found that, by the mercy of Providence, the sea had gone down, and that I was alone in the vessel. At which last discovery I was so terror-struck that I could but stand wringing my hands and bewailing my sad fate, until at last taking heart, I fell to comparing my lot with that of my unhappy camerados, on which I became more cheerful, and, descending to the cabin, made a meal off such dainties as were in the captain's locker."

Having got so far, Defoe remarked that he thought he had given them a fair start, and handed over the story to Dean Swift, who, after premising that he feared he would find himself as much at sea as Master Cyprian Overbeck Wells, continued in this way:

"For two days I drifted about in great distress, fearing that there should be a return of the gale and keeping an eager lookout for my late companions. Upon the third day, towards evening, I observed to my extreme surprise that the ship was under the influence of a very powerful current, which ran to the north-east with such violence that she was carried, now bows on, now stern on, and occasionally drifting sideways like a crab, at a rate which I cannot compute at less than twelve or fifteen knots an hour. For several weeks I was borne away in this manner, until one morning, to my inexpressible joy, I sighted an island upon the starboard quarter. The current would, however, have carried me past it had I not made shift, though single-handed, to set the flying jib so as to turn her bows, and then, clapping on the spritsail, studding sail and foresail, I clewed up the halyards upon the port side, and put the wheel down hard a-starboard, the wind being at the time north-east-half-east."

At the description of this nautical manoeuvre I observed that Smollett grinned, and a gentleman who was sitting higher up the table in the uniform of the Royal Navy, and who I guessed to be Captain Marryat,* became very uneasy and fidgeted in his seat.

"By this means I got clear of the current and was able to steer within a quarter of a mile of the beach, which indeed I might have approached still nearer by making another tack, but being an excellent swimmer I deemed it best to leave the vessel, which was almost waterlogged, and to make the best of my way to the shore.

"I had had my doubts hitherto as to whether this new-found country was inhabited or no, but as I approached nearer to it, being on the summit of a great wave, I perceived a number of figures on the beach, engaged apparently in watching me and my vessel. My joy, however, was considerably lessened when on reaching the land I found that the figures consisted of a vast concourse of animals of various sorts who were standing about in groups, and who hurried down to the water's edge to meet me. I had scarce put my foot upon the sand before I was surrounded by an eager crowd of deer, dogs, wild boars, buffaloes and other creatures, none of whom showed the least fear either of me or of each other, but, on the contrary, were animated by a common feeling of curiosity, as well as, it would appear, by some degree of disgust."

"A second edition," whispered Laurence Sterne to his neighbour. "Gulliver served up cold."

"Did you speak, sir?" asked the Dean very sternly, having evidently overheard the remark.

"My words were not addressed to you, sir," answered Sterne, looking rather frightened.

"They were nonetheless insolent," roared the Dean. "Your Reverence would fain make a Sentimental Journey of the narrative, I doubt not, and find pathos in a dead donkey* – though faith, no man can blame thee for mourning over thy own kith and kin."

"Better that than to wallow in all the filth of Yahooland,"* returned Sterne warmly, and a quarrel would certainly have ensued but for the interposition of the remainder of the company. As it was, the Dean refused indignantly to have any further hand in the story, and Sterne also stood out of it, remarking with a sneer that he was loth to fit a good blade onto a poor handle. Under these circumstances some further unpleasantness might have occurred had not Smollett rapidly taken up the narrative, continuing it in the third person instead of the first:

"Our hero, being considerably alarmed at this strange reception, lost little time in plunging into the sea again and regaining his vessel, being convinced that the worst which might befall him from the elements would be as nothing compared to the dangers of this mysterious island. It was as well that he took this course, for before nightfall his ship was overhauled and he himself picked up by a British man-of-war, the *Lightning*, then returning from the West Indies, where it had formed part of the fleet under the command of Admiral Benbow.* Young Wells, being a likely lad enough, well spoken and high-spirited, was at once entered on the books as officer's servant, in which capacity he both gained great popularity on account of the freedom of his manners and found an opportunity for indulging in those practical pleasantries for which he had all his life been famous.

"Among the quartermasters of the *Lightning* there was one named Jedediah Anchorstock, whose appearance was so remarkable that it quickly attracted the attention of our hero. He was a man of about fifty, dark with exposure to the weather, and so tall that as he came along the 'tween decks he had to bend himself nearly double. The most striking peculiarity of this individual was, however, that in his boyhood some evil-minded person had tattooed eyes all over his countenance with such marvellous skill that it was difficult at a short distance to pick out his real ones among so many counterfeits. On this strange personage Master Cyprian determined to exercise his talents for mischief, the more so as he learnt that he was extremely superstitious, and also that he had left behind him in Portsmouth a strong-minded spouse of whom he stood in mortal terror. With this object he secured one of the sheep which were kept on board for the officers' table, and, pouring a can of rumbo down its throat, reduced it to a state of utter intoxication. He then conveyed it to Anchorstock's berth, and with the assistance of some other imps, as mischievous as himself, dressed it up in a high nightcap and gown, and covered it over with the bedclothes.

"When the quartermaster came down from his watch our hero met him at the door of his berth with an agitated face. 'Mr Anchorstock,' said he, 'can it be that your wife is on board?' 'Wife!' roared the astonished sailor. 'Ye white-faced swab, what d'ye mean?' 'If she's not here in the ship it must be her ghost,' said Cyprian, shaking his head gloomily. 'In the ship! How in thunder could she get into the ship? Why, master, I believe as how you're weak in the upper works – d'ye see? – to as much as think o' such a thing. My Poll is moored head and starn, behind the point at Portsmouth, more'n two thousand mile away.' 'Upon my word,' said our hero, very earnestly, 'I saw a female look out of your cabin not five minutes ago.' 'Ay, ay, Mr Anchorstock,' joined in several of the conspirators. 'We all saw her – a spanking-looking craft with a deadlight mounted on one side.' 'Sure enough,' said Anchorstock, staggered by this accumulation of evidence, 'my Polly's starboard eye was doused for ever by long Sue Williams of the Hard.* But if so be as she be there I must see her, be she ghost or quick'; with which the honest sailor, in much perturbation and trembling in every limb, began to shuffle forward into the cabin, holding the light well in front of him. It chanced, however, that the unhappy sheep, which was quietly engaged in sleeping off the effects of its unusual potations, was awakened by the noise of his approach and, finding herself in such an unusual position, sprang out of bed and rushed furiously for the door, bleating wildly, and rolling about like a brig in a tornado, partly from intoxication and partly from the nightdress which impeded her movements. As Anchorstock saw this extraordinary apparition bearing down upon him, he uttered a yell and fell flat upon his face, convinced that he had to do with a supernatural visitor, the more so as the confederates heightened the effect by a chorus of most ghastly groans and cries. The joke had nearly gone beyond what was originally intended, for the quartermaster lay as one dead, and it was only with the greatest difficulty that he could be brought to his senses. To the end of the voyage he stoutly asserted that he had seen the distant Mrs Anchorstock, remarking with many oaths that though he was too woundily scared to take much note of the features, there was no mistaking the strong smell of rum which was characteristic of his better half.

"It chanced shortly after this to be the King's birthday, an event which was signalized aboard the *Lightning* by the death of the commander under singular circumstances. This officer, who was a real fair-weather Jack, hardly knowing the ship's keel from her ensign, had obtained his position through parliamentary interest, and used it with such tyranny and cruelty that he was universally execrated. So unpopular was he that when a plot was entered into by the whole crew to punish his misdeeds with death, he had not a single friend among six hundred souls to warn him of his danger. It was the custom on board the King's ships that upon his birthday the entire ship's company should be drawn up upon deck, and that at a signal they should discharge their muskets into the air in honour of His Majesty. On this occasion word had been secretly passed round for every man to slip a slug into his firelock, instead of the blank cartridge provided. On the boatswain blowing his whistle the men mustered upon deck and formed line, whilst the captain, standing well in front of them, delivered a few words to them. 'When I give the word,' he concluded, 'you shall discharge your pieces, and by thunder, if any man is a second before or a second after his fellows I shall trice him up to the weather rigging!' With these words he roared 'Fire!' – on which every man levelled his musket straight at his head and pulled the trigger. So accurate was the aim and so short the distance, that more than five hundred bullets struck him simultaneously, blowing away his head and a large portion of his body. There were so many concerned in this matter, and it was so hopeless to trace it to any individual, that the officers were unable to punish anyone for the affair – the more readily as the captain's haughty ways and heartless conduct had made him quite as hateful to them as to the men whom he commanded.

"By his pleasantries and the natural charm of his manners our hero so far won the good wishes of the ship's company that they parted with infinite regret upon their arrival in England. Filial duty, however, urged him to return home and report himself to his father, with which object he posted from Portsmouth to London, intending to proceed thence to Shropshire. As it chanced, however, one of the horses sprained his off foreleg while passing through Chichester, and as no change could be obtained, Cyprian found himself compelled to put up at the Crown and Bull for the night.

"Ods bodikins!" continued Smollett, laughing. "I never could pass a comfortable hostel without stopping,* and so, with your permission, I'll e'en stop here, and whoever wills may lead friend Cyprian to his further adventures. Do you, Sir Walter, give us a touch of the Wizard of the North."*

With these words Smollett produced a pipe, and filling it at Defoe's tobacco pot, waited patiently for the continuation of the story.

"If I must, I must," remarked the illustrious Scotchman, taking a pinch of snuff, "but I must beg leave to put Mr Wells back a few hundred years, for of all things I love the true medieval smack. To proceed then:

"Our hero, being anxious to continue his journey, and learning that it would be some time before any conveyance would be ready, determined to push on alone mounted on his gallant grey steed. Travelling was particularly dangerous at that time, for besides the usual perils which beset wayfarers, the southern parts of England were in a lawless and disturbed state which bordered on insurrection. The young man, however, having loosened his sword in his sheath, so as to be ready for every eventuality, galloped cheerily upon his way, guiding himself to the best of his ability by the light of the rising moon.

"He had not gone far before he realized that the cautions which had been impressed upon him by the landlord, and which he had been inclined to look upon as self-interested advice, were only too well justified. At a spot where the road was particularly rough, and ran across some marshland, he perceived a short distance from him a dark shadow, which his practised eye detected at once as a body of crouching men. Reining up his horse within a few yards of the ambuscade, he wrapped his cloak round his bridle arm and summoned the party to stand forth.

"'What ho, my masters!' he cried. 'Are beds so scarce, then, that ye must hamper the high road of the King with your bodies? Now, by St Ursula of Alpuxerra,* there be those who might think that birds who fly o' nights were after higher game than the moorhen or the woodcock!'

"'Blades and targets, comrades!' exclaimed a tall powerful man, springing into the centre of the road with several companions, and standing in front of the frightened horse. 'Who is this swashbuckler who summons His Majesty's lieges from their repose? A very *soldado*, o' truth. Hark ye, sir, or My Lord, or Thy Grace, or whatsoever title Your Honour's honour may be pleased to approve, thou must curb thy tongue play, or by the seven witches of Gambleside thou may find thyself in but a sorry plight.'

"'I prithee, then, that thou wilt expound to me who and what ye are,' quoth our hero, 'and whether your purpose be such as an honest man may approve of. As to your threats, they turn from my mind as your caitiffly* weapons would shiver upon my hauberk from Milan.'

"'Nay, Allen,' interrupted one of the party, addressing him who seemed to be their leader, 'this is a lad of mettle, and such a one as our honest Jack longs for. But we lure not hawks with empty hands. Look ye, sir, there is game afoot which it may need such bold hunters as thyself to follow. Come with us and take a firkin of canary, and we will find better work for that glaive of thine than getting its owner into broil and bloodshed; for, by my troth! Milan or no Milan, if my curtel axe do but ring against that morion* of thine it will be an ill day for thy father's son.'

"For a moment our hero hesitated as to whether it would best become his knightly traditions to hurl himself against his enemies, or whether it might not be better to obey their requests. Prudence, mingled with a large share of curiosity, eventually carried the day, and, dismounting from his horse, he intimated that he was ready to follow his captors.

"'Spoken like a man!' cried he whom they addressed as Allen. 'Jack Cade* will be right glad of such a recruit. Blood and carrion! but thou hast the thews of a young ox; and I swear, by the haft of my sword, that it might have gone ill with some of us hadst thou not listened to reason!'

"'Nay, not so, good Allen – not so,' squeaked a very small man, who had remained in the background while there was any prospect of a fray, but who now came pushing to the front. 'Hadst thou been alone it might indeed have been so, perchance, but an expert swordsman can disarm at pleasure such a one as this young knight. Well I remember in the Palatinate how I clove to the chine* even such another – the Baron von Slogstaff. He struck at me, look ye, so; but I, with buckler and blade, did, as one might say, deflect it; and then, countering in carte, I returned in tierce,* and so – St Agnes save us! – who comes here?'

"The apparition which frightened the loquacious little man was sufficiently strange to cause a qualm even in the bosom of the knight. Through the darkness there loomed a figure which appeared to be of gigantic size, and a hoarse voice, issuing apparently some distance above the heads of the party, broke roughly on the silence of the night.

"'Now out upon thee, Thomas Allen, and foul be thy fate if thou hast abandoned thy post without good and sufficient cause. By St Anselm of the Holy Grove, thou hadst best have never been born than rouse my spleen this night. Wherefore is it that you and your men are trailing over the moor like a flock of geese when Michaelmas is near?'

"'Good captain,' said Allen, doffing his bonnet, an example followed by others of the band, 'we have captured a goodly youth who was pricking it along the London road. Methought that some word of thanks were meet reward for such service, rather than taunt or threat.'

"'Nay, take it not to heart, bold Allen,' exclaimed their leader, who was none other than the great Jack Cade himself. 'Thou knowest of old that my temper is somewhat choleric, and my tongue not greased with that unguent which oils the mouths of the lip-serving lords of the land. And you,' he continued, turning suddenly upon our hero, 'are you ready to join the great cause which will make England what it was when the learned Alfred reigned in the land?* Zounds, man, speak out, and pick not your phrases.'

"'I am ready to do aught which may become a knight and a gentleman,' said the soldier stoutly.

"'Taxes shall be swept away!' cried Cade excitedly. 'The impost and the anpost – the tithe and the hundred tax.* The poor man's salt box and flour bin shall be as free as the nobleman's cellar. Ha! What sayest thou?'

"'It is but just,' said our hero.

"'Ay, but they give us such justice as the falcon gives the leveret!' roared the orator. 'Down with them, I say – down with every man of them! Noble and judge, priest and king, down with them all!'

"'Nay,' said Sir Overbeck Wells, drawing himself up to his full height, and laying his hand upon the hilt of his sword, 'there I cannot follow thee, but must rather defy thee as traitor and fainéant, seeing that thou art no true man, but one who would usurp the rights of our master the King, whom may the Virgin protect!'

"At these bold words, and the defiance which they conveyed, the rebels seemed for a moment utterly bewildered; but, encouraged by the hoarse shout of their leader, they brandished their weapons and prepared to fall upon the knight, who placed himself in a posture for defence and awaited their attack.

"There now!" cried Sir Walter, rubbing his hands and chuckling. "I've put the chiel in a pretty warm corner, and we'll see which of you moderns can take him oot o't. Ne'er a word more will ye get frae me to help him one way or the other."

"You try your hand, James," cried several voices, and the author in question had got so far as to make an allusion to a solitary horseman who was approaching, when he was interrupted by a tall gentleman a little farther down with a slight stutter and a very nervous manner.

"Excuse me," he said, "but I fancy that I may be able to do something here. Some of my humble productions have been said to excel Sir Walter at his best, and I was undoubtedly stronger all round. I could picture modern society as well as ancient; and as to my plays, why Shakespeare never came near *The Lady of Lyons** for popularity. There is this little thing..." (Here he rummaged among a great pile of papers in front of him.) "Ah! That's a report of mine, when I was in India! Here it is. No, this is one of my speeches in the House,* and this is my criticism on Tennyson. Didn't I warm him up? I can't find what I wanted, but of course you have read them all – *Rienzi*, and *Harold*, and *The Last of the Barons*.* Every schoolboy knows them by heart, as poor Macaulay* would have said. Allow me to give you a sample:

"In spite of the gallant knight's valiant resistance the combat was too unequal to be sustained. His sword was broken by a slash from a brown bill,* and he was borne to the ground. He expected immediate death, but such did not seem to be the intention of the ruffians who had captured him. He was placed upon the back of his own charger and borne, bound hand and foot, over the trackless moor, in the fastnesses of which the rebels secreted themselves.

"In the depths of these wilds there stood a stone building which had once been a farmhouse but, having been for some reason abandoned, had fallen into ruin, and had now become the headquarters of Cade and his men. A large cowhouse near the farm had been utilized as sleeping quarters, and some rough attempts had been made to shield the principal room of the main building from the weather by stopping up the gaping apertures in the walls. In this apartment was spread out a rough meal for the returning rebels, and our hero was thrown, still bound, into an empty outhouse, there to await his fate."

Sir Walter had been listening with the greatest impatience to Bulwer-Lytton's narrative, but when it had reached this point he broke in impatiently.

"We want a touch of your own style, man," he said. "The animal-magnetico-electro-hysterical-biological-mysterious sort of story is all your own, but at present you are just a poor copy of myself, and nothing more."

There was a murmur of assent from the company, and Defoe remarked, "Truly, Master Lytton, there is a plaguey resemblance in the style, which may indeed be but a chance, and yet methinks it is sufficiently marked to warrant such words as our friend hath used."

"Perhaps you will think that this is an imitation also," said Lytton bitterly and, leaning back in his chair with a morose countenance, he continued the narrative in this way:

"Our unfortunate hero had hardly stretched himself upon the straw with which his dungeon was littered, when a secret door opened in the wall and a venerable old man swept majestically into the apartment. The prisoner gazed upon him with astonishment not unmixed with awe, for on his broad brow was printed the seal of much knowledge – such knowledge as it is not granted to a son of man to know. He was clad in a long white robe, crossed and chequered with mystic devices in the Arabic character, while a high scarlet tiara marked with the square and circle enhanced his venerable appearance. 'My son,' he said, turning his piercing and yet dreamy gaze upon Sir Overbeck, 'all things lead to nothing, and nothing is the foundation of all things. Cosmos is impenetrable. Why then should we exist?'

"Astounded at this weighty query, and at the philosophic demeanour of his visitor, our hero made shift to bid him welcome and to demand his name and quality. As the old man answered him his voice rose and fell in musical cadences, like the sighing of the east wind, while an ethereal and aromatic vapour pervaded the apartment.

"'I am the eternal non-ego,' he answered. 'I am the concentrated negative – the everlasting essence of nothing. You see in me that which existed before the beginning of matter many years before the commencement of time. I am the algebraic *x* which represents the infinite divisibility of a finite particle.'

"Sir Overbeck felt a shudder as though an ice-cold hand had been placed upon his brow. 'What is your message?' he whispered, falling prostrate before his mysterious visitor.

"'To tell you that the eternities beget chaos, and that the immensities are at the mercy of the divine Ananke.* Infinitude crouches before a personality. The mercurial essence is the prime mover in spirituality, and the thinker is powerless before the pulsating inanity. The cosmical procession is terminated only by the unknowable and unpronounceable...

"May I ask, Mr Smollett, what you find to laugh at?"

"Gadzooks, master," cried Smollett, who had been sniggering for some time back. "It seems to me that there is little danger of anyone venturing to dispute that style with you."

"It's all your own," murmured Sir Walter.

"And very pretty too," quoth Laurence Sterne, with a malignant grin. "Pray sir, what language do you call it?"

Lytton was so enraged at these remarks, and at the favour with which they appeared to be received, that he endeavoured to stutter out some reply, and then, losing control of himself completely, picked up all his loose papers and strode out of the room, dropping pamphlets and speeches at every step. This incident amused the company so much that they laughed for several minutes without cessation. Gradually the sound of their laughter sounded more and more harshly in my ears, the lights on the table grew dim and the company more misty, until they and their symposium vanished away altogether. I was sitting before the embers of what had been a roaring fire, but was now little more than a heap of grey ashes, and the merry laughter of the august company had changed to the recriminations of my wife, who was shaking me violently by the shoulder and exhorting me to choose some more seasonable spot for my slumbers. So ended the wondrous adventures of Master Cyprian Overbeck Wells, but I still live in the hopes that in some future dream the great masters may themselves finish that which they have begun.

Playing with Fire

I cannot pretend to say what occurred on the 14th of April last at No. 17, Badderly Gardens. Put down in black and white, my surmise might seem too crude, too grotesque, for serious consideration. And yet that something did occur, and that it was of a nature which will leave its mark upon every one of us for the rest of our lives is as certain as the unanimous testimony of five witnesses can make it. I will not enter into any argument or speculation. I will only give a plain statement, which will be submitted to John Moir, Harvey Deacon and Mrs Delamere, and withheld from publication unless they are prepared to corroborate every detail. I cannot obtain the sanction of Paul Le Duc, for he appears to have left the country.

It was John Moir (the well-known senior partner of Moir, Moir and Sanderson) who had originally turned our attention to occult subjects. He had, like many very hard and practical men of business, a mystic side to his nature, which had led him to the examination, and eventually to the acceptance, of those elusive phenomena which are grouped together with much that is foolish, and much that is fraudulent, under the common heading of spiritualism. His researches, which had begun with an open mind, ended unhappily in dogma, and he became as positive and fanatical as any other bigot. He represented in our little group the body of men who have turned these singular phenomena into a new religion.

Mrs Delamere, our medium, was his sister, the wife of Delamere, the rising sculptor. Our experience had shown us that to work on these subjects without a medium was as futile as for an astronomer to make observations without a telescope. On the other hand, the introduction of a paid medium was hateful to all of us. Was it not obvious that he or she would feel bound to return some result for money received, and that the temptation to fraud would be an overpowering one? No phenomena could be relied upon which were produced at a guinea an hour. But, fortunately, Moir had discovered that his sister was mediumistic – in other words, that she was a battery of that animal-magnetic force* which is the only form of energy which is subtle enough to be acted upon from the spiritual plane as well as from our own material one. Of course, when I say this, I do not mean to beg the question;

but I am simply indicating the theories upon which we were ourselves, rightly or wrongly, explaining what we saw. The lady came, not altogether with the approval of her husband, and though she never gave indications of any very great psychic force, we were able, at least, to obtain those usual phenomena of message-tilting which are at the same time so puerile and so inexplicable. Every Sunday evening we met in Harvey Deacon's studio at Badderly Gardens, the next house to the corner of Merton Park Road.

Harvey Deacon's imaginative work in art would prepare anyone to find that he was an ardent lover of everything which was outré and sensational. A certain picturesqueness in the study of the occult had been the quality which had originally attracted him to it, but his attention was speedily arrested by some of those phenomena to which I have referred, and he was coming rapidly to the conclusion that what he had looked upon as an amusing romance and an after-dinner entertainment was really a very formidable reality. He is a man with a remarkably clear and logical brain – a true descendant of his ancestor, the well-known Scotch professor – and he represented in our small circle the critical element, the man who has no prejudices, is prepared to follow facts as far as he can see them and refuses to theorize in advance of his data. His caution annoyed Moir as much as the latter's robust faith amused Deacon, but each in his own way was equally keen upon the matter.

And I? What am I to say that I represented? I was not the devotee. I was not the scientific critic. Perhaps the best that I can claim for myself is that I was the dilettante man about town, anxious to be in the swim of every fresh movement, thankful for any new sensation which would take me out of myself and open up fresh possibilities of existence. I am not an enthusiast myself, but I like the company of those who are. Moir's talk, which made me feel as if we had a private passkey through the door of death, filled me with a vague contentment. The soothing atmosphere of the seance with the darkened lights was delightful to me. In a word, the thing amused me, and so I was there.

It was, as I have said, upon the 14th of April last that the very singular event which I am about to put upon record took place. I was the first of the men to arrive at the studio, but Mrs Delamere was already there, having had afternoon tea with Mrs Harvey Deacon. The two ladies and Deacon himself were standing in front of an unfinished picture of his upon the easel. I am not an expert in art, and I have never professed to understand what Harvey Deacon meant by his pictures; but I could see in this instance that it was all very clever and imaginative, fairies and animals and allegorical figures of all sorts. The ladies were loud in their praises, and indeed the colour effect was a remarkable one.

"What do you think of it, Markham?" he asked.

"Well, it's above me," said I. "These beasts – what are they?"

"Mythical monsters, imaginary creatures, heraldic emblems – a sort of weird, bizarre procession of them."

"With a white horse in front!"

"It's not a horse," said he rather testily – which was surprising, for he was a very good-humoured fellow as a rule, and hardly ever took himself seriously.

"What is it, then?"

"Can't you see the horn in front? It's a unicorn. I told you they were heraldic beasts. Can't you recognize one?"

"Very sorry, Deacon," said I, for he really seemed to be annoyed.

He laughed at his own irritation.

"Excuse me, Markham!" said he. "The fact is that I have had an awful job over the beast. All day I have been painting him in and painting him out, and trying to imagine what a real live, ramping unicorn would look like. At last I got him, as I hoped; so when you failed to recognize it, it took me on the raw."

"Why, of course it's a unicorn," said I, for he was evidently depressed at my obtuseness. "I can see the horn quite plainly, but I never saw a unicorn except beside the Royal Arms,* and so I never thought of the creature. And these others are griffins and cockatrices, and dragons of sorts?"

"Yes, I had no difficulty with them. It was the unicorn which bothered me. However, there's an end of it until tomorrow." He turned the picture round upon the easel, and we all chatted about other subjects.

Moir was late that evening, and when he did arrive he brought with him, rather to our surprise, a small, stout Frenchman, whom he introduced as Monsieur Paul Le Duc. I say to our surprise, for we held a theory that any intrusion into our spiritual circle deranged the conditions, and introduced an element of suspicion. We knew that we could trust each other, but all our results were vitiated by the presence of an outsider. However, Moir soon reconciled us to the innovation. Monsieur Paul Le Duc was a famous student of occultism, a seer, a medium and a mystic. He was travelling in England with a letter of introduction to Moir from the president of the Parisian brothers of the Rosy Cross.* What more natural than that he should bring him to our little seance, or that we should feel honoured by his presence?

He was, as I have said, a small, stout man, undistinguished in appearance, with a broad, smooth, clean-shaven face, remarkable only for a pair of large, brown, velvety eyes, staring vaguely out in front of him. He was well dressed, with the manners of a gentleman, and his curious little turns of English speech set the ladies smiling. Mrs Deacon had a prejudice against our researches and left the room, upon which we lowered the lights, as was our custom, and drew up our chairs to the square mahogany table which stood in the centre of the studio. The light was subdued, but sufficient to allow us to see each other quite plainly. I remember that I could even observe the curious, podgy little square-topped hands which the Frenchman laid upon the table.

"What a fun!" said he. "It is many years since I have sat in this fashion, and it is to me amusing. Madame is medium. Does Madame make the trance?"

"Well, hardly that," said Mrs Delamere. "But I am always conscious of extreme sleepiness."

"It is the first stage. Then you encourage it, and there comes the trance. When the trance comes, then out jumps your little spirit and in jumps another little spirit, and so you have direct talking or writing. You leave your machine to be worked by another. *Hein?** But what have unicorns to do with it?"

Harvey Deacon started in his chair. The Frenchman was moving his head slowly round and staring into the shadows which draped the walls.

"What a fun!" said he. "Always unicorns. Who has been thinking so hard upon a subject so bizarre?"

"This is wonderful!" cried Deacon. "I have been trying to paint one all day. But how could you know it?"

"You have been thinking of them in this room."

"Certainly."

"But thoughts are things, my friend. When you imagine a thing you make a thing. You did not know it, *hein*? But I can see your unicorns because it is not only with my eye that I can see."

"Do you mean to say that I create a thing which has never existed by merely thinking of it?"

"But certainly. It is the fact which lies under all other facts. That is why an evil thought is also a danger."

"They are, I suppose, upon the astral plane?" said Moir.

"Ah, well, these are but words, my friends. They are there – somewhere – everywhere – I cannot tell myself. I see them. I could touch them."

"You could not make *us* see them."

"It is to materialize them. Hold! It is an experiment. But the power is wanting. Let us see what power we have, and then arrange what we shall do. May I place you as I wish?"

"You evidently know a great deal more about it than we do," said Harvey Deacon. "I wish that you would take complete control."

"It may be that the conditions are not good. But we will try what we can do. Madame will sit where she is, I next, and this gentleman beside me. Meester Moir will sit next to Madame, because it is well to have blacks and blondes in turn. So! And now with your permission I will turn the lights all out."

"What is the advantage of the dark?" I asked.

"Because the force with which we deal is a vibration of ether and so also is light. We have the wires all for ourselves now – *hein*? You will not be frightened in the darkness, Madame? What a fun is such a seance!"

At first the darkness appeared to be absolutely pitchy, but in a few minutes our eyes became so far accustomed to it that we could just make out each other's presence – very dimly and vaguely, it is true. I could see nothing else in the room – only the black loom of the motionless figures. We were all taking the matter much more seriously than we had ever done before.

"You will place your hands in front. It is hopeless that we touch, since we are so few round so large a table. You will compose yourself, Madame, and if sleep should come to you, you will not fight against it. And now we sit in silence and we expect – *hein*?"

So we sat in silence and expected, staring out into the blackness in front of us. A clock ticked in the passage. A dog barked intermittently far away. Once or twice a cab rattled past in the street, and the gleam of its lamps through the chink in the curtains was a cheerful break in that gloomy vigil. I felt those physical symptoms with which previous seances had made me familiar – the coldness of the feet, the tingling in the hands, the glow of the palms, the feeling of a cold wind upon the back. Strange little shooting pains came in my forearms, especially as it seemed to me in my left one, which was nearest to our visitor – due no doubt to disturbance of the vascular system, but worthy of some attention all the same. At the same time I was conscious of a strained feeling of expectancy which was almost painful. From the rigid, absolute silence of my companions I gathered that their nerves were as tense as my own.

And then suddenly a sound came out of the darkness – a low, sibilant sound, the quick, thin breathing of a woman. Quicker and thinner yet it came, as between clenched teeth, to end in a loud gasp with a dull rustle of cloth.

"What's that? Is all right?" someone asked in the darkness.

"Yes, all is right," said the Frenchman. "It is Madame. She is in her trance. Now, gentlemen, if you will wait quiet you will see something, I think, which will interest you much."

Still the ticking in the hall. Still the breathing, deeper and fuller now, from the medium. Still the occasional flash, more welcome than ever, of the passing lights of the hansoms. What a gap we were bridging, the half-raised veil of the eternal on the one side and the cabs of London on the other. The table was throbbing with a mighty pulse. It swayed steadily, rhythmically, with an easy swooping, scooping motion under our fingers. Sharp little raps and cracks came from its substance, file-firing, volley-firing, the sounds of a faggot burning briskly on a frosty night.

"There is much power," said the Frenchman. "See it on the table!"

I had thought it was some delusion of my own, but all could see it now. There was a greenish-yellow phosphorescent light – or I should say a luminous vapour rather than a light – which lay over the surface of the table. It rolled and wreathed and undulated in dim glimmering folds, turning and swirling like clouds of smoke. I could see the white, square-ended hands of the French medium in this baleful light.

"What a fun!" he cried. "It is splendid!"

"Shall we call the alphabet?" asked Moir.

"But no – for we can do much better," said our visitor. "It is but a clumsy thing to tilt the table for every letter of the alphabet, and with such a medium as Madame we should do better than that."

"Yes, you will do better," said a voice.

"Who was that? Who spoke? Was that you, Markham?"

"No, I did not speak."

"It was Madame who spoke."

"But it was not her voice."

"Is that you, Mrs Delamere?"

"It is not the medium, but it is the power which uses the organs of the medium," said the strange, deep voice.

"Where is Mrs Delamere? It will not hurt her, I trust."

"The medium is happy in another plane of existence. She has taken my place, as I have taken hers."

"Who are you?"

"It cannot matter to you who I am. I am one who has lived as you are living, and who has died as you will die."

We heard the creak and grate of a cab pulling up next door. There was an argument about the fare, and the cabman grumbled hoarsely down the street. The green-yellow cloud still swirled faintly over the table, dull elsewhere, but glowing into a dim luminosity in the direction of the medium. It seemed to be piling itself up in front of her. A sense of fear and cold struck into my heart. It seemed to me that lightly and flippantly we had approached the most real and august of sacraments, that communion with the dead of which the fathers of the Church had spoken.

"Don't you think we are going too far? Should we not break up this seance?" I cried.

But the others were all earnest to see the end of it. They laughed at my scruples.

"All the powers are made for use," said Harvey Deacon. "If we *can* do this, we *should* do this. Every new departure of knowledge has been called unlawful in its inception. It is right and proper that we should enquire into the nature of death."

"It is right and proper," said the voice.

"There, what more could you ask?" cried Moir, who was much excited. "Let us have a test. Will you give us a test that you are really there?"

"What test do you demand?"

"Well, now – I have some coins in my pocket. Will you tell me how many?"

"We come back in the hope of teaching and of elevating, and not to guess childish riddles."

"Ha, ha, Meester Moir, you catch it that time," cried the Frenchman. "But surely this is very good sense what the control is saying."

"It is a religion, not a game," said the cold, hard voice.

"Exactly – the very view I take of it," cried Moir. "I am sure I am very sorry if I have asked a foolish question. You will not tell me who you are?"

"What does it matter?"

"Have you been a spirit long?"

"Yes."

"How long?"

"We cannot reckon time as you do. Our conditions are different."

"Are you happy?"

"Yes."

"You would not wish to come back to life?"

"No – certainly not."

"Are you busy?"

"We could not be happy if we were not busy."

"What do you do?"

"I have said that the conditions are entirely different."

"Can you give us no idea of your work?"

"We labour for our own improvement and for the advancement of others."

"Do you like coming here tonight?"

"I am glad to come if I can do any good by coming."

"Then to do good is your object?"

"It is the object of all life on every plane."

"You see, Markham, that should answer your scruples."

It did, for my doubts had passed and only interest remained.

"Have you pain in your life?" I asked.

"No, pain is a thing of the body."

"Have you mental pain?"

"Yes, one may always be sad or anxious."

"Do you meet the friends whom you have known on earth?"

"Some of them."

"Why only some of them?"

"Only those who are sympathetic."

"Do husbands meet wives?"

"Those who have truly loved."

"And the others?"

"They are nothing to each other."

"There must be a spiritual connection?"

"Of course."

"Is what we are doing right?"

"If done in the right spirit."

"What is the wrong spirit?"

"Curiosity and levity."

"May harm come of that?"

"Very serious harm."

"What sort of harm?"

"You may call up forces over which you have no control."

"Evil forces?"

"Undeveloped forces."

"You say they are dangerous. Dangerous to body or mind?"

"Sometimes to both."

There was a pause, and the blackness seemed to grow blacker still, while the yellow-green fog swirled and smoked upon the table.

"Any questions you would like to ask, Moir?" said Harvey Deacon.

"Only this – do you pray in your world?"

"One should pray in every world."

"Why?"

"Because it is the acknowledgement of forces outside ourselves."

"What religion do you hold over there?"

"We differ exactly as you do."

"You have no certain knowledge?"

"We have only faith."

"These questions of religion," said the Frenchman, "they are of interest to you serious English people, but they are not so much fun. It seems to me that with this power here we might be able to have some great experience – *hein*? Something of which we could talk."

"But nothing could be more interesting than this," said Moir.

"Well, if you think so, that is very well," the Frenchman answered, peevishly. "For my part, it seems to me that I have heard all this before, and that tonight I should weesh to try some experiment with all this force which is given to us. But if you have other questions, then ask them, and when you are finish we can try something more."

But the spell was broken. We asked and asked, but the medium sat silent in her chair. Only her deep, regular breathing showed that she was there. The mist still swirled upon the table.

"You have disturbed the harmony. She will not answer."

"But we have learnt already all that she can tell – *hein*? For my part I wish to see something I have never seen before."

"What then?"

"You will let me try?"

"What would you do?"

"I have said to you that thoughts are things. Now I wish to *prove* it to you, and to show you that which is only a thought. Yes, yes, I can do it and you will see. Now I ask you only to sit still and say nothing, and keep ever your hands quiet upon the table."

The room was blacker and more silent than ever. The same feeling of apprehension which had lain heavily upon me at the beginning of the seance was back at my heart once more. The roots of my hair were tingling.

"It is working! It is working!" cried the Frenchman, and there was a crack in his voice as he spoke which told me that he also was strung to his tightest.

The luminous fog drifted slowly off the table, and wavered and flickered across the room. There in the farther and darkest corner it gathered and glowed, hardening down into a shining core – a strange, shifty, luminous and yet non-illuminating patch of radiance, bright itself, but throwing no rays into the darkness. It had changed from a greenish-yellow to a dusky sullen red. Then round this centre there coiled a dark, smoky substance, thickening, hardening, growing denser and blacker. And then the light went out, smothered in that which had grown round it.

"It has gone."

"Hush – there's something in the room."

We heard it in the corner where the light had been, something which breathed deeply and fidgeted in the darkness.

"What is it? Le Duc, what have you done?"

"It is all right. No harm will come." The Frenchman's voice was treble with agitation.

"Good Heavens, Moir, there's a large animal in the room. Here it is, close by my chair! Go away! Go away!"

It was Harvey Deacon's voice, and then came the sound of a blow upon some hard object. And then… And then… how can I tell you what happened then?

Some huge thing hurtled against us in the darkness, rearing, stamping, smashing, springing, snorting. The table was splintered. We were scattered in every direction. It clattered and scrambled amongst us, rushing with horrible energy from one corner of the room to another. We were all screaming with fear, grovelling upon our hands and knees to get away from it. Something trod upon my left hand, and I felt the bones splinter under the weight.

"A light! A light!" someone yelled.

"Moir, you have matches, matches!"

"No, I have none. Deacon, where are the matches? For God's sake, the matches!"

"I can't find them. Here, you Frenchman, stop it!"

"It is beyond me. Oh, *mon Dieu*, I cannot stop it. The door! Where is the door?"

My hand, by good luck, lit upon the handle as I groped about in the darkness. The hard-breathing, snorting, rushing creature tore past me and butted with a fearful crash against the oaken partition. The instant that it had passed I turned the handle, and next moment we were all outside, and the door shut behind us. From within came a horrible crashing and rending and stamping.

"What is it? In Heaven's name, what is it?"

"A horse. I saw it when the door opened. But Mrs Delamere?…"

"We must fetch her out. Come on, Markham; the longer we wait the less we shall like it."

He flung open the door and we rushed in. She was there on the ground amidst the splinters of her chair. We seized her and dragged her swiftly out, and as we gained the door I looked over my shoulder into the darkness. There were two strange eyes glowing at us, a rattle of hoofs, and I had just time to slam the door when there came a crash upon it which split it from top to bottom.

"It's coming through! It's coming!"

"Run, run for your lives!" cried the Frenchman.

Another crash, and something shot through the riven door. It was a long white spike, gleaming in the lamplight. For a moment it shone before us, and then with a snap it disappeared again.

"Quick! Quick! This way!" Harvey Deacon shouted. "Carry her in! Here! Quick!"

We had taken refuge in the dining room and shut the heavy oak door. We laid the senseless woman upon the sofa, and as we did so, Moir, the hard man of business, drooped and fainted across the hearthrug. Harvey Deacon was as white as a corpse, jerking and twitching like an epileptic. With a crash we heard the studio door fly to pieces, and the snorting and stamping were in the passage, up and down, up and down, shaking the house with their fury. The Frenchman had sunk his face on his hands, and sobbed like a frightened child.

"What shall we do?" I shook him roughly by the shoulder. "Is a gun any use?"

"No, no. The power will pass. Then it will end."

"You might have killed us all – you unspeakable fool – with your infernal experiments."

"I did not know. How could I tell that it would be frightened? It is mad with terror. It was his fault. He struck it."

Harvey Deacon sprang up. "Good Heavens!" he cried.

A terrible scream sounded through the house.

"It's my wife! Here, I'm going out. If it's the Evil One himself I am going out!"

He had thrown open the door and rushed out into the passage. At the end of it, at the foot of the stairs, Mrs Deacon was lying senseless, struck down by the sight which she had seen. But there was nothing else.

With eyes of horror we looked about us, but all was perfectly quiet and still. I approached the black square of the studio door, expecting with every slow step that some atrocious shape would hurl itself out of it. But nothing came, and all was silent inside the room. Peeping and peering, our hearts in our mouths, we came to the very threshold, and stared into the darkness. There was still no sound, but in one direction there was also no darkness. A luminous, glowing cloud, with an incandescent centre, hovered in the corner of the room. Slowly it dimmed and faded, growing thinner and fainter, until at last the same dense, velvety blackness filled the whole studio. And with the last flickering gleam of that baleful light the Frenchman broke into a shout of joy.

"What a fun!" he cried. "No one is hurt, and only the door broken, and the ladies frightened. But, my friends, we have done what has never been done before."

"And as far as I can help," said Harvey Deacon, "it will certainly never be done again."

And that was what befell on the 14th of April last at No. 17, Badderly Gardens. I began by saying that it would seem too grotesque to dogmatize as to what it was which actually did occur; but I give my impressions, *our* impressions (since they are corroborated by Harvey Deacon and John Moir), for what they are worth. You may, if it pleases you, imagine that we were the victims of an elaborate and extraordinary hoax. Or you may think with us that we underwent a very real and a very terrible experience. Or perhaps you may know more than we do of such occult matters, and can inform us of some similar occurrence. In this latter case a letter to William Markham, 146M, The Albany, would help to throw a light upon that which is very dark to us.

The Ring of Thoth*

Mr John Vansittart Smith, FRS,* of 147A Gower Street, was a man whose energy of purpose and clearness of thought might have placed him in the very first rank of scientific observers. He was the victim, however, of a universal ambition which prompted him to aim at distinction in many subjects rather than pre-eminence in one. In his early days he had shown an aptitude for zoology and for botany which caused his friends to look upon him as a second Darwin, but when a professorship was almost within his reach he had suddenly discontinued his studies and turned his whole attention to chemistry. Here his researches upon the spectra of the metals had won him his fellowship in the Royal Society; but again he played the coquette with his subject, and after a year's absence from the laboratory he joined the Oriental Society and delivered a paper on the hieroglyphic and demotic inscriptions of El-Kab,* thus giving a crowning example both of the versatility and of the inconstancy of his talents.

The most fickle of wooers, however, is apt to be caught at last, and so it was with John Vansittart Smith. The more he burrowed his way into Egyptology the more impressed he became by the vast field which it opened to the enquirer, and by the extreme importance of a subject which promised to throw a light upon the first germs of human civilization and the origin of the greater part of our arts and sciences. So struck was Mr Smith that he straightway married an Egyptological young lady who had written upon the sixth dynasty, and having thus secured a sound base of operations he set himself to collect materials for a work which should unite the research of Lepsius and the ingenuity of Champollion.* The preparation of this magnum opus entailed many hurried visits to the magnificent Egyptian collections of the Louvre, upon the last of which, no longer ago than the middle of last October, he became involved in a most strange and noteworthy adventure.

The trains had been slow and the Channel had been rough, so that the student arrived in Paris in a somewhat befogged and feverish condition. On reaching the Hôtel de France, in the Rue Laffitte, he had thrown himself upon a sofa for a couple of hours, but, finding that he was unable to sleep, he determined, in spite of his fatigue, to make his way to the Louvre, settle the point which he had come to decide and take the evening train back to Dieppe. Having come to this conclusion, he donned his greatcoat, for it was a raw rainy day, and made his way across the Boulevard des Italiens and down the Avenue de l'Opéra. Once in the Louvre he was on familiar ground, and he speedily made his way to the collection of papyri which it was his intention to consult.

The warmest admirers of John Vansittart Smith could hardly claim for him that he was a handsome man. His high-beaked nose and prominent chin had something of the same acute and incisive character which distinguished his intellect. He held his head in a bird-like fashion, and bird-like too was the pecking motion with which, in conversation, he threw out his objections and retorts. As he stood, with the high collar of his greatcoat raised to his ears, he might have seen from the reflection in the glass case before him that his appearance was a singular one. Yet it came upon him as a sudden jar when an English voice behind him exclaimed in very audible tones, "What a queer-looking mortal!"

The student had a large amount of petty vanity in his composition which manifested itself by an ostentatious and overdone disregard of all personal considerations. He straightened his lips and looked rigidly at the roll of papyrus, while his heart filled with bitterness against the whole race of travelling Britons.

"Yes," said another voice, "he really is an extraordinary fellow."

"Do you know," said the first speaker, "one could almost believe that by the continual contemplation of mummies the chap has became half a mummy himself?"

"He has certainly an Egyptian cast of countenance," said the other.

John Vansittart Smith spun round upon his heel with the intention of shaming his countrymen by a corrosive remark or two. To his surprise and relief, the two young fellows who had been conversing had their shoulders turned towards him, and were gazing at one of the Louvre attendants who was polishing some brasswork at the other side of the room.

"Carter will be waiting for us at the Palais-Royal," said one tourist to the other, glancing at his watch, and they clattered away, leaving the student to his labours.

"I wonder what these chatterers call an Egyptian cast of countenance," thought John Vansittart Smith, and he moved his position slightly in order to catch a glimpse of the man's face. He started as his eyes fell upon it. It was indeed the very face with which his studies had made him familiar.

The regular statuesque features, broad brow, well-rounded chin and dusky complexion were the exact counterpart of the innumerable statues, mummy cases and pictures which adorned the walls of the apartment. The thing was beyond all coincidence. The man must be an Egyptian. The national angularity of the shoulders and narrowness of the hips were alone sufficient to identify him.

John Vansittart Smith shuffled towards the attendant with some intention of addressing him. He was not light of touch in conversation, and found it difficult to strike the happy mean between the brusqueness of the superior and the geniality of the equal. As he came nearer, the man presented his side face to him, but kept his gaze still bent upon his work. Vansittart Smith, fixing his eyes upon the fellow's skin, was conscious of a sudden impression that there was something inhuman and preternatural about its appearance. Over the temple and cheekbone it was as glazed and as shiny as varnished parchment. There was no suggestion of pores. One could not fancy a drop of moisture upon that arid surface. From brow to chin, however, it was cross-hatched by a million delicate wrinkles, which shot and interlaced as though Nature in some Maori mood had tried how wild and intricate a pattern she could devise.

"*Où est la collection de Memphis?*"* asked the student with the awkward air of a man who is devising a question merely for the purpose of opening a conversation.

"*C'est là,*"* replied the man brusquely, nodding his head at the other side of the room.

"*Vous êtes un Égyptien, n'est-ce pas?*"* asked the Englishman.

The attendant looked up and turned his strange dark eyes upon his questioner. They were vitreous, with a misty dry shininess, such as Smith had never seen in a human head before. As he gazed into them he saw some strong emotion gather in their depths, which rose and deepened until it broke into a look of something akin both to horror and to hatred.

"*Non, monsieur: je suis français.*"* The man turned abruptly and bent low over his polishing. The student gazed at him for a moment in astonishment, and then, turning to a chair in a retired corner behind one of the doors, he proceeded to make notes of his researches among the papyri. His thoughts, however, refused to return into their natural groove. They would run upon the enigmatical attendant with the sphinx-like face and the parchment skin.

"Where have I seen such eyes?" said Vansittart Smith to himself. "There is something saurian about them, something reptilian. There's the *membrana* *nictitans** of the snakes," he mused, bethinking himself of his zoological studies. "It gives a shiny effect. But there was something more here. There was a sense of power, of wisdom – so I read them – and of weariness, utter weariness, and ineffable despair. It may be all imagination, but I never had so strong an impression. By Jove, I must have another look at them!" He rose and paced round the Egyptian rooms, but the man who had excited his curiosity had disappeared.

The student sat down again in his quiet corner, and continued to work at his notes. He had gained the information which he required from the papyri, and it only remained to write it down while it was still fresh in his memory. For a time his pencil travelled rapidly over the paper, but soon the lines became less level, the words more blurred, and finally the pencil tinkled down upon the floor, and the head of the student dropped heavily forward upon his chest. Tired out by his journey, he slept so soundly in his lonely post behind the door that neither the clanking civil guard, nor the footsteps of sightseers, nor even the loud hoarse bell which gives the signal for closing, were sufficient to arouse him.

Twilight deepened into darkness, the bustle from the Rue de Rivoli waxed and then waned, distant Notre-Dame clanged out the hour of midnight, and still the dark and lonely figure sat silently in the shadow. It was not until close upon one in the morning that, with a sudden gasp and an intaking of the breath, Vansittart Smith returned to consciousness. For a moment it flashed upon him that he had dropped asleep in his study chair at home. The moon was shining fitfully through the unshuttered window, however, and as his eye ran along the lines of mummies and the endless array of polished cases, he remembered clearly where he was and how he came there. The student was not a nervous man. He possessed that love of a novel situation which is peculiar to his race. Stretching out his cramped limbs, he looked at his watch, and burst into a chuckle as he observed the hour. The episode would make an admirable anecdote to be introduced into his next paper as a relief to the graver and heavier speculations. He was a little cold, but wide awake and much refreshed. It was no wonder that the guardians had overlooked him, for the door threw its heavy black shadow right across him.

The complete silence was impressive. Neither outside nor inside was there a creak or a murmur. He was alone with the dead men of a dead civilization. What though the outer city reeked of the garish nineteenth century! In all this chamber there was scarce an article, from the shrivelled ear of wheat to the pigment box of the painter, which had not held its own against four thousand years. Here was the flotsam and jetsam washed up by the great ocean of time from that far-off empire. From stately Thebes, from lordly Luxor, from the great temples of Heliopolis, from a hundred rifled tombs, these relics had been brought. The student glanced round at the long silent figures who flickered vaguely up through the gloom, at the busy toilers who were now so restful, and he fell into a reverent and thoughtful mood. An unwonted sense of his own youth and insignificance came over him. Leaning back in his chair, he gazed dreamily down the long vista of rooms, all silvery with the moonshine, which extend through the whole wing of the widespread building. His eyes fell upon the yellow glare of a distant lamp.

John Vansittart Smith sat up on his chair with his nerves all on edge. The light was advancing slowly towards him, pausing from time to time, and then coming jerkily onwards. The bearer moved noiselessly. In the utter silence there was no suspicion of the pat of a footfall. An idea of robbers entered the Englishman's head. He snuggled up farther into the corner. The light was two rooms off. Now it was in the next chamber, and still there was no sound. With something approaching to a thrill of fear the student observed a face, floating in the air as it were, behind the flare of the lamp. The figure was wrapped in shadow, but the light fell full upon the strange eager face. There was no mistaking the metallic glistening eyes and the cadaverous skin. It was the attendant with whom he had conversed.

Vansittart Smith's first impulse was to come forward and address him. A few words of explanation would set the matter clear, and lead doubtless to his being conducted to some side door from which he might make his way to his hotel. As the man entered the chamber, however, there was something so stealthy in his movements, and so furtive in his expression, that the Englishman altered his intention. This was clearly no ordinary official walking the rounds. The fellow wore felt-soled slippers, stepped with a rising chest and glanced quickly from left to right, while his hurried gasping breathing thrilled the flame of his lamp. Vansittart Smith crouched silently back into the corner and watched him keenly, convinced that his errand was one of secret and probably sinister import.

There was no hesitation in the other's movements. He stepped lightly and swiftly across to one of the great cases and, drawing a key from his pocket, he unlocked it. From the upper shelf he pulled down a mummy, which he bore away with him, and laid it with much care and solicitude upon the ground. By it he placed his lamp, and then squatting down beside it in Eastern fashion he began with long quivering fingers to undo the cerecloths* and bandages which girt it round. As the crackling rolls of linen peeled off one after the other, a strong aromatic odour filled the chamber, and fragments of scented wood and of spices pattered down upon the marble floor.

It was clear to John Vansittart Smith that this mummy had never been unswathed before. The operation interested him keenly. He thrilled all over with curiosity, and his bird-like head protruded farther and farther from behind the door. When, however, the last roll had been removed from the four-thousand-year-old head, it was all that he could do to stifle an outcry of amazement. First, a cascade of long, black, glossy tresses poured over the workman's hands and arms. A second turn of the bandage revealed a low, white forehead, with a pair of delicately arched eyebrows. A third uncovered a pair of bright, deeply fringed eyes, and a straight, well-cut nose, while a fourth and last showed a sweet, full, sensitive mouth, and a beautifully curved chin. The whole face was one of extraordinary loveliness, save for the one blemish that in the centre of the forehead there was a single irregular, coffee-coloured splotch. It was a triumph of the embalmer's art. Vansittart Smith's eyes grew larger and larger as he gazed upon it, and he chirruped in his throat with satisfaction.

Its effect upon the Egyptologist was as nothing, however, compared with that which it produced upon the strange attendant. He threw his hands up into the air, burst into a harsh clatter of words, and then, hurling himself down upon the ground beside the mummy, he threw his arms round her, and kissed her repeatedly upon the lips and brow. "*Ma petite!*" he groaned in French. "*Ma pauvre petite!*"* His voice broke with emotion, and his innumerable wrinkles quivered and writhed, but the student observed in the lamplight that his shining eyes were still dry and tearless as two beads of steel. For some minutes he lay, with a twitching face, crooning and moaning over the beautiful head. Then he broke into a sudden smile, said some words in an unknown tongue, and sprang to his feet with the vigorous air of one who has braced himself for an effort.

In the centre of the room there was a large circular case which contained, as the student had frequently remarked, a magnificent collection of early Egyptian rings and precious stones. To this the attendant strode and, unlocking it, threw it open. On the ledge at the side he placed his lamp, and beside it a small earthenware jar which he had drawn from his pocket. He then took a handful of rings from the case, and with a most serious and anxious face he proceeded to smear each in turn with some liquid substance from the earthen pot, holding them to the light as he did so. He was clearly disappointed with the first lot, for he threw them petulantly back into the case and drew out some more. One of these, a massive ring with a large crystal set in it, he seized and eagerly tested with the contents of the jar. Instantly he uttered a cry of joy, and threw out his arms in a wild gesture which upset the pot and sent the liquid streaming across the floor to the very feet of the Englishman. The attendant drew a red handkerchief from his bosom and, mopping up the mess, he followed it into the corner, where in a moment he found himself face to face with his observer.

"Excuse me," said John Vansittart Smith, with all imaginable politeness, "I have been unfortunate enough to fall asleep behind this door."

"And you have been watching me?" the other asked in English, with a most venomous look on his corpse-like face.

The student was a man of veracity. "I confess," said he, "that I have noticed your movements, and that they have aroused my curiosity and interest in the highest degree."

The man drew a long flamboyant-bladed knife from his bosom. "You have had a very narrow escape," he said. "Had I seen you ten minutes ago, I should have driven this through your heart. As it is, if you touch me or interfere with me in any way you are a dead man."

"I have no wish to interfere with you," the student answered. "My presence here is entirely accidental. All I ask is that you will have the extreme kindness to show me out through some side door." He spoke with great suavity, for the man was still pressing the tip of his dagger against the palm of his left hand, as though to assure himself of its sharpness, while his face preserved its malignant expression.

"If I thought…" said he. "But no, perhaps it is as well. What is your name?"

The Englishman gave it.

"Vansittart Smith," the other repeated. "Are you the same Vansittart Smith who gave a paper in London upon El-Kab? I saw a report of it. Your knowledge of the subject is contemptible."

"Sir!" cried the Egyptologist.

"Yet it is superior to that of many who make even greater pretensions. The whole keystone of our old life in Egypt was not the inscriptions or monuments of which you make so much, but was our hermetic philosophy and mystic knowledge of which you say little or nothing."

"Our old life!" repeated the scholar, wide-eyed – and then suddenly, "Good God, look at the mummy's face!"

The strange man turned and flashed his light upon the dead woman, uttering a long doleful cry as he did so. The action of the air had already undone all the art of the embalmer. The skin had fallen away, the eyes had sunk inwards, the discoloured lips had writhed away from the yellow teeth and the brown mark upon the forehead alone showed that it was indeed the same face which had shown such youth and beauty a few short minutes before.

The man flapped his hands together in grief and horror. Then mastering himself by a strong effort he turned his hard eyes once more upon the Englishman.

"It does not matter," he said, in a shaking voice. "It does not really matter. I came here tonight with the fixed determination to do something. It is now done. All else is as nothing. I have found my quest. The old curse is broken. I can rejoin her. What matter about her inanimate shell, so long as her spirit is awaiting me at the other side of the veil!"

"These are wild words," said Vansittart Smith. He was becoming more and more convinced that he had to do with a madman.

"Time presses, and I must go," continued the other. "The moment is at hand for which I have waited this weary time. But I must show you out first. Come with me."

Taking up the lamp, he turned from the disordered chamber, and led the student swiftly through the long series of the Egyptian, Assyrian and Persian apartments. At the end of the latter he pushed open a small door let into the wall and descended a winding stone stair. The Englishman felt the cold fresh air of the night upon his brow. There was a door opposite him which appeared to communicate with the street. To the right of this another door stood ajar, throwing a spurt of yellow light across the passage. "Come in here!" said the attendant shortly.

Vansittart Smith hesitated. He had hoped that he had come to the end of his adventure. Yet his curiosity was strong within him. He could not leave the matter unsolved, so he followed his strange companion into the lighted chamber.

It was a small room, such as is devoted to a concierge. A wood fire sparkled in the grate. At one side stood a truckle bed, and at the other a coarse wooden chair, with a round table in the centre, which bore the remains of a meal. As the visitor's eye glanced round he could not but remark with an ever-recurring thrill that all the small details of the room were of the most quaint design and antique workmanship. The candlesticks, the vases upon the chimney piece, the fire irons, the ornaments upon the walls were all such as he had been wont to associate with the remote past. The gnarled heavy-eyed man sat himself down upon the edge of the bed, and motioned his guest into the chair.

"There may be design in this," he said, still speaking excellent English. "It may be decreed that I should leave some account behind as a warning to all rash mortals who would set their wits up against the workings of Nature. I leave it with you. Make such use as you will of it. I speak to you now with my feet upon the threshold of the other world.

"I am, as you surmised, an Egyptian – not one of the downtrodden race of slaves who now inhabit the delta of the Nile, but a survivor of that fiercer and harder people who tamed the Hebrew, drove the Ethiopian back into the southern deserts, and built those mighty works which have been the envy and the wonder of all after generations. It was in the reign of Tuthmosis,* sixteen hundred years before the birth of Christ, that I first saw the light. You shrink away from me. Wait, and you will see that I am more to be pitied than to be feared.

"My name was Sosra. My father had been the chief priest of Osiris in the great temple of Abaris, which stood in those days upon the Bubastic branch of the Nile.* I was brought up in the temple and was trained in all those mystic arts which are spoken of in your own Bible. I was an apt pupil. Before I was sixteen I had learnt all which the wisest priest could teach me. From that time on I studied Nature's secrets for myself, and shared my knowledge with no man.

"Of all the questions which attracted me there were none over which I laboured so long as over those which concern themselves with the nature of life. I probed deeply into the vital principle. The aim of medicine had been to drive away disease when it appeared. It seemed to me that a method might be devised which should so fortify the body as to prevent weakness or death from ever taking hold of it. It is useless that I should recount my researches. You would scarce comprehend them if I did. They were carried out partly upon animals, partly upon slaves and partly on myself. Suffice it that their result was to furnish me with a substance which, when injected into the blood, would endow the body with strength to resist the effects of time, of violence or of disease. It would not indeed confer immortality, but its potency would endure for many thousands of years. I used it upon a cat, and afterwards drugged the creature with the most deadly poisons. That cat is alive in Lower Egypt at the present moment. There was nothing of mystery or magic in the matter. It was simply a chemical discovery, which may well be made again.

"Love of life runs high in the young. It seemed to me that I had broken away from all human care now that I had abolished pain and driven death to such a distance. With a light heart I poured the accursed stuff into my veins. Then I looked round for someone whom I could benefit. There was a young priest of Thoth, Parmes by name, who had won my goodwill by his earnest nature and his devotion to his studies. To him I whispered my secret, and at his request I injected him with my elixir. I should now, I reflected, never be without a companion of the same age as myself.

"After this grand discovery I relaxed my studies to some extent, but Parmes continued his with redoubled energy. Every day I could see him working with his flasks and his distiller in the Temple of Thoth, but he said little to me as to the result of his labours. For my own part, I used to walk through the city and look around me with exultation as I reflected that all this was destined to pass away, and that only I should remain. The people would bow to me as they passed me, for the fame of my knowledge had gone abroad.

"There was war at this time, and the Great King had sent down his soldiers to the eastern boundary to drive away the Hyksos.* A governor, too, was sent to Abaris, that he might hold it for the King. I had heard much of the beauty of the daughter of this governor, but one day as I walked out with Parmes we met her, borne upon the shoulders of her slaves. I was struck with love as with lightning. My heart went out from me. I could have thrown myself beneath the feet of her bearers. This was my woman. Life without her was impossible. I swore by the head of Horus that she should be mine. I swore it to the priest of Thoth. He turned away from me with a brow which was as black as midnight.

"There is no need to tell you of our wooing. She came to love me even as I loved her. I learnt that Parmes had seen her before I did, and had shown her that he too loved her, but I could smile at his passion, for I knew that her heart was mine. The white plague had come upon the city and many were stricken, but I laid my hands upon the sick and nursed them without fear or scathe. She marvelled at my daring. Then I told her my secret, and begged her that she would let me use my art upon her.

"'Your flower shall then be unwithered, Atma,' I said. 'Other things may pass away, but you and I, and our great love for each other, shall outlive the tomb of King Chefru.'

"But she was full of timid, maidenly objections. 'Was it right?' she asked. 'Was it not a thwarting of the will of the gods? If the great Osiris had wished that our years should be so long, would he not himself have brought it about?'

"With fond and loving words I overcame her doubts, and yet she hesitated. It was a great question, she said. She would think it over for this one night. In the morning I should know of her resolution. Surely one night was not too much to ask. She wished to pray to Isis for help in her decision.

"With a sinking heart and a sad foreboding of evil I left her with her tirewomen. In the morning, when the early sacrifice was over, I hurried to her house. A frightened slave met me upon the steps. Her mistress was ill, she said, very ill. In a frenzy I broke my way through the attendants, and rushed through hall and corridor to my Atma's chamber. She lay upon her couch, her head high upon the pillow, with a pallid face and a glazed eye. On her forehead there blazed a single angry purple patch. I knew that hell mark of old. It was the scar of the white plague, the sign manual of death.

"Why should I speak of that terrible time? For months I was mad, fevered, delirious, and yet I could not die. Never did an Arab thirst after the sweet wells as I longed after death. Could poison or steel have shortened the thread of my existence, I should soon have rejoined my love in the land with the narrow portal. I tried, but it was of no avail. The accursed influence was too strong upon me. One night as I lay upon my couch, weak and weary, Parmes, the priest of Thoth, came to my chamber. He stood in the circle of the lamplight, and he looked down upon me with eyes which were bright with a mad joy.

"'Why did you let the maiden die?' he asked. 'Why did you not strengthen her as you strengthened me?'

"'I was too late,' I answered. 'But I had forgot. You also loved her. You are my fellow in misfortune. Is it not terrible to think of the centuries which must pass ere we look upon her again? Fools, fools, that we were to take death to be our enemy!'

"'You may say that,' he cried with a wild laugh. 'The words come well from your lips. For me they have no meaning.'

"'What mean you?' I cried, raising myself upon my elbow. 'Surely, friend, this grief has turned your brain.' His face was aflame with joy, and he writhed and shook like one who hath a devil.

"'Do you know whither I go?' he asked.

"'Nay,' I answered, 'I cannot tell.'

"'I go to her,' said he. 'She lies embalmed in the farther tomb by the double palm tree beyond the city wall.'

"'Why do you go there?' I asked.

"'To die!' he shrieked. 'To die! I am not bound by earthen fetters.'

"'But the elixir is in your blood,' I cried.

"'I can defy it,' said he. 'I have found a stronger principle which will destroy it. It is working in my veins at this moment, and in an hour I shall be a dead man. I shall join her, and you shall remain behind.'

"As I looked upon him I could see that he spoke words of truth. The light in his eye told me that he was indeed beyond the power of the elixir.

"'You will teach me!' I cried.

"'Never!' he answered.

"'I implore you, by the wisdom of Thoth, by the majesty of Anubis!'

"'It is useless,' he said coldly.

"'Then I will find it out,' I cried.

"'You cannot,' he answered. 'It came to me by chance. There is one ingredient which you can never get. Save that which is in the ring of Thoth, none will ever more be made.'

"'In the ring of Thoth!' I repeated. 'Where then is the ring of Thoth?'

"'That also you shall never know,' he answered. 'You won her love. Who has won in the end? I leave you to your sordid earth life. My chains are broken. I must go!' He turned upon his heel and fled from the chamber. In the morning came the news that the priest of Thoth was dead.

"My days after that were spent in study. I must find this subtle poison which was strong enough to undo the elixir. From early dawn to midnight I bent over the test tube and the furnace. Above all, I collected the papyri and the chemical flasks of the priest of Thoth. Alas! They taught me little. Here and there some hint or stray expression would raise hope in my bosom, but no good ever came of it. Still, month after month, I struggled on. When my heart grew faint I would make my way to the tomb by the palm trees. There, standing by the dead casket from which the jewel had been rifled, I would feel her sweet presence, and would whisper to her that I would rejoin her if mortal wit could solve the riddle.

"Parmes had said that his discovery was connected with the ring of Thoth. I had some remembrance of the trinket. It was a large and weighty circlet, made not of gold, but of a rarer and heavier metal brought from the mines of Mount Harbal. Platinum, you call it. The ring had, I remembered, a hollow crystal set in it, in which some few drops of liquid might be stored. Now, the secret of Parmes could not have to do with the metal alone, for there were many rings of that metal in the Temple. Was it not more likely that he had stored his precious poison within the cavity of the crystal? I had scarce come to this conclusion before, in hunting through his papers, I came upon one which told me that it was indeed so, and that there was still some of the liquid unused.

"But how to find the ring? It was not upon him when he was stripped for the embalmer. Of that I made sure. Neither was it among his private effects. In vain I searched every room that he had entered, every box and vase and chattel that he had owned. I sifted the very sand of the desert in the places where he had been wont to walk; but, do what I would, I could come upon no traces of the ring of Thoth. Yet it may be that my labours would have overcome all obstacles had it not been for a new and unlooked-for misfortune.

"A great war had been waged against the Hyksos, and the captains of the Great King had been cut off in the desert, with all their bowmen and horsemen. The shepherd tribes were upon us like the locusts in a dry year. From the wilderness of Shur to the great bitter lake there was blood by day and fire by night. Abaris was the bulwark of Egypt, but we could not keep the savages back. The city fell. The governor and the soldiers were put to the sword, and I, with many more, was led away into captivity.

"For years and years I tended cattle in the great plains by the Euphrates. My master died, and his son grew old, but I was still as far from death as ever. At last I escaped upon a swift camel, and made my way back to Egypt. The Hyksos had settled in the land which they had conquered, and their own king ruled over the country. Abaris had been torn down, the city had been burnt, and of the great Temple there was nothing left save an unsightly mound. Everywhere the tombs had been rifled and the monuments destroyed. Of my Atma's grave no sign was left. It was buried in the sands of the desert, and the palm trees which marked the spot had long disappeared. The papers of Parmes and the remains of the Temple of Thoth were either destroyed or scattered far and wide over the deserts of Syria. All search after them was vain.

"From that time I gave up all hope of ever finding the ring or discovering the subtle drug. I set myself to live as patiently as might be until the effect of the elixir should wear away. How can you understand how terrible a thing time is, you who have experience only of the narrow course which lies between the cradle and the grave! I know it to my cost, I who have floated down the whole stream of history. I was old when Ilium fell. I was very old when Herodotus came to Memphis. I was bowed down with years when the new gospel came upon earth. Yet you see me much as other men are, with the cursed elixir still sweetening my blood, and guarding me against that which I would court. Now at last, at last I have come to the end of it!

"I have travelled in all lands and I have dwelt with all nations. Every tongue is the same to me. I learnt them all to help pass the weary time.

I need not tell you how slowly they drifted by, the long dawn of modern civilization, the dreary middle years, the dark times of barbarism. They are all behind me now. I have never looked with the eyes of love upon another woman. Atma knows that I have been constant to her.

"It was my custom to read all that the scholars had to say upon ancient Egypt. I have been in many positions, sometimes affluent, sometimes poor, but I have always found enough to enable me to buy the journals which deal with such matters. Some nine months ago I was in San Francisco, when I read an account of some discoveries made in the neighbourhood of Abaris. My heart leapt into my mouth as I read it. It said that the excavator had busied himself in exploring some tombs recently unearthed. In one there had been found an unopened mummy with an inscription upon the outer case setting forth that it contained the body of the daughter of the governor of the city in the days of Tuthmosis. It added that on removing the outer case there had been exposed a large platinum ring set with a crystal, which had been laid upon the breast of the embalmed woman. This, then, was where Parmes had hid the ring of Thoth. He might well say that it was safe, for no Egyptian would ever stain his soul by moving even the outer case of a buried friend.

"That very night I set off from San Francisco, and in a few weeks I found myself once more at Abaris, if a few sand heaps and crumbling walls may retain the name of the great city. I hurried to the Frenchmen who were digging there and asked them for the ring. They replied that both the ring and the mummy had been sent to the Boulak Museum at Cairo.* To Boulak I went, but only to be told that Mariette Bey* had claimed them and had shipped them to the Louvre. I followed them, and there at last, in the Egyptian chamber, I came, after close upon four thousand years, upon the remains of my Atma, and upon the ring for which I had sought so long.

"But how was I to lay hands upon them? How was I to have them for my very own? It chanced that the office of attendant was vacant. I went to the director. I convinced him that I knew much about Egypt. In my eagerness I said too much. He remarked that a professor's chair would suit me better than a seat in the *conciergerie*. I knew more, he said, than he did. It was only by blundering, and letting him think that he had overestimated my knowledge, that I prevailed upon him to let me move the few effects which I have retained into this chamber. It is my first and my last night here.

"Such is my story, Mr Vansittart Smith. I need not say more to a man of your perception. By a strange chance you have this night looked upon the face of the woman whom I loved in those far-off days. There were many rings with crystals in the case, and I had to test for the platinum to be sure of the one which I wanted. A glance at the crystal has shown me that the liquid is indeed within it, and that I shall at last be able to shake off that accursed health which has been worse to me than the foulest disease. I have nothing more to say to you. I have unburdened myself. You may tell my story or you may withhold it at your pleasure. The choice rests with you. I owe you some amends, for you have had a narrow escape of your life this night. I was a desperate man, and not to be baulked in my purpose. Had I seen you before the thing was done, I might have put it beyond your power to oppose me or to raise an alarm. This is the door. It leads into the Rue de Rivoli. Goodnight."

The Englishman glanced back. For a moment the lean figure of Sosra the Egyptian stood framed in the narrow doorway. The next the door had slammed, and the heavy rasping of a bolt broke on the silent night.

It was on the second day after his return to London that Mr John Vansittart Smith saw the following concise narrative in the Paris correspondence of *The Times*:

> *Curious Occurrence in the Louvre*. Yesterday morning a strange discovery was made in the principal Eastern chamber. The *ouvriers** who are employed to clean out the rooms in the morning found one of the attendants lying dead upon the floor with his arms round one of the mummies. So close was his embrace that it was only with the utmost difficulty that they were separated. One of the cases containing valuable rings had been opened and rifled. The authorities are of opinion that the man was bearing away the mummy with some idea of selling it to a private collector, but that he was struck down in the very act by long-standing disease of the heart. It is said that he was a man of uncertain age and eccentric habits, without any living relations to mourn over his dramatic and untimely end.

The Los Amigos Fiasco

I used to be the leading practitioner of Los Amigos. Of course, everyone has heard of the great electrical generating gear there. The town is widespread, and there are dozens of little townlets and villages all around, which receive their supply from the same centre, so that the works are on a very large scale. The Los Amigos folk say that they are the largest upon earth, but then we claim that for everything in Los Amigos except the jail and the death rate. Those are said to be the smallest.

Now, with so fine an electrical supply, it seemed to be a sinful waste of hemp that the Los Amigos criminals should perish in the old-fashioned manner. And then came the news of the electrocutions in the east, and how the results had not after all been so instantaneous as had been hoped. The western engineers raised their eyebrows when they read of the puny shocks by which these men had perished, and they vowed in Los Amigos that when an irreclaimable came their way he should be dealt handsomely by and have the run of all the big dynamos. There should be no reserve, said the engineers, but he should have all that they had got. And what the result of that would be none could predict, save that it must be absolutely blasting and deadly. Never before had a man been so charged with electricity as they would charge him. He was to be smitten by the essence of ten thunderbolts. Some prophesied combustion, and some disintegration and disappearance. They were waiting eagerly to settle the question by actual demonstration, and it was just at that moment that Duncan Warner came that way.

Warner had been wanted by the law, and by nobody else, for many years. Desperado, murderer, train robber and road agent, he was a man beyond the pale of human pity. He had deserved a dozen deaths, and the Los Amigos folk grudged him so gaudy a one as that. He seemed to feel himself to be unworthy of it, for he made two frenzied attempts at escape. He was a powerful, muscular man, with a lion head, tangled black locks and a sweeping beard which covered his broad chest. When he was tried, there was no finer head in all the crowded court. It's no new thing to find the best face looking from the dock. But his good looks could not balance his bad deeds. His advocate did all he knew, but the cards lay against him, and Duncan Warner was handed over to the mercy of the big Los Amigos dynamos.

I was there at the committee meeting when the matter was discussed. The town council had chosen four experts to look after the arrangements. Three of them were admirable. There was Joseph McConnor, the very man who had designed the dynamos, and there was Joshua Westmacott, the chairman of the Los Amigos Electrical Supply Company, Limited. Then there was myself as the chief medical man, and lastly an old German of the name of Peter Stulpnagel. The Germans were a strong body at Los Amigos, and they all voted for their man. That was how he got on the committee. It was said that he had been a wonderful electrician at home, and he was eternally working with wires and insulators and Leyden jars; but, as he never seemed to get any further, or to have any results worth publishing, he came at last to be regarded as a harmless crank who had made science his hobby. We three practical men smiled when we heard that he had been elected as our colleague, and at the meeting we fixed it all up very nicely among ourselves without much thought of the old fellow who sat with his ears scooped forward in his hands, for he was a trifle hard of hearing, taking no more part in the proceedings than the gentlemen of the press who scribbled their notes on the back benches.

We did not take long to settle it all. In New York a strength of some two thousand volts had been used, and death had not been instantaneous. Evidently their shock had been too weak. Los Amigos should not fall into that error. The charge should be six times greater, and therefore, of course, it would be six times more effective. Nothing could possibly be more logical. The whole concentrated force of the great dynamos should be employed on Duncan Warner.

So we three settled it, and had already risen to break up the meeting when our silent companion opened his mouth for the first time.

"Gentlemen," said he, "you appear to me to show an extraordinary ignorance upon the subject of electricity. You have not mastered the first principles of its actions upon a human being."

The committee was about to break into an angry reply to this brusque comment, but the chairman of the Electrical Company tapped his forehead to claim its indulgence for the crankiness of the speaker.

"Pray tell us, sir," said he, with an ironical smile, "what is there in our conclusions with which you find fault?"

"With your assumption that a large dose of electricity will merely increase the effect of a small dose. Do you not think it possible that it might have an entirely different result? Do you know anything, by actual experiment, of the effect of such powerful shocks?"

"We know it by analogy," said the chairman pompously. "All drugs increase their effect when they increase their dose; for example – for example…"

"Whisky," said Joseph McConnor.

"Quite so. Whisky. You see it there."

Peter Stulpnagel smiled and shook his head.

"Your argument is not very good," said he. "When I used to take whisky, I used to find that one glass would excite me, but that six would send me to sleep, which is just the opposite. Now, suppose that electricity were to act in just the opposite way also, what then?"

We three practical men burst out laughing. We had known that our colleague was queer, but we never had thought that he would be as queer as this.

"What then?" repeated Peter Stulpnagel.

"We'll take our chances," said the chairman.

"Pray consider," said Peter, "that workmen who have touched the wires, and who have received shocks of only a few hundred volts, have died instantly. The fact is well known. And yet when a much greater force was used upon a criminal at New York, the man struggled for some little time. Do you not clearly see that the smaller dose is the more deadly?"

"I think, gentlemen, that this discussion has been carried on quite long enough," said the chairman, rising again. "The point, I take it, has already been decided by the majority of the committee, and Duncan Warner shall be electrocuted on Tuesday by the full strength of the Los Amigos dynamos. Is it not so?"

"I agree," said Joseph McConnor.

"I agree," said I.

"And I protest," said Peter Stulpnagel.

"Then the motion is carried, and your protest will be duly entered in the minutes," said the chairman, and so the sitting was dissolved.

The attendance at the electrocution was a very small one. We four members of the committee were, of course, present with the executioner, who was to act under their orders. The others were the United States marshal, the governor of the jail, the chaplain and three members of the press. The room was a small brick chamber, forming an outhouse to the Central Electrical station. It had been used as a laundry, and had an oven and copper at one side, but no other furniture save a single chair for the condemned man. A metal plate for his feet was placed in front of it, to which ran a thick insulated wire. Above, another wire depended from the ceiling, which could be connected with a small metallic rod projecting from a cap which was to be placed upon his head. When this connection was established Duncan Warner's hour was come.

There was a solemn hush as we waited for the coming of the prisoner. The practical engineers looked a little pale, and fidgeted nervously with the wires. Even the hardened marshal was ill at ease, for a mere hanging was one thing, and this blasting of flesh and blood a very different one. As to the pressmen, their faces were whiter than the sheets which lay before them. The only man who appeared to feel none of the influence of these preparations was the little German crank, who strolled from one to the other with a smile on his lips and mischief in his eyes. More than once he even went so far as to burst into a shout of laughter, until the chaplain sternly rebuked him for his ill-timed levity.

"How can you so far forget yourself, Mr Stulpnagel," said he, "as to jest in the presence of death?"

But the German was quite unabashed.

"If I were in the presence of death I should not jest," said he, "but since I am not I may do what I choose."

This flippant reply was about to draw another and a sterner reproof from the chaplain, when the door was swung open and two warders entered leading Duncan Warner between them. He glanced round him with a set face, stepped resolutely forward, and seated himself upon the chair.

"Touch her off!" said he.

It was barbarous to keep him in suspense. The chaplain murmured a few words in his ear, the attendant placed the cap upon his head, and then, while we all held our breath, the wire and the metal were brought in contact.

"Great Scott!" shouted Duncan Warner.

He had bounded in his chair as the frightful shock crashed through his system. But he was not dead. On the contrary, his eyes gleamed far more brightly than they had done before. There was only one change, but it was a singular one. The black had passed from his hair and beard as the shadow passes from a landscape. They were both as white as snow. And yet there was no other sign of decay. His skin was smooth and plump and lustrous as a child's.

The marshal looked at the committee with a reproachful eye.

"There seems to be some hitch here, gentlemen," said he.

We three practical men looked at each other.

Peter Stulpnagel smiled pensively.

"I think that another one should do it," said I.

Again the connection was made, and again Duncan Warner sprang in his chair and shouted, but, indeed, were it not that he still remained in the chair none of us would have recognized him. His hair and his beard had shredded off in an instant, and the room looked like a barber's shop on a Saturday night. There he sat, his eyes still shining, his skin radiant with the glow of perfect health, but with a scalp as bald as a Dutch cheese, and a chin without so much as a trace of down. He began to revolve one of his arms, slowly and doubtfully at first, but with more confidence as he went on.

"That jint," said he, "has puzzled half the doctors on the Pacific Slope. It's as good as new, and as limber as a hickory twig."

"You are feeling pretty well?" asked the old German.

"Never better in my life," said Duncan Warner cheerily.

The situation was a painful one. The marshal glared at the committee. Peter Stulpnagel grinned and rubbed his hands. The engineers scratched their heads. The bald-headed prisoner revolved his arm and looked pleased.

"I think that one more shock—" began the chairman.

"No, sir," said the marshal. "We've had foolery enough for one morning. We are here for an execution, and an execution we'll have."

"What do you propose?"

"There's a hook handy upon the ceiling. Fetch a rope, and we'll soon set this matter straight."

There was another awkward delay while the warders departed for the cord. Peter Stulpnagel bent over Duncan Warner, and whispered something in his ear. The desperado stared in surprise.

"You don't say?" he asked.

The German nodded.

"What! No ways?"

Peter shook his head, and the two began to laugh as though they shared some huge joke between them.

The rope was brought, and the marshal himself slipped the noose over the criminal's neck. Then the two warders, the assistant and he swung their victim into the air. For half an hour he hung – a dreadful sight – from the ceiling. Then in solemn silence they lowered him down, and one of the warders went out to order the shell* to be brought round. But as he touched ground again what was our amazement when Duncan Warner put his hands up to his neck, loosened the noose and took a long, deep breath.

"Paul Jefferson's sale is goin' well," he remarked, "I could see the crowd from up yonder," and he nodded at the hook in the ceiling.

"Up with him again!" shouted the marshal. "We'll get the life out of him somehow."

In an instant the victim was up at the hook once more.

They kept him there for an hour, but when he came down he was perfectly garrulous.

"Old man Plunket goes too much to the Arcady Saloon," said he. "Three times he's been there in an hour; and him with a family. Old man Plunket would do well to swear off."

It was monstrous and incredible, but there it was. There was no getting round it. The man was there talking when he ought to have been dead. We all sat staring in amazement, but United States Marshal Carpenter was not a man to be euchred* so easily. He motioned the others to one side, so that the prisoner was left standing alone.

"Duncan Warner," said he slowly, "you are here to play your part, and I am here to play mine. Your game is to live if you can, and my game is to carry out the sentence of the law. You've beat us on electricity. I'll give you one there. And you've beat us on hanging, for you seem to thrive on it. But it's my turn to beat you now, for my duty has to be done."

He pulled a six-shooter from his coat as he spoke, and fired all the shots through the body of the prisoner. The room was so filled with smoke that we could see nothing, but when it cleared the prisoner was still standing there, looking down in disgust at the front of his coat.

"Coats must be cheap where you come from," said he. "Thirty dollars it cost me, and look at it now. The six holes in front are bad enough, but four of the balls have passed out, and a pretty fine state the back must be in."

The marshal's revolver fell from his hand, and he dropped his arms to his sides, a beaten man.

"Maybe some of you gentlemen can tell me what this means," said he, looking helplessly at the committee.

Peter Stulpnagel took a step forward.

"I'll tell you all about it," said he.

"You seem to be the only person who knows anything."

"I *am* the only person who knows anything. I should have warned these gentlemen; but, as they would not listen to me, I have allowed them to learn by experience. What you have done with your electricity is that you have increased the man's vitality until he can defy death for centuries."

"Centuries!"

"Yes, it will take the wear of hundreds of years to exhaust the enormous nervous energy with which you have drenched him. Electricity is life, and you have charged him with it to the utmost. Perhaps in fifty years you might execute him, but I am not sanguine about it."

"Great Scott! What shall I do with him?" cried the unhappy marshal.

Peter Stulpnagel shrugged his shoulders.

"It seems to me that it does not much matter what you do with him now," said he.

"Maybe we could drain the electricity out of him again. Suppose we hang him up by the heels?"

"No, no, it's out of the question."

"Well, well, he shall do no more mischief in Los Amigos, anyhow," said the marshal with decision. "He shall go into the new jail. The prison will wear him out."

"On the contrary," said Peter Stulpnagel, "I think that it is much more probable that he will wear out the prison."

It was rather a fiasco, and for years we didn't talk more about it than we could help, but it's no secret now, and I thought you might like to jot down the facts in your casebook.

How It Happened

She was a writing medium. This is what she wrote:

I can remember some things upon that evening most distinctly, and others are like some vague, broken dreams. That is what makes it so difficult to tell a connected story. I have no idea now what it was that had taken me to London and brought me back so late. It just merges into all my other visits to London. But from the time that I got out at the little country station everything is extraordinarily clear. I can live it again – every instant of it.

I remember so well walking down the platform and looking at the illuminated clock at the end which told me that it was half-past eleven. I remember also my wondering whether I could get home before midnight. Then I remember the big motor, with its glaring headlights and glitter of polished brass, waiting for me outside. It was my new thirty-horsepower Robur,* which had only been delivered that day. I remember also asking Perkins, my chauffeur, how she had gone, and his saying that he thought she was excellent.

"I'll try her myself," said I, and I climbed into the driver's seat.

"The gears are not the same," said he. "Perhaps, sir, I had better drive."

"No, I should like to try her," said I.

And so we started on the five-mile drive for home.

My old car had the gears as they used always to be in notches on a bar. In this car you passed the gear lever through a gate to get on the higher ones. It was not difficult to master, and soon I thought that I understood it. It was foolish, no doubt, to begin to learn a new system in the dark, but one often does foolish things, and one has not always to pay the full price for them. I got along very well until I came to Claystall Hill. It is one of the worst hills in England, a mile and a half long and one in six in places, with three fairly sharp curves. My park gates stand at the very foot of it upon the main London road.

We were just over the brow of this hill, where the grade is steepest, when the trouble began. I had been on the top speed, and wanted to get her on the free; but she stuck between gears, and I had to get her back on the top again. By this time she was going at a great rate, so I clapped on both brakes, and one after the other they gave way. I didn't mind so much when I felt my footbrake snap, but when I put all my weight on my side brake, and the lever clanged to its full limit without a catch, it brought a cold sweat out of me. By this time we were fairly tearing down the slope. The lights were brilliant, and I brought her round the first curve all right. Then we did the second one, though it was a close shave for the ditch. There was a mile of straight then with the third curve beneath it, and after that the gate of the park. If I could shoot into that harbour all would be well, for the slope up to the house would bring her to a stand.

Perkins behaved splendidly. I should like that to be known. He was perfectly cool and alert. I had thought at the very beginning of taking the bank, and he read my intention.

"I wouldn't do it, sir," said he. "At this pace it must go over and we should have it on the top of us."

Of course he was right. He got to the electric switch and had it off, so we were in the free; but we were still running at a fearful pace. He laid his hands on the wheel.

"I'll keep her steady," said he, "if you care to jump and chance it. We can never get round that curve. Better jump, sir."

"No," said I. "I'll stick it out. You can jump if you like."

"I'll stick it with you, sir," said he.

If it had been the old car I should have jammed the gear lever into the reverse, and seen what would happen. I expect she would have stripped her gears or smashed up somehow, but it would have been a chance. As it was, I was helpless. Perkins tried to climb across, but you couldn't do it going at that pace. The wheels were whirring like a high wind and the big body creaking and groaning with the strain. But the lights were brilliant, and one could steer to an inch. I remember thinking what an awful and yet majestic sight we should appear to anyone who met us. It was a narrow road, and we were just a great, roaring, golden death to anyone who came in our path.

We got round the corner with one wheel three feet high upon the bank. I thought we were surely over, but after staggering for a moment she righted and darted onwards. That was the third corner and the last one. There was only the park gate now. It was facing us, but, as luck would have it, not facing us directly. It was about twenty yards to the left up the main road into which we ran. Perhaps I could have done it, but I expect that the steering gear had been jarred when we ran on the bank. The wheel did not turn easily. We shot out of the lane. I saw the open gate on the left. I whirled round my wheel with all the strength of my wrists. Perkins and I threw our bodies across, and then the next instant, going at fifty miles an hour, my right front wheel struck full on the right-hand pillar of my own gate. I heard the crash. I was conscious of flying through the air, and then – and then!…

When I became aware of my own existence once more I was among some brushwood in the shadow of the oaks upon the lodge side of the drive. A man was standing beside me. I imagined at first that it was Perkins, but when I looked again I saw that it was Stanley, a man whom I had known at college some years before, and for whom I had a really genuine affection. There was always something peculiarly sympathetic to me in Stanley's personality; and I was proud to think that I had some similar influence upon him. At the present moment I was surprised to see him, but I was like a man in a dream, giddy and shaken and quite prepared to take things as I found them without questioning them.

"What a smash!" I said. "Good Lord, what an awful smash!"

He nodded his head, and even in the gloom I could see that he was smiling the gentle, wistful smile which I connected with him.

I was quite unable to move. Indeed, I had not any desire to try to move. But my senses were exceedingly alert. I saw the wreck of the motor lit up by the moving lanterns. I saw the little group of people and heard the hushed voices. There were the lodge-keeper and his wife, and one or two more. They were taking no notice of me, but were very busy round the car. Then suddenly I heard a cry of pain.

"The weight is on him. Lift it easy," cried a voice.

"It's only my leg!" said another one, which I recognized as Perkins's. "Where's master?" he cried.

"Here I am," I answered, but they did not seem to hear me. They were all bending over something which lay in front of the car.

Stanley laid his hand upon my shoulder, and his touch was inexpressibly soothing. I felt light and happy, in spite of all.

"No pain, of course?" said he.

"None," said I.

"There never is," said he.

And then suddenly a wave of amazement passed over me. Stanley! Stanley! Why, Stanley had surely died of enteric at Bloemfontein in the Boer War!*

"Stanley!" I cried, and the words seemed to choke my throat. "Stanley, you are dead."

He looked at me with the same old gentle, wistful smile.

"So are you," he answered.

Lot No. 249

Of the dealings of Edward Bellingham with William Monkhouse Lee, and of the cause of the great terror of Abercrombie Smith, it may be that no absolute and final judgement will ever be delivered. It is true that we have the full and clear narrative of Smith himself, and such corroboration as he could look for from Thomas Styles the servant, from the Reverend Plumptree Peterson, Fellow of Old's, and from such other people as chanced to gain some passing glance at this or that incident in a singular chain of events. Yet, in the main, the story must rest upon Smith alone, and the most will think that it is more likely that one brain, however outwardly sane, has some subtle warp in its texture, some strange flaw in its workings, than that the path of nature has been overstepped in open day in so famed a centre of learning and light as the University of Oxford. Yet when we think how narrow and how devious this path of nature is, how dimly we can trace it, for all our lamps of science, and how from the darkness which girds it round great and terrible possibilities loom ever shadowly upwards, it is a bold and confident man who will put a limit to the strange bypaths into which the human spirit may wander.

In a certain wing of what we will call Old College in Oxford there is a corner turret of an exceeding great age. The heavy arch which spans the open door has bent downwards in the centre under the weight of its years, and the grey, lichen-blotched blocks of stone are bound and knitted together with withes and strands of ivy, as though the old mother had set herself to brace them up against wind and weather. From the door a stone stair curves upwards spirally, passing two landings and terminating in a third one, its steps all shapeless and hollowed by the tread of so many generations of the seekers after knowledge. Life has flowed like water down this winding stair and, water-like, has left these smooth-worn grooves behind it. From the long-gowned, pedantic scholars of Plantagenet days* down to the young bloods of a later age, how full and strong had been that tide of young English life. And what was left now of all those hopes, those strivings, those fiery energies, save here and there in some old-world churchyard a few scratches upon a stone, and perchance a handful of dust in a mouldering coffin? Yet here were the silent stair and the grey old wall, with bend and saltire and many another heraldic device still to be read upon its surface, like grotesque shadows thrown back from the days that had passed.

In the month of May, in the year 1884, three young men occupied the sets of rooms which opened onto the separate landings of the old stair. Each set consisted simply of a sitting room and of a bedroom, while the two corresponding rooms upon the ground floor were used, the one as a coal cellar and the other as the living room of the servant, or scout, Thomas Styles, whose duty it was to wait upon the three men above him. To right and to left was a line of lecture rooms and of offices, so that the dwellers in the old turret enjoyed a certain seclusion, which made the chambers popular among the more studious undergraduates. Such were the three who occupied them now – Abercrombie Smith above, Edward Bellingham beneath him, and William Monkhouse Lee upon the lowest storey.

It was ten o'clock on a bright spring night, and Abercrombie Smith lay back in his armchair, his feet upon the fender, and his briar-root pipe between his lips. In a similar chair, and equally at his ease, there lounged on the other side of the fireplace his old school friend Jephro Hastie. Both men were in flannels, for they had spent their evening upon the river, but apart from their dress no one could look at their hard-cut, alert faces without seeing that they were open-air men – men whose minds and tastes turned naturally to all that was manly and robust. Hastie, indeed, was stroke of his college boat, and Smith was an even better oar, but a coming examination had already cast its shadow over him and held him to his work, save for the few hours a week which health demanded. A litter of medical books upon the table, with scattered bones, models and anatomical plates, pointed to the extent as well as the nature of his studies, while a couple of single-sticks* and a set of boxing gloves above the mantelpiece hinted at the means by which, with Hastie's help, he might take his exercise in its most compressed and least distant form. They knew each other very well – so well that they could sit now in that soothing silence which is the very highest development of companionship.

"Have some whisky," said Abercrombie Smith at last between two cloudbursts. "Scotch in the jug and Irish in the bottle."

"No, thanks. I'm in for the sculls.* I don't liquor when I'm training. How about you?"

"I'm reading hard. I think it best to leave it alone."

Hastie nodded, and they relapsed into a contented silence.

"By the way, Smith," asked Hastie presently, "have you made the acquaintance of either of the fellows on your stair yet?"

"Just a nod when we pass. Nothing more."

"Hum! I should be inclined to let it stand at that. I know something of them both. Not much, but as much as I want. I don't think I should take them to my bosom if I were you. Not that there's much amiss with Monkhouse Lee."

"Meaning the thin one?"

"Precisely. He is a gentlemanly little fellow. I don't think there is any vice in him. But then you can't know him without knowing Bellingham."

"Meaning the fat one?"

"Yes, the fat one. And he's a man whom I, for one, would rather not know."

Abercrombie Smith raised his eyebrows and glanced across at his companion.

"What's up, then?" he asked. "Drink? Cards? Cad? You used not to be censorious."

"Ah! You evidently don't know the man, or you wouldn't ask. There's something damnable about him – something reptilian. My gorge always rises at him. I should put him down as a man with secret vices – an evil liver. He's no fool, though. They say that he is one of the best men in his line that they have ever had in the college."

"Medicine or classics?"

"Eastern languages. He's a demon at them. Chillingworth met him somewhere above the second cataract last long,* and he told me that he just prattled to the Arabs as if he had been born and nursed and weaned among them. He talked Coptic to the Copts, and Hebrew to the Jews, and Arabic to the Bedouins, and they were all ready to kiss the hem of his frock coat. There are some old hermit johnnies up in those parts who sit on rocks and scowl and spit at the casual stranger. Well, when they saw this chap Bellingham, before he had said five words they just lay down on their bellies and wriggled. Chillingworth said that he never saw anything like it. Bellingham seemed to take it as his right too, and strutted about among them and talked down to them like a Dutch uncle. Pretty good for an undergrad of Old's, wasn't it?"

"Why do you say you can't know Lee without knowing Bellingham?"

"Because Bellingham is engaged to his sister Eveline. Such a bright little girl, Smith! I know the whole family well. It's disgusting to see that brute with her. A toad and a dove, that's what they always remind me of."

Abercrombie Smith grinned and knocked his ashes out against the side of the grate.

"You show every card in your hand, old chap," said he. "What a prejudiced, green-eyed, evil-thinking old man it is! You have really nothing against the fellow except that."

"Well, I've known her ever since she was as long as that cherrywood pipe, and I don't like to see her taking risks. And it is a risk. He looks beastly. And he has a beastly temper, a venomous temper. You remember his row with Long Norton?"

"No, you always forget that I am a freshman."

"Ah, it was last winter. Of course. Well, you know the towpath along by the river. There were several fellows going along it, Bellingham in front, when they came on an old market woman coming the other way. It had been raining – you know what those fields are like when it has rained – and the path ran between the river and a great puddle that was nearly as broad. Well, what does this swine do but keep the path, and push the old girl into the mud, where she and her marketings came to terrible grief. It was a blackguard thing to do, and Long Norton, who is as gentle a fellow as ever stepped, told him what he thought of it. One word led to another, and it ended in Norton laying his stick across the fellow's shoulders. There was the deuce of a fuss about it, and it's a treat to see the way in which Bellingham looks at Norton when they meet now. By Jove, Smith, it's nearly eleven o'clock!"

"No hurry. Light your pipe again."

"Not I. I'm supposed to be in training. Here I've been sitting gossiping when I ought to have been safely tucked up. I'll borrow your skull, if you can share it. Williams has had mine for a month. I'll take the little bones of your ear too, if you are sure you won't need them. Thanks very much. Never mind a bag, I can carry them very well under my arm. Goodnight, my son, and take my tip as to your neighbour."

When Hastie, bearing his anatomical plunder, had clattered off down the winding stair, Abercrombie Smith hurled his pipe into the wastepaper basket and, drawing his chair nearer to the lamp, plunged into a formidable green-covered volume, adorned with great coloured maps of that strange internal kingdom of which we are the hapless and helpless monarchs. Though a freshman at Oxford, the student was not so in medicine, for he had worked for four years at Glasgow and at Berlin, and this coming examination would place him finally as a member of his profession. With his firm mouth, broad forehead and clear-cut, somewhat hard-featured face, he was a man who, if he had no brilliant talent, was yet so dogged, so patient and so strong that he might in the end overtop a more showy genius. A man who can hold his own among Scotchmen and North Germans is not a man to be easily set back. Smith had left a name at Glasgow and at Berlin, and he was bent now upon doing as much at Oxford, if hard work and devotion could accomplish it.

He had sat reading for about an hour, and the hands of the noisy carriage clock upon the side table were rapidly closing together upon the twelve, when a sudden sound fell upon the student's ear – a sharp, rather shrill sound, like the hissing intake of a man's breath who gasps under some strong emotion. Smith laid down his book and slanted his ear to listen. There was no one on either side or above him, so that the interruption came certainly from the neighbour beneath – the same neighbour of whom Hastie had given so unsavoury an account. Smith knew him only as a flabby, pale-faced man of silent and studious habits, a man whose lamp threw a golden bar from the old turret even after he had extinguished his own. This community in lateness had formed a certain silent bond between them. It was soothing to Smith when the hours stole on towards dawning to feel that there was another so close who set as small a value upon his sleep as he did. Even now, as his thoughts turned towards him, Smith's feelings were kindly. Hastie was a good fellow, but he was rough, strong-fibred, with no imagination or sympathy. He could not tolerate departures from what he looked upon as the model type of manliness. If a man could not be measured by a public-school standard, then he was beyond the pale with Hastie. Like so many who are themselves robust, he was apt to confuse the constitution with the character, to ascribe to want of principle what was really a want of circulation. Smith, with his stronger mind, knew his friend's habit, and made allowance for it now as his thoughts turned towards the man beneath him.

There was no return of the singular sound, and Smith was about to turn to his work once more, when suddenly there broke out in the silence of the night a hoarse cry, a positive scream – the call of a man who is moved and shaken beyond all control. Smith sprang out of his chair and dropped his book. He was a man of fairly firm fibre, but there was something in this sudden, uncontrollable shriek of horror which chilled his blood and pringled in his skin. Coming in such a place and at such an hour, it brought a thousand fantastic possibilities into his head. Should he rush down, or was it better to wait? He had all the national hatred of making a scene, and he knew so little of his neighbour that he would not lightly intrude upon his affairs. For a moment he stood in doubt and even as he balanced the matter there was a quick rattle of footsteps upon the stairs, and young Monkhouse Lee, half dressed and as white as ashes, burst into his room.

"Come down!" he gasped. "Bellingham's ill."

Abercrombie Smith followed him closely downstairs into the sitting room, which was beneath his own, and, intent as he was upon the matter in hand, he could not but take an amazed glance around him as he crossed the threshold. It was such a chamber as he had never seen before – a museum rather than a study. Walls and ceiling were thickly covered with a thousand strange relics from Egypt and the East. Tall, angular figures bearing burdens or weapons stalked in an uncouth frieze round the apartments. Above were bull-headed, stork-headed, cat-headed, owl-headed statues, with viper-crowned, almond-eyed monarchs, and strange, beetle-like deities cut out of the blue Egyptian lapis lazuli. Horus and Isis and Osiris peeped down from every niche and shelf, while across the ceiling a true son of Old Nile, a great, hanging-jawed crocodile, was slung in a double noose.

In the centre of this singular chamber was a large, square table, littered with papers, bottles and the dried leaves of some graceful, palm-like plant. These varied objects had all been heaped together in order to make room for a mummy case, which had been conveyed from the wall, as was evident from the gap there, and laid across the front of the table. The mummy itself, a horrid, black, withered thing, like a charred head on a gnarled bush, was lying half out of the case, with its clawlike hand and bony forearm resting upon the table. Propped up against the sarcophagus was an old yellow scroll of papyrus, and in front of it, in a wooden armchair, sat the owner of the room, his head thrown back, his widely opened eyes directed in a horrified stare to the crocodile above him, and his blue, thick lips puffing loudly with every expiration.

"My God! He's dying!" cried Monkhouse Lee distractedly.

He was a slim, handsome young fellow, olive-skinned and dark-eyed, of a Spanish rather than of an English type, with a Celtic intensity of manner which contrasted with the Saxon phlegm of Abercrombie Smith.

"Only a faint, I think," said the medical student. "Just give me a hand with him. You take his feet. Now onto the sofa. Can you kick all those little wooden devils off? What a litter it is! Now he will be all right if we undo his collar and give him some water. What has he been up to at all?"

"I don't know. I heard him cry out. I ran up. I know him pretty well, you know. It is very good of you to come down."

"His heart is going like a pair of castanets," said Smith, laying his hand on the breast of the unconscious man. "He seems to me to be frightened all to pieces. Chuck the water over him! What a face he has got on him!"

It was indeed a strange and most repellent face, for colour and outline were equally unnatural. It was white, not with the ordinary pallor of fear, but with an absolutely bloodless white, like the underside of a sole. He was very fat, but gave the impression of having at some time been considerably fatter, for his skin hung loosely in creases and folds, and was shot with a meshwork of wrinkles. Short, stubbly brown hair bristled up from his scalp, with a pair of thick, wrinkled ears protruding at the sides. His light-grey eyes were still open, the pupils dilated and the balls projecting in a fixed and horrid stare. It seemed to Smith as he looked down upon him that he had never seen Nature's danger signals flying so plainly upon a man's countenance, and his thoughts turned more seriously to the warning which Hastie had given him an hour before.

"What the deuce can have frightened him so?" he asked.

"It's the mummy."

"The mummy? How, then?"

"I don't know. It's beastly and morbid. I wish he would drop it. It's the second fright he has given me. It was the same last winter. I found him just like this, with that horrid thing in front of him."

"What does he want with the mummy, then?"

"Oh, he's a crank, you know. It's his hobby. He knows more about these things than any man in England. But I wish he wouldn't! Ah, he's beginning to come to."

A faint tinge of colour had begun to steal back into Bellingham's ghastly cheeks, and his eyelids shivered like a sail after a calm. He clasped and unclasped his hands, drew a long, thin breath between his teeth, and suddenly, jerking up his head, threw a glance of recognition around him. As his eyes fell upon the mummy, he sprang off the sofa, seized the roll of papyrus, thrust it into a drawer, turned the key, and then staggered back onto the sofa.

"What's up?" he asked. "What do you chaps want?"

"You've been shrieking out and making no end of a fuss," said Monkhouse Lee. "If our neighbour here from above hadn't come down, I'm sure I don't know what I should have done with you."

"Ah, it's Abercrombie Smith," said Bellingham, glancing up at him. "How very good of you to come in! What a fool I am! Oh, my God, what a fool I am!"

He sunk his head onto his hands, and burst into peal after peal of hysterical laughter.

"Look here! Drop it!" cried Smith, shaking him roughly by the shoulder. "Your nerves are all in a jangle. You must drop these little midnight games with mummies, or you'll be going off your chump. You're all on wires now."

"I wonder," said Bellingham, "whether you would be as cool as I am if you had seen…"

"What then?"

"Oh, nothing. I meant that I wonder if you could sit up at night with a mummy without trying your nerves. I have no doubt that you are quite right. I dare say that I have been taking it out of myself too much lately. But I am all right now. Please don't go, though. Just wait for a few minutes until I am quite myself."

"The room is very close," remarked Lee, throwing open the window and letting in the cool night air.

"It's balsamic resin," said Bellingham. He lifted up one of the dried palmate leaves from the table and frizzled it over the chimney of the lamp. It broke away into heavy smoke wreaths, and a pungent, biting odour filled the chamber. "It's the sacred plant – the plant of the priests," he remarked. "Do you know anything of Eastern languages, Smith?"

"Nothing at all. Not a word."

The answer seemed to lift a weight from the Egyptologist's mind.

"By the way," he continued, "how long was it from the time that you ran down until I came to my senses?"

"Not long. Some four or five minutes."

"I thought it could not be very long," said he, drawing a long breath. "But what a strange thing unconsciousness is! There is no measurement to it. I could not tell from my own sensations if it were seconds or weeks. Now that gentleman on the table was packed up in the days of the eleventh dynasty, some forty centuries ago, and yet if he could find his tongue, he would tell us that this lapse of time has been but a closing of the eyes and a reopening of them. He is a singularly fine mummy, Smith."

Smith stepped over to the table and looked down with a professional eye at the black and twisted form in front of him. The features, though horribly discoloured, were perfect, and two little nut-like eyes still lurked in the depths of the black, hollow sockets. The blotched skin was drawn tightly from bone to bone, and a tangled wrap of black coarse hair fell over the ears. Two thin teeth, like those of a rat, overlay the shrivelled lower lip. In its crouching position, with bent joints and craned head, there was a suggestion of energy about the horrid thing which made Smith's gorge rise. The gaunt ribs, with their parchment-like covering, were exposed, and the sunken, leaden-hued abdomen, with the long slit where the embalmer had left his mark; but the lower limbs were wrapped round with coarse yellow bandages. A number of little clove-like pieces of myrrh and of cassia were sprinkled over the body, and lay scattered on the inside of the case.

"I don't know his name," said Bellingham, passing his hand over the shrivelled head. "You see the outer sarcophagus with the inscriptions is missing. Lot 249 is all the title he has now. You see it printed on his case. That was his number in the auction at which I picked him up."

"He has been a very pretty sort of fellow in his day," remarked Abercrombie Smith.

"He has been a giant. His mummy is six feet seven in length, and that would be a giant over there, for they were never a very robust race. Feel these great knotted bones too. He would be a nasty fellow to tackle."

"Perhaps these very hands helped to build the stones into the pyramids," suggested Monkhouse Lee, looking down with disgust in his eyes at the crooked, unclean talons.

"No fear. This fellow has been pickled in natron,* and looked after in the most approved style. They did not serve hodsmen in that fashion. Salt or bitumen was enough for them. It has been calculated that this sort of thing cost about seven hundred and thirty pounds in our money. Our friend was a noble at the least. What do you make of that small inscription near his feet, Smith?"

"I told you that I know no Eastern tongue."

"Ah, so you did. It is the name of the embalmer, I take it. A very conscientious worker he must have been. I wonder how many modern works will survive four thousand years?"

He kept on speaking lightly and rapidly, but it was evident to Abercrombie Smith that he was still palpitating with fear. His hands shook, his lower lip trembled and, look where he would, his eye always came sliding round to his gruesome companion. Through all his fear, however, there was a suspicion of triumph in his tone and manner. His eyes shone, and his footstep, as he paced the room, was brisk and jaunty. He gave the impression of a man who has gone through an ordeal, the marks of which he still bears upon him, but which has helped him to his end.

"You're not going yet?" he cried, as Smith rose from the sofa.

At the prospect of solitude, his fears seemed to crowd back upon him, and he stretched out a hand to detain him.

"Yes, I must go. I have my work to do. You are all right now. I think that with your nervous system you should take up some less morbid study."

"Oh, I am not nervous as a rule – and I have unwrapped mummies before."

"You fainted last time," observed Monkhouse Lee.

"Ah, yes, so I did. Well, I must have a nerve tonic or a course of electricity. You are not going, Lee?"

"I'll do whatever you wish, Ned."

"Then I'll come down with you and have a shakedown on your sofa. Goodnight, Smith. I am so sorry to have disturbed you with my foolishness."

They shook hands, and as the medical student stumbled up the spiral and irregular stair he heard a key turn in a door, and the steps of his two new acquaintances as they descended to the lower floor.

In this strange way began the acquaintance between Edward Bellingham and Abercrombie Smith, an acquaintance which the latter, at least, had no desire to push further. Bellingham, however, appeared to have taken a fancy to his rough-spoken neighbour, and made his advances in such a way that he could hardly be repulsed without absolute brutality. Twice he called to thank Smith for his assistance, and many times afterwards he looked in with books, papers and such other civilities as two bachelor neighbours can offer each other. He was, as Smith soon found, a man of wide reading, with catholic tastes and an extraordinary memory. His manner, too, was so pleasing and suave that one came, after a time, to overlook his repellent appearance. For a jaded and wearied man he was no unpleasant companion, and Smith found himself, after a time, looking forward to his visits, and even returning them.

Clever as he undoubtedly was, however, the medical student seemed to detect a dash of insanity in the man. He broke out at times into a high, inflated style of talk which was in contrast with the simplicity of his life.

"It is a wonderful thing," he cried, "to feel that one can command powers of good and of evil – a ministering angel or a demon of vengeance." And again, of Monkhouse Lee, he said, "Lee is a good fellow, an honest fellow, but he is without strength or ambition. He would not make a fit partner for a man with a great enterprise. He would not make a fit partner for me."

At such hints and innuendoes stolid Smith, puffing solemnly at his pipe, would simply raise his eyebrows and shake his head, with little interjections of medical wisdom as to earlier hours and fresher air.

One habit Bellingham had developed of late which Smith knew to be a frequent herald of a weakening mind. He appeared to be forever talking to himself. At late hours of the night, when there could be no visitor with him, Smith could still hear his voice beneath him in a low, muffled monologue, sunk almost to a whisper, and yet very audible in the silence. This solitary babbling annoyed and distracted the student, so that he spoke more than once to his neighbour about it. Bellingham, however, flushed up at the charge, and denied curtly that he had uttered a sound; indeed, he showed more annoyance over the matter than the occasion seemed to demand.

Had Abercrombie Smith had any doubt as to his own ears he had not to go far to find corroboration. Tom Styles, the little wrinkled manservant who had attended to the wants of the lodgers in the turret for a longer time than any man's memory could carry him, was sorely put to it over the same matter.

"If you please, sir," said he, as he tidied down the top chamber one morning, "do you think Mr Bellingham is all right, sir?"

"All right, Styles?"

"Yes, sir. Right in his head, sir."

"Why should he not be, then?"

"Well, I don't know, sir. His habits has changed of late. He's not the same man he used to be, though I make free to say that he was never quite one of my gentlemen, like Mr Hastie or yourself, sir. He's took to talkin' to himself something awful. I wonder it don't disturb you. I don't know what to make of him, sir."

"I don't know what business it is of yours, Styles."

"Well, I takes an interest, Mr Smith. It may be forward of me, but I can't help it. I feel sometimes as if I was mother and father to my young gentlemen. It all falls on me when things go wrong and the relations come. But Mr Bellingham, sir. I want to know what it is that walks about his room sometimes when he's out and when the door's locked on the outside."

"Eh? You're talking nonsense, Styles."

"Maybe so, sir; but I heard it more'n once with my own ears."

"Rubbish, Styles."

"Very good, sir. You'll ring the bell if you want me."

Abercrombie Smith gave little heed to the gossip of the old manservant, but a small incident occurred a few days later which left an unpleasant effect upon his mind, and brought the words of Styles forcibly to his memory.

Bellingham had come up to see him late one night, and was entertaining him with an interesting account of the rock tombs of Beni-Hassan in

Upper Egypt, when Smith, whose hearing was remarkably acute, distinctly heard the sound of a door opening on the landing below.

"There's some fellow gone in or out of your room," he remarked.

Bellingham sprang up and stood helpless for a moment, with the expression of a man who is half incredulous and half afraid.

"I surely locked it. I am almost positive that I locked it," he stammered. "No one could have opened it."

"Why, I hear someone coming up the steps now," said Smith.

Bellingham rushed out through the door, slammed it loudly behind him, and hurried down the stairs. About halfway down Smith heard him stop, and thought he caught the sound of whispering. A moment later the door beneath him shut, a key creaked in a lock, and Bellingham, with beads of moisture upon his pale face, ascended the stairs once more, and re-entered the room.

"It's all right," he said, throwing himself down in a chair. "It was that fool of a dog. He had pushed the door open. I don't know how I came to forget to lock it."

"I didn't know you kept a dog," said Smith, looking very thoughtfully at the disturbed face of his companion.

"Yes, I haven't had him long. I must get rid of him. He's a great nuisance."

"He must be, if you find it so hard to shut him up. I should have thought that shutting the door would have been enough, without locking it."

"I want to prevent old Styles from letting him out. He's of some value, you know, and it would be awkward to lose him."

"I am a bit of a dog-fancier myself," said Smith, still gazing hard at his companion from the corner of his eyes. "Perhaps you'll let me have a look at it."

"Certainly. But I am afraid it cannot be tonight; I have an appointment. Is that clock right? Then I am a quarter of an hour late already. You'll excuse me, I am sure."

He picked up his cap and hurried from the room. In spite of his appointment, Smith heard him re-enter his own chamber and lock his door upon the inside.

This interview left a disagreeable impression upon the medical student's mind. Bellingham had lied to him, and lied so clumsily that it looked as if he had desperate reasons for concealing the truth. Smith knew that his neighbour had no dog. He knew, also, that the step which he had heard upon the stairs was not the step of an animal. But if it were not, then what could it be? There was old Styles's statement about the something which used to pace the room at times when the owner was absent. Could it be a woman? Smith rather inclined to the view. If so, it would mean disgrace and expulsion to Bellingham if it were discovered by the authorities, so that his anxiety and falsehoods might be accounted for. And yet it was inconceivable that an undergraduate could keep a woman in his rooms without being instantly detected. Be the explanation what it might, there was something ugly about it, and Smith determined, as he turned to his books, to discourage all further attempts at intimacy on the part of his soft-spoken and ill-favoured neighbour.

But his work was destined to interruption that night. He had hardly caught up the broken threads when a firm, heavy footfall came three steps at a time from below, and Hastie, in blazer and flannels, burst into the room.

"Still at it!" said he, plumping down into his wonted armchair. "What a chap you are to stew! I believe an earthquake might come and knock Oxford into a cocked hat, and you would sit perfectly placid with your books among the ruins. However, I won't bore you long. Three whiffs of baccy, and I am off."

"What's the news, then?" asked Smith, cramming a plug of bird's-eye* into his briar with his forefinger.

"Nothing very much. Wilson made seventy for the freshmen against the eleven. They say that they will play him instead of Buddicomb, for Buddicomb is clean off colour. He used to be able to bowl a little, but it's nothing but half-volleys and long hops now."

"Medium right," suggested Smith, with the intense gravity which comes upon a varsity man when he speaks of athletics.

"Inclining to fast, with a work from leg. Comes with the arm about three inches or so. He used to be nasty on a wet wicket. Oh, by the way, have you heard about Long Norton?"

"What's that?"

"He's been attacked."

"Attacked?"

"Yes, just as he was turning out of the High Street, and within a hundred yards of the gate of Old's."

"But who—"

"Ah, that's the rub! If you said 'what', you would be more grammatical. Norton swears that it was not human, and, indeed, from the scratches on his throat, I should be inclined to agree with him."

"What, then? Have we come down to spooks?"

Abercrombie Smith puffed his scientific contempt.

"Well, no; I don't think that is quite the idea, either. I am inclined to think that if any showman has lost a great ape lately, and the brute is in these parts, a jury would find a true bill against it. Norton passes that way every night, you know, about the same hour. There's a tree that hangs low over the path – the big elm from Rainy's garden. Norton thinks the thing dropped on him out of the tree. Anyhow, he was nearly strangled by two arms, which, he says, were as strong and as thin as steel bands. He saw nothing; only those beastly arms that tightened and tightened on him. He yelled his head nearly off, and a couple of chaps came running, and the thing went over the wall like a cat. He never got a fair sight of it the whole time. It gave Norton a shake-up, I can tell you. I tell him it has been as good as a change at the seaside for him."

"A garrotter, most likely," said Smith.

"Very possibly. Norton says not; but we don't mind what he says. The garrotter had long nails, and was pretty smart at swinging himself over walls. By the way, your beautiful neighbour would be pleased if he heard about it. He had a grudge against Norton, and he's not a man, from what I know of him, to forget his little debts. But hallo, old chap, what have you got in your noddle?"

"Nothing," Smith answered curtly.

He had started in his chair, and the look had flashed over his face which comes upon a man who is struck suddenly by some unpleasant idea.

"You looked as if something I had said had taken you on the raw. By the way, you have made the acquaintance of Master B., since I looked in last, have you not? Young Monkhouse Lee told me something to that effect."

"Yes, I know him slightly. He has been up here once or twice."

"Well, you're big enough and ugly enough to take care of yourself. He's not what I should call exactly a healthy sort of johnny, though, no doubt, he's very clever and all that. But you'll soon find out for yourself. Lee is all right: he's a very decent little fellow. Well, so long, old chap! I row Mullins for the vice chancellor's pot on Wednesday week, so mind you come down, in case I don't see you before."

Bovine Smith laid down his pipe and turned stolidly to his books once more. But with all the will in the world he found it very hard to keep his mind upon his work. It would slip away to brood upon the man beneath him, and upon the little mystery which hung round his chambers. Then his thoughts turned to this singular attack of which Hastie had spoken, and to the grudge which Bellingham was said to owe the object of it. The two ideas would persist in rising together in his mind, as though there were some close and intimate connection between them. And yet the suspicion was so dim and vague that it could not be put down in words.

"Confound the chap!" cried Smith, as he shied his book on pathology across the room. "He has spoilt my night's reading, and that's reason enough, if there were no other, why I should steer clear of him in the future."

For ten days the medical student confined himself so closely to his studies that he neither saw nor heard anything of either of the men beneath him. At the hours when Bellingham had been accustomed to visit him, he took care to sport his oak, and though he more than once heard a knocking at his outer door, he resolutely refused to answer it. One afternoon, however, he was descending the stairs when, just as he was passing it, Bellingham's door flew open, and young Monkhouse Lee came out with his eyes sparkling and a dark flush of anger upon his olive cheeks. Close at his heels followed Bellingham, his fat, unhealthy face all quivering with malignant passion.

"You fool!" he hissed. "You'll be sorry."

"Very likely," cried the other. "Mind what I say. It's off! I won't hear of it!"

"You've promised, anyhow."

"Oh, I'll keep that! I won't speak. But I'd rather little Eva was in her grave. Once for all, it's off. She'll do what I say. We don't want to see you again."

So much Smith could not avoid hearing, but he hurried on, for he had no wish to be involved in their dispute. There had been a serious breach between them, that was clear enough, and Lee was going to cause the engagement with his sister to be broken off. Smith thought of Hastie's comparison of the toad and the dove, and was glad to think that the matter was at an end. Bellingham's face when he was in a passion was not pleasant to look upon. He was not a man to whom an innocent girl could be trusted for life. As he walked, Smith wondered languidly what could have caused the quarrel, and what the promise might be which Bellingham had been so anxious that Monkhouse Lee should keep.

It was the day of the sculling match between Hastie and Mullins, and a stream of men were making their way down to the banks of the Isis. A May sun was shining brightly, and the yellow path was barred with the black shadows of the tall elm trees. On either side the grey colleges lay back from the road, the hoary old mothers of minds looking out from their high, mullioned windows at the tide of young life which swept so merrily past them. Black-clad tutors, prim officials, pale reading men, brown-faced, straw-hatted young athletes in white sweaters or many-coloured blazers, all were hurrying towards the blue winding river which curves through the Oxford meadows.

Abercrombie Smith, with the intuition of an old oarsman, chose his position at the point where he knew that the struggle, if there were a struggle, would come. Far off he heard the hum which announced the start, the gathering roar of the approach, the thunder of running feet and the shouts of the men in the boats beneath him. A spray of half-clad, deep-breathing runners shot past him and, craning over their shoulders, he saw Hastie pulling a steady thirty-six, while his opponent, with a jerky forty,* was a good boat's length behind him. Smith gave a cheer for his friend and, pulling out his watch, was starting off again for his chambers, when he felt a touch upon his shoulder, and found that young Monkhouse Lee was beside him.

"I saw you there," he said, in a timid, deprecating way. "I wanted to speak to you, if you could spare me a half-hour. This cottage is mine. I share it with Harrington of King's. Come in and have a cup of tea."

"I must be back presently," said Smith. "I am hard on the grind at present. But I'll come in for a few minutes with pleasure. I wouldn't have come out, only Hastie is a friend of mine."

"So he is of mine. Hasn't he a beautiful style? Mullins wasn't in it. But come into the cottage. It's a little den of a place, but it is pleasant to work in during the summer months."

It was a small, square, white building, with green doors and shutters, and a rustic trelliswork porch, standing back some fifty yards from the river's bank. Inside, the main room was roughly fitted up as a study – deal table, unpainted shelves with books and a few cheap oleographs upon the wall. A kettle sang upon a spirit stove, and there were tea things upon a tray on the table.

"Try that chair and have a cigarette," said Lee. "Let me pour you out a cup of tea. It's so good of you to come in, for I know that your time is a good deal taken up. I wanted to say to you that, if I were you, I should change my rooms at once."

"Eh?"

Smith sat staring with a lighted match in one hand and his unlit cigarette in the other.

"Yes, it must seem very extraordinary, and the worst of it is that I cannot give my reasons, for I am under a solemn promise – a very solemn promise. But I may go so far as to say that I don't think Bellingham is a very safe man to live near. I intend to camp out here as much as I can for a time."

"Not safe! What do you mean?"

"Ah, that's what I mustn't say. But do take my advice, and move your rooms. We had a grand row today. You must have heard us, for you came down the stairs."

"I saw that you had fallen out."

"He's a horrible chap, Smith. That is the only word for him. I have had doubts about him ever since that night when he fainted – you remember, when you came down. I taxed him today, and he told me things that made my hair rise, and wanted me to stand in with him. I'm not strait-laced, but I am a clergyman's son, you know, and I think there are some things which are quite beyond the pale. I only thank God that I found him out before it was too late, for he was to have married into my family."

"This is all very fine, Lee," said Abercrombie Smith curtly. "But either you are saying a great deal too much or a great deal too little."

"I give you a warning."

"If there is real reason for warning, no promise can bind you. If I see a rascal about to blow a place up with dynamite, no pledge will stand in my way of preventing him."

"Ah, but I cannot prevent him, and I can do nothing but warn you."

"Without saying what you warn me against."

"Against Bellingham."

"But that is childish. Why should I fear him, or any man?"

"I can't tell you. I can only entreat you to change your rooms. You are in danger where you are. I don't even say that Bellingham would wish to injure you. But it might happen, for he is a dangerous neighbour just now."

"Perhaps I know more than you think," said Smith, looking keenly at the young man's boyish, earnest face. "Suppose I tell you that someone else shares Bellingham's rooms."

Monkhouse Lee sprang from his chair in uncontrollable excitement.

"You know, then?" he gasped.

"A woman."

Lee dropped back again with a groan.

"My lips are sealed," he said. "I must not speak."

"Well, anyhow," said Smith, rising, "it is not likely that I should allow myself to be frightened out of rooms which suit me very nicely. It would be a little too feeble for me to move out all my goods and chattels because you say that Bellingham might in some unexplained way do me an injury. I think that I'll just take my chance, and stay where I am, and as I see that it's nearly five o'clock, I must ask you to excuse me."

He bade the young student adieu in a few curt words, and made his way homeward through the sweet spring evening, feeling half ruffled, half amused, as any other strong, unimaginative man might who has been menaced by a vague and shadowy danger.

There was one little indulgence which Abercrombie Smith always allowed himself, however closely his work might press upon him. Twice a week, on the Tuesday and the Friday, it was his invariable custom to walk over to Farlingford, the residence of Dr Plumptree Peterson, situated about a mile and a half out of Oxford. Peterson had been a close friend of Smith's elder brother Francis, and as he was a bachelor, fairly well-to-do, with a good cellar and a better library, his house was a pleasant goal for a man who was in need of a brisk walk. Twice a week, then, the medical student would swing out there along the dark country roads, and spend a pleasant hour in Peterson's comfortable study, discussing, over a glass of old port, the gossip of the varsity or the latest developments of medicine or of surgery.

On the day which followed his interview with Monkhouse Lee, Smith shut up his books at a quarter past eight, the hour when he usually started for his friend's house. As he was leaving his room, however, his eyes chanced to fall upon one of the books which Bellingham had lent him, and his conscience pricked him for not having returned it. However repellent the man might be, he should not be treated with discourtesy. Taking the book, he walked downstairs and knocked at his neighbour's door. There was no answer; but on turning the handle he found that it was unlocked. Pleased at the thought of avoiding an interview, he stepped inside, and placed the book with his card upon the table.

The lamp was turned half down, but Smith could see the details of the room plainly enough. It was all much as he had seen it before – the frieze, the animal-headed gods, the hanging crocodile and the table littered over with papers and dried leaves. The mummy case stood upright against the wall, but the mummy itself was missing. There was no sign of any second occupant of the room, and he felt as he withdrew that he had probably done Bellingham an injustice. Had he a guilty secret to preserve, he would hardly leave his door open so that all the world might enter.

The spiral stair was as black as pitch, and Smith was slowly making his way down its irregular steps, when he was suddenly conscious that something had passed him in the darkness. There was a faint sound, a whiff of air, a light brushing past his elbow, but so slight that he could scarcely be certain of it. He stopped and listened, but the wind was rustling among the ivy outside, and he could hear nothing else.

"Is that you, Styles?" he shouted.

There was no answer, and all was still behind him. It must have been a sudden gust of air, for there were crannies and cracks in the old turret. And yet he could almost have sworn that he heard a footfall by his very side. He had emerged into the quadrangle, still turning the matter over in his head, when a man came running swiftly across the smooth-cropped lawn.

"Is that you, Smith?"

"Hullo, Hastie!"

"For God's sake come at once! Young Lee is drowned! Here's Harrington of King's with the news. The doctor is out. You'll do, but come along at once. There may be life in him."

"Have you brandy?"

"No."

"I'll bring some. There's a flask on my table."

Smith bounded up the stairs, taking three at a time, seized the flask, and was rushing down with it, when, as he passed Bellingham's room, his eyes fell upon something which left him gasping and staring upon the landing.

The door, which he had closed behind him, was now open, and right in front of him, with the lamplight shining upon it, was the mummy case. Three minutes ago it had been empty. He could swear to that. Now it framed the lank body of its horrible occupant, who stood, grim and stark, with his black shrivelled face towards the door. The form was lifeless and inert, but it seemed to Smith as he gazed that there still lingered a lurid spark of vitality, some faint sign of consciousness in the little eyes which lurked in the depths of the hollow sockets. So astounded and shaken was he that he had forgotten his errand, and was still staring at the lean, sunken figure when the voice of his friend below recalled him to himself.

"Come on, Smith!" he shouted. "It's life and death, you know. Hurry up! Now, then," he added, as the medical student reappeared, "let us do a sprint. It is well under a mile, and we should do it in five minutes. A human life is better worth running for than a pot."

Neck and neck they dashed through the darkness, and did not pull up until, panting and spent, they had reached the little cottage by the river. Young Lee, limp and dripping like a broken water plant, was stretched upon the sofa, the green scum of the river upon his black hair, and a fringe of white foam upon his leaden-hued lips. Beside him knelt his fellow student, Harrington, endeavouring to chafe some warmth back into his rigid limbs.

"I think there's life in him," said Smith, with his hand to the lad's side. "Put your watch glass to his lips. Yes, there's dimming on it. You take one arm, Hastie. Now work it as I do, and we'll soon pull him round."

For ten minutes they worked in silence, inflating and depressing the chest of the unconscious man. At the end of that time a shiver ran through his body, his lips trembled and he opened his eyes. The three students burst out into an irrepressible cheer.

"Wake up, old chap. You've frightened us quite enough."

"Have some brandy. Take a sip from the flask."

"He's all right now," said his companion Harrington. "Heavens, what a fright I got! I was reading here, and he had gone out for a stroll as far as the river, when I heard a scream and a splash. Out I ran, and by the time I could find him and fish him out, all life seemed to have gone. Then Simpson couldn't get a doctor, for he has a game leg, and I had to run, and I don't know what I'd have done without you fellows. That's right, old chap. Sit up."

Monkhouse Lee had raised himself on his hands, and looked wildly about him.

"What's up?" he asked. "I've been in the water. Ah, yes: I remember."

A look of fear came into his eyes, and he sank his face into his hands.

"How did you fall in?"

"I didn't fall in."

"How then?"

"I was thrown in. I was standing by the bank, and something from behind picked me up like a feather and hurled me in. I heard nothing, and I saw nothing. But I know what it was, for all that."

"And so do I," whispered Smith.

Lee looked up with a quick glance of surprise.

"You've learnt, then?" he said. "You remember the advice I gave you?"

"Yes, and I begin to think that I shall take it."

"I don't know what the deuce you fellows are talking about," said Hastie, "but I think, if I were you, Harrington, I should get Lee to bed at once. It will be time enough to discuss the why and the wherefore when he is a little stronger. I think, Smith, you and I can leave him alone now. I am walking back to college; if you are coming in that direction, we can have a chat."

But it was little chat that they had upon their homeward path. Smith's mind was too full of the incidents of the evening, the absence of the mummy from his neighbour's rooms, the step that passed him on the stair, the reappearance – the extraordinary, inexplicable reappearance of the grisly thing – and then this attack upon Lee, corresponding so closely to the previous outrage upon another man against whom Bellingham bore a grudge. All this settled in his thoughts, together with the many little incidents which had previously turned him against his neighbour, and the singular circumstances under which he was first called in to him. What had been a dim suspicion, a vague, fantastic conjecture, had suddenly taken form, and stood out in his mind as a grim fact, a thing not to be denied. And yet, how monstrous it was! How unheard of! How entirely beyond all bounds of human experience. An impartial judge, or even the friend who walked by his side, would simply tell him that his eyes had deceived him, that the mummy had been there all the time, that young Lee had tumbled into the river as any other man tumbles into a river, and that a blue pill* was the best thing for a disordered liver. He felt that he would have said as much if the positions had been reversed. And yet he could swear that Bellingham was a murderer at heart, and that he wielded a weapon such as no man had ever used in all the grim history of crime.

Hastie had branched off to his rooms with a few crisp and emphatic comments upon his friend's unsociability, and Abercrombie Smith crossed the quadrangle to his corner turret with a strong feeling of repulsion for his chambers and their associations. He would take Lee's advice, and move his quarters as soon as possible, for how could a man study when his ear was ever straining for every murmur or footstep in the room below? He observed, as he crossed over the lawn, that the light was still shining in Bellingham's window, and as he passed up the staircase the door opened, and the man himself looked out at him. With his fat, evil face he was like some bloated spider fresh from the weaving of his poisonous web.

"Good evening," said he. "Won't you come in?"

"No," cried Smith fiercely.

"No? You are busy as ever? I wanted to ask you about Lee. I was sorry to hear that there was a rumour that something was amiss with him."

His features were grave, but there was the gleam of a hidden laugh in his eyes as he spoke. Smith saw it, and he could have knocked him down for it.

"You'll be sorrier still to hear that Monkhouse Lee is doing very well, and is out of all danger," he answered. "Your hellish tricks have not come off this time. Oh, you needn't try to brazen it out. I know all about it."

Bellingham took a step back from the angry student, and half-closed the door as if to protect himself.

"You are mad," he said. "What do you mean? Do you assert that I had anything to do with Lee's accident?"

"Yes," thundered Smith. "You and that bag of bones behind you: you worked it between you. I tell you what it is, Master B., they have given up burning folk like you, but we still keep a hangman, and – by George! – if any man in this college meets his death while you are here, I'll have you up, and if you don't swing for it, it won't be my fault. You'll find that your filthy Egyptian tricks won't answer in England."

"You're a raving lunatic," said Bellingham.

"All right. You just remember what I say, for you'll find that I'll be better than my word."

The door slammed, and Smith went fuming up to his chamber, where he locked the door upon the inside, and spent half the night in smoking his old briar and brooding over the strange events of the evening.

Next morning Abercrombie Smith heard nothing of his neighbour, but Harrington called upon him in the afternoon to say that Lee was almost himself again. All day Smith stuck fast to his work, but in the evening he determined to pay the visit to his friend Dr Peterson upon which he had started the night before. A good walk and a friendly chat would be welcome to his jangled nerves.

Bellingham's door was shut as he passed, but glancing back when he was some distance from the turret, he saw his neighbour's head at the window outlined against the lamplight, his face pressed apparently against the glass as he gazed out into the darkness. It was a blessing to be away from all contact with him, if but for a few hours, and Smith stepped out briskly, and breathed the soft spring air into his lungs. The half-moon lay in the west between two Gothic pinnacles, and threw upon the silvered street a dark tracery from the stonework above. There was a brisk breeze, and light, fleecy clouds drifted swiftly across the sky. Old's was on the very border of the town, and in five minutes Smith found himself beyond the houses and between the hedges of a May-scented Oxfordshire lane.

It was a lonely and little-frequented road which led to his friend's house. Early as it was, Smith did not meet a single soul upon his way. He walked briskly along until he came to the avenue gate, which opened into the long gravel drive leading up to Farlingford. In front of him he could see the cosy red light of the windows glimmering through the foliage. He stood with his hand upon the iron latch of the swinging gate, and he glanced back at the road along which he had come. Something was coming swiftly down it.

It moved in the shadow of the hedge, silently and furtively, a dark, crouching figure, dimly visible against the black background. Even as he gazed back at it, it had lessened its distance by twenty paces, and was fast closing upon him. Out of the darkness he had a glimpse of a scraggy neck, and of two eyes that will ever haunt him in his dreams. He turned, and with a cry of terror he ran for his life up the avenue. There were the red lights, the signals of safety, almost within a stone's throw of him. He was a famous runner, but never had he run as he ran that night.

The heavy gate had swung into place behind him, but he heard it dash open again before his pursuer. As he rushed madly and wildly through the night, he could hear a swift, dry patter behind him, and could see, as he threw back a glance, that this horror was bounding like a tiger at his heels, with blazing eyes and one stringy arm out-thrown. Thank God, the door was ajar. He could see the thin bar of light which shot from the lamp in the hall. Nearer yet sounded the clatter from behind. He heard a hoarse gurgling at his very shoulder. With a shriek he flung himself against the door, slammed and bolted it behind him, and sank half-fainting onto the hall chair.

"My goodness, Smith, what's the matter?" asked Peterson, appearing at the door of his study.

"Give me some brandy."

Peterson disappeared, and came rushing out again with a glass and a decanter.

"You need it," he said, as his visitor drank off what he poured out for him. "Why, man, you are as white as a cheese."

Smith laid down his glass, rose up, and took a deep breath.

"I am my own man again now," said he. "I was never so unmanned before. But, with your leave, Peterson, I will sleep here tonight, for I don't think I could face that road again except by daylight. It's weak, I know, but I can't help it."

Peterson looked at his visitor with a very questioning eye.

"Of course you shall sleep here if you wish. I'll tell Mrs Burney to make up the spare bed. Where are you off to now?"

"Come up with me to the window that overlooks the door. I want you to see what I have seen."

They went up to the window of the upper hall, whence they could look down upon the approach to the house. The drive and the fields on either side lay quiet and still, bathed in the peaceful moonlight.

"Well, really, Smith," remarked Peterson, "it is well that I know you to be an abstemious man. What in the world can have frightened you?"

"I'll tell you presently. But where can it have gone? Ah, now, look, look! See the curve of the road just beyond your gate."

"Yes, I see; you needn't pinch my arm off. I saw someone pass. I should say a man, rather thin, apparently, and tall, very tall. But what of him? And what of yourself? You are still shaking like an aspen leaf."

"I have been within hand grip of the Devil, that's all. But come down to your study, and I shall tell you the whole story."

He did so. Under the cheery lamplight, with a glass of wine on the table beside him, and the portly form and florid face of his friend in front, he narrated, in their order, all the events, great and small, which had formed so singular a chain, from the night on which he had found Bellingham fainting in front of the mummy case until this horrid experience of an hour ago.

"There now," he said as he concluded, "that's the whole black business. It is monstrous and incredible, but it is true."

Dr Plumptree Peterson sat for some time in silence with a very puzzled expression upon his face.

"I never heard of such a thing in my life, never!" he said at last. "You have told me the facts. Now tell me your inferences."

"You can draw your own."

"But I should like to hear yours. You have thought over the matter, and I have not."

"Well, it must be a little vague in detail, but the main points seem to me to be clear enough. This fellow Bellingham, in his Eastern studies, has got hold of some infernal secret by which a mummy – or possibly only this particular mummy – can be temporarily brought to life. He was trying this disgusting business on the night when he fainted. No doubt the sight of the creature moving had shaken his nerve, even though he had expected it. You remember that almost the first words he said were to call out upon himself as a fool. Well, he got more hardened afterwards, and carried the matter through without fainting. The vitality which he could put into it was evidently only a passing thing, for I have seen it continually in its case as dead as this table. He has some elaborate process, I fancy, by which he brings the thing to pass. Having done it, he naturally bethought him that he might use the creature as an agent. It has intelligence and it has strength. For some purpose he took Lee into his confidence; but Lee, like a decent Christian, would have nothing to do with such a business. Then they had a row, and Lee vowed that he would tell his sister of Bellingham's true character. Bellingham's game was to prevent him, and he nearly managed it, by setting this creature of his on his track. He had already tried its powers upon another man – Norton – towards whom he had a grudge. It is the merest chance that he has not two murders upon his soul.

Then, when I taxed him with the matter, he had the strongest reasons for wishing to get me out of the way before I could convey my knowledge to anyone else. He got his chance when I went out, for he knew my habits and where I was bound for. I have had a narrow shave, Peterson, and it is mere luck you didn't find me on your doorstep in the morning. I'm not a nervous man as a rule, and I never thought to have the fear of death put upon me as it was tonight."

"My dear boy, you take the matter too seriously," said his companion. "Your nerves are out of order with your work, and you make too much of it. How could such a thing as this stride about the streets of Oxford, even at night, without being seen?"

"It has been seen. There is quite a scare in the town about an escaped ape, as they imagine the creature to be. It is the talk of the place."

"Well, it's a striking chain of events. And yet, my dear fellow, you must allow that each incident in itself is capable of a more natural explanation."

"What! Even my adventure of tonight?"

"Certainly. You come out with your nerves all unstrung, and your head full of this theory of yours. Some gaunt, half-famished tramp steals after you, and seeing you run, is emboldened to pursue you. Your fears and imagination do the rest."

"It won't do, Peterson; it won't do."

"And again, in the instance of your finding the mummy case empty, and then a few moments later with an occupant, you know that it was lamplight, that the lamp was half turned down, and that you had no special reason to look hard at the case. It is quite possible that you may have overlooked the creature in the first instance."

"No, no; it is out of the question."

"And then Lee may have fallen into the river, and Norton been garrotted. It is certainly a formidable indictment that you have against Bellingham; but if you were to place it before a police magistrate, he would simply laugh in your face."

"I know he would. That is why I mean to take the matter into my own hands."

"Eh?"

"Yes, I feel that a public duty rests upon me and, besides, I must do it for my own safety, unless I choose to allow myself to be hunted by this beast out of the college, and that would be a little too feeble. I have quite made up my mind what I shall do. And first of all, may I use your paper and pens for an hour?"

"Most certainly. You will find all that you want upon that side table."

Abercrombie Smith sat down before a sheet of foolscap, and for an hour, and then for a second hour, his pen travelled swiftly over it. Page after page was finished and tossed aside while his friend leant back in his armchair, looking across at him with patient curiosity. At last, with an exclamation of satisfaction, Smith sprang to his feet, gathered his papers up into order, and laid the last one upon Peterson's desk.

"Kindly sign this as a witness," he said.

"A witness? Of what?"

"Of my signature, and of the date. The date is the most important. Why, Peterson, my life might hang upon it."

"My dear Smith, you are talking wildly. Let me beg you to go to bed."

"On the contrary, I never spoke so deliberately in my life. And I will promise to go to bed the moment you have signed it."

"But what is it?"

"It is a statement of all that I have been telling you tonight. I wish you to witness it."

"Certainly," said Peterson, signing his name under that of his companion. "There you are! But what is the idea?"

"You will kindly retain it, and produce it in case I am arrested."

"Arrested? For what?"

"For murder. It is quite on the cards. I wish to be ready for every event. There is only one course open to me, and I am determined to take it."

"For Heaven's sake, don't do anything rash!"

"Believe me, it would be far more rash to adopt any other course. I hope that we won't need to bother you, but it will ease my mind to know that you have this statement of my motives. And now I am ready to take your advice and to go to roost, for I want to be at my best in the morning."

Abercrombie Smith was not an entirely pleasant man to have as an enemy. Slow and easy-tempered, he was formidable when driven to action. He brought to every purpose in life the same deliberate resoluteness which had distinguished him as a scientific student. He had laid his studies aside for a day, but he intended that the day should not be wasted. Not a word did he say to his host as to his plans, but by nine o'clock he was well on his way to Oxford.

In the High Street he stopped at Clifford's, the gun-maker's, and bought a heavy revolver, with a box of central-fire cartridges. Six of them he slipped into the chambers and, half-cocking the weapon, placed it in the pocket of his coat. He then made his way to Hastie's rooms, where the big oarsman was lounging over his breakfast, with the *Sporting Times* propped up against the coffee pot.

"Hullo! What's up?" he asked. "Have some coffee?"

"No, thank you. I want you to come with me, Hastie, and do what I ask you."

"Certainly, my boy."

"And bring a heavy stick with you."

"Hullo!" Hastie stared. "Here's a hunting crop that would fell an ox."

"One other thing. You have a box of amputating knives. Give me the longest of them."

"There you are. You seem to be fairly on the war trail. Anything else?"

"No, that will do." Smith placed the knife inside his coat, and led the way to the quadrangle. "We are neither of us chickens, Hastie," said he. "I think I can do this job alone, but I take you as a precaution. I am going to have a little talk with Bellingham. If I have only him to deal with, I won't, of course, need you. If I shout, however, up you come, and lam out with your whip as hard as you can lick. Do you understand?"

"All right. I'll come if I hear you bellow."

"Stay here, then. I may be a little time, but don't budge until I come down."

"I'm a fixture."

Smith ascended the stairs, opened Bellingham's door and stepped in. Bellingham was seated behind his table, writing. Beside him, among his litter of strange possessions, towered the mummy case, with its sale number 249 still stuck upon its front, and its hideous occupant stiff and stark within it. Smith looked very deliberately round him, closed the door, and then, stepping across to the fireplace, struck a match and set the fire alight. Bellingham sat staring, with amazement and rage upon his bloated face.

"Well, really now, you make yourself at home," he gasped.

Smith sat himself deliberately down, placing his watch upon the table, drew out his pistol, cocked it and laid it in his lap. Then he took the long amputating knife from his bosom, and threw it down in front of Bellingham.

"Now, then," said he, "just get to work and cut up that mummy."

"Oh, is that it?" said Bellingham with a sneer.

"Yes, that is it. They tell me that the law can't touch you. But I have a law that will set matters straight. If in five minutes you have not set to work, I swear by the God who made me that I will put a bullet through your brain!"

"You would murder me?"

Bellingham had half risen, and his face was the colour of putty.

"Yes."

"And for what?"

"To stop your mischief. One minute has gone."

"But what have I done?"

"I know and you know."

"This is mere bullying."

"Two minutes are gone."

"But you must give reasons. You are a madman – a dangerous madman. Why should I destroy my own property? It is a valuable mummy."

"You must cut it up, and you must burn it."

"I will do no such thing."

"Four minutes are gone."

Smith took up the pistol and he looked towards Bellingham with an inexorable face. As the second hand stole round, he raised his hand, and the finger twitched upon the trigger.

"There! There! I'll do it!" screamed Bellingham.

In frantic haste he caught up the knife and hacked at the figure of the mummy, ever glancing round to see the eye and the weapon of his terrible visitor bent upon him. The creature crackled and snapped under every stab of the keen blade. A thick yellow dust rose up from it. Spices and dried essences rained down upon the floor. Suddenly, with a rending crack, its backbone snapped asunder, and it fell, a brown heap of sprawling limbs, upon the floor.

"Now into the fire!" said Smith.

The flames leapt and roared as the dried and tinder-like debris was piled upon it. The little room was like the stokehole of a steamer and the sweat ran down the faces of the two men; but still the one stooped and worked, while the other sat watching him with a set face. A thick, fat smoke oozed out from the fire, and a heavy smell of burnt rosin and singed hair filled the air. In a quarter of an hour a few charred and brittle sticks were all that was left of lot No. 249.

"Perhaps that will satisfy you," snarled Bellingham, with hate and fear in his little grey eyes as he glanced back at his tormentor.

"No, I must make a clean sweep of all your materials. We must have no more devil's tricks. In with all these leaves! They may have something to do with it."

"And what now!" asked Bellingham, when the leaves also had been added to the blaze.

"Now the roll of papyrus which you had on the table that night. It is in that drawer, I think."

"No, no," shouted Bellingham. "Don't burn that! Why, man, you don't know what you do. It is unique: it contains wisdom which is nowhere else to be found."

"Out with it!"

"But look here, Smith, you can't really mean it. I'll share the knowledge with you. I'll teach you all that is in it. Or, stay, let me only copy it before you burn it!"

Smith stepped forward and turned the key in the drawer. Taking out the yellow, curled roll of paper, he threw it into the fire, and pressed it down with his heel. Bellingham screamed, and grabbed at it; but Smith pushed him back and stood over it until it was reduced to a formless grey ash.

"Now, Master B.," said he, "I think I have pretty well drawn your teeth. You'll hear from me again, if you return to your old tricks. And now good morning, for I must go back to my studies."

And such is the narrative of Abercrombie Smith as to the singular events which occurred in Old College, Oxford, in the spring of '84. As Bellingham left the university immediately afterwards, and was last heard of in the Sudan, there is no one who can contradict his statement. But the wisdom of men is small, and the ways of Nature are strange, and who shall put a bound to the dark things which may be found by those who seek for them?

"De Profundis"*

So long as the oceans are the ligaments which bind together the great broadcast British Empire, so long will there be a dash of romance in our minds. For the soul is swayed by the waters, as the waters are by the moon, and when the great highways of an empire are along such roads as these, so full of strange sights and sounds, with danger ever running like a hedge on either side of the course, it is a dull mind indeed which does not bear away with it some trace of such a passage. And now, Britain lies far beyond herself, for the three-mile limit of every seaboard is her frontier, which has been won by hammer and loom and pick rather than by arts of war. For it is written in history that neither king nor army can bar the path to the man who, having twopence in his strongbox, and knowing well where he can turn it to threepence, sets his mind to that one end. And as the frontier has broadened the mind of Britain has broadened too, spreading out until all men can see that the ways of the island are continental, even as those of the Continent are insular.

But for this a price must be paid, and the price is a grievous one. As the beast of old must have one young human life as a tribute every year, so to our Empire we throw from day to day the pick and flower of our youth. The engine is worldwide and strong, but the only fuel that will drive it is the lives of British men. Thus it is that in the grey old cathedrals, as we look round upon the brasses on the walls, we see strange names, such names as they who reared those walls had never heard, for it is in Peshawur, and Umballah, and Korti, and Fort Pearson* that the youngsters die, leaving only a precedent and a brass behind them. But if every man had his obelisk, even where he lay, then no frontier line need be drawn, for a cordon of British graves would ever show how high the Anglo-Celtic tide had lapped.

This, then, as well as the waters which join us to the world, has done something to tinge us with romance. For when so many have their loved ones over the seas, walking amid hillmen's bullets, or swamp malaria, where death is sudden and distance great, then mind communes with mind, and strange stories arise of dream, presentiment or vision, where the mother sees her dying son, and is past the first bitterness of her grief ere the message comes which should have broken the news. The learned have of late looked into the matter and have even labelled it with a name;* but what can we know more of it save that a poor stricken soul, when hard-pressed and driven, can shoot across the earth some ten-thousand-mile-distant picture of its trouble to the mind which is most akin to it. Far be it from me to say that there lies no such power within us, for of all things which the brain will grasp the last will be itself; but yet it is well to be very cautious over such matters, for once at least I have known that which was within the laws of nature seem to be far upon the further side of them.

John Vansittart was the younger partner of the firm of Hudson and Vansittart, coffee exporters of the island of Ceylon, three-quarters Dutchman by descent, but wholly English in his sympathies. For years I had been his agent in London, and when in '72 he came over to England for a three months' holiday, he turned to me for the introductions which would enable him to see something of town and country life. Armed with seven letters he left my offices, and for many weeks scrappy notes from different parts of the country let me know that he had found favour in the eyes of my friends. Then came word of his engagement to Emily Lawson, of a cadet branch of the Hereford Lawsons, and at the very tail of the first flying rumour the news of his absolute marriage, for the wooing of a wanderer must be short, and the days were already crowding on towards the date when he must be upon his homeward journey. They were to return together to Colombo in one of the firm's own thousand-ton barque-rigged sailing ships, and this was to be their princely honeymoon, at once a necessity and a delight.

Those were the royal days of coffee-planting in Ceylon, before a single season and a rotting fungus drove a whole community through years of despair to one of the greatest commercial victories which pluck and ingenuity ever won.* Not often is it that men have the heart when their one great industry is withered to rear up in a few years another as rich to take its place, and the tea fields of Ceylon are as true a monument to courage as is the lion at Waterloo. But in '72 there was no cloud yet above the skyline, and the hopes of the planters were as high and as bright as the hillsides on which they reared their crops. Vansittart came down to London with his young and beautiful wife. I was introduced, dined with them, and it was finally arranged that I, since business called me also to Ceylon, should be a fellow passenger with them on the *Eastern Star*, which was timed to sail on the following Monday.

It was on the Sunday evening that I saw him again. He was shown up into my rooms about nine o'clock at night, with the air of a man who is bothered and out of sorts. His hand, as I shook it, was hot and dry.

"I wish, Atkinson," said he, "that you could give me a little lime juice and water. I have a beastly thirst upon me, and the more I take the more I seem to want."

I rang and ordered a carafe and glasses. "You are flushed," said I. "You don't look the thing."

"No, I'm clean off colour. Got a touch of rheumatism in my back, and don't seem to taste my food. It is this vile London that is choking me. I'm not used to breathing air which has been used up by four million lungs all sucking away on every side of you." He flapped his crooked hands before his face, like a man who really struggles for his breath.

"A touch of the sea will soon set you right."

"Yes, I'm of one mind with you there. That's the thing for me. I want no other doctor. If I don't get to sea tomorrow I'll have an illness. There are no two ways about it." He drank off a tumbler of lime juice, and clapped his two hands with his knuckles doubled up into the small of his back.

"That seems to ease me," said he, looking at me with a filmy eye. "Now I want your help, Atkinson, for I am rather awkwardly placed."

"As how?"

"This way. My wife's mother got ill and wired for her. I couldn't go – you know best yourself how tied I have been – so she had to go alone. Now I've had another wire to say that she can't come tomorrow, but that she will pick up the ship at Falmouth on Wednesday. We put in there, you know, though I count it hard, Atkinson, that a man should be asked to believe in a mystery, and cursed if he can't do it. Cursed, mind you, no less." He leant forward and began to draw a catchy breath like a man who is poised on the very edge of a sob.

Then first it came into my mind that I had heard much of the hard-drinking life of the island, and that from brandy came these wild words and fevered hands. The flushed cheek and the glazing eye were those of one whose drink is strong upon him. Sad it was to see so noble a young man in the grip of that most bestial of all the devils.

"You should lie down," I said, with some severity.

He screwed up his eyes like a man who is striving to wake himself, and looked up with an air of surprise.

"So I shall presently," said he, quite rationally. "I felt quite swimmy just now, but I am my own man again now. Let me see, what was I talking about? Oh, ah, of course, about the wife. She joins the ship at Falmouth. Now I want to go round by water. I believe my health depends upon it. I just want a little clean first-lung air to set me on my feet again. I ask you, like a good fellow, to go to Falmouth by rail, so that in case we should be late you may be there to look after the wife. Put up at the Royal Hotel, and I will wire her that you are there. Her sister will bring her down, so that it will be all plain sailing."

"I'll do it with pleasure," said I. "In fact, I would rather go by rail, for we shall have enough and to spare of the sea before we reach Colombo. I believe too that you badly need a change. Now, I should go and turn in, if I were you."

"Yes, I will. I sleep aboard tonight. You know," he continued, as the film settled down again over his eyes, "I've not slept well the last few nights. I've been troubled with theolololog – that is to say, theolological – hang it," with a desperate effort, "with the doubts of theolologicians. Wondering why the Almighty made us, you know, and why He made our heads swimmy, and fixed little pains into the small of our backs. Maybe I'll do better tonight." He rose and steadied himself with an effort against the corner of the chair back.

"Look here, Vansittart," said I gravely, stepping up to him, and laying my hand upon his sleeve, "I can give you a shakedown here. You are not fit to go out. You are all over the place. You've been mixing your drinks."

"Drinks!" He stared at me stupidly.

"You used to carry your liquor better than this."

"I give you my word, Atkinson, that I have not had a drain for two days. It's not drink. I don't know what it is. I suppose you think this is drink." He took up my hand in his burning grasp, and passed it over his own forehead.

"Great Lord!" said I.

His skin felt like a thin sheet of velvet beneath which lies a close-packed layer of small shot. It was smooth to the touch at any one place but, to a finger passed along it, rough as a nutmeg grater.

"It's all right," said he, smiling at my startled face. "I've had the prickly heat nearly as bad."

"But this is never prickly heat."

"No, it's London. It's breathing bad air. But tomorrow it'll be all right. There's a surgeon aboard, so I shall be in safe hands. I must be off now."

"Not you," said I, pushing him back into a chair. "This is past a joke. You don't move from here until a doctor sees you. Just stay where you are."

I caught up my hat and, rushing round to the house of a neighbouring physician, I brought him back with me. The room was empty and Vansittart gone. I rang the bell. The servant said that the gentleman had ordered a cab the instant that I had left, and had gone off in it. He had told the cabman to drive to the docks.

"Did the gentleman seem ill?" I asked.

"Ill!" The man smiled. "No, sir, he was singin' his 'ardest all the time."

The information was not as reassuring as my servant seemed to think, but I reflected that he was going straight back to the *Eastern Star*, and that there was a doctor aboard of her, so that there was nothing which I could do in the matter. Nonetheless, when I thought of his thirst, his burning hands, his heavy eye, his tripping speech and, lastly, of that leprous forehead, I carried with me to bed an unpleasant memory of my visitor and his visit.

At eleven o'clock next day I was at the docks, but the *Eastern Star* had already moved down the river, and was nearly at Gravesend. To Gravesend I went by train, but only to see her topmasts far off, with a plume of smoke from a tug in front of her. I would hear no more of my friend until I rejoined him at Falmouth. When I got back to my offices, a telegram was awaiting me from Mrs Vansittart, asking me to meet her, and next evening found us both at the Royal Hotel, Falmouth, where we were to wait for the *Eastern Star.* Ten days passed, and there came no news of her.

They were ten days which I am not likely to forget. On the very day that the *Eastern Star* had cleared from the Thames, a furious easterly gale had sprung up, and blew on from day to day for the greater part of a week without the sign of a lull. Such a screaming, raving, long-drawn storm has never been known on the southern coast. From our hotel windows the sea view was all banked in haze, with a little rain-swept half-circle under our very eyes, churned and lashed into one tossing stretch of foam. So heavy was the wind upon the waves that little sea could rise, for the crest of each billow was torn shrieking from it, and lashed broadcast over the bay. Clouds, wind, sea, all were rushing to the west, and there, looking down at this mad jumble of elements, I waited on day after day, my sole companion a white, silent woman, with terror in her eyes, her forehead pressed ever against the window, her gaze from early morning to the fall of night fixed upon that wall of grey haze through which the loom of a vessel might come. She said nothing, but that face of hers was one long wail of fear.

On the fifth day I took counsel with an old seaman. I should have preferred to have done so alone, but she saw me speak with him and was at our side in an instant, with parted lips and a prayer in her eyes.

"Seven days out from London," said he, "and five in the gale. Well, the Channel's swept clear by this wind. There's three things for it. She may have popped into port on the French side. That's like enough."

"No, no – he knew we were here. He would have telegraphed."

"Ah, yes, so he would. Well, then, he might have run for it, and if he did that he won't be very far from Madeira by now. That'll be it, marm, you may depend."

"Or else? You said there was a third chance."

"Did I, marm. No, only two, I think. I don't think I said anything of a third. Your ship's out there, depend upon it, away out in the Atlantic, and you'll hear of it time enough, for the weather is breaking. Now don't you fret, marm, and wait quiet, and you'll find a real blue Cornish sky tomorrow."

The old seaman was right in his surmise, for the next day broke calm and bright, with only a low dwindling cloud in the west to mark the last trailing wreaths of the storm wrack.* But still there came no word from the sea, and no sign of the ship. Three more weary days had passed, the weariest that I have ever spent, when there came a seafaring man to the hotel with a letter. I gave a shout of joy. It was from the captain of the *Eastern Star*. As I read the first lines of it I whisked my hand over it, but she laid her own upon it and drew it away. "I have seen it," said she in a cold, quiet voice. "I may as well see the rest too."

> DEAR SIR – said the letter – Mr Vansittart is down with the smallpox, and we are blown so far on our course that we don't know what to do, he being off his head and unfit to tell us. By dead reckoning we are but three hundred miles from Funchal, so I take it that it is best that we should push on there, get Mr V. into hospital, and wait in the Bay until you come. There's a sailing ship due from Falmouth to Funchal in a few days' time, as I understand. This goes by the brig *Marian* of Falmouth, and five pounds is due to the master.
>
> Yours respectfully,
>
> JNO. HINES

She was a wonderful woman that, only a chit of a girl fresh from school, but as quiet and strong as a man. She said nothing – only pressed her lips together tight, and put on her bonnet.

"You are going out?" I asked.

"Yes."

"Can I be of use?"

"No, I am going to the doctor's."

"To the doctor's?"

"Yes. To learn how to nurse a smallpox case."

She was busy at that all the evening, and next morning we were off with a fine ten-knot breeze in the barque *Rose of Sharon* for Madeira. For five days we made good time, and were no great way from the island; but on the sixth there fell a calm, and we lay without motion on a sea of oil, heaving slowly, but making not a foot of way.

At ten o'clock that night Emily Vansittart and I stood leaning on the starboard railing of the poop, with a full moon shining at our backs, and casting a black shadow of the barque, and of our own two heads, upon the shining water. From the shadow a broadening path of moonshine stretched away to the lonely skyline, flickering and shimmering in the gentle heave of the swell. We were talking with bent heads, chatting of the calm, of the chances of wind, of the look of the sky, when there came a sudden plop, like a rising salmon, and there, in the clear light, John Vansittart sprang out of the water and looked up at us.

I never saw anything clearer in my life than I saw that man. The moon shone full upon him, and he was but three oars' length away. His face was more puffed than when I had seen him last, mottled here and there with dark scabs, his mouth and eyes open as one who is struck with some overpowering surprise. He had some white stuff streaming from his shoulders, and one hand was raised to his ear, the other crooked across his breast. I saw him leap from the water into the air, and in the dead calm the waves of his coming lapped up against the sides of the vessel. Then his figure sank back into the water again, and I heard a rending, crackling sound like a bundle of brushwood snapping in the fire on a frosty night. There were no signs of him when I looked again, but a swift swirl and eddy on the still sea still marked the spot where he had been. How long I stood there, tingling to my fingertips, holding up an unconscious woman with one hand, clutching at the rail of the vessel with the other, was more than I could afterwards tell. I had been noted as a man of slow and unresponsive emotions, but this time at least I was shaken to the core. Once and twice I struck my foot upon the deck to be certain that I was indeed the master of my own senses, and that this was not some mad prank of an unruly brain. As I stood, still marvelling, the woman shivered, opened her eyes, gasped, and then, standing erect with her hands upon the rail, looked out over the moonlit sea with a face which had aged ten years in a summer night.

"You saw his vision?" she murmured.

"I saw something."

"It was he! It was John! He is dead!"

I muttered some lame words of doubt.

"Doubtless he died at this hour," she whispered. "In hospital at Madeira. I have read of such things. His thoughts were with me. His vision came to me. Oh, my John, my dear, dear, lost John!"

She broke out suddenly into a storm of weeping, and I led her down into her cabin, where I left her with her sorrow. That night a brisk breeze blew up from the east, and in the evening of the next day we passed the two islets of Los Desertos,* and dropped anchor at sundown in the Bay of Funchal. The *Eastern Star* lay no great distance from us, with the quarantine flag flying from her main, and her Jack halfway up her peak.

"You see," said Mrs Vansittart quickly. She was dry-eyed now, for she had known how it would be.

That night we received permission from the authorities to move on board the *Eastern Star*. The captain, Hines, was waiting upon deck with confusion and grief contending upon his bluff face as he sought for words with which to break this heavy tidings, but she took the story from his lips.

"I know that my husband is dead," she said. "He died yesterday night, about ten o'clock, in hospital at Madeira, did he not?"

The seaman stared aghast. "No, marm, he died eight days ago at sea, and we had to bury him out there, for we lay in a belt of calm, and could not say when we might make the land."

Well, those are the main facts about the death of John Vansittart, and his appearance to his wife somewhere about lat. 35 N. and long. 15 W. A clearer case of a wraith has seldom been made out, and since then it has been told as such, and put into print as such, and endorsed by a learned society as such, and so floated off with many others to support the recent theory of telepathy. For myself, I hold telepathy to be proved, but I would snatch this one case from amid the evidence, and say that I do not think that it was the wraith of John Vansittart, but John Vansittart himself whom we saw that night leaping into the moonlight out of the depths of the Atlantic. It has ever been my belief that some strange chance – one of those chances which seem so improbable and yet so constantly occur – had becalmed us over the very spot where the man had been buried a week before. For the rest, the surgeon tells me that the leaden weight was not too firmly fixed, and that seven days bring about changes which fetch a body to the surface. Coming from the depth to which the weight would have sunk it, he explains that it might well attain such a velocity as to carry it clear of the water. Such is my own explanation of the matter, and if you ask me what then became of the body, I must recall to you that snapping, crackling sound, with the swirl in the water. The shark is a surface feeder and is plentiful in those parts.

The Lift

Flight Commander Stangate should have been happy. He had come safely through the war without a hurt, and with a good name in the most heroic of services. He had only just turned thirty, and a great career seemed to lie ahead of him. Above all, beautiful Mary MacLean was walking by his side, and he had her promise that she was there for life. What could a young man ask for more? And yet there was a heavy load upon his heart.

He could not explain it himself, and endeavoured to reason himself out of it. There was the blue sky above him, the blue sea in front, the beautiful gardens with their throngs of happy pleasure-seekers around. Above all, there was that sweet face turned upon him with questioning concern. Why could he not raise himself to so joyful an environment? He made effort after effort, but they were not convincing enough to deceive the quick instinct of a loving woman.

"What is it, Tom?" she asked anxiously. "I can see that something is clouding you. Do tell me if I can help you in any way."

He laughed in shamefaced fashion.

"It is such a sin to spoil our little outing," he said. "I could kick myself round these gardens when I think of it. Don't worry, my darling, for I know the cloud will roll off. I suppose I am a creature of nerves, though I should have got past that by now. The Flying Service is supposed either to break you or to warrant you for life."

"It is nothing definite, then?"

"No, it is nothing definite. That's the worst of it. You could fight it more easily if it was. It's just a dead, heavy depression here in my chest and across my forehead. But do forgive me, dear girl! What a brute I am to shadow you like this."

"But I love to share even the smallest trouble."

"Well, it's gone – vamoosed – vanished. We will talk about it no more."

She gave him a swift, penetrating glance.

"No, no, Tom: your brow shows, as well as feels. Tell me, dear, have you often felt like this? You really look very ill. Sit here, dear, in the shade and tell me of it."

They sat together in the shadow of the great latticed Tower* which reared itself six hundred feet high beside them.

"I have an absurd faculty," said he. "I don't know that I have ever mentioned it to anyone before. But when imminent danger is threatening me I got these strange forebodings. Of course it is absurd today in these peaceful surroundings. It only shows how queerly these things work. But it is the first time that it has deceived me."

"When had you it before?"

"When I was a lad it seized me one morning. I was nearly drowned that afternoon. I had it when the burglar came to Morton Hall and I got a bullet through my coat. Then twice in the war when I was overmatched and escaped by a miracle, I had this strange feeling before ever I climbed into my machine. Then it lifts quite suddenly, like a mist in the sunshine. Why, it is lifting now. Look at me! Can't you see that it is so?"

She could indeed. He had turned in a minute from a haggard man to a laughing boy. She found herself laughing in sympathy. A rush of high spirits and energy had swept away his strange foreboding and filled his whole soul with the vivid, dancing joy of youth.

"Thank goodness!" he cried. "I think it is your dear eyes that have done it. I could not stand that wistful look in them. What a silly, foolish nightmare it all has been! There's an end for ever in my belief in presentiments. Now, dear girl, we have just time for one good turn before luncheon. After that the gardens get so crowded that it is hopeless to do anything. Shall we have a sideshow, or the great wheel, or the flying boat, or what?"

"What about the Tower?" she asked, glancing upwards. "Surely that glorious air and the view from the top would drive the last wisps of cloud out of your mind."

He looked at his watch.

"Well, it's past twelve, but I suppose we could do it all in an hour. But it doesn't seem to be working. What about it, conductor?"

The man shook his head and pointed to a little knot of people who were assembled at the entrance.

"They've all been waiting, sir. It's hung up, but the gear is being overhauled, and I expect the signal every minute. If you join the others I promise it won't be long."

They had hardly reached the group when the steel face of the lift rolled aside – a sign that there was hope in the future. The motley crowd drifted through the opening and waited expectantly upon the wooden platform. They were not numerous, for the gardens are not crowded until the afternoon, but they were fair samples of the kindly, good-humoured north-country folk who take their annual holiday at Northam. Their faces were all upturned now, and they were watching with keen interest a man who was descending the steel framework. It seemed a dangerous, precarious business, but he came as swiftly as an ordinary mortal upon a staircase.

"My word!" said the conductor, glancing up. "Jim has got a move on this morning."

"Who is he?" asked Commander Stangate.

"That's Jim Barnes, sir, the best workman that ever went on a scaffold. He fair lives up there. Every bolt and rivet are under his care. He's a wonder, is Jim."

"But don't argue religion with him," said one of the group.

The attendant laughed.

"Ah, you know him, then," said he. "No, don't argue religion with him."

"Why not?" asked the officer.

"Well, he takes it very hard, he does. He's the shining light of his sect."

"It ain't hard to be that," said the knowing one. "I've heard there are only six folk in the fold. He's one of those who picture heaven as the exact size of their own backstreet conventicle and everyone else left outside it."

"Better not tell him so while he's got that hammer in his hand," said the conductor in a hurried whisper. "Hallo, Jim, how goes it this morning?"

The man slid swiftly down the last thirty feet, and then balanced himself on a crossbar while he looked at the little group in the lift. As he stood there, clad in a leather suit, with his pliers and other tools dangling from his brown belt, he was a figure to please the eye of an artist. The man was very tall and gaunt, with great straggling limbs and every appearance of giant strength. His face was a remarkable one, noble and yet sinister, with dark eyes and hair, a prominent hooked nose and a beard which flowed over his chest. He steadied himself with one knotted hand, while the other held a steel hammer dangling by his knee.

"It's all ready aloft," said he. "I'll go up with you if I may." He sprang down from his perch and joined the others in the lift.

"I suppose you are always watching it," said the young lady.

"That is what I am engaged for, miss. From morning to night, and often from night to morning, I am up here. There are times when I feel as if I were not a man at all, but a fowl of the air. They fly round me, the creatures, as I lie out on the girders, and they cry to me until I find myself crying back to the poor soulless things."

"It's a great charge," said the commander, glancing up at the wonderful tracery of steel outlined against the deep-blue sky.

"Aye, sir, and there is not a nut nor a screw that is not in my keeping. Here's my hammer to ring them true and my spanner to wrench them tight. As the Lord over the earth, so am I – even I – over the Tower, with power of life and power of death, aye of death and of life."

The hydraulic machinery had begun to work and the lift very slowly ascended. As it mounted, the glorious panorama of the coast and bay gradually unfolded itself. So engrossing was the view that the passengers hardly noticed it when the platform stopped abruptly between stages at the five-hundred-foot level. Barnes, the workman, muttered that something must be amiss, and springing like a cat across the gap which separated them from the trelliswork of metal he clambered out of sight. The motley little party, suspended in mid-air, lost something of their British shyness under such unwonted conditions and began to compare notes with each other. One couple, who addressed each other as Dolly and Billy, announced to the company that they were the particular stars of the Hippodrome bill, and kept their neighbours tittering with their rather obvious wit. A buxom mother, her precocious son and two married couples upon holiday formed an appreciative audience.

"You'd like to be a sailor, would you?" said Billy the comedian, in answer to some remark of the boy. "Look 'ere, my nipper, you'll end up as a blooming corpse if you ain't careful. See 'im standin' at the edge. At this hour of the morning I can't bear to watch it."

"What's the hour got to do with it?" asked a stout commercial traveller.

"My nerves are worth nothin' before midday. Why, lookin' down there, and seein' those folk like dots, puts me all in a twitter. My family is all alike in the mornin'."

"I expect," said Dolly, a high-coloured young woman, "that they're all alike the evening before."

There was a general laugh, which was led by the comedian.

"You got it across that time, Dolly. It's KO for Battling Billy – still senseless when last heard of. If my family is laughed at I'll leave the room."

"It's about time we did," said the commercial traveller, who was a red-faced, choleric person. "It's a disgrace the way they hold us up. I'll write to the company."

"Where's the bell-push?" said Billy. "I'm goin' to ring."

"What for – the waiter?" asked the lady.

"For the conductor, the chauffeur, whoever it is that drives the old bus up and down. Have they run out of petrol, or broke the mainspring, or what?"

"We have a fine view, anyhow," said the commander.

"Well, I've had that," remarked Billy. "I'm done with it, and I'm for getting on."

"I'm getting nervous," cried the stout mother. "I do hope there is nothing wrong with the lift."

"I say, hold on to the slack of my coat, Dolly. I'm going to look over and chance it. Oh, Lord, it makes me sick and giddy! There's a horse down under, and it ain't bigger than a mouse. I don't see anyone lookin' after us. Where's old Isaiah the prophet who came up with us?"

"He shinned out of it mighty quick when he thought trouble was coming."

"Look here," said Dolly, looking very perturbed, "this is a nice thing, I don't think. Here we are five hundred foot up, and stuck for the day as like as not. I'm due for the matinée at the Hippodrome. I'm sorry for the company if they don't get me down in time for that. I'm billed all over the town for a new song."

"A new one! What's that, Dolly?"

"A real pot o' ginger, I tell you. It's called 'On the Road to Ascot'. I've got a hat four foot across to sing it in."

"Come on, Dolly, let's have a rehearsal while we wait."

"No, no – the young lady here wouldn't understand."

"I'd be very glad to hear it," cried Mary MacLean. "Please don't let me prevent you."

"The words were written to the hat. I couldn't sing the verses without the hat. But there's a nailin' good chorus to it:

"'If you want a little mascot
When you're on the way to Ascot,
Try the lady with the cartwheel hat.'"

She had a tuneful voice and a sense of rhythm which set everyone nodding. "Try it now all together," she cried; and the strange little haphazard company sang it with all their lungs.

"I say," said Billy, "that ought to wake somebody up. What? Let's try a shout all together."

It was a fine effort, but there was no response. It was clear that the management down below was quite ignorant or impotent. No sound came back to them.

The passengers became alarmed. The commercial traveller was rather less rubicund. Billy still tried to joke, but his efforts were not well received. The officer in his blue uniform at once took his place as rightful leader in a crisis. They all looked to him and appealed to him.

"What would you advise, sir? You don't think there's any danger of it coming down, do you?"

"Not the least. But it's awkward to be stuck here all the same. I think I could jump across onto that girder. Then perhaps I could see what is wrong."

"No, no, Tom – for goodness' sake, don't leave us!"

"Some people have a nerve," said Billy. "Fancy jumping across a five-hundred-foot drop!"

"I dare say the gentleman did worse things in the war."

"Well, I wouldn't do it myself – not if they starred me in the bills. It's all very well for old Isaiah. It's his job, and I wouldn't do him out of it."

Three sides of the lift were shut in with wooden partitions, pierced with windows for the view. The fourth side, facing the sea, was clear. Stangate leant over as far as he could and looked upwards. As he did so there came from above him a peculiar sonorous metallic twang, as if a mighty harp string had been struck. Some distance up – a hundred feet, perhaps – he could see a long brown corded arm, which was working furiously among the wire cordage above. The form was beyond his view, but he was fascinated by this bare sinewy arm which tugged and pulled and sagged and stabbed.

"It's all right," he said, and a general sigh of relief broke from his strange comrades at his words. "There is someone above us setting things right."

"It's old Isaiah," said Billy, stretching his neck round the corner. "I can't see him, but it's his arm for a dollar. What's he got in his hand? Looks like a screwdriver or something. No, by George, it's a file."

As he spoke there came another sonorous twang from above. There was a troubled frown upon the officer's brow.

"I say, dash it all, that's the very sound our steel hawser made when it parted, strand by strand, at Dixmude.* What the deuce is the fellow about? Heh, there! What are you trying to do?"

The man had ceased his work and was now slowly descending the iron trellis.

"All right, he's coming," said Stangate to his startled companions. "It's all right, Mary. Don't be frightened, any of you. It's absurd to suppose he would really weaken the cord that holds us."

A pair of high boots appeared from above. Then came the leathern breeches, the belt with its dangling tools, the muscular form and, finally, the fierce, swarthy eagle face of the workman. His coat was off and his shirt open, showing the hairy chest. As he appeared there came another sharp snapping vibration from above. The man made his way down in leisurely fashion, and then, balancing himself upon the cross-girder and leaning against the side piece, he stood with folded arms, looking from under his heavy black brows at the huddled passengers upon the platform.

"Hallo!" said Stangate. "What's the matter?"

The man stood impassive and silent, with something indescribably menacing in his fixed, unwinking stare.

The flying officer grew angry.

"Hallo! Are you deaf?" he cried. "How long do you mean to have us stuck here?"

The man stood silent. There was something devilish in his appearance.

"I'll complain of you, my lad," said Billy, in a quivering voice. "This won't stop here, I can promise you."

"Look here!" cried the officer. "We have ladies here and you are alarming them. Why are we stuck here? Has the machinery gone wrong?"

"You are here," said the man, "because I have put a wedge against the hawser above you."

"You fouled the line! How dared you do such a thing! What right have you to frighten the women and put us all to this inconvenience? Take that wedge out this instant, or it will be the worse for you."

The man was silent.

"Do you hear what I say? Why the devil don't you answer? Is this a joke or what? We've had about enough of it, I tell you."

Mary MacLean had gripped her lover by the arm in an agony of sudden panic.

"Oh, Tom!" she cried. "Look at his eyes – look at his horrible eyes! The man is a maniac."

The workman stirred suddenly into sinister life. His dark face broke into writhing lines of passion, and his fierce eyes glowed like embers, while he shook one long arm in the air.

"Behold," he cried, "those who are mad to the children of this world are in very truth the Lord's anointed and the dwellers in the inner temple. Lo, I am one who is prepared to testify even to the uttermost, for of a verity the day has now come when the humble will be exalted and the wicked will be cut off in their sins!"

"Mother! Mother!" cried the little boy, in terror.

"There, there! It's all right, Jack," said the buxom woman, and then, in a burst of womanly wrath: "What d'you want to make the child cry for? You're a pretty man, you are!"

"Better he should cry now than in the outer darkness. Let him seek safety while there is yet time."

The officer measured the gap with a practised eye. It was a good eight feet across, and the fellow could push him over before he could steady himself. It would be a desperate thing to attempt. He tried soothing words once more.

"See here, my lad, you've carried this joke too far. Why should you wish to injure us? Just shin up and get that wedge out, and we will agree to say no more about it."

Another rending snap came from above.

"By George, the hawser is going!" cried Stangate. "Here! Stand aside! I'm coming over to see to it."

The workman had plucked the hammer from his belt, and waved it furiously in the air.

"Stand back, young man! Stand back! Or come – if you would hasten your end."

"Tom, Tom, for God's sake, don't spring! Help! Help!"

The passengers all joined in the cry for aid. The man smiled malignly as he watched them.

"There is no one to help. They could not come if they would. You would be wiser to turn to your own souls that ye he not cast to the burning. Lo, strand by strand the cable snaps which holds you. There is yet another, and with each that goes there is more strain upon the rest. Five minutes of time, and all eternity beyond."

A moan of fear rose from the prisoners in the lift. Stangate felt a cold sweat upon his brow as he passed his arm round the shrinking girl. If this vindictive devil could only be coaxed away for an instant he would spring across and take his chance in a hand-to-hand fight.

"Look here, my friend! We give you best!" he cried. "We can do nothing. Go up and cut the cable if you wish. Go on – do it now, and get it over!"

"That you may come across unharmed. Having set my hand to the work, I will not draw back from it."

Fury seized the young officer.

"You devil!" he cried. "What do you stand there grinning for? I'll give you something to grin about. Give me a stick, one of you."

The man waved his hammer.

"Come, then! Come to judgement!" he howled.

"He'll murder you, Tom! Oh, for God's sake, don't! If we must die, let us die together."

"I wouldn't try it, sir," cried Billy. "He'll strike you down before you get a footing. Hold up, Dolly, my dear! Faintin' won't 'elp us. You speak to him, miss. Maybe he'll listen to you."

"Why should you wish to hurt us?" said Mary. "What have we ever done to you? Surely you will be sorry afterwards if we are injured. Now do be kind and reasonable and help us to get back to the ground."

For a moment there may have been some softening in the man's fierce eyes as he looked at the sweet face which was upturned to him. Then his features set once more into their grim lines of malice.

"My hand is set to the work, woman. It is not for the servant to look back from his task."

"But why should this be your task?"

"Because there is a voice within me which tells me so. In the night-time I have heard it, and in the daytime too, when I have lain out alone upon the girders and seen the wicked dotting the streets beneath me, each busy on his own evil intent. 'John Barnes, John Barnes,' said the voice. 'You are here that you may give a sign to a sinful generation – such a sign as shall show them that the Lord liveth and that there is a judgement upon sin.' Who am I that I should disobey the voice of the Lord?"

"The voice of the Devil," said Stangate. "What is the sin of this lady, or of these others, that you should seek their lives?"

"You are as the others, neither better nor worse. All day they pass me, load by load, with foolish cries and empty songs and vain babble of voices. Their thoughts are set upon the things of the flesh. Too long have I stood aside and watched and refused to testify. But now the day of wrath is come and the sacrifice is ready. Think not that a woman's tongue can turn me from my task."

"It is useless!" Mary cried. "Useless! I read death in his eyes."

Another cord had snapped.

"Repent! Repent!" cried the madman. "One more, and it is over!"

Commander Stangate felt as if it were all some extraordinary dream – some monstrous nightmare. Could it be possible that he, after all his escapes of death in warfare, was now, in the heart of peaceful England, at the mercy of a homicidal lunatic, and that his dear girl, the one being whom he would shield from the very shadow of danger, was helpless before this horrible man? All his energy and manhood rose up in him for one last effort.

"Here, we won't be killed like sheep in the shambles!"* he cried, throwing himself against the wooden wall of the lift and kicking with all his force. "Come on, boys! Kick it! Beat it! It's only matchboarding, and it is giving. Smash it down! Well done! Once more all together! There she goes! Now for the side! Out with it! Splendid!"

First the back and then the side of the little compartment had been knocked out, and the splinters dropped down into the abyss. Barnes danced upon his girder, his hammer in the air.

"Strive not!" he shrieked. "It avails not. The day is surely come."

"It's not two feet from the side girder," cried the officer. "Get across! Quick! Quick! All of you. I'll hold this devil off!" He had seized a stout stick from the commercial traveller and faced the madman, daring him to spring across.

"Your turn now, my friend!" he hissed. "Come on, hammer and all! I'm ready for you."

Above him he heard another snap, and the frail platform began to rock. Glancing over his shoulder, he saw that his companions were all safe upon the side girder. A strange line of terrified castaways they appeared as they clung in an ungainly row to the trelliswork of steel. But their feet were on the iron support. With two quick steps and a spring he was at their side. At the same instant the murderer, hammer in hand, jumped the gap. They had one vision of him there – a vision which will haunt their dreams – the convulsed face, the blazing eyes, the wind-tossed raven locks. For a moment he balanced himself upon the swaying platform. The next, with a rending crash, he and it were gone. There was a long silence and then, far down, the thud and clatter of a mighty fall.

With white faces, the forlorn group clung to the cold steel bars and gazed down into the terrible abyss. It was the commander who broke the silence.

"They'll send for us now. It's all safe," he cried, wiping his brow. "But, by Jove, it was a close call!"

TALES OF TERROR
AND MYSTERY

TALES OF TERROR

The Horror of the Heights

(which includes the manuscript known as the Joyce-Armstrong Fragment)

The idea that the extraordinary narrative which has been called the Joyce-Armstrong Fragment is an elaborate practical joke evolved by some unknown person, cursed by a perverted and sinister sense of humour, has now been abandoned by all who have examined the matter. The most macabre and imaginative of plotters would hesitate before linking his morbid fancies with the unquestioned and tragic facts which reinforce the statement. Though the assertions contained in it are amazing and even monstrous, it is nonetheless forcing itself upon the general intelligence that they are true, and that we must readjust our ideas to the new situation. This world of ours appears to be separated by a slight and precarious margin of safety from a most singular and unexpected danger. I will endeavour in this narrative, which reproduces the original document in its necessarily somewhat fragmentary form, to lay before the reader the whole of the facts up to date, prefacing my statement by saying that, if there be any who doubt the narrative of Joyce-Armstrong, there can be no question at all as to the facts concerning Lieutenant Myrtle, RN,* and Mr Hay Connor, who undoubtedly met their end in the manner described.

The Joyce-Armstrong Fragment was found in the field which is called Lower Haycock, lying one mile to the westward of the village of Withyham, upon the Kent and Sussex border. It was on 15th September last that an agricultural labourer, James Flynn, in the employment of Mathew Dodd, farmer, of the Chauntry Farm, Withyham, perceived a briar pipe lying near the footpath which skirts the hedge in Lower Haycock. A few paces farther on he picked up a pair of broken binocular glasses. Finally, among some nettles in the ditch, he caught sight of a flat, canvas-backed book, which proved to be a notebook with detachable leaves, some of which had come loose and were fluttering along the base of the hedge. These he collected, but some, including the first, were never recovered, and leave a deplorable hiatus in this all-important statement. The notebook was taken by the labourer to his master, who in turn showed it to Dr J.H. Atherton, of Hartfield. This gentleman at once recognized the need for an expert examination, and the manuscript was forwarded to the Aero Club* in London, where it now lies.

The first two pages of the manuscript are missing. There is also one torn away at the end of the narrative, though none of these affect the general coherence of the story. It is conjectured that the missing opening is concerned with the record of Mr Joyce-Armstrong's qualifications as an aeronaut, which can be gathered from other sources and are admitted to be unsurpassed among the air pilots of England. For many years he has been looked upon as among the most daring and the most intellectual of flying men, a combination which has enabled him to both invent and test several new devices, including the common gyroscopic attachment which is known by his name. The main body of the manuscript is written neatly in ink, but the last few lines are in pencil and are so ragged as to be hardly legible – exactly, in fact, as they might be expected to appear if they were scribbled off hurriedly from the seat of a moving aeroplane. There are, it may be added, several stains, both on the last page and on the outside cover, which have been pronounced by the Home Office experts to be blood – probably human and certainly mammalian. The fact that something closely resembling the organism of malaria was discovered in this blood, and that Joyce-Armstrong is known to have suffered from intermittent fever, is a remarkable example of the new weapons which modern science has placed in the hands of our detectives.

And now a word as to the personality of the author of this epoch-making statement. Joyce-Armstrong, according to the few friends who really knew something of the man, was a poet and a dreamer as well as a mechanic and an inventor. He was a man of considerable wealth, much of which he had spent in the pursuit of his aeronautical hobby. He had four private aeroplanes in his hangars near Devizes, and is said to have made no fewer than 170 ascents in the course of last year. He was a retiring man with dark moods, in which he would avoid the society of his fellows. Captain Dangerfield, who knew him better than anyone, says that there were times when his eccentricity threatened to develop into something more serious. His habit of carrying a shotgun with him in his aeroplane was one manifestation of it.

Another was the morbid effect which the fall of Lieutenant Myrtle had upon his mind. Myrtle, who was attempting the height record, fell from an altitude of something over 30,000 feet. Horrible to narrate, his head was entirely obliterated, though his body and limbs preserved their configuration. At every gathering of airmen, Joyce-Armstrong, according to Dangerfield, would ask, with an enigmatic smile: "And where, pray, is Myrtle's head?"

On another occasion after dinner, at the mess of the Flying School on Salisbury Plain, he started a debate as to what will be the most permanent danger which airmen will have to encounter. Having listened to successive opinions as to air pockets, faulty construction and over-banking, he ended by shrugging his shoulders and refusing to put forward his own views, though he gave the impression that they differed from any advanced by his companions.

It is worth remarking that after his own complete disappearance it was found that his private affairs were arranged with a precision which may show that he had a strong premonition of disaster. With these essential explanations I will now give the narrative exactly as it stands, beginning at page three of the blood-soaked notebook:

Nevertheless, when I dined at Rheims with Coselli and Gustav Raymond I found that neither of them was aware of any particular danger in the higher layers of the atmosphere. I did not actually say what was in my thoughts, but I got so near to it that if they had any corresponding idea they could not have failed to express it. But then they are two empty, vainglorious fellows with no thought beyond seeing their silly names in the newspaper. It is interesting to note that neither of them had ever been much beyond the 20,000-foot level. Of course, men have been higher than this both in balloons and in the ascent of mountains. It must be well above that point that the aeroplane enters the danger zone – always presuming that my premonitions are correct.

Aeroplaning has been with us now for more than twenty years, and one might well ask: why should this peril be only revealing itself in our day? The answer is obvious. In the old days of weak engines, when a hundred-horsepower Gnome or Green* was considered ample for every need, the flights were very restricted. Now that 300 horsepower is the rule rather than the exception, visits to the upper layers have become easier and more common. Some of us can remember how, in our youth, Garros* made a worldwide reputation by attaining 19,000 feet, and it was considered a remarkable achievement to fly over the Alps. Our standard now has been immeasurably raised, and there are twenty high flights for one in former years. Many of them have been undertaken with impunity. The

30,000-foot level has been reached time after time with no discomfort beyond cold and asthma. What does this prove? A visitor might descend upon this planet a thousand times and never see a tiger. Yet tigers exist, and if he chanced to come down into a jungle he might be devoured. There are jungles of the upper air, and there are worse things than tigers which inhabit them. I believe in time they will map these jungles accurately out. Even at the present moment I could name two of them. One of them lies over the Pau-Biarritz district of France. Another is just over my head as I write here in my house in Wiltshire. I rather think there is a third in the Homburg-Wiesbaden district.

It was the disappearance of the airmen that first set me thinking. Of course, everyone said that they had fallen into the sea, but that did not satisfy me at all. First, there was Verrier in France; his machine was found near Bayonne, but they never got his body. There was the case of Baxter also, who vanished, though his engine and some of the iron fixings were found in a wood in Leicestershire. In that case, Dr Middleton of Amesbury, who was watching the flight with a telescope, declares that just before the clouds obscured the view he saw the machine, which was at an enormous height, suddenly rise perpendicularly upwards in a succession of jerks in a manner that he would have thought to be impossible. That was the last seen of Baxter. There was a correspondence in the papers, but it never led to anything. There were several other similar cases, and then there was the death of Hay Connor. What a cackle there was about an unsolved mystery of the air, and what columns in the halfpenny papers, and yet how little was ever done to get to the bottom of the business! He came down in a tremendous *vol plané** from an unknown height. He never got off his machine and died in his pilot's seat. Died of what? "Heart disease," said the doctors. Rubbish! Hay Connor's heart was as sound as mine is. What did Venables say? Venables was the only man who was at his side when he died. He said that he was shivering and looked like a man who had been badly scared. "Died of fright," said Venables, but could not imagine what he was frightened about. Only said one word to Venables, which sounded like "Monstrous". They could make nothing of that at the inquest. But I could make something of it. Monsters! That was the last word of poor Harry Hay Connor. And he *did* die of fright, just as Venables thought.

And then there was Myrtle's head. Do you really believe – does anybody really believe – that a man's head could be driven clean into his body by the force of a fall? Well, perhaps it may be possible, but I, for one, have never believed that it was so with Myrtle. And the grease upon his clothes – "all slimy with grease," said somebody at the inquest. Queer that nobody got thinking after that! I did – but then I had been thinking for a good long time. I've made three ascents – how Dangerfield used to chaff me about my shotgun – but I've never been high enough. Now, with this new, light Paul Veroner machine and its 175 Robur,* I should easily touch the 30,000 tomorrow. I'll have a shot at the record. Maybe I shall have a shot at something else as well. Of course, it's dangerous. If a fellow wants to avoid danger he had best keep out of flying altogether and subside finally into flannel slippers and a dressing gown. But I'll visit the air jungle tomorrow – and if there's anything there I shall know it. If I return, I'll find myself a bit of a celebrity. If I don't, this notebook may explain what I am trying to do, and how I lost my life in doing it. But no drivel about accidents or mysteries, if *you* please.

I chose my Paul Veroner monoplane for the job. There's nothing like a monoplane when real work is to be done. Beaumont* found that out in very early days. For one thing it doesn't mind damp, and the weather looks as if we should be in the clouds all the time. It's a bonny little model and answers my hand like a tender-mouthed horse. The engine is a ten-cylinder rotary Robur working up to 175. It has all the modern improvements – enclosed fuselage, high-curved landing skids, brakes, gyroscopic steadiers and three speeds, worked by an alteration of the angle of the planes upon the Venetian-blind principle. I took a shotgun with me and a dozen cartridges filled with buckshot. You should have seen the face of Perkins, my old mechanic, when I directed him to put them in. I was dressed like an Arctic explorer, with two jerseys under my overalls, thick socks inside my padded boots, a storm cap with flaps and my talc goggles.* It was stifling outside the hangars, but I was going for the summit of the Himalayas, and had to dress for the part. Perkins knew there was something on and implored me to take him with me. Perhaps I should if I were using the biplane, but a monoplane is a one-man show – if you want to get the last foot of lift out of it. Of course, I took an oxygen bag; the man who goes for the altitude record without one will either be frozen or smothered – or both.

I had a good look at the planes, the rudder bar and the elevating lever before I got in. Everything was in order so far as I could see. Then I switched on my engine and found that she was running sweetly. When they let her go she rose almost at once upon the lowest speed. I circled my home field once or twice just to warm her up, and then, with a wave to Perkins and the others, I flattened out my planes and put her on her highest. She skimmed like a swallow downwind for eight or ten miles until I turned her nose up a little and she began to climb in a great spiral for the cloud bank above me. It's all-important to rise slowly and adapt yourself to the pressure as you go.

It was a close, warm day for an English September, and there was the hush and heaviness of impending rain. Now and then there came sudden puffs of wind from the south-west – one of them so gusty and unexpected that it caught me napping and turned me half round for an instant. I remember the time when gusts and whirls and air pockets used to be things of danger – before we learnt to put an overmastering power into our engines. Just as I reached the cloud banks, with the altimeter marking 3,000, down came the rain. My word, how it poured! It drummed upon my wings and lashed against my face, blurring my glasses so that I could hardly see. I got down onto a low speed, for it was painful to travel against it. As I got higher it became hail, and I had to turn tail to it. One of my cylinders was out of action – a dirty plug, I should imagine, but still I was rising steadily with plenty of power. After a bit the trouble passed, whatever it was, and I heard the full, deep-throated purr – the ten singing as one. That's where the beauty of our modern silencers comes in. We can at last control our engines by ear. How they squeal and squeak and sob when they are in trouble! All those cries for help were wasted in the old days, when every sound was swallowed up by the monstrous racket of the machine. If only the early aviators could come back to see the beauty and perfection of the mechanism which have been bought at the cost of their lives!

About nine thirty I was nearing the clouds. Down below me, all blurred and shadowed with rain, lay the vast expanse of Salisbury Plain. Half a dozen flying machines were doing hackwork at the thousand-foot level, looking like little black swallows against the green background. I dare say they were wondering what I was doing up in cloudland. Suddenly a grey curtain drew across beneath me and the wet folds of vapours were swirling round my face. It was clammily cold and miserable. But I was above the hailstorm, and that was something gained. The cloud was as dark and thick as a London fog. In my anxiety to get clear, I cocked her nose up until the automatic alarm bell rang, and I actually began to slide backwards. My sopped and dripping wings had made me heavier than I thought, but presently I was in lighter cloud, and soon had cleared the first layer. There was a second – opal-coloured and fleecy – at a great height above my head, a white, unbroken ceiling above and a dark, unbroken floor below, with the monoplane labouring upwards upon a vast spiral between them. It is deadly lonely in these cloud spaces. Once a great flight of some small water birds went past me, flying very fast to the westwards. The quick whir of their wings and their musical cry were cheery to my ear. I fancy that they were teal, but I am a wretched zoologist. Now that we humans have become birds we must really learn to know our brethren by sight.

The wind down beneath me whirled and swayed the broad cloud plain. Once a great eddy formed in it, a whirlpool of vapour, and through it, as down a funnel, I caught sight of the distant world. A large white biplane was passing at a vast depth beneath me. I fancy it was the morning mail service betwixt Bristol and London. Then the drift swirled inwards again and the great solitude was unbroken.

Just after ten I touched the lower edge of the upper cloud stratum. It consisted of fine diaphanous vapour drifting swiftly from the westward. The wind had been steadily rising all this time and it was now blowing a sharp breeze – twenty-eight an hour by my gauge. Already it was very cold, though my altimeter only marked 9,000. The engines were working beautifully, and we went droning steadily upwards. The cloud bank was thicker than I had expected, but at last it thinned out into a golden mist before me, and then in an instant I had shot out from it, and there was an unclouded sky and a brilliant sun above my head – all blue and gold above, all shining silver below, one vast, glimmering plain as far as my eyes could reach. It was a quarter past ten o'clock, and the barograph needle pointed to 12,800. Up I went and up, my ears concentrated upon the deep purring of my motor, my eyes busy always with the watch, the revolution indicator, the petrol lever and the oil pump. No wonder aviators are said to be a fearless race. With so many things to think of there is no time to trouble about oneself. About this time I noted how unreliable is the compass when above a certain height from earth. At 15,000 feet mine was pointing east and a point south. The sun and the wind gave me my true bearings.

I had hoped to reach an eternal stillness in these high altitudes, but with every thousand feet of ascent the gale grew stronger. My machine groaned and trembled in every joint and rivet as she faced it, and swept away like a sheet of paper when I banked her on the turn, skimming downwind at a greater pace, perhaps, than ever mortal man has moved. Yet I had always to turn again and tack up in the wind's eye, for it was not merely a height record that I was after. By all my calculations it was above little Wiltshire that my air jungle lay, and all my labour might be lost if I struck the outer layers at some farther point.

When I reached the 19,000-foot level, which was about midday, the wind was so severe that I looked with some anxiety to the stays of my wings, expecting momentarily to see them snap or slacken. I even cast loose the parachute behind me, and fastened its hook into the ring of my leathern belt, so as to be ready for the worst. Now was the time when a bit of scamped work by the mechanic is paid for by the life of the aeronaut. But she held together bravely. Every cord and strut was humming and vibrating like so many harp strings, but it was glorious to see how, for all the beating and the buffeting, she was still the conqueror of Nature and the mistress of the sky. There is surely something divine in man himself that he should rise so superior to the limitations which Creation seemed to impose – rise, too, by such unselfish, heroic devotion as this air conquest has shown. Talk of human degeneration! When has such a story as this been written in the annals of our race?

These were the thoughts in my head as I climbed that monstrous, inclined plane with the wind sometimes beating in my face and sometimes whistling behind my ears, while the cloudland beneath me fell away to such a distance that the folds and hummocks of silver had all smoothed out into one flat, shining plain. But suddenly I had a horrible and unprecedented experience. I have known before what it is to be in what our neighbours have called a *tourbillon*,* but never on such a scale as this. That huge, sweeping river of wind of which I have spoken had, as it appears, whirlpools within it which were as monstrous as itself. Without a moment's warning I was dragged suddenly into the heart of one. I spun round for a minute or two with such velocity that I almost lost my senses, and then fell suddenly, left wing foremost, down the vacuum funnel in the centre. I dropped like a stone, and lost nearly a thousand feet. It was only my belt that kept me in my seat, and the shock and breathlessness left me hanging half insensible over the side of the fuselage. But I am always capable of a supreme effort – it is my one great merit as an aviator. I was conscious that the descent was slower. The whirlpool was a cone rather than a funnel, and I had come to the apex. With a terrific wrench, throwing my weight all to one side, I levelled my planes and brought her head away from the wind. In an instant I had shot out of the eddies and was skimming down the sky. Then, shaken but victorious, I turned her nose up and began once more my steady grind on the upward spiral. I took a large sweep to avoid the danger spot of the whirlpool, and soon I was safely above it. Just after one o'clock I was 21,000 feet above the sea level. To my great joy I had topped the gale, and with every hundred feet of ascent the air grew stiller. On the other hand, it was very cold, and I was conscious of that peculiar nausea which goes with rarefaction of the air. For the first time I unscrewed the mouth of my oxygen bag and took an occasional whiff of the glorious gas. I could feel it running like a cordial through my veins, and I was exhilarated almost to the point of drunkenness. I shouted and sang as I soared upwards into the cold, still outer world.

It is very clear to me that the insensibility which came upon Glaisher, and in a lesser degree upon Coxwell,* when, in 1862, they ascended in a balloon to the height of 30,000 feet, was due to the extreme speed with which a perpendicular ascent is made. Doing it at an easy gradient and accustoming oneself to the lessened barometric pressure by slow degrees, there are no such dreadful symptoms. At the same great height I found that even without my oxygen inhaler I could breathe without undue distress. It was bitterly cold, however, and my thermometer was at zero Fahrenheit. At one thirty I was nearly seven miles above the surface of the earth, and still ascending steadily. I found, however, that the rarefied air was giving markedly less support to my planes, and that my angle of ascent had to be considerably lowered in consequence. It was already clear that even with my light weight and strong engine power there was a point in front of me where I should be held. To make matters worse, one of my sparking plugs was in trouble again and there was intermittent misfiring in the engine. My heart was heavy with the fear of failure.

It was about that time that I had a most extraordinary experience. Something whizzed past me in a trail of smoke and exploded with a loud, hissing sound, sending forth a cloud of steam. For the instant I could not imagine what had happened. Then I remembered that the earth is forever being bombarded by meteor stones, and would be hardly inhabitable were they not in nearly every case turned to vapour in the outer layers of the atmosphere. Here is a new danger for the high-altitude man, for two others passed me when I was nearing the 40,000-foot mark. I cannot doubt that at the edge of the earth's envelope the risk would be a very real one.

My barograph needle marked 41,300 when I became aware that I could go no farther. Physically, the strain was not as yet greater than I could bear, but my machine had reached its limit. The attenuated air gave no firm support to the wings, and the least tilt developed into sideslip, while she seemed sluggish on her controls. Possibly, had the engine been at its best, another thousand feet might have been within our capacity, but it was still misfiring, and two out of the ten cylinders appeared to be out of action. If I had not already reached the zone for which I was searching then I should never see it upon this journey. But was it not possible that I had attained it? Soaring in circles like a monstrous hawk upon the 40,000-foot level I let the monoplane guide herself, and with my Mannheim glass* I made a careful observation of my surroundings. The heavens were perfectly clear; there was no indication of those dangers which I had imagined.

I have said that I was soaring in circles. It struck me suddenly that I would do well to take a wider sweep and open up a new air tract. If the hunter entered an earth jungle he would drive through it if he wished to find his game. My reasoning had led me to believe that the air jungle which I had imagined lay somewhere over Wiltshire. This should be to the south and west of me. I took my bearings from the sun, for the compass was hopeless and no trace of earth was to be seen – nothing but the distant, silver cloud plain. However, I got my direction as best I might and kept her head straight to the mark. I reckoned that my petrol supply would not last for more than another hour or so, but I could afford to use it to the last drop, since a single magnificent *vol plané* could at any time take me to the earth.

Suddenly I was aware of something new. The air in front of me had lost its crystal clearness. It was full of long, ragged wisps of something which I can only compare to very fine cigarette smoke. It hung about in wreaths and coils, turning and twisting slowly in the sunlight. As the monoplane shot through it, I was aware of a faint taste of oil upon my lips, and there was a greasy scum upon the woodwork of the machine. Some infinitely fine organic matter appeared to be suspended in the atmosphere. There was no life there. It was inchoate and diffuse, extending for many square acres and then fringing off into the void. No, it was not life. But might it not be the remains of life? Above all, might it not be the food of life, of monstrous life, even as the humble grease of the ocean is the food for the mighty whale? The thought was in my mind when my eyes looked upwards and I saw the most wonderful vision that ever man has seen. Can I hope to convey it to you even as I saw it myself last Thursday?

Conceive a jellyfish such as sails in our summer seas, bell-shaped and of enormous size – far larger, I should judge, than the dome of St Paul's. It was of a light-pink colour veined with a delicate green, but the whole huge fabric so tenuous that it was but a fairy outline against the dark-blue sky. It pulsated with a delicate and regular rhythm. From it there depended two long, drooping, green tentacles, which swayed slowly backwards and forwards. This gorgeous vision passed gently with noiseless dignity over my head, as light and fragile as a soap bubble, and drifted upon its stately way.

I had half-turned my monoplane, that I might look after this beautiful creature, when, in a moment, I found myself amidst a perfect fleet of them, of all sizes, but none so large as the first. Some were quite small, but the majority about as big as an average balloon, and with much the same curvature at the top. There was in them a delicacy of texture and colouring which reminded me of the finest Venetian glass. Pale shades of pink and green were the prevailing tints, but all had a lovely iridescence where the sun shimmered through their dainty forms. Some hundreds of them drifted past me, a wonderful fairy squadron of strange, unknown argosies of the sky – creatures whose forms and substance were so attuned to these pure heights that one could not conceive anything so delicate within actual sight or sound of earth.

But soon my attention was drawn to a new phenomenon – the serpents of the outer air. These were long, thin, fantastic coils of vapour-like material, which turned and twisted with great speed, flying round and round at such a pace that the eyes could hardly follow them. Some of these ghost-like creatures were twenty or thirty feet long, but it was difficult to tell their girth, for their outline was so hazy that it seemed to fade away into the air around them. These air snakes were of a very light grey or smoke colour, with some darker lines within, which gave the impression of a definite organism. One of them whisked past my very face, and I was conscious of a cold, clammy contact, but their composition was so unsubstantial that I could not connect them with any thought of physical danger, any more than the beautiful bell-like creatures which had preceded them. There was no more solidity in their frames than in the floating spume from a broken wave.

But a more terrible experience was in store for me. Floating downwards from a great height there came a purplish patch of vapour, small as I saw it first, but rapidly enlarging as it approached me, until it appeared to be hundreds of square feet in size. Though fashioned of some transparent, jelly-like substance, it was nonetheless of much more definite outline and solid consistence than anything which I had seen before. There were more traces, too, of a physical organization, especially two vast, shadowy, circular plates upon either side, which may have been eyes, and a perfectly solid white projection between them which was as curved and cruel as the beak of a vulture.

The whole aspect of this monster was formidable and threatening, and it kept changing its colour from a very light mauve to a dark, angry purple so thick that it cast a shadow as it drifted between my monoplane and the sun. On the upper curve of its huge body there were three great projections which I can only describe as enormous bubbles, and I was convinced as I looked at them that they were charged with some extremely light gas which served to buoy up the misshapen and semi-solid mass in the rarefied air. The creature moved swiftly along, keeping pace easily with the monoplane, and for twenty miles or more it formed my horrible escort, hovering over me like a bird of prey which is waiting to pounce. Its method of progression – done so swiftly that it was not easy to follow – was to throw out a long, glutinous streamer in front of it, which in turn seemed to draw forward the rest of the writhing body. So elastic and gelatinous was it that never for two successive minutes was it the same shape, and yet each change made it more threatening and loathsome than the last.

I knew that it meant mischief. Every purple flush of its hideous body told me so. The vague, goggling eyes which were turned always upon me were cold and merciless in their viscid hatred. I dipped the nose of my monoplane downwards to escape it. As I did so, as quick as a flash there shot out a long tentacle from this mass of floating blubber, and it fell as light and sinuous as a whiplash across the front of my machine. There was a loud hiss as it lay for a moment across the hot engine, and it whisked itself into the air again, while the huge, flat body drew itself together as if in sudden pain. I dipped to a *vol piqué*,* but again a tentacle fell over the monoplane and was shorn off by the propeller as easily as it might have cut through a smoke wreath. A long, gliding, sticky, serpent-like coil came from behind and caught me round the waist, dragging me out of the fuselage. I tore at it, my fingers sinking into the smooth, glue-like surface, and for an instant I disengaged myself, but only to be caught round the boot by another coil, which gave me a jerk that tilted me almost onto my back.

As I fell over I blazed off both barrels of my gun, though, indeed, it was like attacking an elephant with a peashooter to imagine that any human weapon could cripple that mighty bulk. And yet I aimed better than I knew, for, with a loud report, one of the great blisters upon the creature's back exploded with the puncture of the buckshot. It was very clear that my conjecture was right, and that these vast, clear bladders were distended with some lifting gas, for in an instant the huge, cloud-like body turned sideways, writhing desperately to find its balance, while the white beak snapped and gaped in horrible fury. But already I had shot away on the steepest glide that I dared to attempt, my engine still full on, the flying propeller and the force of gravity shooting me downwards like an aerolite. Far behind me I saw a dull, purplish smudge growing swiftly smaller and merging into the blue sky behind it. I was safe out of the deadly jungle of the outer air.

Once out of danger I throttled my engine, for nothing tears a machine to pieces quicker than running on full power from a height. It was a glorious, spiral *vol plané* from nearly eight miles of altitude – first to the level of the silver cloud bank, then to that of the storm cloud beneath it and, finally, in beating rain, to the surface of the earth. I saw the Bristol Channel beneath me as I broke from the clouds, but, having still some petrol in my tank, I got twenty miles inland before I found myself stranded in a field half a mile from the village of Ashcombe. There I got three tins of petrol from a passing motor car, and at ten minutes past six that evening I alighted gently in my own home meadow at Devizes, after such a journey as no mortal upon earth has ever yet taken and lived to tell the tale. I have seen the beauty and I have seen the horror of the heights – and greater beauty or greater horror than that is not within the ken of man.

And now it is my plan to go once again before I give my results to the world. My reason for this is that I must surely have something to show by way of proof before I lay such a tale before my fellow men. It is true that others will soon follow and will confirm what I have said, and yet I should wish to carry conviction from the first. Those lovely iridescent bubbles of the air should not be hard to capture. They drift slowly upon their way, and the swift monoplane could intercept their leisurely course. It is likely enough that they would dissolve in the heavier layers of the atmosphere, and that some small heap of amorphous jelly might be all that I should bring to earth with me. And yet something there would surely be by which I could substantiate my story. Yes, I will go, even if I run a risk by doing so. These purple horrors would not seem to be numerous. It is probable that I shall not see one. If I do I shall dive at once. At the worst there is always the shotgun and my knowledge of…

Here a page of the manuscript is unfortunately missing. On the next page is written, in large, straggling writing:

"Forty-three thousand feet. I shall never see earth again. They are beneath me, three of them. God help me; it is a dreadful death to die!"

Such in its entirety is the Joyce-Armstrong Statement. Of the man nothing has since been seen. Pieces of his shattered monoplane have been picked up in the preserves of Mr Budd-Lushington upon the borders of Kent and Sussex, within a few miles of the spot where the notebook was discovered. If the unfortunate aviator's theory is correct that this air jungle, as he called it, existed only over the south-west of England, then it would seem that he had fled from it at the full speed of his monoplane, but had been overtaken and devoured by these horrible creatures at some spot in the outer atmosphere above the place where the grim relics were found. The picture of that monoplane skimming down the sky, with the nameless terrors flying as swiftly beneath it and cutting it off always from the earth while they gradually closed in upon their victim, is one upon which a man who valued his sanity would prefer not to dwell. There are many, as I am aware, who still jeer at the facts which I have here set down, but even they must admit that Joyce-Armstrong has disappeared, and I would commend to them his own words: "This notebook may explain what I am trying to do, and how I lost my life in doing it. But no drivel about accidents or mysteries, if *you* please."

The Leather Funnel

My friend, Lionel Dacre, lived in the Avenue de Wagram, Paris. His house was that small one, with the iron railings and grass plot in front of it, on the left-hand side as you pass down from the Arc de Triomphe. I fancy that it had been there long before the avenue was constructed, for the grey tiles were stained with lichens, and the walls were mildewed and discoloured with age. It looked a small house from the street, five windows in front, if I remember right, but it deepened into a single long chamber at the back. It was here that Dacre had that singular library of occult literature, and the fantastic curiosities which served as a hobby for himself, and an amusement for his friends. A wealthy man of refined and eccentric tastes, he had spent much of his life and fortune in gathering together what was said to be a unique private collection of Talmudic, cabbalistic and magical works, many of them of great rarity and value. His tastes leant towards the marvellous and the monstrous, and I have heard that his experiments in the direction of the unknown have passed all the bounds of civilization and of decorum. To his English friends he never alluded to such matters, and took the tone of the student and virtuoso; but a Frenchman whose tastes were of the same nature has assured me that the worst excesses of the black mass have been perpetrated in that large and lofty hall, which is lined with the shelves of his books, and the cases of his museum.

Dacre's appearance was enough to show that his deep interest in these psychic matters was intellectual rather than spiritual. There was no trace of asceticism upon his heavy face, but there was much mental force in his huge, dome-like skull, which curved upward from amongst his thinning locks, like a snow peak above its fringe of fir trees. His knowledge was greater than his wisdom, and his powers were far superior to his character. The small bright eyes, buried deeply in his fleshy face, twinkled with intelligence and an unabated curiosity of life, but they were the eyes of a sensualist and an egotist. Enough of the man, for he is dead now, poor devil, dead at the very time that he had made sure that he had at last discovered the elixir of life. It is not with his complex character that I have to deal, but with the very strange and inexplicable incident which had its rise in my visit to him in the early spring of the year '82.

I had known Dacre in England, for my researches in the Assyrian Room of the British Museum had been conducted at the time when he was endeavouring to establish a mystic and esoteric meaning in the Babylonian tablets, and this community of interests had brought us together. Chance remarks had led to daily conversation, and that to something verging upon friendship. I had promised him that on my next visit to Paris I would call upon him. At the time when I was able to fulfil my compact I was living in a cottage at Fontainebleau, and as the evening trains were inconvenient, he asked me to spend the night in his house.

"I have only that one spare couch," said he, pointing to a broad sofa in his large salon. "I hope that you will manage to be comfortable there."

It was a singular bedroom, with its high walls of brown volumes, but there could be no more agreeable furniture to a bookworm like myself, and there is no scent so pleasant to my nostrils as that faint, subtle reek which comes from an ancient book. I assured him that I could desire no more charming chamber, and no more congenial surroundings.

"If the fittings are neither convenient nor conventional, they are at least costly," said he, looking round at his shelves. "I have expended nearly a quarter of a million of money upon these objects which surround you. Books, weapons, gems, carvings, tapestries, images – there is hardly a thing here which has not its history, and it is generally one worth telling."

He was seated as he spoke at one side of the open fireplace, and I at the other. His reading table was on his right, and the strong lamp above it ringed it with a very vivid circle of golden light. A half-rolled palimpsest lay in the centre, and around it were many quaint articles of bric-a-brac. One of these was a large funnel, such as is used for filling wine casks. It appeared to be made of black wood, and to be rimmed with discoloured brass.

"That is a curious thing," I remarked. "What is the history of that?"

"Ah!" said he. "It is the very question which I have had occasion to ask myself. I would give a good deal to know. Take it in your hands and examine it."

I did so, and found that what I had imagined to be wood was in reality leather, though age had dried it into an extreme hardness. It was a large funnel, and might hold a quart when full. The brass rim encircled the wide end, but the narrow was also tipped with metal.

"What do you make of it?" asked Dacre.

"I should imagine that it belonged to some vintner or maltster in the Middle Ages," said I. "I have seen in England leathern drinking flagons of the seventeenth century – 'blackjacks' as they were called – which were of the same colour and hardness as this filler."

"I dare say the date would be about the same," said Dacre, "and, no doubt, also, it was used for filling a vessel with liquid. If my suspicions are correct, however, it was a queer vintner who used it, and a very singular cask which was filled. Do you observe nothing strange at the spout end of the funnel?"

As I held it to the light I observed that at a spot some five inches above the brass tip the narrow neck of the leather funnel was all haggled and scored, as if someone had notched it round with a blunt knife. Only at that point was there any roughening of the dead black surface.

"Someone has tried to cut off the neck."

"Would you call it a cut?"

"It is torn and lacerated. It must have taken some strength to leave these marks on such tough material, whatever the instrument may have been. But what do you think of it? I can tell that you know more than you say."

Dacre smiled, and his little eyes twinkled with knowledge.

"Have you included the psychology of dreams among your learned studies?" he asked.

"I did not even know that there was such a psychology."

"My dear sir, that shelf above the gem case is filled with volumes, from Albertus Magnus* onward, which deal with no other subject. It is a science in itself."

"A science of charlatans."

"The charlatan is always the pioneer. From the astrologer came the astronomer, from the alchemist the chemist, from the mesmerist the experimental psychologist. The quack of yesterday is the professor of tomorrow. Even such subtle and elusive things as dreams will in time be reduced to system and order. When that time comes the researchers of our friends on the bookshelf yonder will no longer be the amusement of the mystic, but the foundations of a science."

"Supposing that is so, what has the science of dreams to do with a large, black, brass-rimmed funnel?"

"I will tell you. You know that I have an agent who is always on the look-out for rarities and curiosities for my collection. Some days ago he heard of a dealer upon one of the Quais who had acquired some old rubbish found in a cupboard in an ancient house at the back of the Rue Mathurin, in the Quartier Latin. The dining room of this old house is decorated with a coat of arms, chevrons and bars rouge upon a field argent, which prove, upon enquiry, to be the shield of Nicolas de la Reynie,* a high official of King Louis XIV. There can be no doubt that the other articles in the cupboard date back to the early days of that king. The inference is, therefore, that they were all the property of this Nicolas de la Reynie, who was, as I understand, the gentleman specially concerned with the maintenance and execution of the draconic laws of that epoch."*

"What then?"

"I would ask you now to take the funnel into your hands once more and to examine the upper brass rim. Can you make out any lettering upon it?"

There were certainly some scratches upon it, almost obliterated by time. The general effect was of several letters, the last of which bore some resemblance to a *B*.

"You make it a *B*?"

"Yes, I do."

"So do I. In fact, I have no doubt whatever that it is a *B*."

"But the nobleman you mentioned would have had *R* for his initial."

"Exactly! That's the beauty of it. He owned this curious object, and yet he had someone else's initials upon it. Why did he do this?"

"I can't imagine – can you?"

"Well, I might, perhaps, guess. Do you observe something drawn a little farther along the rim?"

"I should say it was a crown."

"It is undoubtedly a crown; but if you examine it in a good light, you will convince yourself that it is not an ordinary crown. It is a heraldic crown – a badge of rank – and it consists of an alternation of four pearls and strawberry leaves, the proper badge of a marquis. We may infer, therefore, that the person whose initials end in B was entitled to wear that coronet."

"Then this common leather filler belonged to a marquis?"

Dacre gave a peculiar smile.

"Or to some member of the family of a marquis," said he. "So much we have clearly gathered from this engraved rim."

"But what has all this to do with dreams?" I do not know whether it was from a look upon Dacre's face, or from some subtle suggestion in his manner, but a feeling of repulsion, of unreasoning horror, came upon me as I looked at the gnarled old lump of leather.

"I have more than once received important information through my dreams," said my companion in the didactic manner which he loved to affect. "I make it a rule now when I am in doubt upon any material point to place the article in question beside me as I sleep, and to hope for some enlightenment. The process does not appear to me to be very obscure, though it has not yet received the blessing of orthodox science. According to my theory, any object which has been intimately associated with any supreme paroxysm of human emotion, whether it be joy or pain, will retain a certain atmosphere or association which it is capable of communicating to a sensitive mind. By a sensitive mind I do not mean an abnormal one, but such a trained and educated mind as you or I possess."

"You mean, for example, that if I slept beside that old sword upon the wall, I might dream of some bloody incident in which that very sword took part?"

"An excellent example, for, as a matter of fact, that sword was used in that fashion by me, and I saw in my sleep the death of its owner, who perished in a brisk skirmish, which I have been unable to identify, but which occurred at the time of the wars of the Frondists.* If you think of it, some of our popular observances show that the fact has already been recognized by our ancestors, although we, in our wisdom, have classed it among superstitions."

"For example?"

"Well, the placing of the bride's cake beneath the pillow in order that the sleeper may have pleasant dreams. That is one of several instances which you will find set forth in a small brochure which I am myself writing upon the subject. But to come back to the point, I slept one night with this funnel beside me, and I had a dream which certainly throws a curious light upon its use and origin."

"What did you dream?"

"I dreamt..." He paused, and an intent look of interest came over his massive face. "By Jove, that's well thought of," said he. "This really will be an exceedingly interesting experiment. You are yourself a psychic subject – with nerves which respond readily to any impression."

"I have never tested myself in that direction."

"Then we shall test you tonight. Might I ask you as a very great favour, when you occupy that couch tonight, to sleep with this old funnel placed by the side of your pillow?"

The request seemed to me a grotesque one; but I have myself, in my complex nature, a hunger after all which is bizarre and fantastic. I had not the faintest belief in Dacre's theory, nor any hopes for success in such an experiment; yet it amused me that the experiment should be made.

Dacre, with great gravity, drew a small stand to the head of my settee, and placed the funnel upon it. Then, after a short conversation, he wished me goodnight and left me.

I sat for some little time smoking by the smouldering fire, and turning over in my mind the curious incident which had occurred, and the strange experience which might lie before me. Sceptical as I was, there was something impressive in the assurance of Dacre's manner, and my extraordinary surroundings, the huge room with the strange and often sinister objects which were hung round it, struck solemnity into my soul. Finally I undressed and, turning out the lamp, I lay down. After long tossing I fell asleep. Let me try to describe as accurately as I can the scene which came to me in my dreams. It stands out now in my memory more clearly than anything which I have seen with my waking eyes.

There was a room which bore the appearance of a vault. Four spandrels from the corners ran up to join a sharp, cup-shaped roof. The architecture was rough, but very strong. It was evidently part of a great building.

Three men in black, with curious, top-heavy, black velvet hats, sat in a line upon a red-carpeted dais. Their faces were very solemn and sad. On the left stood two long-gowned men with portfolios in their hands, which seemed to be stuffed with papers. Upon the right, looking towards me, was a small woman with blond hair and singular, light-blue eyes – the eyes of a child. She was past her first youth, but could not yet be called middle-aged. Her figure was inclined to stoutness and her bearing was proud and confident. Her face was pale, but serene. It was a curious face, comely and yet feline, with a subtle suggestion of cruelty about the straight, strong little mouth and chubby jaw. She was draped in some sort of loose, white gown. Beside her stood a thin, eager priest, who whispered in her ear and continually raised a crucifix before her eyes. She turned her head and looked fixedly past the crucifix at the three men in black, who were, I felt, her judges.

As I gazed, the three men stood up and said something, but I could distinguish no words, though I was aware that it was the central one who was speaking. They then swept out of the room, followed by the two men with the papers. At the same instant several rough-looking fellows in stout jerkins came bustling in and removed first the red carpet and then the boards which formed the dais, so as to entirely clear the room. When this screen was removed, I saw some singular articles of furniture behind it. One looked like a bed with wooden rollers at each end, and a winch handle to regulate its length. Another was a wooden horse. There were several other curious objects, and a number of swinging cords which played over pulleys. It was not unlike a modern gymnasium.

When the room had been cleared there appeared a new figure upon the scene. This was a tall, thin person clad in black, with a gaunt and austere face. The aspect of the man made me shudder. His clothes were all shining with grease and mottled with stains. He bore himself with a slow and impressive dignity, as if he took command of all things from the instant of his entrance. In spite of his rude appearance and sordid dress, it was now *his* business, *his* room, his to command. He carried a coil of light ropes over his left forearm. The lady looked him up and down with a searching glance, but her expression was unchanged. It was confident – even defiant. But it was very different with the priest. His face was ghastly white, and I saw the moisture glisten and run on his high, sloping forehead. He threw up his hands in prayer and he stooped continually to mutter frantic words in the lady's ear.

The man in black now advanced and, taking one of the cords from his left arm, he bound the woman's hands together. She held them meekly towards him as he did so. Then he took her arm with a rough grip and led her towards the wooden horse, which was little higher than her waist. Onto this she was lifted and laid, with her back upon it and her face to the ceiling, while the priest, quivering with horror, had rushed out of the room. The woman's lips were moving rapidly, and though I could hear nothing I knew that she was praying. Her feet hung down on either side of the horse, and I saw that the rough varlets in attendance had fastened cords to her ankles and secured the other ends to iron rings in the stone floor.

My heart sank within me as I saw these ominous preparations, and yet I was held by the fascination of horror, and I could not take my eyes from the strange spectacle. A man had entered the room with a bucket of water in either hand. Another followed with a third bucket. They were laid beside the wooden horse. The second man had a wooden dipper – a bowl with a straight handle – in his other hand. This he gave to the man in black. At the same moment one of the varlets approached with a dark object in his hand, which even in my dream filled me with a vague feeling of familiarity. It was a leathern filler. With horrible energy he thrust it – but I could stand no more. My hair stood on end with horror. I writhed, I struggled, I broke through the bonds of sleep, and I burst with a shriek into my own life, and found myself lying shivering with terror in the huge library, with the moonlight flooding through the window and throwing strange silver-and-black traceries upon the opposite wall. Oh, what a blessed relief to feel that I was back in the nineteenth century – back out of that medieval vault into a world where men had human hearts within their bosoms. I sat up on my couch, trembling in every limb, my mind divided between thankfulness and horror. To think that such things were ever done – that they *could* be done without God striking the villains dead. Was it all a fantasy, or did it really stand for something which had happened in the black, cruel days of the world's history? I sank my throbbing head upon my shaking hands. And then, suddenly, my heart seemed to stand still in my bosom, and I could not even scream, so great was my terror. Something was advancing towards me through the darkness of the room.

It is a horror coming upon a horror which breaks a man's spirit. I could not reason, I could not pray; I could only sit like a frozen image and glare at the dark figure which was coming down the great room. And then it moved out into the white lane of moonlight, and I breathed once more. It was Dacre, and his face showed that he was as frightened as myself.

"Was that you? For God's sake what's the matter?" he asked in a husky voice.

"Oh, Dacre, I am glad to see you! I have been down into hell. It was dreadful."

"Then it was you who screamed?"

"I dare say it was."

"It rang through the house. The servants are all terrified." He struck a match and lit the lamp. "I think we may get the fire to burn up again," he added, throwing some logs upon the embers. "Good God, my dear chap, how white you are! You look as if you had seen a ghost."

"So I have – several ghosts."

"The leather funnel has acted, then?"

"I wouldn't sleep near the infernal thing again for all the money you could offer me."

Dacre chuckled.

"I expected that you would have a lively night of it," said he. "You took it out of me in return, for that scream of yours wasn't a very pleasant sound at two in the morning. I suppose from what you say that you have seen the whole dreadful business."

"What dreadful business?"

"The torture of the water – the 'Extraordinary Question', as it was called in the genial days of 'le Roi-Soleil'.* Did you stand it out to the end?"

"No, thank God, I awoke before it really began."

"Ah! It is just as well for you. I held out till the third bucket. Well, it is an old story, and they are all in their graves now anyhow, so what does it matter how they got there? I suppose that you have no idea what it was that you have seen?"

"The torture of some criminal. She must have been a terrible malefactor indeed if her crimes are in proportion to her penalty."

"Well, we have that small consolation," said Dacre, wrapping his dressing gown round him and crouching closer to the fire. "They *were* in proportion to her penalty. That is to say, if I am correct in the lady's identity."

"How could you possibly know her identity?"

For answer Dacre took down an old vellum-covered volume from the shelf.

"Just listen to this," said he. "It is in the French of the seventeenth century, but I will give a rough translation as I go. You will judge for yourself whether I have solved the riddle or not.

"'The prisoner was brought before the Grand Chambers and Tournelles of Parliament, sitting as a court of justice, charged with the murder of Master Dreux d'Aubray, her father, and of her two brothers, MM d'Aubray, one being civil lieutenant and the other a counsellor of Parliament. In person it seemed hard to believe that she had really done such wicked deeds, for she was of a mild appearance, and of short stature, with a fair skin and blue eyes. Yet the court, having found her guilty, condemned her to the ordinary and to the extraordinary question in order that she might be forced to name her accomplices, after which she should be carried in a cart to the Place de Grève, there to have her head cut off, her body being afterwards burnt and her ashes scattered to the winds.'

"The date of this entry is 16th July 1676."

"It is interesting," said I, "but not convincing. How do you prove the two women to be the same?"

"I am coming to that. The narrative goes on to tell of the woman's behaviour when questioned. 'When the executioner approached her she recognized him by the cords which he held in his hands, and she at once held out her own hands to him, looking at him from head to foot without uttering a word.' How's that?"

"Yes, it was so."

"'She gazed without wincing upon the wooden horse and rings which had twisted so many limbs and caused so many shrieks of agony. When her eyes fell upon the three pails of water, which were all ready for her, she said with a smile, "All that water must have been brought here for the purpose of drowning me, Monsieur. You have no idea, I trust, of making a person of my small stature swallow it all."' Shall I read the details of the torture?"

"No, for Heaven's sake, don't."

"Here is a sentence which must surely show you that what is here recorded is the very scene which you have gazed upon tonight: 'The good Abbé Pirot, unable to contemplate the agonies which were suffered by his penitent, had hurried from the room.' Does that convince you?"

"It does entirely. There can be no question that it is indeed the same event. But who, then, is this lady whose appearance was so attractive and whose end was so horrible?"

For answer Dacre came across to me, and placed the small lamp upon the table which stood by my bed. Lifting up the ill-omened filler, he turned the brass rim so that the light fell full upon it. Seen in this way, the engraving seemed clearer than on the night before.

"We have already agreed that this is the badge of a marquis or of a marquise," said he. "We have also settled that the last letter is *B*."

"It is undoubtedly so."

"I now suggest to you that the other letters from left to right are, *M*, *M*, a small *d*, *A*, a small *d*, and then the final *B*."

"Yes, I am sure that you are right. I can make out the two small *d*s quite plainly."

"What I have read to you tonight," said Dacre, "is the official record of the trial of Marie-Madeleine d'Aubray, Marquise de Brinvilliers,* one of the most famous poisoners and murderers of all time."

I sat in silence, overwhelmed at the extraordinary nature of the incident, and at the completeness of the proof with which Dacre had exposed its real meaning. In a vague way I remembered some details of the woman's career, her unbridled debauchery, the cold-blooded and protracted torture of her sick father, the murder of her brothers for motives of petty gain. I recollected also that the bravery of her end had done something to atone for the horror of her life, and that all Paris had sympathized with her last moments, and blessed her as a martyr within a few days of the time when they had cursed her as a murderess. One objection, and one only, occurred to my mind.

"How came her initials and her badge of rank upon the filler? Surely they did not carry their medieval homage to the nobility to the point of decorating instruments of torture with their titles?"

"I was puzzled with the same point," said Dacre, "but it admits of a simple explanation. The case excited extraordinary interest at the time, and nothing could be more natural than that La Reynie, the head of the police, should retain this filler as a grim souvenir. It was not often that a marchioness of France underwent the extraordinary question. That he should engrave her initials upon it for the information of others was surely a very ordinary proceeding upon his part."

"And this?" I asked, pointing to the marks upon the leathern neck.

"She was a cruel tigress," said Dacre, as he turned away. "I think it is evident that like other tigresses her teeth were both strong and sharp."

The New Catacomb

"Look here, Burger," said Kennedy, "I do wish that you would confide in me."

The two famous students of Roman remains sat together in Kennedy's comfortable room overlooking the Corso. The night was cold, and they had both pulled up their chairs to the unsatisfactory Italian stove which threw out a zone of stuffiness rather than of warmth. Outside under the bright winter stars lay the modern Rome, the long, double chain of the electric lamps, the brilliantly lit cafés, the rushing carriages and the dense throng upon the footpaths. But inside, in the sumptuous chamber of the rich young English archaeologist, there was only old Rome to be seen. Cracked and timeworn friezes hung upon the walls, grey old busts of senators and soldiers with their fighting heads and their hard, cruel faces peered out from the corners. On the centre table, amidst a litter of inscriptions, fragments and ornaments, there stood the famous reconstruction by Kennedy of the Baths of Caracalla,* which excited such interest and admiration when it was exhibited in Berlin. Amphorae hung from the ceiling, and a litter of curiosities strewed the rich red Turkey carpet. And of them all there was not one which was not of the most unimpeachable authenticity and of the utmost rarity and value; for Kennedy, though little more than thirty, had a European reputation in this particular branch of research, and was, moreover, provided with that long purse which either proves to be a fatal handicap to the student's energies or, if his mind is still true to its purpose, gives him an enormous advantage in the race for fame. Kennedy had often been seduced by whim and pleasure from his studies, but his mind was an incisive one, capable of long and concentrated efforts which ended in sharp reactions of sensuous languor. His handsome face, with its high, white forehead, its aggressive nose and its somewhat loose and sensual mouth, was a fair index of the compromise between strength and weakness in his nature.

Of a very different type was his companion, Julius Burger. He came of a curious blend, a German father and an Italian mother, with the robust qualities of the north mingling strangely with the softer graces of the south. Blue Teutonic eyes lightened his sun-browned face, and above them rose a square, massive forehead, with a fringe of close yellow curls lying round it. His strong, firm jaw was clean-shaven, and his companion had frequently remarked how much it suggested those old Roman busts which peered out from the shadows in the corners of his chamber. Under its bluff German strength there lay always a suggestion of Italian subtlety, but the smile was so honest, and the eyes so frank, that one understood that this was only an indication of his ancestry, with no actual bearing upon his character. In age and in reputation, he was on the same level as his English companion, but his life and his work had both been far more arduous. Twelve years before, he had come as a poor student to Rome, and had lived ever since upon some small endowment for research which had been awarded to him by the University of Bonn. Painfully, slowly and doggedly, with extraordinary tenacity and single-mindedness, he had climbed from rung to rung of the ladder of fame, until now he was a member of the Berlin Academy, and there was every reason to believe that he would shortly be promoted to the chair of the greatest of German universities. But the singleness of purpose which had brought him to the same high level as the rich and brilliant Englishman had caused him in everything outside their work to stand infinitely below him. He had never found a pause in his studies in which to cultivate the social graces. It was only when he spoke of his own subject that his face was filled with life and soul. At other times he was silent and embarrassed, too conscious of his own limitations in larger subjects, and impatient of that small talk which is the conventional refuge of those who have no thoughts to express.

And yet for some years there had been an acquaintanceship which appeared to be slowly ripening into a friendship between these two very different rivals. The base and origin of this lay in the fact that in their own studies each was the only one of the younger men who had knowledge and enthusiasm enough to properly appreciate the other. Their common interests and pursuits had brought them together, and each had been attracted by the other's knowledge. And then gradually something had been added to this. Kennedy had been amused by the frankness and simplicity of his rival, while Burger in turn had been fascinated by the brilliancy and vivacity which had made Kennedy such a favourite in Roman society. I say "had", because just at the moment, the young Englishman was somewhat under a cloud. A love affair, the details of which had never quite come out, had indicated a heartlessness and callousness upon his part which shocked many of his friends. But in the bachelor circles of students and artists in which he preferred to move there is no very rigid code of honour in such matters, and though a head might be shaken or a pair of shoulders shrugged over the flight of two and the return of one, the general sentiment was probably one of curiosity and perhaps of envy rather than of reprobation.

"Look here, Burger," said Kennedy, looking hard at the placid face of his companion, "I do wish that you would confide in me."

As he spoke he waved his hand in the direction of a rug which lay upon the floor. On the rug stood a long, shallow fruit basket of the light wickerwork which is used in the Campagna, and this was heaped with a litter of objects, inscribed tiles, broken inscriptions, cracked mosaics, torn papyri, rusty metal ornaments, which to the uninitiated might have seemed to have come straight from a dustman's bin, but which a specialist would have speedily recognized as unique of their kind. The pile of odds and ends in the flat wickerwork basket supplied exactly one of those missing links of social development which are of such interest to the student. It was the German who had brought them in, and the Englishman's eyes were hungry as he looked at them.

"I won't interfere with your treasure trove, but I should very much like to hear about it," he continued, while Burger very deliberately lit a cigar. "It is evidently a discovery of the first importance. These inscriptions will make a sensation throughout Europe."

"For every one here there are a million there!" said the German. "There are so many that a dozen savants might spend a lifetime over them, and build up a reputation as solid as the Castle of St Angelo."*

Kennedy sat thinking with his fine forehead wrinkled and his fingers playing with his long, fair moustache.

"You have given yourself away, Burger!" said he at last. "Your words can only apply to one thing. You have discovered a new catacomb."

"I had no doubt that you had already come to that conclusion from an examination of these objects."

"Well, they certainly appeared to indicate it, but your last remarks make it certain. There is no place except a catacomb which could contain so vast a store of relics as you describe."

"Quite so. There is no mystery about that. I *have* discovered a new catacomb."

"Where?"

"Ah, that is my secret, my dear Kennedy. Suffice it that it is so situated that there is not one chance in a million of anyone else coming upon it. Its date is different from that of any known catacomb, and it has been reserved for the burial of the highest Christians, so that the remains and the relics are quite different from anything which has ever been seen before. If I was not aware of your knowledge and of your energy, my friend, I would not hesitate, under the pledge of secrecy, to tell you everything about it. But as it is, I think that I must certainly prepare my own report of the matter before I expose myself to such formidable competition."

Kennedy loved his subject with a love which was almost a mania – a love which held him true to it, amidst all the distractions which come to a wealthy and dissipated young man. He had ambition, but his ambition was secondary to his mere abstract joy and interest in everything which concerned the old life and history of the city. He yearned to see this new underworld which his companion had discovered.

"Look here, Burger," said he earnestly, "I assure you that you can trust me most implicitly in the matter. Nothing would induce me to put pen to paper about anything which I see until I have your express permission. I quite understand your feeling and I think it is most natural, but you have really nothing whatever to fear from me. On the other hand, if you don't tell me I shall make a systematic search, and I shall most certainly discover it. In that case, of course, I should make what use I liked of it, since I should be under no obligation to you."

Burger smiled thoughtfully over his cigar.

"I have noticed, friend Kennedy," said he, "that when I want information over any point you are not always so ready to supply it."

"When did you ever ask me anything that I did not tell you? You remember, for example, my giving you the material for your paper about the Temple of the Vestals."*

"Ah, well, that was not a matter of much importance. If I were to question you upon some intimate thing, would you give me an answer, I wonder? This new catacomb is a very intimate thing to me, and I should certainly expect some sign of confidence in return."

"What you are driving at I cannot imagine," said the Englishman, "but if you mean that you will answer my question about the catacomb if I answer any question which you may put to me I can assure you that I will certainly do so."

"Well, then," said Burger, leaning luxuriously back in his settee, and puffing a blue tree of cigar smoke into the air, "tell me all about your relations with Miss Mary Saunderson."

Kennedy sprang up in his chair and glared angrily at his impassive companion.

"What the devil do you mean?" he cried. "What sort of a question is this? You may mean it as a joke, but you never made a worse one."

"No, I don't mean it as a joke," said Burger simply. "I am really rather interested in the details of the matter. I don't know much about the world and women and social life and that sort of thing, and such an incident has the fascination of the unknown for me. I know you, and I knew her by sight – I had even spoken to her once or twice. I should very much like to hear from your own lips exactly what it was which occurred between you."

"I won't tell you a word."

"That's all right. It was only my whim to see if you would give up a secret as easily as you expected me to give up my secret of the new catacomb. You wouldn't, and I didn't expect you to. But why should you expect otherwise of me? There's St John's clock* striking ten. It is quite time that I was going home."

"No, wait a bit, Burger," said Kennedy. "This is really a ridiculous caprice of yours to wish to know about an old love affair which has burnt out months ago. You know we look upon a man who kisses and tells as the greatest coward and villain possible."

"Certainly," said the German, gathering up his basket of curiosities, "when he tells anything about a girl which is previously unknown he must be so. But in this case, as you must be aware, it was a public matter which was the common talk of Rome, so that you are not really doing Miss Mary Saunderson any injury by discussing her case with me. But still, I respect your scruples, and so goodnight!"

"Wait a bit, Burger," said Kennedy, laying his hand upon the other's arm. "I am very keen upon this catacomb business, and I can't let it drop quite so easily. Would you mind asking me something else in return – something not quite so eccentric this time?"

"No, no, you have refused, and there is an end of it," said Burger, with his basket on his arm. "No doubt you are quite right not to answer, and no doubt I am quite right also – and so again, my dear Kennedy, goodnight!"

The Englishman watched Burger cross the room, and he had his hand on the handle of the door before his host sprang up with the air of a man who is making the best of that which cannot be helped.

"Hold on, old fellow," said he. "I think you are behaving in a most ridiculous fashion; but still, if this is your condition, I suppose that I must submit to it. I hate saying anything about a girl, but, as you say, it is all over Rome, and I don't suppose I can tell you anything which you do not know already. What was it you wanted to know?"

The German came back to the stove and, laying down his basket, he sank into his chair once more.

"May I have another cigar?" said he. "Thank you very much! I never smoke when I work, but I enjoy a chat much more when I am under the influence of tobacco. Now, as regards this young lady, with whom you had this little adventure. What in the world has become of her?"

"She is at home with her own people."

"Oh, really – in England?"

"Yes."

"What part of England – London?"

"No, Twickenham."

"You must excuse my curiosity, my dear Kennedy, and you must put it down to my ignorance of the world. No doubt it is quite a simple thing to persuade a young lady to go off with you for three weeks or so, and then to hand her over to her own family at – what did you call the place?"

"Twickenham."

"Quite so – at Twickenham. But it is something so entirely outside my own experience that I cannot even imagine how you set about it. For example, if you had loved this girl your love could hardly disappear in three weeks, so I presume that you could not have loved her at all. But if you did not love her why should you make this great scandal which has damaged you and ruined her?"

Kennedy looked moodily into the red eye of the stove.

"That's a logical way of looking at it, certainly," said he. "Love is a big word, and it represents a good many different shades of feeling. I liked her, and – well, you say you've seen her – you know how charming she could look. But still I am willing to admit, looking back, that I could never have really loved her."

"Then, my dear Kennedy, why did you do it?"

"The adventure of the thing had a great deal to do with it."

"What! You are so fond of adventures!"

"Where would the variety of life be without them? It was for an adventure that I first began to pay my attentions to her. I've chased a good deal of game in my time, but there's no chase like that of a pretty woman. There was the piquant difficulty of it also, for, as she was the companion of Lady Emily Rood, it was almost impossible to see her alone. On the top of all the other obstacles which attracted me, I learnt from her own lips very early in the proceedings that she was engaged."

"*Mein Gott!* To whom?"

"She mentioned no names."

"I do not think that anyone knows that. So that made the adventure more alluring, did it?"

"Well, it did certainly give a spice to it. Don't you think so?"

"I tell you that I am very ignorant about these things."

"My dear fellow, you can remember that the apple you stole from your neighbour's tree was always sweeter than that which fell from your own. And then I found that she cared for me."

"What – at once?"

"Oh, no, it took about three months of sapping and mining. But at last I won her over. She understood that my judicial separation from my wife made it impossible for me to do the right thing by her – but she came all the same, and we had a delightful time, as long as it lasted."

"But how about the other man?"

Kennedy shrugged his shoulders.

"I suppose it is the survival of the fittest," said he. "If he had been the better man she would not have deserted him. Let's drop the subject, for I have had enough of it!"

"Only one other thing. How did you get rid of her in three weeks?"

"Well, we had both cooled down a bit, you understand. She absolutely refused, under any circumstances, to come back to face the people she had known in Rome. Now, of course, Rome is necessary to me, and I was already pining to be back at my work – so there was one obvious cause of separation. Then, again, her old father turned up at the hotel in London, and there was a scene, and the whole thing became so unpleasant that really – though I missed her dreadfully at first – I was very glad to slip out of it. Now, I rely upon you not to repeat anything of what I have said."

"My dear Kennedy, I should not dream of repeating it. But all that you say interests me very much, for it gives me an insight into your way of looking at things, which is entirely different from mine, for I have seen so little of life. And now you want to know about my new catacomb. There's no use my trying to describe it, for you would never find it by that. There is only one thing, and that is for me to take you there."

"That would be splendid."

"When would you like to come?"

"The sooner the better. I am all impatience to see it."

"Well, it is a beautiful night – though a trifle cold. Suppose we start in an hour. We must be very careful to keep the matter to ourselves. If anyone saw us hunting in couples they would suspect that there was something going on."

"We can't be too cautious," said Kennedy. "Is it far?"

"Some miles."

"Not too far to walk?"

"Oh, no, we could walk there easily."

"We had better do so, then. A cabman's suspicions would be aroused if he dropped us both at some lonely spot in the dead of the night."

"Quite so. I think it would be best for us to meet at the gate of the Appian Way at midnight. I must go back to my lodgings for the matches and candles and things."

"All right, Burger! I think it is very kind of you to let me into this secret, and I promise you that I will write nothing about it until you have published your report. Goodbye for the present! You will find me at the gate at twelve."

The cold, clear air was filled with the musical chimes from that city of clocks as Burger, wrapped in an Italian overcoat, with a lantern hanging from his hand, walked up to the rendezvous. Kennedy stepped out of the shadow to meet him.

"You are ardent in work as well as in love!" said the German, laughing.

"Yes – I have been waiting here for nearly half an hour."

"I hope you left no clue as to where we were going."

"Not such a fool! By Jove, I am chilled to the bone! Come on, Burger, let us warm ourselves by a spurt of hard walking."

Their footsteps sounded loud and crisp upon the rough stone paving of the disappointing road which is all that is left of the most famous highway of the world. A peasant or two going home from the wine shop, and a few carts of country produce coming up to Rome, were the only things which they met. They swung along, with the huge tombs looming up through the darkness upon each side of them, until they had come as far as the Catacombs of St Callixtus,* and saw against a rising moon the great circular bastion of Cecilia Metella* in front of them. Then Burger stopped with his hand to his side.

"Your legs are longer than mine, and you are more accustomed to walking," said he, laughing. "I think that the place where we turn off is somewhere here. Yes, this is it, round the corner of the trattoria. Now, it is a very narrow path, so perhaps I had better go in front and you can follow."

He had lit his lantern, and by its light they were enabled to follow a narrow and devious track which wound across the marshes of the Campagna. The great Aqueduct of old Rome lay like a monstrous caterpillar across the moonlit landscape, and their road led them under one of its huge arches and past the circle of crumbling bricks which marks the old arena. At last Burger stopped at a solitary wooden cow house, and he drew a key from his pocket.

"Surely your catacomb is not inside a house!" cried Kennedy.

"The entrance to it is. That is just the safeguard which we have against anyone else discovering it."

"Does the proprietor know of it?"

"Not he. He had found one or two objects which made me almost certain that his house was built on the entrance to such a place. So I rented it from him and did my excavations for myself. Come in, and shut the door behind you."

It was a long, empty building, with the mangers of the cows along one wall. Burger put his lantern down on the ground, and shaded its light in all directions save one by draping his overcoat round it.

"It might excite remark if anyone saw a light in this lonely place," said he. "Just help me to move this boarding."

The flooring was loose in the corner, and plank by plank the two savants raised it and leant it against the wall. Below there was a square aperture and a stair of old stone steps which led away down into the bowels of the earth.

"Be careful!" cried Burger, as Kennedy, in his impatience, hurried down them. "It is a perfect rabbits' warren below, and if you were once to lose your way there the chances would be a hundred to one against your ever coming out again. Wait until I bring the light."

"How do you find your own way if it is so complicated?"

"I had some very narrow escapes at first, but I have gradually learnt to go about. There is a certain system to it, but it is one which a lost man, if he were in the dark, could not possibly find out. Even now I always spin out a ball of string behind me when I am going far into the catacomb. You can see for yourself that it is difficult, but every one of these passages divides and subdivides a dozen times before you go a hundred yards."

They had descended some twenty feet from the level of the byre, and they were standing now in a square chamber cut out of the soft tufa. The lantern cast a flickering light, bright below and dim above, over the cracked brown walls. In every direction were the black openings of passages which radiated from this common centre.

"I want you to follow me closely, my friend," said Burger. "Do not loiter to look at anything upon the way, for the place to which I will take you contains all that you can see, and more. It will save time for us to go there direct."

He led the way down one of the corridors, and the Englishman followed closely at his heels. Every now and then the passage bifurcated, but Burger was evidently following some secret marks of his own, for he neither stopped nor hesitated. Everywhere along the walls, packed like the berths upon an emigrant ship, lay the Christians of old Rome. The yellow light flickered over the shrivelled features of the mummies, and gleamed upon rounded skulls and long, white arm bones crossed over fleshless chests. And everywhere as he passed Kennedy looked with wistful eyes upon inscriptions, funeral vessels, pictures, vestments, utensils, all lying as pious hands had placed them so many centuries ago. It was apparent to him, even in those hurried, passing glances, that this was the earliest and finest of the catacombs, containing such a storehouse of Roman remains as had never before come at one time under the observation of the student.

"What would happen if the light went out?" he asked, as they hurried onwards.

"I have a spare candle and a box of matches in my pocket. By the way, Kennedy, have you any matches?"

"No; you had better give me some."

"Oh, that is all right. There is no chance of our separating."

"How far are we going? It seems to me that we have walked at least a quarter of a mile."

"More than that, I think. There is really no limit to the tombs – at least, I have never been able to find any. This is a very difficult place, so I think that I will use our ball of string."

He fastened one end of it to a projecting stone and he carried the coil in the breast of his coat, paying it out as he advanced. Kennedy saw that it was no unnecessary precaution, for the passages had become more complex and tortuous than ever, with a perfect network of intersecting corridors. But these all ended in one large circular hall with a square pedestal of tufa topped with a slab of marble at one end of it.

"By Jove!" cried Kennedy in an ecstasy, as Burger swung his lantern over the marble. "It is a Christian altar – probably the first one in existence. Here is the little consecration cross cut upon the corner of it. No doubt this circular space was used as a church."

"Precisely," said Burger. "If I had more time I should like to show you all the bodies which are buried in these niches upon the walls, for they are the early popes and bishops of the Church, with their mitres, their croziers and full canonicals. Go over to that one and look at it!"

Kennedy went across, and stared at the ghastly head which lay loosely on the shredded and mouldering mitre.

"This is most interesting," said he, and his voice seemed to boom against the concave vault. "As far as my experience goes, it is unique. Bring the lantern over, Burger, for I want to see them all."

But the German had strolled away, and was standing in the middle of a yellow circle of light at the other side of the hall.

"Do you know how many wrong turnings there are between this and the stairs?" he asked. "There are over two thousand. No doubt it was one of the means of protection which the Christians adopted. The odds are two thousand to one against a man getting out, even if he had a light; but if he were in the dark it would, of course, be far more difficult."

"So I should think."

"And the darkness is something dreadful. I tried it once for an experiment. Let us try it again!" He stooped to the lantern, and in an instant it was as if an invisible hand was squeezed tightly over each of Kennedy's eyes. Never had he known what such darkness was. It seemed to press upon him and to smother him. It was a solid obstacle against which the body shrank from advancing. He put his hands out to push it back from him.

"That will do, Burger," said he, "let's have the light again."

But his companion began to laugh, and in that circular room the sound seemed to come from every side at once.

"You seem uneasy, friend Kennedy," said he.

"Go on, man, light the candle!" said Kennedy impatiently.

"It's very strange, Kennedy, but I could not in the least tell by the sound in which direction you stand. Could you tell where I am?"

"No; you seem to be on every side of me."

"If it were not for this string which I hold in my hand I should not have a notion which way to go."

"I dare say not. Strike a light, man, and have an end of this nonsense."

"Well, Kennedy, there are two things which I understand that you are very fond of. The one is an adventure, and the other is an obstacle to surmount. The adventure must be the finding of your way out of this catacomb. The obstacle will be the darkness and the two thousand wrong turns which make the way a little difficult to find. But you need not hurry, for you have plenty of time, and when you halt for a rest now and then, I should like you just to think of Miss Mary Saunderson, and whether you treated her quite fairly."

"You devil, what do you mean?" roared Kennedy. He was running about in little circles and clasping at the solid blackness with both hands.

"Goodbye," said the mocking voice, and it was already at some distance. "I really do not think, Kennedy, even by your own showing that you did the right thing by that girl. There was only one little thing which you appeared not to know, and I can supply it. Miss Saunderson was engaged to a poor ungainly devil of a student, and his name was Julius Burger."

There was a rustle somewhere, the vague sound of a foot striking a stone, and then there fell silence upon that old Christian church – a stagnant, heavy silence which closed round Kennedy and shut him in like water round a drowning man.

Some two months afterwards the following paragraph made the round of the European press:

> One of the most interesting discoveries of recent years is that of the new catacomb in Rome, which lies some distance to the east of the well-known vaults of St Callixtus. The finding of this important burial place, which is exceeding rich in most interesting early Christian remains, is due to the energy and sagacity of Dr Julius Burger, the young German specialist, who is rapidly taking the first place as an authority upon ancient Rome. Although the first to publish his discovery, it appears that a less fortunate adventurer had anticipated Dr Burger. Some months ago Mr Kennedy, the well-known English student, disappeared suddenly from his rooms in the Corso, and it was conjectured that his association with a recent scandal had driven him to leave Rome. It appears now that he had in reality fallen a victim to that fervid love of archaeology which had raised him to a distinguished place among living scholars. His body was discovered in the heart of the new catacomb, and it was evident from the condition of his feet and boots that he had tramped for days through the tortuous corridors which make these subterranean tombs so dangerous to explorers. The deceased gentleman had, with inexplicable rashness, made his way into this labyrinth without, as far as can be discovered, taking with him either candles or matches, so that his sad fate was the natural result of his own temerity. What makes the matter more painful is that Dr Julius Burger was an intimate friend of the deceased. His joy at the extraordinary find which he has been so fortunate as to make has been greatly marred by the terrible fate of his comrade and fellow worker.

The Case of Lady Sannox

The relations between Douglas Stone and the notorious Lady Sannox were very well known both among the fashionable circles of which she was a brilliant member and the scientific bodies which numbered him among their most illustrious confrères. There was naturally, therefore, a very widespread interest when it was announced one morning that the lady had absolutely and for ever taken the veil, and that the world would see her no more. When, at the very tail of this rumour, there came the assurance that the celebrated operating surgeon, the man of steel nerves, had been found in the morning by his valet, seated on one side of his bed, smiling pleasantly upon the universe, with both legs jammed into one side of his breeches and his great brain about as valuable as a cap full of porridge, the matter was strong enough to give quite a little thrill of interest to folk who had never hoped that their jaded nerves were capable of such a sensation.

Douglas Stone in his prime was one of the most remarkable men in England. Indeed, he could hardly be said to have ever reached his prime, for he was but nine-and-thirty at the time of this little incident. Those who knew him best were aware that, famous as he was as a surgeon, he might have succeeded with even greater rapidity in any of a dozen lines of life. He could have cut his way to fame as a soldier, struggled to it as an explorer, bullied for it in the courts or built it out of stone and iron as an engineer. He was born to be great, for he could plan what another man dare not do, and he could do what another man dare not plan. In surgery none could follow him. His nerve, his judgement, his intuition were things apart. Again and again his knife cut away death, but grazed the very springs of life in doing it, until his assistants were as white as the patient. His energy, his audacity, his full-blooded self-confidence – does not the memory of them still linger to the south of Marylebone Road and the north of Oxford Street?

His vices were as magnificent as his virtues, and infinitely more picturesque. Large as was his income, and it was the third-largest of all professional men in London, it was far beneath the luxury of his living. Deep in his complex nature lay a rich vein of sensualism, at the sport of which he placed all the prizes of his life. The eye, the ear, the touch, the palate, all were his masters. The bouquet of old vintages, the scent of rare exotics, the curves and tints of the daintiest potteries of Europe, it was to these that the quick-running stream of gold was transformed. And then there came his sudden mad passion for Lady Sannox, when a single interview with two challenging glances and a whispered word set him ablaze. She was the loveliest woman in London and the only one to him. He was one of the handsomest men in London, but not the only one to her. She had a liking for new experiences, and was gracious to most men who wooed her. It may have been cause or it may have been effect that Lord Sannox looked fifty, though he was but six-and-thirty.

He was a quiet, silent, neutral-tinted man, this lord, with thin lips and heavy eyelids, much given to gardening and full of home-like habits. He had at one time been fond of acting, had even rented a theatre in London, and on its boards had first seen Miss Marion Dawson, to whom he had offered his hand, his title and the third of a county. Since his marriage this early hobby had become distasteful to him. Even in private theatricals it was no longer possible to persuade him to exercise the talent which he had often shown that he possessed. He was happier with a spud* and a watering can among his orchids and chrysanthemums.

It was quite an interesting problem whether he was absolutely devoid of sense, or miserably wanting in spirit. Did he know his lady's ways and condone them, or was he a mere blind, doting fool? It was a point to be discussed over the teacups in snug little drawing rooms, or with the aid of a cigar in the bow windows of clubs. Bitter and plain were the comments among men upon his conduct. There was but one who had a good word to say for him, and he was the most silent member in the smoking room. He had seen him break in a horse at the university, and it seemed to have left an impression upon his mind.

But when Douglas Stone became the favourite all doubts as to Lord Sannox's knowledge or ignorance were set for ever at rest. There was no subterfuge about Stone. In his high-handed, impetuous fashion, he set all caution and discretion at defiance. The scandal became notorious. A learned body intimated that his name had been struck from the list of its vice presidents. Two friends implored him to consider his professional credit. He cursed them all three, and spent forty guineas on a bangle to take with him to the lady. He was at her house every evening, and she drove in his carriage in the afternoons. There was not an attempt on either side to conceal their relations; but there came at last a little incident to interrupt them.

It was a dismal winter's night, very cold and gusty, with the wind whooping in the chimneys and blustering against the window panes. A thin spatter of rain tinkled on the glass with each fresh sough of the gale, drowning for the instant the dull gurgle and drip from the eaves. Douglas Stone had finished his dinner, and sat by his fire in the study, a glass of rich port upon the malachite table at his elbow. As he raised it to his lips, he held it up against the lamplight, and watched with the eye of a connoisseur the tiny scales of beeswing which floated in its rich ruby depths. The fire, as it spurted up, threw fitful lights upon his bold, clear-cut face, with its widely opened grey eyes, its thick and yet firm lips and the deep, square jaw, which had something Roman in its strength and its animalism. He smiled from time to time as he nestled back in his luxurious chair. Indeed, he had a right to feel well pleased, for, against the advice of six colleagues, he had performed an operation that day of which only two cases were on record, and the result had been brilliant beyond all expectation. No other man in London would have had the daring to plan, or the skill to execute, such a heroic measure.

But he had promised Lady Sannox to see her that evening and it was already half-past eight. His hand was outstretched to the bell to order the carriage when he heard the dull thud of the knocker. An instant later there was the shuffling of feet in the hall, and the sharp closing of a door.

"A patient to see you, sir, in the consulting room," said the butler.

"About himself?"

"No, sir, I think he wants you to go out."

"It is too late," cried Douglas Stone peevishly. "I won't go."

"This is his card, sir."

The butler presented it upon the gold salver which had been given to his master by the wife of a prime minister.

"'Hamil Ali, Smyrna.' Hum! The fellow is a Turk, I suppose."

"Yes, sir. He seems as if he came from abroad, sir. And he's in a terrible way."

"Tut, tut! I have an engagement. I must go somewhere else. But I'll see him. Show him in here, Pim."

A few moments later the butler swung open the door and ushered in a small and decrepit man, who walked with a bent back and with the forward push of the face and blink of the eyes which goes with extreme short sight. His face was swarthy, and his hair and beard of the deepest black. In one hand he held a turban of white muslin striped with red, in the other a small chamois-leather bag.

"Good evening," said Douglas Stone, when the butler had closed the door. "You speak English, I presume?"

"Yes, sir. I am from Asia Minor, but I speak English when I speak slow."

"You wanted me to go out, I understand?"

"Yes, sir. I wanted very much that you should see my wife."

"I could come in the morning, but I have an engagement which prevents me from seeing your wife tonight."

The Turk's answer was a singular one. He pulled the string which closed the mouth of the chamois-leather bag, and poured a flood of gold onto the table.

"There are one hundred pounds there," said he, "and I promise you that it will not take you an hour. I have a cab ready at the door."

Douglas Stone glanced at his watch. An hour would not make it too late to visit Lady Sannox. He had been there later. And the fee was an extraordinarily high one. He had been pressed by his creditors lately, and he could not afford to let such a chance pass. He would go.

"What is the case?" he asked.

"Oh, it is so sad a one! So sad a one! You have not, perhaps, heard of the daggers of the Almohades?"*

"Never."

"Ah, they are Eastern daggers of a great age and of a singular shape, with the hilt like what you call a stirrup. I am a curiosity dealer, you understand, and that is why I have come to England from Smyrna,* but next week I go back once more. Many things I brought with me, and I have a few things left, but among them, to my sorrow, is one of these daggers."

"You will remember that I have an appointment, sir," said the surgeon, with some irritation. "Pray confine yourself to the necessary details."

"You will see that it is necessary. Today my wife fell down in a faint in the room in which I keep my wares, and she cut her lower lip upon this cursed dagger of Almohades."

"I see," said Douglas Stone, rising. "And you wish me to dress the wound?"

"No, no, it is worse than that."

"What then?"

"These daggers are poisoned."

"Poisoned!"

"Yes, and there is no man, East or West, who can tell now what is the poison or what the cure. But all that is known I know, for my father was in this trade before me, and we have had much to do with these poisoned weapons."

"What are the symptoms?"

"Deep sleep, and death in thirty hours."

"And you say there is no cure. Why then should you pay me this considerable fee?"

"No drug can cure, but the knife may."

"And how?"

"The poison is slow of absorption. It remains for hours in the wound."

"Washing, then, might cleanse it?"

"No more than in a snakebite. It is too subtle and too deadly."

"Excision of the wound, then?"

"That is it. If it be on the finger, take the finger off. So said my father always. But think of where this wound is, and that it is my wife. It is dreadful!"

But familiarity with such grim matters may take the finer edge from a man's sympathy. To Douglas Stone this was already an interesting case, and he brushed aside as irrelevant the feeble objections of the husband.

"It appears to be that or nothing," said he brusquely. "It is better to lose a lip than a life."

"Ah, yes, I know that you are right. Well, well, it is kismet, and it must be faced. I have the cab, and you will come with me and do this thing."

Douglas Stone took his case of bistouries* from a drawer, and placed it with a roll of bandage and a compress of lint in his pocket. He must waste no more time if he were to see Lady Sannox.

"I am ready," said he, pulling on his overcoat. "Will you take a glass of wine before you go out into this cold air?"

His visitor shrank away, with a protesting hand upraised.

"You forget that I am a Mussulman, and a true follower of the Prophet," said he. "But tell me what is the bottle of green glass which you have placed in your pocket?"

"It is chloroform."

"Ah, that also is forbidden to us. It is a spirit, and we make no use of such things."

"What! You would allow your wife to go through an operation without an anaesthetic?"

"Ah! She will feel nothing, poor soul. The deep sleep has already come on, which is the first working of the poison. And then I have given her of our Smyrna opium. Come, sir, for already an hour has passed."

As they stepped out into the darkness, a sheet of rain was driven in upon their faces, and the hall lamp, which dangled from the arm of a marble caryatid, went out with a fluff. Pim, the butler, pushed the heavy door to, straining hard with his shoulder against the wind, while the two men groped their way towards the yellow glare which showed where the cab was waiting. An instant later they were rattling upon their journey.

"Is it far?" asked Douglas Stone.

"Oh, no. We have a very little quiet place off the Euston Road."

The surgeon pressed the spring of his repeater and listened to the little tings which told him the hour. It was a quarter past nine. He calculated the distances, and the short time which it would take him to perform so trivial an operation. He ought to reach Lady Sannox by ten o'clock. Through the fogged windows he saw the blurred gas lamps dancing past, with occasionally the broader glare of a shopfront. The rain was pelting and rattling upon the leathern top of the carriage, and the wheels swashed as they rolled through puddle and mud. Opposite to him the white headgear of his companion gleamed faintly through the obscurity. The surgeon felt in his pockets and arranged his needles, his ligatures and his safety pins, that no time might be wasted when they arrived. He chafed with impatience and drummed his foot upon the floor.

But the cab slowed down at last and pulled up. In an instant Douglas Stone was out, and the Smyrna merchant's toe was at his very heel.

"You can wait," said he to the driver.

It was a mean-looking house in a narrow and sordid street. The surgeon, who knew his London well, cast a swift glance into the shadows, but there was nothing distinctive – no shop, no movement, nothing but a double line of dull, flat-faced houses, a double stretch of wet flagstones which gleamed in the lamplight and a double rush of water in the gutters which swirled and gurgled towards the sewer gratings. The door which faced them was blotched and discoloured, and a faint light in the fan pane above it served to show the dust and the grime which covered it. Above, in one of the bedroom windows, there was a dull yellow glimmer. The merchant knocked loudly, and, as he turned his dark face towards the light, Douglas Stone could see that it was contracted with anxiety. A bolt was drawn, and an elderly woman with a taper stood in the doorway, shielding the thin flame with her gnarled hand.

"Is all well?" gasped the merchant.

"She is as you left her, sir."

"She has not spoken?"

"No, she is in a deep sleep."

The merchant closed the door, and Douglas Stone walked down the narrow passage, glancing about him in some surprise as he did so. There was no oilcloth, no mat, no hatrack. Deep grey dust and heavy festoons of cobwebs met his eyes everywhere. Following the old woman up the winding stair, his firm footfall echoed harshly through the silent house. There was no carpet.

The bedroom was on the second landing. Douglas Stone followed the old nurse into it, with the merchant at his heels. Here, at least, there was furniture and to spare. The floor was littered and the corners piled with Turkish cabinets, inlaid tables, coats of chainmail, strange pipes and grotesque weapons. A single small lamp stood upon a bracket on the wall. Douglas Stone took it down and, picking his way among the lumber, walked over to a couch in the corner, on which lay a woman dressed in the Turkish fashion, with yashmak* and veil. The lower part of the face was exposed, and the surgeon saw a jagged cut which zigzagged along the border of the underlip.

"You will forgive the yashmak," said the Turk. "You know our views about woman in the East."

But the surgeon was not thinking about the yashmak. This was no longer a woman to him. It was a case. He stooped and examined the wound carefully.

"There are no signs of irritation," said he. "We might delay the operation until local symptoms develop."

The husband wrung his hands in uncontrollable agitation.

"Oh, sir, sir!" he cried. "Do not trifle. You do not know. It is deadly. I know, and I give you my assurance that an operation is absolutely necessary. Only the knife can save her."

"And yet I am inclined to wait," said Douglas Stone.

"That is enough," the Turk cried angrily. "Every minute is of importance, and I cannot stand here and see my wife allowed to sink. It only remains for me to give you my thanks for having come, and to call in some other surgeon before it is too late."

Douglas Stone hesitated. To refund that hundred pounds was no pleasant matter. But of course if he left the case he must return the money. And if the Turk were right and the woman died, his position before a coroner might be an embarrassing one.

"You have had personal experience of this poison?" he asked.

"I have."

"And you assure me that an operation is needful."

"I swear it by all that I hold sacred."

"The disfigurement will be frightful."

"I can understand that the mouth will not be a pretty one to kiss."

Douglas Stone turned fiercely upon the man. The speech was a brutal one. But the Turk has his own fashion of talk and of thought, and there was no time for wrangling. Douglas Stone drew a bistoury from his case, opened it and felt the keen straight edge with his forefinger. Then he held the lamp closer to the bed. Two dark eyes were gazing up at him through the slit in the yashmak. They were all iris, and the pupil was hardly to be seen. "You have given her a very heavy dose of opium."

"Yes, she has had a good dose."

He glanced again at the dark eyes which looked straight at his own. They were dull and lustreless but, even as he gazed, a little shifting sparkle came into them, and the lips quivered.

"She is not absolutely unconscious," said he.

"Would it not be well to use the knife while it will be painless?"

The same thought had crossed the surgeon's mind. He grasped the wounded lip with his forceps, and with two swift cuts he took out a broad V-shaped piece. The woman sprang up on the couch with a dreadful gurgling scream. Her covering was torn from her face. It was a face that he knew. In spite of that protruding upper lip and that slobber of blood, it was a face that he knew. She kept on putting her hand up to the gap and screaming. Douglas Stone sat down at the foot of the couch with his knife and his forceps. The room was whirling round, and he had felt something go like a ripping seam behind his ear. A bystander would have said that his face was the more ghastly of the two. As in a dream, or as if he had been looking at something at the play, he was conscious that the Turk's hair and beard lay upon the table, and that Lord Sannox was leaning against the wall with his hand to his side, laughing silently. The screams had died away now, and the dreadful head had dropped back again upon the pillow, but Douglas Stone still sat motionless, and Lord Sannox still chuckled quietly to himself.

"It was really very necessary for Marion, this operation," said he, "not physically, but morally, you know, morally."

Douglas Stone stooped forwards and began to play with the fringe of the coverlet. His knife tinkled down upon the ground, but he still held the forceps and something more.

"I had long intended to make a little example," said Lord Sannox suavely. "Your note of Wednesday miscarried, and I have it here in my pocketbook.

I took some pains in carrying out my idea. The wound, by the way, was from nothing more dangerous than my signet ring."

He glanced keenly at his silent companion, and cocked the small revolver which he held in his coat pocket. But Douglas Stone was still picking at the coverlet.

"You see you have kept your appointment after all," said Lord Sannox.

And at that Douglas Stone began to laugh. He laughed long and loudly. But Lord Sannox did not laugh now. Something like fear sharpened and hardened his features. He walked from the room, and he walked on tiptoe. The old woman was waiting outside.

"Attend to your mistress when she awakes," said Lord Sannox.

Then he went down to the street. The cab was at the door, and the driver raised his hand to his hat.

"John," said Lord Sannox, "you will take the doctor home first. He will want leading downstairs, I think. Tell his butler that he has been taken ill at a case."

"Very good, sir."

"Then you can take Lady Sannox home."

"And how about yourself, sir?"

"Oh, my address for the next few months will be Hotel di Roma, Venice. Just see that the letters are sent on. And tell Stevens to exhibit all the purple chrysanthemums next Monday, and to wire me the result."

The Terror of Blue John Gap

The following narrative was found among the papers of Dr James Hardcastle, who died of phthisis on 4th February 1908, at 36 Upper Coventry Flats, South Kensington. Those who knew him best, while refusing to express an opinion upon this particular statement, are unanimous in asserting that he was a man of a sober and scientific turn of mind, absolutely devoid of imagination, and most unlikely to invent any abnormal series of events. The paper was contained in an envelope, which was docketed "A Short Account of the Circumstances Which Occurred Near Miss Allerton's Farm in North-West Derbyshire in the Spring of Last Year". The envelope was sealed, and on the other side was written in pencil:

> DEAR SEATON,
>
> It may interest, and perhaps pain you, to know that the incredulity with which you met my story has prevented me from ever opening my mouth upon the subject again. I leave this record after my death, and perhaps strangers may be found to have more confidence in me than my friend.

Enquiry has failed to elicit who this Seaton may have been. I may add that the visit of the deceased to Allerton's Farm, and the general nature of the alarm there, apart from his particular explanation, have been absolutely established. With this foreword I append his account exactly as he left it. It is in the form of a diary, some entries in which have been expanded, while a few have been erased.

17th April: Already I feel the benefit of this wonderful upland air. The farm of the Allertons lies fourteen hundred and twenty feet above sea level, so it may well be a bracing climate. Beyond the usual morning cough I have very little discomfort and, what with the fresh milk and the home-grown mutton, I have every chance of putting on weight. I think Saunderson will be pleased.

The two Miss Allertons are charmingly quaint and kind, two dear little hard-working old maids who are ready to lavish all the heart which might have gone out to husband and to children upon an invalid stranger. Truly, the old maid is a most useful person, one of the reserve forces of the community. They talk of the superfluous woman, but what would the poor superfluous man do without her kindly presence? By the way, in their simplicity they very quickly let out the reason why Saunderson recommended their farm. The professor rose from the ranks himself, and I believe that in his youth he was not above scaring crows in these very fields.

It is a most lonely spot, and the walks are picturesque in the extreme. The farm consists of grazing land lying at the bottom of an irregular valley. On each side are the fantastic limestone hills, formed of rock so soft that you can break it away with your hands. All this country is hollow. Could you strike it with some gigantic hammer it would boom like a drum, or possibly cave in altogether and expose some huge subterranean sea. A great sea there must surely be, for on all sides the streams run into the mountain itself, never to reappear. There are gaps everywhere amid the rocks, and when you pass through them you find yourself in great caverns, which wind down into the bowels of the earth. I have a small bicycle lamp, and it is a perpetual joy to me to carry it into these weird solitudes, and to see the wonderful silver and black effects when I throw its light upon the stalactites which drape the lofty roofs. Shut off the lamp, and you are in the blackest darkness. Turn it on, and it is a scene from the *Arabian Nights*.

But there is one of these strange openings in the earth which has a special interest, for it is the handiwork, not of nature, but of man. I had never heard of Blue John when I came to these parts. It is the name given to a peculiar mineral of a beautiful purple shade, which is only found at one or two places in the world. It is so rare that an ordinary vase of Blue John would be valued at a great price. The Romans, with that extraordinary instinct of theirs, discovered that it was to be found in this valley, and sank a horizontal shaft deep into the mountainside. The opening of their mine has been called Blue John Gap,* a clean-cut arch in the rock, the mouth all overgrown with bushes. It is a goodly passage which the Roman miners have cut, and it intersects some of the great water-worn caves, so that if you enter Blue John Gap you would do well to mark your steps and to have a good store of candles, or you may never make your way back to the daylight again. I have not yet gone deeply into it, but this very day I stood at the mouth of the arched tunnel and, peering down into the black recesses beyond, I vowed that when my health returned I would devote some holiday to exploring those mysterious depths and finding out for myself how far the Romans had penetrated into the Derbyshire hills.

Strange how superstitious these countrymen are! I should have thought better of young Armitage, for he is a man of some education and character, and a very fine fellow for his station in life. I was standing at the Blue John Gap when he came across the field to me.

"Well, doctor," said he, "you're not afraid, anyhow."

"Afraid!" I answered. "Afraid of what?"

"Of it," said he, with a jerk of his thumb towards the black vault, "of the Terror that lives in the Blue John Cave."

How absurdly easy it is for a legend to arise in a lonely countryside! I examined him as to the reasons for his weird belief. It seems that from time to time sheep have been missing from the fields, carried bodily away, according to Armitage. That they could have wandered away of their own accord and disappeared among the mountains was an explanation to which he would not listen. On one occasion a pool of blood had been found, and some tufts of wool. That also, I pointed out, could be explained in a perfectly natural way. Further, the nights upon which sheep disappeared were invariably very dark, cloudy nights with no moon. This I met with the obvious retort that those were the nights which a commonplace sheep-stealer would naturally choose for his work. On one occasion a gap had been made in a wall, and some of the stones scattered for a considerable distance. Human agency again, in my opinion. Finally, Armitage clinched all his arguments by telling me that he had actually heard the Creature – indeed, that anyone could hear it who remained long enough at the Gap. It was a distant roaring of an immense volume. I could not but smile at this, knowing, as I do, the strange reverberations which come out of an underground water system running amid the chasms of a limestone formation. My incredulity annoyed Armitage so that he turned and left me with some abruptness.

And now comes the queer point about the whole business. I was still standing near the mouth of the cave turning over in my mind the various statements of Armitage, and reflecting how readily they could be explained away, when suddenly, from the depth of the tunnel beside me, there issued a most extraordinary sound. How shall I describe it? First of all, it seemed to be a great distance away, far down in the bowels of the earth. Secondly, in spite of this suggestion of distance, it was very loud. Lastly, it was not a boom, nor a crash, such as one would associate with falling water or tumbling rock, but it was a high whine, tremulous and vibrating, almost like the whinnying of a horse. It was certainly a most remarkable experience, and one which for a moment, I must admit, gave a new significance to Armitage's words. I waited by the Blue John Gap for half an hour or more, but there was no return of the sound, so at last I wandered back to the farmhouse, rather mystified by what had occurred. Decidedly I shall explore that cavern when my strength is restored. Of course, Armitage's explanation is too absurd for discussion, and yet that sound was certainly very strange. It still rings in my ears as I write.

20th April: In the last three days I have made several expeditions to the Blue John Gap, and have even penetrated some short distance, but my bicycle lantern is so small and weak that I dare not trust myself very far. I shall do the thing more systematically. I have heard no sound at all, and could almost believe that I had been the victim of some hallucination suggested, perhaps, by Armitage's conversation. Of course, the whole idea is absurd, and yet I must confess that those bushes at the entrance of the cave do present an appearance as if some heavy creature had forced its way through them. I begin to be keenly interested. I have said nothing to the Miss Allertons, for they are quite superstitious enough already, but I have bought some candles, and mean to investigate for myself.

I observed this morning that among the numerous tufts of sheep's wool which lay among the bushes near the cavern there was one which was smeared with blood. Of course, my reason tells me that if sheep wander into such rocky places they are likely to injure themselves, and yet somehow that splash of crimson gave me a sudden shock, and for a moment I found myself shrinking back in horror from the old Roman arch. A fetid breath seemed to ooze from the black depths into which I peered. Could it indeed be possible that some nameless thing, some dreadful presence, was lurking down yonder? I should have been incapable of such feelings in the days of my strength, but one grows more nervous and fanciful when one's health is shaken.

For the moment I weakened in my resolution, and was ready to leave the secret of the old mine, if one exists, for ever unsolved. But tonight my interest has returned and my nerves grown more steady. Tomorrow I trust that I shall have gone more deeply into this matter.

22nd April: Let me try and set down as accurately as I can my extraordinary experience of yesterday. I started in the afternoon, and made my way to the Blue John Gap. I confess that my misgivings returned as I gazed into its depths, and I wished that I had brought a companion to share my exploration. Finally, with a return of resolution, I lit my candle, pushed my way through the briars and descended into the rocky shaft.

It went down at an acute angle for some fifty feet, the floor being covered with broken stone. Thence there extended a long, straight passage cut in the solid rock. I am no geologist, but the lining of this corridor was certainly of some harder material than limestone, for there were points where I could actually see the tool marks which the old miners had left in their excavation, as fresh as if they had been done yesterday. Down this strange, old-world corridor I stumbled, my feeble flame throwing a dim circle of light around me, which made the shadows beyond the more threatening and obscure. Finally, I came to a spot where the Roman tunnel opened into a water-worn cavern – a huge hall, hung with long white icicles of lime deposit. From this central chamber I could dimly perceive that a number of passages worn by the subterranean streams wound away into the depths of the earth. I was standing there wondering whether I had better return, or whether I dare venture farther into this dangerous labyrinth, when my eyes fell upon something at my feet which strongly arrested my attention.

The greater part of the floor of the cavern was covered with boulders of rock or with hard incrustations of lime, but at this particular point there had been a drip from the distant roof, which had left a patch of soft mud. In the very centre of this there was a huge mark – an ill-defined blotch, deep, broad and irregular, as if a great boulder had fallen upon it. No loose stone lay near, however, nor was there anything to account for the impression. It was far too large to be caused by any possible animal, and besides, there was only the one, and the patch of mud was of such a size that no reasonable stride could have covered it. As I rose from the examination of that singular mark and then looked round into the black shadows which hemmed me in, I must confess that I felt for a moment a most unpleasant sinking of my heart, and that, do what I could, the candle trembled in my outstretched hand.

I soon recovered my nerve, however, when I reflected how absurd it was to associate so huge and shapeless a mark with the track of any known animal. Even an elephant could not have produced it. I determined, therefore, that I would not be scared by vague and senseless fears from carrying out my exploration. Before proceeding, I took good note of a curious rock formation in the wall by which I could recognize the entrance of the Roman tunnel. The precaution was very necessary, for the great cave, so far as I could see it, was intersected by passages. Having made sure of my position, and reassured myself by examining my spare candles and my matches, I advanced slowly over the rocky and uneven surface of the cavern.

And now I come to the point where I met with such sudden and desperate disaster. A stream, some twenty feet broad, ran across my path, and I walked for some little distance along the bank to find a spot where I could cross dry-shod. Finally, I came to a place where a single flat boulder lay near the centre, which I could reach in a stride. As it chanced, however, the rock had been cut away and made top-heavy by the rush of the stream, so that it tilted over as I landed on it and shot me into the ice-cold water. My candle went out, and I found myself floundering about in utter and absolute darkness.

I staggered to my feet again, more amused than alarmed by my adventure. The candle had fallen from my hand, and was lost in the stream, but I had two others in my pocket, so that it was of no importance. I got one of them ready, and drew out my box of matches to light it. Only then did I realize my position. The box had been soaked in my fall into the river. It was impossible to strike the matches.

A cold hand seemed to close round my heart as I realized my position. The darkness was opaque and horrible. It was so utter that one put one's hand up to one's face as if to press off something solid. I stood still, and by an effort I steadied myself. I tried to reconstruct in my mind a map of the floor of the cavern as I had last seen it. Alas! The bearings which had impressed themselves upon my mind were high on the wall, and not to be found by touch. Still, I remembered in a general way how the sides were situated, and I hoped that by groping my way along them I should at last come to the opening of the Roman tunnel. Moving very slowly, and continually striking against the rocks, I set out on this desperate quest.

But I very soon realized how impossible it was. In that black, velvety darkness one lost all one's bearings in an instant. Before I had made a dozen paces, I was utterly bewildered as to my whereabouts. The rippling of the stream, which was the one sound audible, showed me where it lay, but the moment that I left its bank I was utterly lost. The idea of finding my way back in absolute darkness through that limestone labyrinth was clearly an impossible one.

I sat down upon a boulder and reflected upon my unfortunate plight. I had not told anyone that I proposed to come to the Blue John mine, and it was unlikely that a search party would come after me. Therefore I must trust to my own resources to get clear of the danger. There was only one hope, and that was that the matches might dry. When I fell into the river, only half of me had got thoroughly wet. My left shoulder had remained above the water. I took the box of matches, therefore, and put it into my left armpit. The moist air of the cavern might possibly be counteracted by the heat of my body, but even so, I knew that I could not hope to get a light for many hours. Meanwhile there was nothing for it but to wait.

By good luck I had slipped several biscuits into my pocket before I left the farmhouse. These I now devoured, and washed them down with a draught from that wretched stream which had been the cause of all my misfortunes. Then I felt about for a comfortable seat among the rocks, and, having discovered a place where I could get a support for my back, I stretched out my legs and settled myself down to wait. I was wretchedly damp and cold, but I tried to cheer myself with the reflection that modern science prescribed open windows and walks in all weather for my disease. Gradually, lulled by the monotonous gurgle of the stream, and by the absolute darkness, I sank into an uneasy slumber.

How long this lasted I cannot say. It may have been for an hour, it may have been for several. Suddenly I sat up on my rock couch, with every nerve thrilling and every sense acutely on the alert. Beyond all doubt I had heard a sound – some sound very distinct from the gurgling of the waters. It had passed, but the reverberation of it still lingered in my ear. Was it a search party? They would most certainly have shouted, and vague as this sound was which had wakened me, it was very distinct from the human voice. I sat palpitating and hardly daring to breathe. There it was again! And again! Now it had become continuous. It was a tread – yes, surely it was the tread of some living creature. But what a tread it was! It gave one the impression of enormous weight carried upon sponge-like feet, which gave forth a muffled but ear-filling sound. The darkness was as complete as ever, but the tread was regular and decisive. And it was coming beyond all question in my direction.

My skin grew cold, and my hair stood on end as I listened to that steady and ponderous footfall. There was some creature there, and surely by the speed of its advance, it was one which could see in the dark. I crouched low on my rock and tried to blend myself into it. The steps grew nearer still, then stopped, and presently I was aware of a loud lapping and gurgling. The creature was drinking at the stream. Then again there was silence, broken by a succession of long sniffs and snorts of tremendous volume and energy. Had it caught the scent of me? My own nostrils were filled by a low fetid odour, mephitic and abominable. Then I heard the steps again. They were on my side of the stream now. The stones rattled within a few yards of where I lay. Hardly daring to breathe, I crouched upon my rock. Then the steps drew away. I heard the splash as it returned across the river, and the sound died away into the distance in the direction from which it had come.

For a long time I lay upon the rock, too much horrified to move. I thought of the sound which I had heard coming from the depths of the cave, of Armitage's fears, of the strange impression in the mud, and now came this final and absolute proof that there was indeed some inconceivable monster, something utterly unearthly and dreadful, which lurked in the hollow of the mountain. Of its nature or form I could frame no conception, save that it was both light-footed and gigantic. The combat between my reason, which told me that such things could not be, and my senses, which told me that they were, raged within me as I lay. Finally, I was almost ready to persuade myself that this experience had been part of some evil dream, and that my abnormal condition might have conjured up a hallucination. But there remained one final experience which removed the last possibility of doubt from my mind.

I had taken my matches from my armpit and felt them. They seemed perfectly hard and dry. Stooping down into a crevice of the rocks, I tried one of them. To my delight it took fire at once. I lit the candle, and, with a terrified backward glance into the obscure depths of the cavern, I hurried in the direction of the Roman passage. As I did so I passed the patch of mud on which I had seen the huge imprint. Now I stood astonished before it, for there were three similar imprints upon its surface, enormous in size, irregular in outline, of a depth which indicated the ponderous weight which had left them. Then a great terror surged over me. Stooping and shading my candle with my hand, I ran in a frenzy of fear to the rocky archway, hastened up it, and never stopped until, with weary feet and panting lungs, I rushed up the final slope of stones, broke through the tangle of briars and flung myself exhausted upon the soft grass under the peaceful light of the stars. It was three in the morning when I reached the farmhouse, and today I am all unstrung and quivering after my terrific adventure. As yet I have told no one. I must move warily in the matter. What would the poor lonely women, or the uneducated yokels here think of it if I were to tell them my experience? Let me go to someone who can understand and advise.

25th April: I was laid up in bed for two days after my incredible adventure in the cavern. I use the adjective with a very definite meaning, for I have had an experience since which has shocked me almost as much as the other. I have said that I was looking round for someone who could advise me. There is a Dr Mark Johnson who practises some few miles away, to whom I had a note of recommendation from Professor Saunderson. To him I drove, when I was strong enough to get about, and I recounted to him my whole strange experience. He listened intently, and then carefully examined me, paying special attention to my reflexes and to the pupils of my eyes. When he had finished, he refused to discuss my adventure, saying that it was entirely beyond him, but he gave me the card of a Mr Picton at Castleton, with the advice that I should instantly go to him and tell him the story exactly as I had done to himself. He was, according to my adviser, the very man who was pre-eminently suited to help me. I went on to the station, therefore, and made my way to the little town, which is some ten miles away. Mr Picton appeared to be a man of importance, as his brass plate was displayed upon the door of a considerable building on the outskirts of the town. I was about to ring his bell, when some misgiving came into my mind and, crossing to a neighbouring shop, I asked the man behind the counter if he could tell me anything of Mr Picton. "Why," said he, "he is the best mad doctor in Derbyshire, and yonder is his asylum." You can imagine that it was not long before I had shaken the dust of Castleton from my feet and returned to the farm, cursing all unimaginative pedants who cannot conceive that there may be things in creation which have never yet chanced to come across their mole's vision. After all, now that I am cooler, I can afford to admit that I have been no more sympathetic to Armitage than Dr Johnson has been to me.

27th April: When I was a student I had the reputation of being a man of courage and enterprise. I remember that when there was a ghost hunt at Coltbridge it was I who sat up in the haunted house. Is it advancing years (after all, I am only thirty-five), or is it this physical malady which has caused degeneration? Certainly my heart quails when I think of that horrible cavern in the hill, and the certainty that it has some monstrous occupant. What shall I do? There is not an hour in the day that I do not debate the question. If I say nothing, then the mystery remains unsolved. If I do say anything, then I have the alternative of mad alarm over the whole countryside, or of absolute incredulity which may end in consigning me to an asylum. On the whole, I think that my best course is to wait, and to prepare for some expedition which shall be more deliberate and better thought out than the last. As a first step I have been to Castleton and obtained a few essentials – a large acetylene lantern for one thing, and a good double-barrelled sporting rifle for another. The latter I have hired, but I have bought a dozen heavy game cartridges, which would bring down a rhinoceros. Now I am ready for my troglodyte friend. Give me better health and a little spate of energy, and I shall try conclusions with him yet. But who and what is he? Ah, there is the question which stands between me and my sleep! How many theories do I form, only to discard each in turn! It is all so utterly unthinkable. And yet the cry, the footmark, the tread in the cavern – no reasoning can get past these. I think of the old-world legends of dragons and of other monsters. Were they, perhaps, not such fairy tales as we have thought? Can it be that there is some fact which underlies them, and am I, of all mortals, the one who is chosen to expose it?

3rd May: For several days I have been laid up by the vagaries of an English spring, and during those days there have been developments, the true and sinister meaning of which no one can appreciate save myself. I may say that we have had cloudy and moonless nights of late, which according to my information were the seasons upon which sheep disappeared. Well, sheep *have* disappeared. Two of Miss Allerton's, one of old Pearson's of the Cat Walk and one of Mrs Moulton's. Four in all during three nights. No trace is left of them at all, and the countryside is buzzing with rumours of gypsies and of sheep-stealers.

But there is something more serious than that. Young Armitage has disappeared also. He left his moorland cottage early on Wednesday night and has never been heard of since. He was an unattached man, so there is less sensation than would otherwise be the case. The popular explanation is that he owes money, and has found a situation in some other part of the country, whence he will presently write for his belongings. But I have grave misgivings. Is it not much more likely that the recent tragedy of the sheep has caused him to take some steps which may have ended in his own destruction? He may, for example, have lain in wait for the creature and been carried off by it into the recesses of the mountains. What an inconceivable fate for a civilized Englishman of the twentieth century! And yet I feel that it is possible and even probable. But in that case, how far am I answerable both for his death and for any other mishap which may occur? Surely with the knowledge I already possess it must be my duty to see that something is done, or if necessary to do it myself. It must be the latter, for this morning I went down to the local police station and told my story. The inspector entered it all in a large book and bowed me out with commendable gravity, but I heard a burst of laughter before I had got down his garden path. No doubt he was recounting my adventure to his family.

10th June: I am writing this, propped up in bed, six weeks after my last entry in this journal. I have gone through a terrible shock both to mind and body, arising from such an experience as has seldom befallen a human being before. But I have attained my end. The danger from the Terror which dwells in the Blue John Gap has passed, never to return. Thus much at least I, a broken invalid, have done for the common good. Let me now recount what occurred as clearly as I may.

The night of Friday, 3rd May, was dark and cloudy – the very night for the monster to walk. About eleven o'clock I went from the farmhouse with my lantern and my rifle, having first left a note upon the table of my bedroom in which I said that, if I were missing, search should be made for me in the direction of the Gap. I made my way to the mouth of the Roman shaft and, having perched myself among the rocks close to the opening, I shut off my lantern and waited patiently with my loaded rifle ready to my hand.

It was a melancholy vigil. All down the winding valley I could see the scattered lights of the farmhouses, and the church clock of Chapel-le-Dale tolling the hours came faintly to my ears. These tokens of my fellow men served only to make my own position seem the more lonely, and to call for a greater effort to overcome the terror which tempted me continually to get back to the farm and abandon for ever this dangerous quest. And yet there lies deep in every man a rooted self-respect which makes it hard for him to turn back from that which he has once undertaken. This feeling of personal pride was my salvation now, and it was that alone which held me fast when every instinct of my nature was dragging me away. I am glad now that I had the strength. In spite of all that it has cost me, my manhood is at least above reproach.

Twelve o'clock struck in the distant church, then one, then two. It was the darkest hour of the night. The clouds were drifting low, and there was not a star in the sky. An owl was hooting somewhere among the rocks, but no other sound, save the gentle sough of the wind, came to my ears. And then suddenly I heard it! From far away down the tunnel came those muffled steps, so soft and yet so ponderous. I heard also the rattle of stones as they gave way under that giant tread. They drew nearer. They were close upon me. I heard the crashing of the bushes round the entrance, and then dimly through the darkness I was conscious of the loom of some enormous shape, some monstrous inchoate creature, passing swiftly and very silently out from the tunnel. I was paralysed with fear and amazement. Long as I had waited, now that it had actually come I was unprepared for the shock. I lay motionless and breathless, whilst the great dark mass whisked by me and was swallowed up in the night.

But now I nerved myself for its return. No sound came from the sleeping countryside to tell of the horror which was loose. In no way could I judge how far off it was, what it was doing or when it might be back. But not a second time should my nerve fail me, not a second time should it pass unchallenged. I swore it between my clenched teeth as I laid my cocked rifle across the rock.

And yet it nearly happened. There was no warning of approach now as the creature passed over the grass. Suddenly, like a dark, drifting shadow, the huge bulk loomed up once more before me, making for the entrance of the cave. Again came that paralysis of volition which held my crooked forefinger impotent upon the trigger. But with a desperate effort I shook it off. Even as the brushwood rustled, and the monstrous beast blended with the shadow of the Gap, I fired at the retreating form. In the blaze of the gun I caught a glimpse of a great shaggy mass, something with rough and bristling hair of a withered grey colour, fading away to white in its lower parts, the huge body supported upon short, thick, curving legs. I had just that glance, and then I heard the rattle of the stones as the creature tore down into its burrow. In an instant, with a triumphant revulsion of feeling, I had cast my fears to the wind, and uncovering my powerful lantern, with my rifle in my hand, I sprang down from my rock and rushed after the monster down the old Roman shaft.

My splendid lamp cast a brilliant flood of vivid light in front of me, very different from the yellow glimmer which had aided me down the same passage only twelve days before. As I ran, I saw the great beast lurching along before me, its huge bulk filling up the whole space from wall to wall. Its hair looked like coarse faded oakum, and hung down in long, dense masses which swayed as it moved. It was like an enormous unclipped sheep in its fleece, but in size it was far larger than the largest elephant, and its breadth seemed to be nearly as great as its height. It fills me with amazement now to think that I should have dared to follow such a horror into the bowels of the earth, but when one's blood is up, and when one's quarry seems to be flying, the old primeval hunting spirit awakes and prudence is cast to the wind. Rifle in hand, I ran at the top of my speed upon the trail of the monster.

I had seen that the creature was swift. Now I was to find out to my cost that it was also very cunning. I had imagined that it was in panic flight and that I had only to pursue it. The idea that it might turn upon me never entered my excited brain. I have already explained that the passage down which I was racing opened into a great central cave. Into this I rushed, fearful lest I should lose all trace of the beast. But he had turned upon his own traces, and in a moment we were face to face.

That picture, seen in the brilliant white light of the lantern, etched for ever upon my brain. He had reared up on his hind legs as a bear would do, and stood above me, enormous, menacing – such a creature as no nightmare had ever brought to my imagination. I have said that he reared like a bear, and there was something bear-like – if one could conceive a bear which was tenfold the bulk of any bear seen upon earth – in his whole pose and attitude, in his great crooked forelegs with their ivory-white claws, in his rugged skin and in his red, gaping mouth, fringed with monstrous fangs. Only in one point did he differ from the bear, or from any other creature which walks the earth, and even at that supreme moment a shudder of horror passed over me as I observed that the eyes which glistened in the glow of my lantern were huge, projecting bulbs, white and sightless. For a moment his great paws swung over my head. The next he fell forward upon me, I and my broken lantern crashed to the earth, and I remember no more.

When I came to myself I was back in the farmhouse of the Allertons. Two days had passed since my terrible adventure in the Blue John Gap. It seems that I had lain all night in the cave insensible from concussion of the brain, with my left arm and two ribs badly fractured. In the morning my note had been found, a search party of a dozen farmers assembled, and I had been tracked down and carried back to my bedroom, where I had lain in high delirium ever since. There was, it seems, no sign of the creature, and no bloodstain which would show that my bullet had found him as he passed. Save for my own plight and the marks upon the mud, there was nothing to prove that what I said was true.

Six weeks have now elapsed, and I am able to sit out once more in the sunshine. Just opposite me is the steep hillside, grey with shaly rock, and yonder on its flank is the dark cleft which marks the opening of the Blue John Gap. But it is no longer a source of terror. Never again through that ill-omened tunnel shall any strange shape flit out into the world of men. The educated and the scientific, the Dr Johnsons and the like, may smile at my narrative, but the poorer folk of the countryside had never a doubt as to its truth. On the day after my recovering consciousness they assembled in their hundreds round the Blue John Gap. As the *Castleton Courier* said:

> It was useless for our correspondent, or for any of the adventurous gentlemen who had come from Matlock, Buxton and other parts to offer to descend, to explore the cave to the end, and to finally test the extraordinary narrative of Dr James Hardcastle. The country people had taken the matter into their own hands, and from an early hour of the morning they had worked hard in stopping up the entrance of the tunnel. There is a sharp slope where the shaft begins, and great boulders, rolled along by many willing hands, were thrust down it until the Gap was absolutely sealed. So ends the episode which has caused such excitement throughout the country. Local opinion is fiercely divided upon the subject. On the one hand are those who point to Dr Hardcastle's impaired health, and to the possibility of cerebral lesions of tubercular origin giving rise to strange hallucinations. Some *idée fixe*, according to these gentlemen, caused the doctor to wander down the tunnel, and a fall among the rocks was sufficient to account for his injuries. On the other hand, a legend of a strange creature in the Gap has existed for some months back, and the farmers look upon Dr Hardcastle's narrative and his personal injuries as a final corroboration. So the matter stands, and so the matter will continue to stand, for no definite solution seems to us to be now possible. It transcends human wit to give any scientific explanation which could cover the alleged facts.

Perhaps before the *Courier* published these words they would have been wise to send their representative to me. I have thought the matter out, as no one else has occasion to do, and it is possible that I might have removed some of the more obvious difficulties of the narrative and brought it one degree nearer to scientific acceptance. Let me then write down the only explanation which seems to me to elucidate what I know to my cost to have been a series of facts. My theory may seem to be wildly improbable, but at least no one can venture to say that it is impossible.

My view is – and it was formed, as is shown by my diary, before my personal adventure – that in this part of England there is a vast subterranean lake or sea, which is fed by the great number of streams which pass down through the limestone. Where there is a large collection of water there must also be some evaporation, mists or rain, and a possibility of vegetation. This in turn suggests that there may be animal life, arising, as the vegetable life would also do, from those seeds and types which had been introduced at an early period of the world's history, when communication with the outer air was more easy. This place had then developed a fauna and flora of its own, including such monsters as the one which I had seen, which may well have been the old cave bear, enormously enlarged and modified by its new environment. For countless aeons the internal and the external creation had kept apart, growing steadily away from each other. Then there had come some rift in the depths of the mountain which had enabled one creature to wander up and, by means of the Roman tunnel, to reach the open air. Like all subterranean life, it had lost the power of sight, but this had no doubt been compensated for by nature in other directions. Certainly it had some means of finding its way about, and of hunting down the sheep upon the hillside. As to its choice of dark nights, it is part of my theory that light was painful to those great white eyeballs, and that it was only a pitch-black world which it could tolerate. Perhaps, indeed, it was the glare of my lantern which saved my life at that awful moment when we were face to face. So I read the riddle. I leave these facts behind me, and if you can explain them, do so; or if you choose to doubt them, do so. Neither your belief nor your incredulity can alter them, nor affect one whose task is nearly over.

So ended the strange narrative of Dr James Hardcastle.

The Brazilian Cat

It is hard luck on a young fellow to have expensive tastes, great expectations, aristocratic connections but no actual money in his pocket, and no profession by which he may earn any. The fact was that my father, a good, sanguine, easy-going man, had such confidence in the wealth and benevolence of his bachelor elder brother, Lord Southerton, that he took it for granted that I, his only son, would never be called upon to earn a living for myself. He imagined that if there were not a vacancy for me on the great Southerton estates, at least there would be found some post in that diplomatic service which still remains the special preserve of our privileged classes. He died too early to realize how false his calculations had been. Neither my uncle nor the state took the slightest notice of me, or showed any interest in my career. An occasional brace of pheasants, or basket of hares, was all that ever reached me to remind me that I was heir to Otwell House and one of the richest estates in the country. In the meantime, I found myself a bachelor and man about town, living in a suite of apartments in Grosvenor Mansions, with no occupation save that of pigeon-shooting and polo-playing at Hurlingham. Month by month I realized that it was more and more difficult to get the brokers to renew my bills, or to cash any further post-obits upon an unentailed property. Ruin lay right across my path, and every day I saw it clearer, nearer and more absolutely unavoidable.

What made me feel my own poverty the more was that, apart from the great wealth of Lord Southerton, all my other relations were fairly well-to-do. The nearest of these was Everard King, my father's nephew and my own first cousin, who had spent an adventurous life in Brazil, and had now returned to his country to settle down on his fortune. We never knew how he made his money, but he appeared to have plenty of it, for he bought the estate of Greylands, near Clipton-on-the-Marsh, in Suffolk. For the first year of his residence in England he took no more notice of me than my miserly uncle; but at last, one summer morning, to my very great relief and joy, I received a letter asking me to come down that very day and spend a short visit at Greylands Court. I was expecting a rather long visit to Bankruptcy Court at the time, and this interruption seemed almost providential. If I could only get on terms with this unknown relative of mine, I might pull through yet. For the family credit he could not let me go entirely to the wall. I ordered my valet to pack my valise, and I set off the same evening for Clipton-on-the-Marsh.

After changing at Ipswich, a little local train deposited me at a small, deserted station lying amidst a rolling grassy country with a sluggish and winding river curving in and out amidst the valleys, between high, silted banks, which showed that we were within reach of the tide. No carriage was awaiting me (I found afterwards that my telegram had been delayed), so I hired a dog cart at the local inn. The driver, an excellent fellow, was full of my relative's praises, and I learnt from him that Mr Everard King was already a name to conjure with in that part of the country. He had entertained the schoolchildren, he had thrown his grounds open to visitors, he had subscribed to charities – in short, his benevolence had been so universal that my driver could only account for it on the supposition that he had parliamentary ambitions.

My attention was drawn away from my driver's panegyric by the appearance of a very beautiful bird which settled on a telegraph post beside the road. At first I thought that it was a jay, but it was larger, with a brighter plumage. The driver accounted for its presence at once by saying that it belonged to the very man whom we were about to visit. It seems that the acclimatization of foreign creatures was one of his hobbies, and that he had brought with him from Brazil a number of birds and beasts which he was endeavouring to rear in England. When once we had passed the gates of Greylands Park we had ample evidence of this taste of his. Some small spotted deer, a curious wild pig known, I believe, as a peccary, a gorgeously feathered oriole, some sort of armadillo and a singular lumbering intoed* beast like a very fat badger, were among the creatures which I observed as we drove along the winding avenue.

Mr Everard King, my unknown cousin, was standing in person upon the steps of his house, for he had seen us in the distance and guessed that it was I. His appearance was very homely and benevolent, short and stout, forty-five years old, perhaps, with a round, good-humoured face, burnt brown with the tropical sun, and shot with a thousand wrinkles. He wore white linen clothes, in true planter style, with a cigar between his lips, and a large panama hat upon the back of his head. It was such a figure as one associates with a verandaed bungalow, and it looked curiously out of place in front of this broad, stone English mansion, with its solid wings and its Palladio pillars* before the doorway.

"My dear!" he cried, glancing over his shoulder. "My dear, here is our guest! Welcome, welcome to Greylands! I am delighted to make your acquaintance, Cousin Marshall, and I take it as a great compliment that you should honour this sleepy little country place with your presence."

Nothing could be more hearty than his manner, and he set me at my ease in an instant. But it needed all his cordiality to atone for the frigidity and even rudeness of his wife, a tall, haggard woman, who came forward at his summons. She was, I believe, of Brazilian extraction, though she spoke excellent English, and I excused her manners on the score of her ignorance of our customs. She did not attempt to conceal, however, either then or afterwards, that I was no very welcome visitor at Greylands Court. Her actual words were, as a rule, courteous, but she was the possessor of a pair of particularly expressive dark eyes, and I read in them very clearly from the first that she heartily wished me back in London once more.

However, my debts were too pressing and my designs upon my wealthy relative were too vital for me to allow them to be upset by the ill temper of his wife, so I disregarded her coldness and reciprocated the extreme cordiality of his welcome. No pains had been spared by him to make me comfortable. My room was a charming one. He implored me to tell him anything which could add to my happiness. It was on the tip of my tongue to inform him that a blank cheque would materially help towards that end, but I felt that it might be premature in the present state of our acquaintance. The dinner was excellent, and as we sat together afterwards over his Havanas and coffee, which latter he told me was specially prepared upon his own plantation, it seemed to me that all my driver's eulogies were justified, and that I had never met a more large-hearted and hospitable man.

But, in spite of his cheery good nature, he was a man with a strong will and a fiery temper of his own. Of this I had an example upon the following morning. The curious aversion which Mrs Everard King had conceived towards me was so strong that her manner at breakfast was almost offensive. But her meaning became unmistakable when her husband had quitted the room.

"The best train in the day is at twelve fifteen," said she.

"But I was not thinking of going today," I answered, frankly – perhaps even defiantly, for I was determined not to be driven out by this woman.

"Oh, if it rests with you..." said she, and stopped with a most insolent expression in her eyes.

"I am sure," I answered, "that Mr Everard King would tell me if I were outstaying my welcome."

"What's this? What's this?" said a voice, and there he was in the room. He had overheard my last words, and a glance at our faces had told him the rest. In an instant his chubby, cheery face set into an expression of absolute ferocity.

"Might I trouble you to walk outside, Marshall?" said he. (I may mention that my own name is Marshall King.)

He closed the door behind me, and then, for an instant, I heard him talking in a low voice of concentrated passion to his wife. This gross breach of hospitality had evidently hit upon his tenderest point. I am no eavesdropper, so I walked out onto the lawn. Presently I heard a hurried step behind me, and there was the lady, her face pale with excitement, and her eyes red with tears.

"My husband has asked me to apologize to you, Mr Marshall King," said she, standing with downcast eyes before me.

"Please do not say another word, Mrs King."

Her dark eyes suddenly blazed out at me.

"You fool!" she hissed, with frantic vehemence, and turning on her heel swept back to the house.

The insult was so outrageous, so insufferable, that I could only stand staring after her in bewilderment. I was still there when my host joined me. He was his cheery, chubby self once more.

"I hope that my wife has apologized for her foolish remarks," said he.

"Oh, yes – yes, certainly!"

He put his hand through my arm and walked with me up and down the lawn.

"You must not take it seriously," said he. "It would grieve me inexpressibly if you curtailed your visit by one hour. The fact is – there is no reason why there should be any concealment between relatives – that my poor dear wife is incredibly jealous. She hates that anyone – male or female – should for an instant come between us. Her ideal is a desert island and an eternal tête-à-tête. That gives you the clue to her actions, which are, I confess, upon this particular point, not very far removed from mania. Tell me that you will think no more of it."

"No, no, certainly not."

"Then light this cigar and come round with me and see my little menagerie."

The whole afternoon was occupied by this inspection, which included all the birds, beasts and even reptiles which he had imported. Some were free, some in cages, a few actually in the house. He spoke with enthusiasm of his successes and his failures, his births and his deaths, and he would cry out in his delight, like a schoolboy, when, as we walked, some gaudy bird would flutter up from the grass or some curious beast slink into the cover. Finally he led me down a corridor which extended from one wing of the house. At the end of this there was a heavy door with a sliding shutter in it, and beside it there projected from the wall an iron handle attached to a wheel and a drum. A line of stout bars extended across the passage.

"I am about to show you the jewel of my collection," said he. "There is only one other specimen in Europe, now that the Rotterdam cub is dead. It is a Brazilian cat."

"But how does that differ from any other cat?"

"You will soon see that," said he, laughing. "Will you kindly draw that shutter and look through?"

I did so, and found that I was gazing into a large, empty room, with stone flags and small, barred windows upon the farther wall. In the centre of this room, lying in the middle of a golden patch of sunlight, there was stretched a huge creature, as large as a tiger, but as black and sleek as ebony. It was simply a very enormous and very well-kept black cat, and it cuddled up and basked in that yellow pool of light exactly as a cat would do. It was so graceful, so sinewy and so gently and smoothly diabolical that I could not take my eyes from the opening.

"Isn't he splendid?" said my host enthusiastically.

"Glorious! I never saw such a noble creature."

"Some people call it a black puma, but really it is not a puma at all. That fellow is nearly eleven feet from tail to tip. Four years ago he was a little ball of black fluff, with two yellow eyes staring out of it. He was sold me as a newborn cub up in the wild country at the headwaters of the Rio Negro.* They speared his mother to death after she had killed a dozen of them."

"They are ferocious, then?"

"The most absolutely treacherous and bloodthirsty creatures upon earth. You talk about a Brazilian cat to an upcountry Indian and see him get the jumps. They prefer humans to game. This fellow has never tasted living blood yet, but when he does he will be a terror. At present he won't stand anyone but me in his den. Even Baldwin, the groom, dare not go near him. As to me, I am his mother and father in one."

As he spoke he suddenly, to my astonishment, opened the door and slipped in, closing it instantly behind him. At the sound of his voice the huge, lithe creature rose, yawned and rubbed its round, black head affectionately against his side, while he patted and fondled it.

"Now, Tommy, into your cage!" said he.

The monstrous cat walked over to one side of the room and coiled itself up under a grating. Everard King came out and, taking the iron handle which I have mentioned, he began to turn it. As he did so the line of bars in the corridor began to pass through a slot in the wall and closed up the front of this grating, so as to make an effective cage. When it was in position he opened the door once more and invited me into the room, which was heavy with the pungent, musty smell peculiar to the great Carnivora.

"That's how we work it," said he. "We give him the run of the room for exercise, and then at night we put him in his cage. You can let him out by turning the handle from the passage, or you can, as you have seen, coop him up in the same way. No, no, you should not do that!"

I had put my hand between the bars to pat the glossy, heaving flank. He pulled it back, with a serious face.

"I assure you that he is not safe. Don't imagine that because I can take liberties with him anyone else can. He is very exclusive in his friends – aren't you, Tommy? Ah, he hears his lunch coming to him! Don't you, boy?"

A step sounded in the stone-flagged passage, and the creature had sprung to his feet, and was pacing up and down the narrow cage, his yellow eyes gleaming, and his scarlet tongue rippling and quivering over the white line of his jagged teeth. A groom entered with a coarse joint upon a tray, and thrust it through the bars to him. He pounced lightly upon it, carried it off to the corner, and there, holding it between his paws, tore and wrenched at it, raising his bloody muzzle every now and then to look at us. It was a malignant and yet fascinating sight.

"You can't wonder that I am fond of him, can you?" said my host, as we left the room, "especially when you consider that I have had the rearing of him. It was no joke bringing him over from the centre of South America; but here he is safe and sound – and, as I have said, far the most perfect specimen in Europe. The people at the zoo are dying to have him, but I really can't part with him. Now, I think that I have inflicted my hobby upon you long enough, so we cannot do better than follow Tommy's example and go to our lunch."

My South American relative was so engrossed by his grounds and their curious occupants that I hardly gave him credit at first for having any interests outside them. That he had some, and pressing ones, was soon borne in upon me by the number of telegrams which he received. They arrived at all hours, and were always opened by him with the utmost eagerness and anxiety upon his face. Sometimes I imagined that it must be the turf,* and sometimes the Stock Exchange, but certainly he had some very urgent business going forwards which was not transacted upon the Downs of Suffolk. During the six days of my visit he had never fewer than three or four telegrams a day, and sometimes as many as seven or eight.

I had occupied these six days so well that by the end of them I had succeeded in getting upon the most cordial terms with my cousin. Every night we had sat up late in the billiard room, he telling me the most extraordinary stories of his adventures in America – stories so desperate and reckless that I could hardly associate them with the brown little chubby man before me. In return, I ventured upon some of my own reminiscences of London life, which interested him so much that he vowed he would come up to Grosvenor Mansions and stay with me. He was anxious to see the faster side of city life, and certainly, though I say it, he could not have chosen a more competent guide. It was not until the last day of my visit that I ventured to approach that which was on my mind. I told him frankly about my pecuniary difficulties and my impending ruin, and I asked his advice – though I hoped for something more solid. He listened attentively, puffing hard at his cigar.

"But surely," said he, "you are the heir of our relative, Lord Southerton?"

"I have every reason to believe so, but he would never make me any allowance."

"No, no, I have heard of his miserly ways. My poor Marshall, your position has been a very hard one. By the way, have you heard any news of Lord Southerton's health lately?"

"He has always been in a critical condition ever since my childhood."

"Exactly – a creaking hinge if ever there was one. Your inheritance may be a long way off. Dear me, how awkwardly situated you are!"

"I had some hopes, sir, that you, knowing all the facts, might be inclined to advance—"

"Don't say another word, my dear boy," he cried, with the utmost cordiality. "We shall talk it over tonight, and I give you my word that whatever is in my power shall be done."

I was not sorry that my visit was drawing to a close, for it is unpleasant to feel that there is one person in the house who eagerly desires your departure. Mrs King's sallow face and forbidding eyes had become more and more hateful to me. She was no longer actively rude – her fear of her husband prevented her – but she pushed her insane jealousy to the extent of ignoring me, never addressing me, and in every way making my stay at Greylands as uncomfortable as she could. So offensive was her manner during that last day that I should certainly have left had it not been for that interview with my host in the evening which would, I hoped, retrieve my broken fortunes.

It was very late when it occurred, for my relative, who had been receiving even more telegrams than usual during the day, went off to his study after dinner, and only emerged when the household had retired to bed. I heard him go round locking the doors, as his custom was of a night, and finally he joined me in the billiard room. His stout figure was wrapped in a dressing gown, and he wore a pair of red Turkish slippers without any heels. Settling down into an armchair, he brewed himself a glass of grog, in which I could not help noticing that the whisky considerably predominated over the water.

"My word!" said he. "What a night!"

It was, indeed. The wind was howling and screaming round the house, and the latticed windows rattled and shook as if they were coming in. The glow of the yellow lamps and the flavour of our cigars seemed the brighter and more fragrant for the contrast.

"Now, my boy," said my host, "we have the house and the night to ourselves. Let me have an idea of how your affairs stand, and I will see what can be done to set them in order. I wish to hear every detail."

Thus encouraged, I entered into a long exposition, in which all my tradesmen and creditors, from my landlord to my valet, figured in turn. I had notes in my pocketbook, and I marshalled my facts and gave, I flatter myself, a very businesslike statement of my own unbusinesslike ways and lamentable position. I was depressed, however, to notice that my companion's eyes were vacant and his attention elsewhere. When he did occasionally throw out a remark it was so entirely perfunctory and pointless that I was sure he had not in the least followed my remarks. Every now and then he roused himself and put on some show of interest, asking me to repeat or to explain more fully, but it was always to sink once more into the same brown study. At last he rose and threw the end of his cigar into the grate.

"I'll tell you what, my boy," said he. "I never had a head for figures, so you will excuse me. You must jot it all down upon paper, and let me have a note of the amount. I'll understand it when I see it in black and white."

The proposal was encouraging. I promised to do so.

"And now it's time we were in bed. By Jove, there's one o'clock striking in the hall."

The tingling of the chiming clock broke through the deep roar of the gale. The wind was sweeping past with the rush of a great river.

"I must see my cat before I go to bed," said my host. "A high wind excites him. Will you come?"

"Certainly," said I.

"Then tread softly and don't speak, for everyone is asleep."

We passed quietly down the lamplit Persian-rugged hall, and through the door at the farther end. All was dark in the stone corridor, but a stable lantern hung on a hook, and my host took it down and lit it. There was no grating visible in the passage, so I knew that the beast was in its cage.

"Come in!" said my relative, and opened the door.

A deep growling as we entered showed that the storm had really excited the creature. In the flickering light of the lantern we saw it, a huge black mass coiled in the corner of its den and throwing a squat, uncouth shadow upon the whitewashed wall. Its tail switched angrily among the straw.

"Poor Tommy is not in the best of tempers," said Everard King, holding up the lantern and looking in at him. "What a black devil he looks, doesn't he? I must give him a little supper to put him in a better humour. Would you mind holding the lantern for a moment?"

I took it from his hand and he stepped to the door.

"His larder is just outside here," said he. "You will excuse me for an instant, won't you?" He passed out, and the door shut with a sharp metallic click behind him.

That hard crisp sound made my heart stand still. A sudden wave of terror passed over me. A vague perception of some monstrous treachery turned me cold. I sprang to the door, but there was no handle upon the inner side.

"Here!" I cried. "Let me out!"

"All right! Don't make a row!" said my host from the passage. "You've got the light all right."

"Yes, but I don't care about being locked in alone like this."

"Don't you?" I heard his hearty, chuckling laugh. "You won't be alone long."

"Let me out, sir!" I repeated angrily. "I tell you I don't allow practical jokes of this sort."

"Practical is the word," said he, with another hateful chuckle. And then suddenly I heard, amidst the roar of the storm, the creak and whine of the winch handle turning, and the rattle of the grating as it passed through the slot. Great God, he was letting loose the Brazilian cat!

In the light of the lantern I saw the bars sliding slowly before me. Already there was an opening a foot wide at the farther end. With a scream I seized the last bar with my hands and pulled with the strength of a madman.

I *was* a madman with rage and horror. For a minute or more I held the thing motionless. I knew that he was straining with all his force upon the handle, and that the leverage was sure to overcome me. I gave inch by inch, my feet sliding along the stones, and all the time I begged and prayed this inhuman monster to save me from this horrible death. I conjured him by his kinship. I reminded him that I was his guest; I begged to know what harm I had ever done him. His only answers were the tugs and jerks upon the handle, each of which, in spite of all my struggles, pulled another bar through the opening. Clinging and clutching, I was dragged across the whole front of the cage, until at last, with aching wrists and lacerated fingers, I gave up the hopeless struggle. The grating clanged back as I released it, and an instant later I heard the shuffle of the Turkish slippers in the passage, and the slam of the distant door. Then everything was silent.

The creature had never moved during this time. He lay still in the corner, and his tail had ceased switching. This apparition of a man adhering to his bars and dragged screaming across him had apparently filled him with amazement. I saw his great eyes staring steadily at me. I had dropped the lantern when I seized the bars, but it still burned upon the floor, and I made a movement to grasp it, with some idea that its light might protect me. But the instant I moved, the beast gave a deep and menacing growl. I stopped and stood still, quivering with fear in every limb. The cat (if one may call so fearful a creature by so homely a name) was not more than ten feet from me. The eyes glimmered like two discs of phosphorus in the darkness. They appalled and yet fascinated me. I could not take my own eyes from them. Nature plays strange tricks with us at such moments of intensity, and those glimmering lights waxed and waned with a steady rise and fall. Sometimes they seemed to be tiny points of extreme brilliancy – little electric sparks in the black obscurity – then they would widen and widen until all that corner of the room was filled with their shifting and sinister light. And then suddenly they went out altogether.

The beast had closed its eyes. I do not know whether there may be any truth in the old idea of the dominance of the human gaze, or whether the huge cat was simply drowsy, but the fact remains that, far from showing any symptom of attacking me, it simply rested its sleek, black head upon its huge forepaws and seemed to sleep. I stood, fearing to move lest I should rouse it into malignant life once more. But at least I was able to think clearly now that the baleful eyes were off me. Here I was shut up for the night with the ferocious beast. My own instincts, to say nothing of the words of the plausible villain who laid this trap for me, warned me that the animal was as savage as its master. How could I stave it off until morning? The door was hopeless, and so were the narrow, barred windows. There was no shelter anywhere in the bare, stone-flagged room. To cry for assistance was absurd. I knew that this den was an outhouse, and that the corridor which connected it with the house was at least a hundred feet long. Besides, with that gale thundering outside, my cries were not likely to be heard. I had only my own courage and my own wits to trust to.

And then, with a fresh wave of horror, my eyes fell upon the lantern. The candle had burnt low, and was already beginning to gutter. In ten minutes it would be out. I had only ten minutes then in which to do something, for I felt that if I were once left in the dark with that fearful beast I should be incapable of action. The very thought of it paralysed me. I cast my despairing eyes round this chamber of death, and they rested upon one spot which seemed to promise, I will not say safety, but less immediate and imminent danger than the open floor.

I have said that the cage had a top as well as a front, and this top was left standing when the front was wound through the slot in the wall. It consisted of bars at a few inches' interval, with stout wire netting between, and it rested upon a strong stanchion at each end. It stood now as a great barred canopy over the crouching figure in the corner. The space between this iron shelf and the roof may have been from two to three feet. If I could only get up there, squeezed in between bars and ceiling, I should have only one vulnerable side. I should be safe from below, from behind, and from each side. Only on the open face of it could I be attacked. There, it is true, I had no protection whatever; but at least I should be out of the brute's path when he began to pace about his den. He would have to come out of his way to reach me. It was now or never, for if once the light were out it would be impossible. With a gulp in my throat I sprang up, seized the iron edge of the top, and swung myself panting onto it. I writhed in face downwards, and found myself looking straight into the terrible eyes and yawning jaws of the cat. Its fetid breath came up into my face like the steam from some foul pot.

It appeared, however, to be rather curious than angry. With a sleek ripple of its long, black back it rose, stretched itself, and then, rearing itself on its hind legs, with one forepaw against the wall, it raised the other and drew its claws across the wire meshes beneath me. One sharp, white hook tore through my trousers – for I may mention that I was still in evening dress – and dug a furrow in my knee. It was not meant as an attack, but rather as an experiment, for upon my giving a sharp cry of pain he dropped down again and, springing lightly into the room, he began walking swiftly round it, looking up every now and again in my direction. For my part I shuffled backwards until I lay with my back against the wall, screwing myself into the smallest space possible. The farther I got the more difficult it was for him to attack me.

He seemed more excited now that he had begun to move about, and he ran swiftly and noiselessly round and round the den, passing continually underneath the iron couch upon which I lay. It was wonderful to see so great a bulk passing like a shadow, with hardly the softest thudding of velvety pads. The candle was burning low – so low that I could hardly see the creature. And then, with a last flare and splutter it went out altogether. I was alone with the cat in the dark!

It helps one to face a danger when one knows that one has done all that possibly can be done. There is nothing for it then but to quietly await the result. In this case, there was no chance of safety anywhere except the precise spot where I was. I stretched myself out, therefore, and lay silently, almost breathlessly, hoping that the beast might forget my presence if I did nothing to remind him. I reckoned that it must already be two o'clock. At four it would be full dawn. I had not more than two hours to wait for daylight.

Outside, the storm was still raging, and the rain lashed continually against the little windows. Inside, the poisonous and fetid air was overpowering. I could neither hear nor see the cat. I tried to think about other things – but only one had power enough to draw my mind from my terrible position. That was the contemplation of my cousin's villainy, his unparalleled hypocrisy, his malignant hatred of me. Beneath that cheerful face there lurked the spirit of a medieval assassin. And as I thought of it I saw more clearly how cunningly the thing had been arranged. He had apparently gone to bed with the others. No doubt he had his witnesses to prove it. Then, unknown to them, he had slipped down, had lured me into this den and abandoned me. His story would be so simple. He had left me to finish my cigar in the billiard room. I had gone down on my own account to have a last look at the cat. I had entered the room without observing that the cage was opened, and I had been caught. How could such a crime be brought home to him? Suspicion, perhaps – but proof, never!

How slowly those dreadful two hours went by! Once I heard a low, rasping sound, which I took to be the creature licking its own fur. Several times those greenish eyes gleamed at me through the darkness, but never in a fixed stare, and my hopes grew stronger that my presence had been forgotten or ignored. At last the least faint glimmer of light came through the windows – I first dimly saw them as two grey squares upon the black wall, then grey turned to white, and I could see my terrible companion once more. And he, alas, could see me!

It was evident to me at once that he was in a much more dangerous and aggressive mood than when I had seen him last. The cold of the morning had irritated him, and he was hungry as well. With a continual growl he paced swiftly up and down the side of the room which was farthest from my refuge, his whiskers bristling angrily, and his tail switching and lashing. As he turned at the corners his savage eyes always looked upwards at me with a dreadful menace. I knew then that he meant to kill me. Yet I found myself even at that moment admiring the sinuous grace of the devilish thing, its long, undulating, rippling movements, the gloss of its beautiful flanks, the vivid, palpitating scarlet of the glistening tongue which hung from the jet-black muzzle. And all the time that deep, threatening growl was rising and rising in an unbroken crescendo. I knew that the crisis was at hand.

It was a miserable hour to meet such a death – so cold, so comfortless, shivering in my light dress clothes upon this gridiron of torment upon which I was stretched. I tried to brace myself to it, to raise my soul above it, and at the same time, with the lucidity which comes to a perfectly desperate man, I cast round for some possible means of escape. One thing was clear to me. If that front of the cage was only back in its position once more, I could find a sure refuge behind it. Could I possibly pull it back? I hardly dared to move for fear of bringing the creature upon me. Slowly, very slowly, I put my hand forward until it grasped the edge of the front, the final bar which protruded through the wall. To my surprise it came quite easily to my jerk. Of course the difficulty of drawing it out arose from the fact that I was clinging to it. I pulled again, and three inches of it came through. It ran apparently on wheels. I pulled again… and then the cat sprang!

It was so quick, so sudden, that I never saw it happen. I simply heard the savage snarl, and in an instant afterwards the blazing yellow eyes, the flattened black head with its red tongue and flashing teeth were within reach of me. The impact of the creature shook the bars upon which I lay, until I thought (as far as I could think of anything at such a moment) that they were coming down. The cat swayed there for an instant, the head and front paws quite close to me, the hind paws clawing to find a grip upon the edge of the grating. I heard the claws rasping as they clung to the wire netting, and the breath of the beast made me sick. But its bound had been miscalculated. It could not retain its position. Slowly, grinning with rage, and scratching madly at the bars, it swung backwards and dropped heavily upon the floor. With a growl it instantly faced round to me and crouched for another spring.

I knew that the next few moments would decide my fate. The creature had learnt by experience. It would not miscalculate again. I must act promptly, fearlessly, if I were to have a chance for life. In an instant I had formed my plan. Pulling off my dress coat, I threw it down over the head of the beast. At the same moment I dropped over the edge, seized the end of the front grating, and pulled it frantically out of the wall.

It came more easily than I could have expected. I rushed across the room, bearing it with me; but, as I rushed, the accident of my position put me upon the outer side. Had it been the other way, I might have come off scatheless. As it was, there was a moment's pause as I stopped it and tried to pass in through the opening which I had left. That moment was enough to give time to the creature to toss off the coat with which I had blinded him and to spring upon me. I hurled myself through the gap and pulled the rails to behind me, but he seized my leg before I could entirely withdraw it. One stroke of that huge paw tore off my calf as a shaving of wood curls off before a plane. The next moment, bleeding and fainting, I was lying among the foul straw with a line of friendly bars between me and the creature which ramped so frantically against them.

Too wounded to move, and too faint to be conscious of fear, I could only lie, more dead than alive, and watch it. It pressed its broad, black chest against the bars and angled for me with its crooked paws as I have seen a kitten do before a mousetrap. It ripped my clothes but, stretch as it would, it could not quite reach me. I have heard of the curious numbing effect produced by wounds from the great Carnivora, and now I was destined to experience it, for I had lost all sense of personality, and was as interested in the cat's failure or success as if it were some game which I was watching. And then gradually my mind drifted away into strange vague dreams, always with that black face and red tongue coming back into them, and so I lost myself in the nirvana of delirium, the blessed relief of those who are too sorely tried.

Tracing the course of events afterwards, I conclude that I must have been insensible for about two hours. What roused me to consciousness once more was that sharp metallic click which had been the precursor of my terrible experience. It was the shooting back of the spring lock. Then, before my senses were clear enough to entirely apprehend what they saw,

I was aware of the round, benevolent face of my cousin peering in through the open door. What he saw evidently amazed him. There was the cat crouching on the floor. I was stretched upon my back in my shirtsleeves within the cage, my trousers torn to ribbons and a great pool of blood all round me. I can see his amazed face now, with the morning sunlight upon it. He peered at me, and peered again. Then he closed the door behind him, and advanced to the cage to see if I were really dead.

I cannot undertake to say what happened. I was not in a fit state to witness or to chronicle such events. I can only say that I was suddenly conscious that his face was away from me – that he was looking towards the animal.

"Good old Tommy!" he cried. "Good old Tommy!"

Then he came near the bars, with his back still towards me.

"Down, you stupid beast!" he roared. "Down, sir! Don't you know your master?"

Suddenly even in my bemuddled brain a remembrance came of those words of his when he had said that the taste of blood would turn the cat into a fiend. My blood had done it, but he was to pay the price.

"Get away!" he screamed. "Get away, you devil! Baldwin! Baldwin! Oh, my God!"

And then I heard him fall, and rise, and fall again, with a sound like the ripping of sacking. His screams grew fainter until they were lost in the worrying snarl. And then, after I thought that he was dead, I saw, as in a nightmare, a blinded, tattered, blood-soaked figure running wildly round the room – and that was the last glimpse which I had of him before I fainted once again.

I was many months in my recovery – in fact, I cannot say that I have ever recovered, for to the end of my days I shall carry a stick as a sign of my night with the Brazilian cat. Baldwin, the groom, and the other servants could not tell what had occurred, when, drawn by the death cries of their master, they found me behind the bars, and his remains – or what they afterwards discovered to be his remains – in the clutch of the creature which he had reared. They stalled him off with hot irons, and afterwards shot him through the loophole of the door before they could finally extricate me. I was carried to my bedroom, and there, under the roof of my would-be murderer, I remained between life and death for several weeks. They had sent for a surgeon from Clipton and a nurse from London, and in a month I was able to be carried to the station, and so conveyed back once more to Grosvenor Mansions.

I have one remembrance of that illness, which might have been part of the ever-changing panorama conjured up by a delirious brain were it not so definitely fixed in my memory. One night, when the nurse was absent, the door of my chamber opened, and a tall woman in blackest mourning slipped into the room. She came across to me, and as she bent her sallow face I saw by the faint gleam of the night light that it was the Brazilian woman whom my cousin had married. She stared intently into my face, and her expression was more kindly than I had ever seen it.

"Are you conscious?" she asked.

I feebly nodded – for I was still very weak.

"Well, then, I only wished to say to you that you have yourself to blame. Did I not do all I could for you? From the beginning I tried to drive you from the house. By every means, short of betraying my husband, I tried to save you from him. I knew that he had a reason for bringing you here. I knew that he would never let you get away again. No one knew him as I knew him, who had suffered from him so often. I did not dare to tell you all this. He would have killed me. But I did my best for you. As things have turned out, you have been the best friend that I have ever had. You have set me free, and I fancied that nothing but death would do that. I am sorry if you are hurt, but I cannot reproach myself. I told you that you were a fool – and a fool you have been." She crept out of the room, the bitter, singular woman, and I was never destined to see her again. With what remained from her husband's property she went back to her native land, and I have heard that she afterwards took the veil at Pernambuco.*

It was not until I had been back in London for some time that the doctors pronounced me to be well enough to do business. It was not a very welcome permission to me, for I feared that it would be the signal for an inrush of creditors; but it was Summers, my lawyer, who first took advantage of it.

"I am very glad to see that Your Lordship is so much better," said he. "I have been waiting a long time to offer my congratulations."

"What do you mean, Summers? This is no time for joking."

"I mean what I say," he answered. "You have been Lord Southerton for the last six weeks, but we feared that it would retard your recovery if you were to learn it."

Lord Southerton! One of the richest peers in England! I could not believe my ears. And then suddenly I thought of the time which had elapsed, and how it coincided with my injuries.

"Then Lord Southerton must have died about the same time that I was hurt?"

"His death occurred upon that very day." Summers looked hard at me as I spoke, and I am convinced – for he was a very shrewd fellow – that he had guessed the true state of the case. He paused for a moment as if awaiting a confidence from me, but I could not see what was to be gained by exposing such a family scandal.

"Yes, a very curious coincidence," he continued, with the same knowing look. "Of course, you are aware that your cousin Everard King was the next heir to the estates. Now, if it had been you instead of him who had been torn to pieces by this tiger, or whatever it was, then of course he would have been Lord Southerton at the present moment."

"No doubt," said I.

"And he took such an interest in it," said Summers. "I happen to know that the late Lord Southerton's valet was in his pay, and that he used to have telegrams from him every few hours to tell him how he was getting on. That would be about the time when you were down there. Was it not strange that he should wish to be so well informed, since he knew that he was not the direct heir?"

"Very strange," said I. "And now, Summers, if you will bring me my bills and a new chequebook, we will begin to get things into order."

TALES OF MYSTERY

The Lost Special

The confession of Herbert de Lernac, now lying under sentence of death at Marseilles, has thrown a light upon one of the most inexplicable crimes of the century – an incident which is, I believe, absolutely unprecedented in the criminal annals of any country. Although there is a reluctance to discuss the matter in official circles, and little information has been given to the press, there are still indications that the statement of this arch-criminal is corroborated by the facts, and that we have at last found a solution for a most astounding business. As the matter is eight years old, and as its importance was somewhat obscured by a political crisis which was engaging the public attention at the time, it may be as well to state the facts as far as we have been able to ascertain them. They are collated from the Liverpool papers of that date, from the proceedings at the inquest upon John Slater, the engine driver, and from the records of the London and West Coast Railway Company, which have been courteously put at my disposal. Briefly, they are as follows:

On 3rd June 1890, a gentleman, who gave his name as Monsieur Louis Caratal, desired an interview with Mr James Bland, the superintendent of the London and West Coast Central Station in Liverpool. He was a small man, middle-aged and dark, with a stoop which was so marked that it suggested some deformity of the spine. He was accompanied by a friend, a man of imposing physique, whose deferential manner and constant attention showed that his position was one of dependence. This friend or companion, whose name did not transpire, was certainly a foreigner, and probably, from his swarthy complexion, either a Spaniard or a South American. One peculiarity was observed in him. He carried in his left hand a small black leather dispatch box, and it was noticed by a sharp-eyed clerk in the central office that this box was fastened to his wrist by a strap. No importance was attached to the fact at the time, but subsequent events endowed it with some significance. Monsieur Caratal was shown up to Mr Bland's office, while his companion remained outside.

Monsieur Caratal's business was quickly dispatched. He had arrived that afternoon from Central America. Affairs of the utmost importance demanded that he should be in Paris without the loss of an unnecessary hour. He had missed the London express. A special must be provided. Money was of no importance. Time was everything. If the company would speed him on his way, they might make their own terms.

Mr Bland struck the electric bell, summoned Mr Potter Hood, the traffic manager, and had the matter arranged in five minutes. The train would start in three quarters of an hour. It would take that time to ensure that the line should be clear. The powerful engine called *Rochdale* (No. 247 on the company's register) was attached to two carriages, with a guard's van behind. The first carriage was solely for the purpose of decreasing the inconvenience arising from the oscillation. The second was divided, as usual, into four compartments, a first-class, a first-class smoking, a second-class and a second-class smoking. The first compartment, which was nearest to the engine, was the one allotted to the travellers. The other three were empty. The guard of the special train was James McPherson, who had been some years in the service of the company. The stoker, William Smith, was a new hand.

Monsieur Caratal, upon leaving the superintendent's office, rejoined his companion, and both of them manifested extreme impatience to be off. Having paid the money asked, which amounted to fifty pounds five shillings, at the usual special rate of five shillings a mile, they demanded to be shown the carriage, and at once took their seats in it, although they were assured that the better part of an hour must elapse before the line could be cleared. In the meantime a singular coincidence had occurred in the office which Monsieur Caratal had just quitted.

A request for a special is not a very uncommon circumstance in a rich commercial centre, but that two should be required upon the same afternoon was most unusual. It so happened, however, that Mr Bland had hardly dismissed the first traveller before a second entered with a similar request. This was a Mr Horace Moore, a gentlemanly man of military appearance, who alleged that the sudden serious illness of his wife in London made it absolutely imperative that he should not lose an instant in starting upon the journey. His distress and anxiety were so evident that Mr Bland did all that was possible to meet his wishes. A second special was out of the question, as the ordinary local service was already somewhat deranged by the first. There was the alternative, however, that Mr Moore should share the expense of Monsieur Caratal's train, and should travel in the other empty first-class compartment, if Monsieur Caratal objected to having him in the one which he occupied. It was difficult to see any objection to such an arrangement, and yet Monsieur Caratal, upon the suggestion being made to him by Mr Potter Hood, absolutely refused to consider it for an instant. The train was his, he said, and he would insist upon the exclusive use of it. All argument failed to overcome his ungracious objections, and finally the plan had to be abandoned. Mr Horace Moore left the station in great distress, after learning that his only course was to take the ordinary slow train which leaves Liverpool at six o'clock. At 4.31 exactly by the station clock, the special train, containing the crippled Monsieur Caratal and his gigantic companion, steamed out of the Liverpool station. The line was at that time clear, and there should have been no stoppage before Manchester.

The trains of the London and West Coast Railway run over the lines of another company as far as this town, which should have been reached by the special rather before six o'clock. At a quarter after six considerable surprise and some consternation were caused amongst the officials at Liverpool by the receipt of a telegram from Manchester to say that it had not yet arrived. An enquiry directed to St Helens, which is a third of the way between the two cities, elicited the following reply:

> To James Bland, Superintendent, Central L&WC, Liverpool. – Special passed here at 4.52, well up to time. – Dowser, St Helens.

This telegram was received at 6.40. At 6.50 a second message was received from Manchester:

> No sign of special as advised by you.

And then ten minutes later a third, more bewildering:

> Presume some mistake as to proposed running of special. Local train from St Helens timed to follow it has just arrived and has seen nothing of it. Kindly wire advices. – Manchester.

The matter was assuming a most amazing aspect, although in some respects the last telegram was a relief to the authorities at Liverpool. If an accident had occurred to the special, it seemed hardly possible that the local train could have passed down the same line without observing it. And yet, what was the alternative? Where could the train be? Had it possibly been sidetracked for some reason in order to allow the slower train to go past? Such an explanation was possible if some small repair had to be effected.

A telegram was dispatched to each of the stations between St Helens and Manchester, and the superintendent and traffic manager waited in the utmost suspense at the instrument for the series of replies which would enable them to say for certain what had become of the missing train. The answers came back in the order of questions, which was the order of the stations beginning at the St Helens end:

> Special passed here five o'clock. – Collins Green.
>
> Special passed here six past five. – Earlestown.
>
> Special passed here 5.10. – Newton.
>
> Special passed here 5.20. – Kenyon Junction.
>
> No special train has passed here. – Barton Moss.

The two officials stared at each other in amazement.

"This is unique in my thirty years of experience," said Mr Bland.

"Absolutely unprecedented and inexplicable, sir. The special has gone wrong between Kenyon Junction and Barton Moss."

"And yet there is no siding, so far as my memory serves me, between the two stations. The special must have run off the metals."

"But how could the 4.50 parliamentary* pass over the same line without observing it?"

"There's no alternative, Mr Hood. It *must* be so. Possibly the local train may have observed something which may throw some light upon the matter. We will wire to Manchester for more information, and to Kenyon Junction with instructions that the line be examined instantly as far as Barton Moss."

The answer from Manchester came within a few minutes.

> No news of missing special. Driver and guard of slow train positive no accident between Kenyon Junction and Barton Moss. Line quite clear, and no sign of anything unusual. – Manchester.

"That driver and guard will have to go," said Mr Bland grimly. "There has been a wreck and they have missed it. The special has obviously run off the metals without disturbing the line – how it could have done so passes my comprehension – but so it must be, and we shall have a wire from Kenyon or Barton Moss presently to say that they have found her at the bottom of an embankment."

But Mr Bland's prophecy was not destined to be fulfilled. Half an hour passed, and then there arrived the following message from the stationmaster of Kenyon Junction:

> There are no traces of the missing special. It is quite certain that she passed here, and that she did not arrive at Barton Moss. We have detached engine from goods train, and I have myself ridden down the line, but all is clear, and there is no sign of any accident.

Mr Bland tore his hair in his perplexity.

"This is rank lunacy, Hood!" he cried. "Does a train vanish into thin air in England in broad daylight? The thing is preposterous. An engine, a tender, two carriages, a van, five human beings – and all lost on a straight line of railway! Unless we get something positive within the next hour I'll take Inspector Collins, and go down myself."

And then at last something positive did occur. It took the shape of another telegram from Kenyon Junction.

> Regret to report that the dead body of John Slater, driver of the special train, has just been found among the gorse bushes at a point two and a quarter miles from the Junction. Had fallen from his engine, pitched down the embankment, and rolled among bushes. Injuries to his head, from the fall, appear to be cause of death. Ground has now been carefully examined, and there is no trace of the missing train.

The country was, as has already been stated, in the throes of a political crisis, and the attention of the public was further distracted by the important and sensational developments in Paris, where a huge scandal threatened to destroy the government and to wreck the reputations of many of the leading men in France. The papers were full of these events, and the singular disappearance of the special train attracted less attention than would have been the case in more peaceful times. The grotesque nature of the event helped to detract from its importance, for the papers were disinclined to believe the facts as reported to them. More than one of the London journals treated the matter as an ingenious hoax, until the coroner's inquest upon the unfortunate driver (an inquest which elicited nothing of importance) convinced them of the tragedy of the incident.

Mr Bland, accompanied by Inspector Collins, the senior detective officer in the service of the company, went down to Kenyon Junction the same evening, and their research lasted throughout the following day, but was attended with purely negative results. Not only was no trace found of the missing train, but no conjecture could be put forward which could possibly explain the facts. At the same time, Inspector Collins's official report (which lies before me as I write) served to show that the possibilities were more numerous than might have been expected.

In the stretch of railway between these two points (said he) the country is dotted with ironworks and collieries. Of these, some are being worked and some have been abandoned. There are no fewer than twelve which have small gauge lines which run trolley cars down to the main line. These can, of course, be disregarded. Besides these, however, there are seven which have, or have had, proper lines running down and connecting with points to the main line, so as to convey their produce from the mouth of the mine to the great centres of distribution. In every case these lines are only a few miles in length. Out of the seven, four belong to collieries which are worked out, or at least to shafts which are no longer used. These are the Redgauntlet, Hero, Slough of Despond and Heartsease mines, the latter having ten years ago been one of the principal mines in Lancashire. These four side lines may be eliminated from our inquiry, for, to prevent possible accidents, the rails nearest to the main line have been taken up, and there is no longer any connection. There remain three other side lines leading

(a) to the Carnstock Ironworks,
(b) to the Big Ben Colliery,
(c) to the Perseverance Colliery.

Of these the Big Ben line is not more than a quarter of a mile long, and ends at a dead wall of coal awaiting removal from the mouth of the mine. Nothing had been seen or heard there of any special. The Carnstock Ironworks line was blocked all day upon 3rd June by sixteen truckloads of haematite. It is a single line, and nothing could have passed. As to the Perseverance line, it is a large double line, which does a considerable traffic, for the output of the mine is very large. On 3rd June this traffic proceeded as usual; hundreds of men, including a gang of railway platelayers, were working along the two miles and a quarter

> which constitute the total length of the line, and it is inconceivable that an unexpected train could have come down there without attracting universal attention. It may be remarked in conclusion that this branch line is nearer to St Helens than the point at which the engine driver was discovered, so that we have every reason to believe that the train was past that point before misfortune overtook her.
>
> As to John Slater, there is no clue to be gathered from his appearance or injuries. We can only say that, so far as we can see, he met his end by falling off his engine, though why he fell, or what became of the engine after his fall, is a question upon which I do not feel qualified to offer an opinion.

In conclusion, the inspector offered his resignation to the board, being much nettled by an accusation of incompetence in the London papers.

A month elapsed, during which both the police and the company prosecuted their inquiries without the slightest success. A reward was offered and a pardon promised in case of crime, but they were both unclaimed. Every day the public opened their papers with the conviction that so grotesque a mystery would at last be solved, but week after week passed by, and a solution remained as far off as ever. In broad daylight, upon a June afternoon in the most thickly inhabited portion of England, a train with its occupants had disappeared as completely as if some master of subtle chemistry had volatilized it into gas. Indeed, among the various conjectures which were put forward in the public press, there were some which seriously asserted that supernatural, or at least preternatural, agencies had been at work, and that the deformed Monsieur Caratal was probably a person who was better known under a less polite name. Others fixed upon his swarthy companion as being the author of the mischief, but what it was exactly which he had done could never be clearly formulated in words.

Amongst the many suggestions put forward by various newspapers or private individuals, there were one or two which were feasible enough to attract the attention of the public. One which appeared in *The Times*, over the signature of an amateur reasoner of some celebrity at that date, attempted to deal with the matter in a critical and semi-scientific manner. An extract must suffice, although the curious can see the whole letter in the issue of 3rd July.

"It is one of the elementary principles of practical reasoning," he remarked,

> that when the impossible has been eliminated, the residuum, however improbable, must contain the truth.* It is certain that the train left Kenyon Junction. It is certain that it did not reach Barton Moss. It is in the highest degree unlikely, but still possible, that it may have taken one of the seven available side lines. It is obviously impossible for a train to run where there are no rails, and, therefore, we may reduce our improbables to the three open lines, namely the Carnstock Ironworks, the Big Ben and the Perseverance. Is there a secret society of colliers, an English Camorra,* which is capable of destroying both train and passengers? It is improbable, but it is not impossible. I confess that I am unable to suggest any other solution. I should certainly advise the company to direct all their energies towards the observation of those three lines, and of the workmen at the end of them. A careful supervision of the pawnbrokers' shops of the district might possibly bring some suggestive facts to light.

The suggestion coming from a recognized authority upon such matters created considerable interest, and a fierce opposition from those who considered such a statement to be a preposterous libel upon an honest and deserving set of men. The only answer to this criticism was a challenge to the objectors to lay any more feasible explanations before the public. In reply to this two others were forthcoming (*Times*, 7th and 9th July). The first suggested that the train might have run off the metals and be lying submerged in the Lancashire and Staffordshire Canal, which runs parallel to the railway for some hundreds of yards. This suggestion was thrown out of court by the published depth of the canal, which was entirely insufficient to conceal so large an object. The second correspondent wrote calling attention to the bag which appeared to be the sole luggage which the travellers had brought with them, and suggesting that some novel explosive of immense and pulverizing power might have been concealed in it. The obvious absurdity, however, of supposing that the whole train might be blown to dust while the metals remained uninjured reduced any such explanation to a farce. The investigation had drifted into this hopeless position when a new and most unexpected incident occurred.

This was nothing less than the receipt by Mrs McPherson of a letter from her husband, James McPherson, who had been the guard of the missing train. The letter, which was dated 5th July 1890, was posted from New York and came to hand upon 14th July. Some doubts were expressed as to its genuine character, but Mrs McPherson was positive as to the writing, and the fact that it contained a remittance of a hundred dollars in five-dollar notes was enough in itself to discount the idea of a hoax. No address was given in the letter, which ran in this way:

> MY DEAR WIFE,
>
> I have been thinking a great deal, and I find it very hard to give you up. The same with Lizzie. I try to fight against it, but it will always come back to me. I send you some money which will change into twenty English pounds. This should be enough to bring both Lizzie and you across the Atlantic, and you will find the Hamburg boats which stop at Southampton very good boats, and cheaper than Liverpool. If you could come here and stop at the Johnston House I would try and send you word how to meet, but things are very difficult with me at present, and I am not very happy, finding it hard to give you both up. So no more at present, from your loving husband,
>
> JAMES McPHERSON

For a time it was confidently anticipated that this letter would lead to the clearing-up of the whole matter, the more so as it was ascertained that a passenger who bore a close resemblance to the missing guard had travelled from Southampton under the name of Summers in the Hamburg and New York liner *Vistula*, which started upon 7th June. Mrs McPherson and her sister Lizzie Dolton went across to New York as directed and stayed for three weeks at the Johnston House, without hearing anything from the missing man. It is probable that some injudicious comments in the press may have warned him that the police were using them as a bait. However this may be, it is certain that he neither wrote nor came, and the women were eventually compelled to return to Liverpool.

And so the matter stood, and has continued to stand up to the present year of 1898. Incredible as it may seem, nothing has transpired during these eight years which has shed the least light upon the extraordinary disappearance of the special train which contained Monsieur Caratal and his companion. Careful inquiries into the antecedents of the two travellers have only established the fact that Monsieur Caratal was well known as a financier and political agent in Central America, and that during his voyage to Europe he had betrayed extraordinary anxiety to reach Paris. His companion, whose name was entered upon the passenger lists as Eduardo Gomez, was a man whose record was a violent one, and whose reputation was that of a bravo and a bully. There was evidence to show, however, that he was honestly devoted to the interests of Monsieur Caratal, and that the latter, being a man of puny physique, employed the other as a guard and protector. It may be added that no information came from Paris as to what the objects of Monsieur Caratal's hurried journey may have been. This comprises all the facts of the case up to the publication in the Marseille papers of the recent confession of Herbert de Lernac, now under sentence of death for the murder of a merchant named Bonvalot. This statement may be literally translated as follows:

It is not out of mere pride or boasting that I give this information, for if that were my object I could tell a dozen actions of mine which are quite as splendid; but I do it in order that certain gentlemen in Paris may understand that I, who am able here to tell about the fate of Monsieur Caratal, can also tell in whose interest and at whose request the deed was done, unless the reprieve which I am awaiting comes to me very quickly. Take warning, Messieurs, before it is too late! You know Herbert de Lernac, and you are aware that his deeds are as ready as his words. Hasten then, or you are lost!

At present I shall mention no names – if you only heard the names, what would you not think! – but I shall merely tell you how cleverly I did it. I was true to my employers then, and no doubt they will be true to me now. I hope so, and until I am convinced that they have betrayed me, these names, which would convulse Europe, shall not be divulged. But on that day... well, I say no more!

In a word, then, there was a famous trial in Paris, in the year 1890, in connection with a monstrous scandal in politics and finance. How monstrous that scandal was can never be known save by such confidential agents as myself. The honour and careers of many of the chief men in France were at stake. You have seen a group of ninepins standing, all so rigid, and prim, and unbending. Then there comes the ball from far away and pop, pop, pop – there are your ninepins on the floor. Well, imagine some of the greatest men in France as these ninepins and then this Monsieur Caratal was the ball which could be seen coming from far away. If he arrived, then it was pop, pop, pop for all of them. It was determined that he should not arrive.

I do not accuse them all of being conscious of what was to happen. There were, as I have said, great financial as well as political interests at stake, and a syndicate was formed to manage the business. Some subscribed to the syndicate who hardly understood what were its objects. But others understood very well, and they can rely upon it that I have not forgotten their names. They had ample warning that Monsieur Caratal was coming long before he left South America, and they knew that the evidence which he held would certainly mean ruin to all of them. The syndicate had the command of an unlimited amount of money – absolutely unlimited, you understand. They looked round for an agent who was capable of wielding this gigantic power. The man chosen must be inventive, resolute, adaptive – a man in a million. They chose Herbert de Lernac, and I admit that they were right.

My duties were to choose my subordinates, to use freely the power which money gives and to make certain that Monsieur Caratal should never arrive in Paris. With characteristic energy I set about my commission within an hour of receiving my instructions, and the steps which I took were the very best for the purpose which could possibly be devised.

A man whom I could trust was dispatched instantly to South America to travel home with Monsieur Caratal. Had he arrived in time the ship would never have reached Liverpool, but – alas! – it had already started before my agent could reach it. I fitted out a small armed brig to intercept it, but again I was unfortunate. Like all great organizers I was, however, prepared for failure, and had a series of alternatives prepared, one or the other of which must succeed. You must not underrate the difficulties of my undertaking, or imagine that a mere commonplace assassination would meet the case. We must destroy not only Monsieur Caratal, but Monsieur Caratal's documents, and Monsieur Caratal's companions also, if we had reason to believe that he had communicated his secrets to them. And you must remember that they were on the alert, and keenly suspicious of any such attempt. It was a task which was in every way worthy of me, for I am always most masterful where another would be appalled.

I was all ready for Monsieur Caratal's reception in Liverpool, and I was the more eager because I had reason to believe that he had made arrangements by which he would have a considerable guard from the moment that he arrived in London. Anything which was to be done must be done between the moment of his setting foot upon the Liverpool quay and that of his arrival at the London and West Coast terminus in London. We prepared six plans, each more elaborate than the last – which plan would be used would depend upon his own movements. Do what he would, we were ready for him. If he had stayed in Liverpool, we were ready. If he took an ordinary train, an express or a special, all was ready. Everything had been foreseen and provided for.

You may imagine that I could not do all this myself. What could I know of the English railway lines? But money can procure willing agents all the world over, and I soon had one of the acutest brains in England to assist me. I will mention no names, but it would be unjust to claim all the credit for myself. My English ally was worthy of such an alliance. He knew the London and West Coast line thoroughly, and he had the command of a band of workers who were trustworthy and intelligent. The idea was his, and my own judgement was only required in the details. We bought over several officials, amongst whom the most important was James McPherson, whom we had ascertained to be the guard most likely to be employed upon a special train. Smith, the stoker, was also in our employ. John Slater, the engine driver, had been approached, but had been found to be obstinate and dangerous, so we desisted. We had no certainty that Monsieur Caratal would take a special, but we thought it very probable, for it was of the utmost importance to him that he should reach Paris without delay. It was for this contingency, therefore, that we made special preparations – preparations which were complete down to the last detail long before his steamer had sighted the shores of England. You will be amused to learn that there was one of my agents in the pilot boat which brought that steamer to its moorings.

The moment that Caratal arrived in Liverpool we knew that he suspected danger and was on his guard. He had brought with him as an escort a dangerous fellow named Gomez, a man who carried weapons and was prepared to use them. This fellow carried Caratal's confidential papers for him, and was ready to protect either them or his master. The probability was that Caratal had taken him into his counsels, and that to remove Caratal without removing Gomez would be a mere waste of energy. It was necessary that they should be involved in a common fate, and our plans to that end were much facilitated by their request for a special train. On that special train you will understand that two out of the three servants of the company were really in our employ, at a price which would make them independent for a lifetime. I do not go so far as to say that the English are more honest than any other nation, but I have found them more expensive to buy.

I have already spoken of my English agent – who is a man with a considerable future before him, unless some complaint of the throat carries him off before his time. He had charge of all arrangements at Liverpool, whilst I was stationed at the inn at Kenyon, where I awaited a cipher signal to act. When the special was arranged for, my agent instantly telegraphed to me and warned me how soon I should have everything ready. He himself under the name of Horace Moore applied immediately for a special also, in the hope that he would be sent down with Monsieur Caratal, which might under certain circumstances have been helpful to us. If, for example, our great coup had failed, it would then have become the duty of my agent to have shot them both and destroyed their papers. Caratal was on his guard, however, and refused to admit any other traveller. My agent then left the station, returned by another entrance, entered the guard's van on the side farthest from the platform and travelled down with McPherson the guard.

In the meantime you will be interested to know what my movements were. Everything had been prepared for days before, and only the finishing touches were needed. The side line which we had chosen had once joined the main line, but it had been disconnected. We had only to replace a few rails to connect it once more. These rails had been laid down as far as could be done without danger of attracting attention, and now it was merely a case of completing a juncture with the line, and arranging the points as they had been before. The sleepers had never been removed, and the rails, fishplates* and rivets were all ready, for we had taken them from a siding on the abandoned portion of the line. With my small but competent band of workers, we had everything ready long before the special arrived. When it did arrive, it ran off upon the small side line so easily that the jolting of the points appears to have been entirely unnoticed by the two travellers.

Our plan had been that Smith, the stoker, should chloroform John Slater, the driver, so that he should vanish with the others. In this respect, and in this respect only, our plans miscarried – I except the criminal folly of McPherson in writing home to his wife. Our stoker did his business so clumsily that Slater in his struggles fell off the engine, and though fortune was with us so far that he broke his neck in the fall, still he remained as a blot upon that which would otherwise have been one of those complete masterpieces which are only to be contemplated in silent admiration. The criminal expert will find in John Slater the one flaw in all our admirable combinations. A man who has had as many triumphs as I can afford to be frank, and I therefore lay my finger upon John Slater, and I proclaim him to be a flaw.

But now I have got our special train upon the small line two kilometres, or rather more than one mile, in length, which leads, or rather used to lead, to the abandoned Heartsease mine, once one of the largest coal mines in England. You will ask how it is that no one saw the train upon this unused line. I answer that along its entire length it runs through a deep cutting, and that, unless someone had been on the edge of that cutting, he could not have seen it. There *was* someone on the edge of that cutting. I was there. And now I will tell you what I saw.

My assistant had remained at the points in order that he might superintend the switching-off of the train. He had four armed men with him, so that if the train ran off the line – we thought it probable, because the points were very rusty – we might still have resources to fall back upon. Having once seen it safely on the side line, he handed over the responsibility to me. I was waiting at a point which overlooks the mouth of the mine, and I was also armed, as were my two companions. Come what might, you see, I was always ready.

The moment that the train was fairly on the side line, Smith, the stoker, slowed down the engine, and then, having turned it onto the fullest speed again, he and McPherson, with my English lieutenant, sprang off before it was too late. It may be that it was this slowing down which first attracted the attention of the travellers, but the train was running at full speed again before their heads appeared at the open window. It makes me smile to think how bewildered they must have been. Picture to yourself your own feelings if, on looking out of your luxurious carriage, you suddenly perceived that the lines upon which you ran were rusted and corroded, red and yellow with disuse and decay! What a catch must have come in their breath as in a second it flashed upon them that it was not Manchester but death which was waiting for them at the end of that sinister line. But the train was running with frantic speed, rolling and rocking over the rotten line, while the wheels made a frightful screaming sound upon the rusted surface. I was close to them, and could see their faces. Caratal was praying, I think – there was something like a rosary dangling out of his hand. The other roared like a bull who smells the blood of the slaughterhouse. He saw us standing on the bank, and he beckoned to us like a madman. Then he tore at his wrist and threw his dispatch box out of the window in our direction. Of course, his meaning was obvious. Here was the evidence, and they would promise to be silent if their lives were spared. It would have been very agreeable if we could have done so, but business is business. Besides, the train was now as much beyond our control as theirs.

He ceased howling when the train rattled round the curve and they saw the black mouth of the mine yawning before them. We had removed the boards which had covered it, and we had cleared the square entrance. The rails had formerly run very close to the shaft for the convenience of loading the coal, and we had only to add two or three lengths of rail in order to lead to the very brink of the shaft. In fact, as the lengths would not quite fit, our line projected about three feet over the edge. We saw the two heads at the window: Caratal below, Gomez above; but they had both been struck silent by what they saw. And yet they could not withdraw their heads. The sight seemed to have paralysed them.

I had wondered how the train running at a great speed would take the pit into which I had guided it, and I was much interested in watching it. One of my colleagues thought that it would actually jump it, and indeed it was not very far from doing so. Fortunately, however, it fell short, and the buffers of the engine struck the other lip of the shaft with a tremendous crash. The funnel flew off into the air. The tender, carriages and van were all smashed up into one jumble, which, with the remains of the engine, choked for a minute or so the mouth of the pit. Then something gave way in the middle, and the whole mass of green iron, smoking coals, brass fittings, wheels, woodwork and cushions all crumbled together and crashed down into the mine. We heard the rattle, rattle, rattle, as the debris struck against the walls, and then, quite a long time afterwards, there came a deep roar as the remains of the train struck the bottom. The boiler may have burst, for a sharp crash came after the roar, and then a dense cloud of steam and smoke swirled up out of the black depths, falling in a spray as thick as rain all round us. Then the vapour shredded off into thin wisps, which floated away in the summer sunshine, and all was quiet again in the Heartsease mine.

And now, having carried out our plans so successfully, it only remained to leave no trace behind us. Our little band of workers at the other end had already ripped up the rails and disconnected the side line, replacing everything as it had been before. We were equally busy at the mine. The funnel and other fragments were thrown in, the shaft was planked over as it used to be, and the lines which led to it were torn up and taken away. Then, without flurry, but without delay, we all made our way out of the country, most of us to Paris, my English colleague to Manchester and McPherson to Southampton, whence he emigrated to America. Let the English papers of that date tell how thoroughly we had done our work, and how completely we had thrown the cleverest of their detectives off our track.

You will remember that Gomez threw his bag of papers out of the window, and I need not say that I secured that bag and brought them to my employers. It may interest my employers now, however, to learn that out of that bag I took one or two little papers as a souvenir of the occasion. I have no wish to publish these papers; but, still, it is every man for himself in this world, and what else can I do if my friends will not come to my aid when I want them? Messieurs, you may believe that Herbert de Lernac is quite as formidable when he is against you as when he is with you, and that he is not a man to go to the guillotine until he has seen that every one of you is en route for New Caledonia. For your own sake, if not for mine, make haste, Monsieur de ——, and General ——, and Baron —— (you can fill up the blanks for yourselves as you read this). I promise you that in the next edition there will be no blanks to fill.

PS: As I look over my statement there is only one omission which I can see. It concerns the unfortunate man McPherson, who was foolish enough to write to his wife and to make an appointment with her in New York. It can be imagined that when interests like ours were at stake, we could not leave them to the chance of whether a man in that class of life would or would not give away his secrets to a woman. Having once broken his oath by writing to his wife, we could not trust him any more. We took steps therefore to ensure that he should not see his wife. I have sometimes thought that it would be a kindness to write to her and to assure her that there is no impediment to her marrying again.

The Beetle-Hunter

A curious experience? said the doctor. Yes, my friends, I have had one very curious experience. I never expect to have another, for it is against all doctrines of chances that two such events would befall any one man in a single lifetime. You may believe me or not, but the thing happened exactly as I tell it.

I had just become a medical man, but I had not started in practice, and I lived in rooms in Gower Street. The street has been renumbered since then, but it was in the only house which has a bow window, upon the left-hand side as you go down from the Metropolitan station.* A widow named Murchison kept the house at that time, and she had three medical students and one engineer as lodgers. I occupied the top room, which was the cheapest, but cheap as it was it was more than I could afford. My small resources were dwindling away, and every week it became more necessary that I should find something to do. Yet I was very unwilling to go into general practice, for my tastes were all in the direction of science, and especially of zoology, towards which I had always a strong leaning. I had almost given the fight up and resigned myself to being a medical drudge for life, when the turning point of my struggles came in a very extraordinary way.

One morning I had picked up the *Standard* and was glancing over its contents. There was a complete absence of news, and I was about to toss the paper down again, when my eyes were caught by an advertisement at the head of the personal column. It was worded in this way:

> Wanted for one or more days the services of a medical man. It is essential that he should be a man of strong physique, of steady nerves, and of a resolute nature. Must be an entomologist – coleopterist preferred. Apply, in person, at 77B Brook Street. Application must be made before twelve o'clock today.

Now, I have already said that I was devoted to zoology. Of all branches of zoology, the study of insects was the most attractive to me, and of all insects beetles were the species with which I was most familiar. Butterfly collectors are numerous, but beetles are far more varied, and more accessible in these islands than are butterflies. It was this fact which had attracted my attention to them, and I had myself made a collection which numbered some hundred varieties. As to the other requisites of the advertisement, I knew that my nerves could be depended upon, and I had won the weight-throwing competition at the inter-hospital sports. Clearly, I was the very man for the vacancy. Within five minutes of my having read the advertisement I was in a cab and on my way to Brook Street.

As I drove, I kept turning the matter over in my head and trying to make a guess as to what sort of employment it could be which needed such curious qualifications. A strong physique, a resolute nature, a medical training and a knowledge of beetles – what connection could there be between these various requisites? And then there was the disheartening fact that the situation was not a permanent one, but terminable from day to day, according to the terms of the advertisement. The more I pondered over it the more unintelligible did it become; but at the end of my meditations I always came back to the ground fact that, come what might, I had nothing to lose, that I was completely at the end of my resources, and that I was ready for any adventure, however desperate, which would put a few honest sovereigns into my pocket. The man fears to fail who has to pay for his failure, but there was no penalty which Fortune could exact from me. I was like the gambler with empty pockets, who is still allowed to try his luck with the others.

No. 77B Brook Street was one of those dingy and yet imposing houses, dun-coloured and flat-faced, with the intensely respectable and solid air which marks the Georgian builder. As I alighted from the cab, a young man came out of the door and walked swiftly down the street. In passing me, I noticed that he cast an inquisitive and somewhat malevolent glance at me, and I took the incident as a good omen, for his appearance was that of a rejected candidate, and if he resented my application it meant that the vacancy was not yet filled up. Full of hope, I ascended the broad steps and rapped with the heavy knocker.

A footman in powder and livery opened the door. Clearly I was in touch with people of wealth and fashion.

"Yes, sir?" said the footman.

"I came in answer to—"

"Quite so, sir," said the footman. "Lord Linchmere will see you at once in the library."

Lord Linchmere! I had vaguely heard the name, but could not for the instant recall anything about him. Following the footman, I was shown into a large, book-lined room in which there was seated behind a writing desk a small man with a pleasant, clean-shaven, mobile face and long hair shot with grey, brushed back from his forehead. He looked me up and down with a very shrewd, penetrating glance, holding the card which the footman had given him in his right hand. Then he smiled pleasantly, and I felt that externally at any rate I possessed the qualifications which he desired.

"You have come in answer to my advertisement, Dr Hamilton?" he asked.

"Yes, sir."

"Do you fulfil the conditions which are there laid down?"

"I believe that I do."

"You are a powerful man, or so I should judge from your appearance."

"I think that I am fairly strong."

"And resolute?"

"I believe so."

"Have you ever known what it was to be exposed to imminent danger?"

"No, I don't know that I ever have."

"But you think you would be prompt and cool at such a time?"

"I hope so."

"Well, I believe that you would. I have the more confidence in you because you do not pretend to be certain as to what you would do in a position that was new to you. My impression is that, so far as personal qualities go, you are the very man of whom I am in search. That being settled, we may pass on to the next point."

"Which is?"

"To talk to me about beetles."

I looked across to see if he was joking, but, on the contrary, he was leaning eagerly forward across his desk, and there was an expression of something like anxiety in his eyes.

"I am afraid that you do not know about beetles," he cried.

"On the contrary, sir, it is the one scientific subject about which I feel that I really do know something."

"I am overjoyed to hear it. Please talk to me about beetles."

I talked. I do not profess to have said anything original upon the subject, but I gave a short sketch of the characteristics of the beetle, and ran over the more common species, with some allusions to the specimens in my own little collection and to the article upon 'Burying Beetles' which I had contributed to the *Journal of Entomological Science*.

"What! Not a collector?" cried Lord Linchmere. "You don't mean that you are yourself a collector?" His eyes danced with pleasure at the thought. "You are certainly the very man in London for my purpose. I thought that among five millions of people there must be such a man, but the difficulty is to lay one's hands upon him. I have been extraordinarily fortunate in finding you."

He rang a gong upon the table, and the footman entered.

"Ask Lady Rossiter to have the goodness to step this way," said His Lordship, and a few moments later the lady was ushered into the room. She was a small, middle-aged woman, very like Lord Linchmere in appearance, with the same quick, alert features and grey-black hair. The expression of anxiety, however, which I had observed upon his face was very much more marked upon hers. Some great grief seemed to have cast its shadow over her features. As Lord Linchmere presented me she turned her face full upon me, and I was shocked to observe a half-healed scar extending for two inches over her right eyebrow. It was partly concealed by plaster, but nonetheless I could see that it had been a serious wound and not long inflicted.

"Dr Hamilton is the very man for our purpose, Evelyn," said Lord Linchmere. "He is actually a collector of beetles, and he has written articles upon the subject."

"Really!" said Lady Rossiter. "Then you must have heard of my husband. Everyone who knows anything about beetles must have heard of Sir Thomas Rossiter."

For the first time a thin little ray of light began to break into the obscure business. Here, at last, was a connection between these people and beetles. Sir Thomas Rossiter – he was the greatest authority upon the subject in the world. He had made it his lifelong study, and had written a most exhaustive work upon it. I hastened to assure her that I had read and appreciated it.

"Have you met my husband?" she asked.

"No, I have not."

"But you shall," said Lord Linchmere with decision.

The lady was standing beside the desk, and she put her hand upon his shoulder. It was obvious to me as I saw their faces together that they were brother and sister.

"Are you really prepared for this, Charles? It is noble of you, but you fill me with fears." Her voice quavered with apprehension, and he appeared to me to be equally moved, though he was making strong efforts to conceal his agitation.

"Yes, yes, dear, it is all settled, it is all decided. In fact, there is no other possible way, that I can see."

"There is one obvious way."

"No, no, Evelyn, I shall never abandon you – never. It will come right – depend upon it; it will come right, and surely it looks like the interference of Providence that so perfect an instrument should be put into our hands."

My position was embarrassing, for I felt that for the instant they had forgotten my presence. But Lord Linchmere came back suddenly to me and to my engagement.

"The business for which I want you, Dr Hamilton, is that you should put yourself absolutely at my disposal. I wish you to come for a short journey with me, to remain always at my side, and to promise to do without question whatever I may ask you, however unreasonable it may appear to you to be."

"That is a good deal to ask," said I.

"Unfortunately I cannot put it more plainly, for I do not myself know what turn matters may take. You may be sure, however, that you will not be asked to do anything which your conscience does not approve; and I promise you that, when all is over, you will be proud to have been concerned in so good a work."

"If it ends happily," said the lady.

"Exactly – if it ends happily," His Lordship repeated.

"And terms?" I asked.

"Twenty pounds a day."

I was amazed at the sum, and must have showed my surprise upon my features.

"It is a rare combination of qualities, as must have struck you when you first read the advertisement," said Lord Linchmere. "Such varied gifts may well command a high return, and I do not conceal from you that your duties might be arduous or even dangerous. Besides, it is possible that one or two days may bring the matter to an end."

"Please God!" sighed his sister.

"So now, Dr Hamilton, may I rely upon your aid?"

"Most undoubtedly," said I. "You have only to tell me what my duties are."

"Your first duty will be to return to your home. You will pack up whatever you may need for a short visit to the country. We start together from Paddington Station at 3.40 this afternoon."

"Do we go far?"

"As far as Pangbourne. Meet me at the bookstall at 3.30. I shall have the tickets. Goodbye, Dr Hamilton! And, by the way, there are two things which I should be very glad if you would bring with you, in case you have them. One is your case for collecting beetles, and the other is a stick, and the thicker and heavier the better."

You may imagine that I had plenty to think of from the time that I left Brook Street until I set out to meet Lord Linchmere at Paddington. The whole fantastic business kept arranging and rearranging itself in kaleidoscopic forms inside my brain, until I had thought out a dozen explanations, each of them more grotesquely improbable than the last. And yet I felt that the truth must be something grotesquely improbable also. At last I gave up all attempts at finding a solution, and contented myself with exactly carrying out the instructions which I had received. With a hand valise, specimen case and a loaded cane, I was waiting at the Paddington bookstall when Lord Linchmere arrived. He was an even smaller man than I had thought – frail and peaky, with a manner which was more nervous than it had been in the morning. He wore a long, thick travelling ulster, and I observed that he carried a heavy blackthorn cudgel in his hand.

"I have the tickets," said he, leading the way up the platform. "This is our train. I have engaged a carriage, for I am particularly anxious to impress one or two things upon you while we travel down."

And yet all that he had to impress upon me might have been said in a sentence, for it was that I was to remember that I was there as a protection to himself, and that I was not on any consideration to leave him for an instant. This he repeated again and again as our journey drew to a close, with an insistence which showed that his nerves were thoroughly shaken.

"Yes," he said at last, in answer to my looks rather than to my words, "I *am* nervous, Dr Hamilton. I have always been a timid man, and my timidity depends upon my frail physical health. But my soul is firm, and I can bring myself up to face a danger which a less nervous man might shrink from. What I am doing now is done from no compulsion, but entirely from a sense of duty, and yet it is, beyond doubt, a desperate risk. If things should go wrong, I will have some claims to the title of martyr."

This eternal reading of riddles was too much for me. I felt that I must put a term to it.

"I think it would be very much better, sir, if you were to trust me entirely," said I. "It is impossible for me to act effectively when I do not know what are the objects which we have in view, or even where we are going."

"Oh, as to where we are going, there need be no mystery about that," said he. "We are going to Delamere Court, the residence of Sir Thomas Rossiter, with whose work you are so conversant. As to the exact object of our visit, I do not know that at this stage of the proceedings anything would be gained, Dr Hamilton, by taking you into my complete confidence. I may tell you that we are acting – I say 'we' because my sister, Lady Rossiter, takes the same view as myself – with the one object of preventing anything in the nature of a family scandal. That being so, you can understand that I am loth to give any explanations which are not absolutely necessary. It would be a different matter, Dr Hamilton, if I were asking your advice. As matters stand, it is only your active help which I need, and I will indicate to you from time to time how you can best give it."

There was nothing more to be said, and a poor man can put up with a good deal for twenty pounds a day, but I felt nonetheless that Lord Linchmere was acting rather scurvily towards me. He wished to convert me into a passive tool, like the blackthorn in his hand. With his sensitive disposition, I could imagine, however, that scandal would be abhorrent to him, and I realized that he would not take me into his confidence until no other course was open to him. I must trust to my own eyes and ears to solve the mystery, but I had every confidence that I should not trust to them in vain.

Delamere Court lies a good five miles from Pangbourne station, and we drove for that distance in an open fly. Lord Linchmere sat in deep thought during the time, and he never opened his mouth until we were close to our destination. When he did speak it was to give me a piece of information which surprised me.

"Perhaps you are not aware," said he, "that I am a medical man like yourself?"

"No, sir, I did not know it."

"Yes, I qualified in my younger days, when there were several lives between me and the peerage. I have not had occasion to practise, but I have found it a useful education, all the same. I never regretted the years which I devoted to medical study. These are the gates of Delamere Court."

We had come to two high pillars crowned with heraldic monsters which flanked the opening of a winding avenue. Over the laurel bushes and rhododendrons I could see a long, many-gabled mansion, girdled with ivy, and toned to the warm, cheery, mellow glow of old brickwork. My eyes were still fixed in admiration upon this delightful house when my companion plucked nervously at my sleeve.

"Here's Sir Thomas," he whispered. "Please talk beetle all you can."

A tall, thin figure, curiously angular and bony, had emerged through a gap in the hedge of laurels. In his hand he held a spud, and he wore gauntleted gardener's gloves. A broad-brimmed, grey hat cast his face into shadow, but it struck me as exceedingly austere, with an ill-nourished beard and harsh, irregular features. The fly pulled up and Lord Linchmere sprang out.

"My dear Thomas, how are you?" said he heartily.

But the heartiness was by no means reciprocal. The owner of the grounds glared at me over his brother-in-law's shoulder, and I caught broken scraps of sentences – "well-known wishes... hatred of strangers... unjustifiable intrusion... perfectly inexcusable." Then there was a muttered explanation, and the two of them came over together to the side of the fly.

"Let me present you to Sir Thomas Rossiter, Dr Hamilton," said Lord Linchmere. "You will find that you have a strong community of tastes."

I bowed. Sir Thomas stood very stiffly, looking at me severely from under the broad brim of his hat.

"Lord Linchmere tells me that you know something about beetles," said he. "What do you know about beetles?"

"I know what I have learnt from your work upon the coleoptera, Sir Thomas," I answered.

"Give me the names of the better-known species of the British *scarabaei*,"* said he.

I had not expected an examination, but fortunately I was ready for one. My answers seemed to please him, for his stern features relaxed.

"You appear to have read my book with some profit, sir," said he. "It is a rare thing for me to meet anyone who takes an intelligent interest in such matters. People can find time for such trivialities as sport or society, and yet the beetles are overlooked. I can assure you that the greater part of the idiots in this part of the country are unaware that I have ever written a book at all – I, the first man who ever described the true function of the elytra.* I am glad to see you, sir, and I have no doubt that I can show you some specimens which will interest you." He stepped into the fly and drove up with us to the house, expounding to me as we went some recent researches which he had made into the anatomy of the ladybird.

I have said that Sir Thomas Rossiter wore a large hat drawn down over his brows. As he entered the hall he uncovered himself, and I was at once aware of a singular characteristic which the hat had concealed. His forehead, which was naturally high, and higher still on account of receding hair, was in a continual state of movement. Some nervous weakness kept the muscles in a constant spasm, which sometimes produced a mere twitching and sometimes a curious rotary movement unlike anything which I had ever seen before. It was strikingly visible as he turned towards us after entering the study, and seemed the more singular from the contrast with the hard, steady, grey eyes which looked out from underneath those palpitating brows.

"I am sorry," said he, "that Lady Rossiter is not here to help me to welcome you. By the way, Charles, did Evelyn say anything about the date of her return?"

"She wished to stay in town for a few more days," said Lord Linchmere. "You know how ladies' social duties accumulate if they have been for some time in the country. My sister has many old friends in London at present."

"Well, she is her own mistress, and I should not wish to alter her plans, but I shall be glad when I see her again. It is very lonely here without her company."

"I was afraid that you might find it so, and that was partly why I ran down. My young friend, Dr Hamilton, is so much interested in the subject which you have made your own, that I thought you would not mind his accompanying me."

"I lead a retired life, Dr Hamilton, and my aversion to strangers grows upon me," said our host. "I have sometimes thought that my nerves are not so good as they were. My travels in search of beetles in my younger days took me into many malarious and unhealthy places. But a brother coleopterist like yourself is always a welcome guest, and I shall be delighted if you will look over my collection, which I think that I may without exaggeration describe as the best in Europe."

And so no doubt it was. He had a huge, oaken cabinet arranged in shallow drawers, and here, neatly ticketed and classified, were beetles from every corner of the earth, black, brown, blue, green and mottled. Every now and then as he swept his hand over the lines and lines of impaled insects he would catch up some rare specimen and, handling it with as much delicacy and reverence as if it were a precious relic, he would hold forth upon its peculiarities and the circumstances under which it came into his possession. It was evidently an unusual thing for him to meet with a sympathetic listener, and he talked and talked until the spring evening had deepened into night, and the gong announced that it was time to dress for dinner. All the time Lord Linchmere said nothing, but he stood at his brother-in-law's elbow, and I caught him continually shooting curious little questioning glances into his face. And his own features expressed some strong emotion, apprehension, sympathy, expectation: I seemed to read them all. I was sure that Lord Linchmere was fearing something and awaiting something, but what that something might be I could not imagine.

The evening passed quietly but pleasantly, and I should have been entirely at my ease if it had not been for that continual sense of tension upon the part of Lord Linchmere. As to our host, I found that he improved upon acquaintance. He spoke constantly with affection of his absent wife, and also of his little son, who had recently been sent to school. The house, he said, was not the same without them. If it were not for his scientific studies, he did not know how he could get through the days. After dinner we smoked for some time in the billiard room, and finally went early to bed.

And then it was that, for the first time, the suspicion that Lord Linchmere was a lunatic crossed my mind. He followed me into my bedroom, when our host had retired.

"Doctor," said he, speaking in a low, hurried voice, "you must come with me. You must spend the night in my bedroom."

"What do you mean?"

"I prefer not to explain. But this is part of your duties. My room is close by, and you can return to your own before the servant calls you in the morning."

"But why?" I asked.

"Because I am nervous of being alone," said he. "That's the reason, since you must have a reason."

It seemed rank lunacy, but the argument of those twenty pounds would overcome many objections. I followed him to his room.

"Well," said I, "there's only room for one in that bed."

"Only one shall occupy it," said he.

"And the other?"

"Must remain on watch."

"Why?" said I. "One would think you expected to be attacked."

"Perhaps I do."

"In that case, why not lock your door?"

"Perhaps I *want* to be attacked."

It looked more and more like lunacy. However, there was nothing for it but to submit. I shrugged my shoulders and sat down in the armchair beside the empty fireplace.

"I am to remain on watch, then?" said I ruefully.

"We will divide the night. If you will watch until two, I will watch the remainder."

"Very good."

"Call me at two o'clock, then."

"I will do so."

"Keep your ears open, and if you hear any sounds wake me instantly – instantly, you hear?"

"You can rely upon it." I tried to look as solemn as he did.

"And for God's sake don't go to sleep," said he, and so, taking off only his coat, he threw the coverlet over him and settled down for the night.

It was a melancholy vigil, and made more so by my own sense of its folly. Supposing that by any chance Lord Linchmere had cause to suspect that he was subject to danger in the house of Sir Thomas Rossiter, why on earth could he not lock his door and so protect himself? His own answer that he might wish to be attacked was absurd. Why should he possibly wish to be attacked? And who would wish to attack him? Clearly, Lord Linchmere was suffering from some singular delusion, and the result was that on an imbecile pretext I was to be deprived of my night's rest. Still, however absurd, I was determined to carry out his injunctions to the letter as long as I was in his employment. I sat, therefore, beside the empty fireplace, and listened to a sonorous chiming clock somewhere down the passage, which gurgled and struck every quarter of an hour. It was an endless vigil. Save for that single clock, an absolute silence reigned throughout the great house. A small lamp stood on the table at my elbow, throwing a circle of light round my chair, but leaving the corners of the room draped in shadow. On the bed Lord Linchmere was breathing peacefully. I envied him his quiet sleep, and again and again my own eyelids drooped, but every time my sense of duty came to my help, and I sat up, rubbing my eyes and pinching myself with a determination to see my irrational watch to an end.

And I did so. From down the passage came the chimes of two o'clock, and I laid my hand upon the shoulder of the sleeper. Instantly he was sitting up, with an expression of the keenest interest upon his face.

"You have heard something?"

"No, sir. It is two o'clock."

"Very good. I will watch. You can go to sleep."

I lay down under the coverlet as he had done and was soon unconscious. My last recollection was of that circle of lamplight, and of the small, hunched-up figure and strained, anxious face of Lord Linchmere in the centre of it.

How long I slept I do not know; but I was suddenly aroused by a sharp tug at my sleeve. The room was in darkness, but a hot smell of oil told me that the lamp had only that instant been extinguished.

"Quick! Quick!" said Lord Linchmere's voice in my ear.

I sprang out of bed, he still dragging at my arm.

"Over here!" he whispered, and pulled me into a corner of the room. "Hush! Listen!"

In the silence of the night I could distinctly hear that someone was coming down the corridor. It was a stealthy step, faint and intermittent, as of a man who paused cautiously after every stride. Sometimes for half a minute there was no sound, and then came the shuffle and creak which told of a fresh advance. My companion was trembling with excitement. His hand, which still held my sleeve, twitched like a branch in the wind.

"What is it?" I whispered.

"It's he!"

"Sir Thomas?"

"Yes."

"What does he want?"

"Hush! Do nothing until I tell you."

I was conscious now that someone was trying the door. There was the faintest little rattle from the handle, and then I dimly saw a thin slit of subdued light. There was a lamp burning somewhere far down the passage, and it just sufficed to make the outside visible from the darkness of our room. The greyish slit grew broader and broader, very gradually, very gently, and then outlined against it I saw the dark figure of a man. He was squat and crouching, with the silhouette of a bulky and misshapen dwarf. Slowly the door swung open with this ominous shape framed in the centre of it. And then, in an instant, the crouching figure shot up, there was a tiger spring across the room and thud, thud, thud, came three tremendous blows from some heavy object upon the bed.

I was so paralysed with amazement that I stood motionless and staring until I was aroused by a yell for help from my companion. The open door shed enough light for me to see the outline of things, and there was little Lord Linchmere with his arms round the neck of his brother-in-law, holding bravely on to him like a game bull terrier with its teeth into a gaunt deerhound. The tall, bony man dashed himself about, writhing round and round to get a grip upon his assailant; but the other, clutching on from behind, still kept his hold, though his shrill, frightened cries showed how unequal he felt the contest to be. I sprang to the rescue, and the two of us managed to throw Sir Thomas to the ground, though he made his teeth meet in my shoulder. With all my youth and weight and strength, it was a desperate struggle before we could master his frenzied struggles; but at last we secured his arms with the waist cord of the dressing gown which he was wearing. I was holding his legs while Lord Linchmere was endeavouring to relight the lamp, when there came the pattering of many feet in the passage, and the butler and two footmen, who had been alarmed by the cries, rushed into the room. With their aid we had no further difficulty in securing our prisoner, who lay foaming and glaring upon the ground. One glance at his face was enough to prove that he was a dangerous maniac, while the short, heavy hammer which lay beside the bed showed how murderous had been his intentions.

"Do not use any violence!" said Lord Linchmere, as we raised the struggling man to his feet. "He will have a period of stupor after this excitement. I believe that it is coming on already." As he spoke the convulsions became less violent, and the madman's head fell forward upon his breast, as if he were overcome by sleep. We led him down the passage and stretched him upon his own bed, where he lay unconscious, breathing heavily.

"Two of you will watch him," said Lord Linchmere. "And now, Dr Hamilton, if you will return with me to my room, I will give you the explanation which my horror of scandal has perhaps caused me to delay too long. Come what may, you will never have cause to regret your share in this night's work.

"The case may be made clear in a very few words," he continued, when we were alone. "My poor brother-in-law is one of the best fellows upon earth, a loving husband and an estimable father, but he comes from a stock which is deeply tainted with insanity. He has more than once had homicidal outbreaks, which are the more painful because his inclination is always to attack the very person to whom he is most attached. His son was sent away to school to avoid this danger, and then came an attempt upon my sister, his wife, from which she escaped with injuries that you may have observed when you met her in London. You understand that he knows nothing of the matter when he is in his sound senses, and would ridicule the suggestion that he could under any circumstances injure those whom he loves so dearly. It is often, as you know, a characteristic of such maladies that it is absolutely impossible to convince the man who suffers from them of their existence.

"Our great object was, of course, to get him under restraint before he could stain his hands with blood, but the matter was full of difficulty. He is a recluse in his habits, and would not see any medical man. Besides, it was necessary for our purpose that the medical man should convince himself of his insanity; and he is sane as you or I, save on these very rare occasions. But, fortunately, before he has these attacks he always shows certain premonitory symptoms, which are providential danger signals, warning us to be upon our guard. The chief of these is that nervous contortion of the forehead which you must have observed. This is a phenomenon which always appears from three to four days before his attacks of frenzy. The moment it showed itself his wife came into town on some pretext, and took refuge in my house in Brook Street.

"It remained for me to convince a medical man of Sir Thomas's insanity, without which it was impossible to put him where he could do no harm. The first problem was how to get a medical man into his house. I bethought me of his interest in beetles, and his love for anyone who shared his tastes. I advertised, therefore, and was fortunate enough to find in you the very man I wanted. A stout companion was necessary, for I knew that the lunacy could only be proved by a murderous assault, and I had every reason to believe that that assault would be made upon myself, since he had the warmest regard for me in his moments of sanity. I think your intelligence will supply all the rest. I did not know that the attack would come by night, but I thought it very probable, for the crises of such cases usually do occur in the early hours of the morning. I am a very nervous man myself, but I saw no other way in which I could remove this terrible danger from my sister's life. I need not ask you whether you are willing to sign the lunacy papers."

"Undoubtedly. But *two* signatures are necessary."

"You forget that I am myself a holder of a medical degree. I have the papers on a side table here, so if you will be good enough to sign them now, we can have the patient removed in the morning."

So that was my visit to Sir Thomas Rossiter, the famous beetle-hunter, and that was also my first step upon the ladder of success, for Lady Rossiter and Lord Linchmere have proved to be staunch friends, and they have never forgotten my association with them in the time of their need. Sir Thomas is out and said to be cured, but I still think that if I spent another night at Delamere Court, I should be inclined to lock my door upon the inside.

The Man with the Watches

There are many who will still bear in mind the singular circumstances which, under the heading of the Rugby Mystery, filled many columns of the daily press in the spring of the year 1892. Coming as it did at a period of exceptional dullness, it attracted perhaps rather more attention than it deserved, but it offered to the public that mixture of the whimsical and the tragic which is most stimulating to the popular imagination. Interest drooped, however, when, after weeks of fruitless investigation, it was found that no final explanation of the facts was forthcoming, and the tragedy seemed from that time to the present to have finally taken its place in the dark catalogue of inexplicable and unexpiated crimes. A recent communication (the authenticity of which appears to be above question) has, however, thrown some new and clear light upon the matter. Before laying it before the public it would be as well, perhaps, that I should refresh their memories as to the singular facts upon which this commentary is founded. These facts were briefly as follows:

At five o'clock on the evening of 18th March in the year already mentioned a train left Euston Station for Manchester. It was a rainy, squally day, which grew wilder as it progressed, so it was by no means the weather in which anyone would travel who was not driven to do so by necessity. The train, however, is a favourite one among Manchester businessmen who are returning from town, for it does the journey in four hours and twenty minutes, with only three stoppages upon the way. In spite of the inclement evening it was, therefore, fairly well filled upon the occasion of which I speak. The guard of the train was a tried servant of the company – a man who had worked for twenty-two years without blemish or complaint. His name was John Palmer.

The station clock was upon the stroke of five, and the guard was about to give the customary signal to the engine driver when he observed two belated passengers hurrying down the platform. The one was an exceptionally tall man, dressed in a long, black overcoat with astrakhan collar and cuffs. I have already said that the evening was an inclement one, and the tall traveller had the high, warm collar turned up to protect his throat against the bitter March wind. He appeared, as far as the guard could judge by so hurried an inspection, to be a man between fifty and sixty years of age, who had retained a good deal of the vigour and activity of his youth. In one hand he carried a brown leather Gladstone bag. His companion was a lady, tall and erect, walking with a vigorous step which outpaced the gentleman beside her. She wore a long, fawn-coloured dust cloak, a black, close-fitting toque and a dark veil which concealed the greater part of her face. The two might very well have passed as father and daughter. They walked swiftly down the line of carriages, glancing in at the windows, until the guard, John Palmer, overtook them.

"Now, then, sir, look sharp, the train is going," said he.

"First-class," the man answered.

The guard turned the handle of the nearest door. In the carriage which he had opened, there sat a small man with a cigar in his mouth. His appearance seems to have impressed itself upon the guard's memory, for he was prepared, afterwards, to describe or to identify him. He was a man of thirty-four or thirty-five years of age, dressed in some grey material, sharp-nosed, alert, with a ruddy, weather-beaten face, and a small, closely cropped black beard. He glanced up as the door was opened. The tall man paused with his foot upon the step.

"This is a smoking compartment. The lady dislikes smoke," said he, looking round at the guard.

"All right! Here you are, sir!" said John Palmer. He slammed the door of the smoking carriage, opened that of the next one, which was empty, and thrust the two travellers in. At the same moment he sounded his whistle and the wheels of the train began to move. The man with the cigar was at the window of his carriage, and said something to the guard as he rolled past him, but the words were lost in the bustle of the departure. Palmer stepped into the guard's van, as it came up to him, and thought no more of the incident.

Twelve minutes after its departure the train reached Willesden Junction, where it stopped for a very short interval. An examination of the tickets has made it certain that no one either joined or left it at this time, and no passenger was seen to alight upon the platform. At 5.14 the journey to Manchester was resumed, and Rugby was reached at 6.50, the express being five minutes late.

At Rugby the attention of the station officials was drawn to the fact that the door of one of the first-class carriages was open. An examination of that compartment, and of its neighbour, disclosed a remarkable state of affairs.

The smoking carriage in which the short, red-faced man with the black beard had been seen was now empty. Save for a half-smoked cigar, there was no trace whatever of its recent occupant. The door of this carriage was fastened. In the next compartment, to which attention had been originally drawn, there was no sign either of the gentleman with the astrakhan collar or of the young lady who accompanied him. All three passengers had disappeared. On the other hand, there was found upon the floor of this carriage – the one in which the tall traveller and the lady had been – a young man, fashionably dressed and of elegant appearance. He lay with his knees drawn up, and his head resting against the farther door, an elbow upon either seat. A bullet had penetrated his heart and his death must have been instantaneous. No one had seen such a man enter the train, and no railway ticket was found in his pocket, neither were there any markings upon his linen, nor papers nor personal property which might help to identify him. Who he was, whence he had come and how he had met his end were each as great a mystery as what had occurred to the three people who had started an hour and a half before from Willesden in those two compartments.

I have said that there was no personal property which might help to identify him, but it is true that there was one peculiarity about this unknown young man which was much commented upon at the time. In his pockets were found no fewer than six valuable gold watches, three in the various pockets of his waistcoat, one in his ticket pocket, one in his breast pocket and one small one set in a leather strap and fastened round his left wrist. The obvious explanation that the man was a pickpocket, and that this was his plunder, was discounted by the fact that all six were of American make and of a type which is rare in England. Three of them bore the mark of the Rochester Watchmaking Company; one was by Mason, of Elmira; one was unmarked; and the small one, which was highly jewelled and ornamented, was from Tiffany, of New York. The other contents of his pocket consisted of an ivory knife with a corkscrew by Rodgers, of Sheffield; a small, circular mirror, one inch in diameter; a readmission slip to the Lyceum Theatre; a silver boxful of vesta matches; and a brown leather cigar case containing two cheroots – also two pounds fourteen shillings in money. It was clear, then, that whatever motives may have led to his death, robbery was not among them. As already mentioned, there were no markings upon the man's linen, which appeared to be new, and no tailor's name upon his coat. In appearance he was young, short, smooth-cheeked and delicately featured. One of his front teeth was conspicuously stopped with gold.

On the discovery of the tragedy an examination was instantly made of the tickets of all passengers, and the number of the passengers themselves was counted. It was found that only three tickets were unaccounted for, corresponding to the three travellers who were missing. The express was then allowed to proceed, but a new guard was sent with it, and John Palmer was detained as a witness at Rugby. The carriage which included the two compartments in question was uncoupled and sidetracked. Then, on the arrival of Inspector Vane, of Scotland Yard, and of Mr Henderson, a detective in the service of the railway company, an exhaustive inquiry was made into all the circumstances.

That crime had been committed was certain. The bullet, which appeared to have come from a small pistol or revolver, had been fired from some little distance, as there was no scorching of the clothes. No weapon was found in the compartment (which finally disposed of the theory of suicide), nor was there any sign of the brown leather bag which the guard had seen in the hand of the tall gentleman. A lady's parasol was found upon the rack, but no other trace was to be seen of the travellers in either of the sections. Apart from the crime, the question of how or why three passengers (one of them a lady) could get out of the train, and one other get in during the unbroken run between Willesden and Rugby, was one which excited the utmost curiosity among the general public, and gave rise to much speculation in the London press.

John Palmer, the guard, was able at the inquest to give some evidence which threw a little light upon the matter. There was a spot between Tring and Cheddington, according to his statement, where, on account of some repairs to the line, the train had for a few minutes slowed down to a pace not exceeding eight or ten miles an hour. At that place it might be possible for a man, or even for an exceptionally active woman, to have left the train without serious injury. It was true that a gang of platelayers was there, and that they had seen nothing, but it was their custom to stand in the middle between the metals, and the open carriage door was upon the far side, so that it was conceivable that someone might have alighted unseen, as the darkness would by that time be drawing in. A steep embankment would instantly screen anyone who sprang out from the observation of the navvies.

The guard also deposed that there was a good deal of movement upon the platform at Willesden Junction, and that though it was certain that no one had either joined or left the train there, it was still quite possible that some of the passengers might have changed unseen from one compartment to another. It was by no means uncommon for a gentleman to finish his cigar in a smoking carriage and then to change to a clearer atmosphere. Supposing that the man with the black beard had done so at Willesden (and the half-smoked cigar upon the floor seemed to favour the supposition), he would naturally go into the nearest section, which would bring him into the company of the two other actors in this drama. Thus the first stage of the affair might be surmised without any great breach of probability. But what the second stage had been, or how the final one had been arrived at, neither the guard nor the experienced detective officers could suggest.

A careful examination of the line between Willesden and Rugby resulted in one discovery which might or might not have a bearing upon the tragedy. Near Tring, at the very place where the train slowed down, there was found at the bottom of the embankment a small pocket Testament, very shabby and worn. It was printed by the Bible Society of London, and bore an inscription: "From John to Alice. 13th Jan. 1856", upon the flyleaf. Underneath was written: "James. 4th July 1859", and beneath that again: "Edward. 1st Nov. 1869", all the entries being in the same handwriting. This was the only clue, if it could be called a clue, which the police obtained, and the coroner's verdict of "Murder by a person or persons unknown" was the unsatisfactory ending of a singular case. Advertisement, rewards and enquiries proved equally fruitless, and nothing could be found which was solid enough to form the basis for a profitable investigation.

It would be a mistake, however, to suppose that no theories were formed to account for the facts. On the contrary, the press, both in England and in America, teemed with suggestions and suppositions, most of which were obviously absurd. The fact that the watches were of American make, and some peculiarities in connection with the gold stopping of his front tooth, appeared to indicate that the deceased was a citizen of the United States, though his linen, clothes and boots were undoubtedly of British manufacture. It was surmised, by some, that he was concealed under the seat, and that, being discovered, he was for some reason, possibly because he had overheard their guilty secrets, put to death by his fellow passengers. When coupled with generalities as to the ferocity and cunning of anarchical and other secret societies, this theory sounded as plausible as any.

The fact that he should be without a ticket would be consistent with the idea of concealment, and it was well known that women played a prominent part in the Nihilistic propaganda.* On the other hand, it was clear, from the guard's statement, that the man must have been hidden there *before* the others arrived, and how unlikely the coincidence that conspirators should stray exactly into the very compartment in which a spy was already concealed! Besides, this explanation ignored the man in the smoking carriage, and gave no reason at all for his simultaneous disappearance. The police had little difficulty in showing that such a theory would not cover the facts, but they were unprepared in the absence of evidence to advance any alternative explanation.

There was a letter in the *Daily Gazette*, over the signature of a well-known criminal investigator, which gave rise to a considerable discussion at the time. He had formed a hypothesis which had at least ingenuity to recommend it, and I cannot do better than append it in his own words.

> Whatever may be the truth (said he) it must depend upon some bizarre and rare combination of events, so we need have no hesitation in postulating such events in our explanation. In the absence of data we must abandon the analytic or scientific method of investigation, and must approach it in the synthetic fashion. In a word, instead of taking known events and deducing from them what has occurred, we must build up a fanciful explanation if it will only be consistent with known events. We can then test this explanation by any fresh facts which may arise. If they all fit into their places, the probability is that we are upon the right track, and with each fresh fact this probability increases in a geometrical progression until the evidence becomes final and convincing.
>
> Now, there is one most remarkable and suggestive fact which has not met with the attention which it deserves. There is a local train running through Harrow and King's Langley, which is timed in such a way that the express must have overtaken it at or about the period when it eased down its speed to eight miles an hour on account of the repairs of the line. The two trains would at that time be travelling in the same direction at a similar rate of speed and upon parallel lines. It is within everyone's experience how, under such circumstances, the occupant of each carriage can see very plainly the passengers in the other carriages opposite to him. The lamps of the express had been lit at Willesden, so that each compartment was brightly illuminated, and most visible to an observer from outside.
>
> Now, the sequence of events as I reconstruct them would be after this fashion. This young man with the abnormal number of watches was alone in the carriage of the slow train. His ticket, with his papers and gloves and other things, was, we will suppose, on the seat beside him. He was probably an American, and also probably a man of weak intellect. The excessive wearing of jewellery is an early symptom in some forms of mania.

As he sat watching the carriages of the express which were (on account of the state of the line) going at the same pace as himself, he suddenly saw some people in it whom he knew. We will suppose for the sake of our theory that these people were a woman whom he loved and a man whom he hated – and who in return hated him. The young man was excitable and impulsive. He opened the door of his carriage, stepped from the footboard of the local train to the footboard of the express, opened the other door, and made his way into the presence of these two people. The feat (on the supposition that the trains were going at the same pace) is by no means so perilous as it might appear.

Having now got our young man, without his ticket, into the carriage in which the elder man and the young woman are travelling, it is not difficult to imagine that a violent scene ensued. It is possible that the pair were also Americans, which is the more probable as the man carried a weapon – an unusual thing in England. If our supposition of incipient mania is correct, the young man is likely to have assaulted the other. As the upshot of the quarrel the elder man shot the intruder, and then made his escape from the carriage, taking the young lady with him. We will suppose that all this happened very rapidly, and that the train was still going at so slow a pace that it was not difficult for them to leave it. A woman might leave a train going at eight miles an hour. As a matter of fact, we know that this woman did do so.

And now we have to fit in the man in the smoking carriage. Presuming that we have, up to this point, reconstructed the tragedy correctly, we shall find nothing in this other man to cause us to reconsider our conclusions. According to my theory, this man saw the young fellow cross from one train to the other, saw him open the door, heard the pistol shot, saw the two fugitives spring out onto the line, realized that murder had been done, and sprang out himself in pursuit. Why he has never been heard of since – whether he met his own death in the pursuit, or whether, as is more likely, he was made to realize that it was not a case for his interference – is a detail which we have at present no means of explaining. I acknowledge that there are some difficulties in the way. At first sight, it might seem improbable that at such a moment a murderer would burden himself in his flight with a brown leather bag. My answer is that he was well aware that if the bag were found his identity would be established. It was absolutely necessary for him to take it with him. My theory stands or falls upon one point, and I call upon the railway company to make strict enquiry as to whether a ticket was found unclaimed in the local train through Harrow and King's Langley upon 18th March. If such a ticket were found my case is proved. If not, my theory may still be the correct one, for it is conceivable either that he travelled without a ticket or that his ticket was lost.

To this elaborate and plausible hypothesis the answer of the police and of the company was, first, that no such ticket was found; secondly, that the slow train would never run parallel to the express; and, thirdly, that the local train had been stationary in King's Langley station when the express, going at fifty miles an hour, had flashed past it. So perished the only satisfying explanation, and five years have elapsed without supplying a new one. Now, at last, there comes a statement which covers all the facts, and which must be regarded as authentic. It took the shape of a letter dated from New York, and addressed to the same criminal investigator whose theory I have quoted. It is given here *in extenso*, with the exception of the two opening paragraphs, which are personal in their nature:

You'll excuse me if I'm not very free with names. There's less reason now than there was five years ago when Mother was still living. But for all that, I had rather cover up our tracks all I can. But I owe you an explanation, for if your idea of it was wrong, it was a mighty ingenious one all the same. I'll have to go back a little so as you may understand all about it.

My people came from Bucks, England, and emigrated to the States in the early Fifties. They settled in Rochester, in the state of New York, where my father ran a large dry-goods store. There were only two sons: myself, James, and my brother, Edward. I was ten years older than my brother, and after my father died I sort of took the place of a father to him, as an elder brother would. He was a bright, spirited boy, and just one of the most beautiful creatures that ever lived. But there was always a soft spot in him, and it was like mould in cheese, for it spread and spread, and nothing that you could do would stop it. Mother saw it just as clearly as I did, but she went on spoiling him all the same, for he had such a way with him that you could refuse him nothing. I did all I could to hold him in, and he hated me for my pains.

At last he fairly got his head, and nothing that we could do would stop him. He got off into New York, and went rapidly from bad to worse. At first he was only fast, and then he was criminal; and then, at the end of a year or two, he was one of the most notorious young crooks in the city. He had formed a friendship with Sparrow MacCoy, who was at the head of his profession as a bunco-steerer, green-goods man* and general rascal. They took to card-sharping, and frequented some of the best hotels in New York. My brother was an excellent actor (he might have made an honest name for himself if he had chosen), and he would take the parts of a young Englishman of title, of a simple lad from the West, or of a college undergraduate, whichever suited Sparrow MacCoy's purpose. And then one day he dressed himself as a girl, and he carried it off so well, and made himself such a valuable decoy, that it was their favourite game afterwards. They had made it right with Tammany* and with the police, so it seemed as if nothing could ever stop them, for those were in the days before the Lexow Commission,* and if you only had a pull, you could do pretty nearly everything you wanted.

And nothing would have stopped them if they had only stuck to cards and New York, but they must needs come up Rochester way, and forge a name upon a cheque. It was my brother that did it, though everyone knew that it was under the influence of Sparrow MacCoy. I bought up that cheque, and a pretty sum it cost me. Then I went to my brother, laid it before him on the table, and swore to him that I would prosecute if he did not clear out of the country. At first he simply laughed. I could not prosecute, he said, without breaking our mother's heart, and he knew that I would not do that. I made him understand, however, that our mother's heart was being broken in any case, and that I had set firm on the point that I would rather see him in Rochester jail than in a New York hotel. So at last he gave in, and he made me a solemn promise that he would see Sparrow MacCoy no more, that he would go to Europe, and that he would turn his hand to any honest trade that I helped him to get. I took him down right away to an old family friend, Joe Willson, who is an exporter of American watches and clocks, and I got him to give Edward an agency in London, with a small salary and a 15-per-cent commission on all business. His manner and appearance were so good that he won the old man over at once, and within a week he was sent off to London with a case full of samples.

It seemed to me that this business of the cheque had really given my brother a fright, and that there was some chance of his settling down into an honest line of life. My mother had spoken with him, and what she said had touched him, for she had always been the best of mothers to him and he had been the great sorrow of her life. But I knew that this man Sparrow MacCoy had a great influence over Edward and my chance of keeping the lad straight lay in breaking the connection between them. I had a friend in the New York detective force, and through him I kept a watch upon MacCoy. When, within a fortnight of my brother's sailing, I heard that MacCoy had taken a berth in the *Etruria*, I was as certain as if he had told me that he was going over to England for the purpose of coaxing Edward back again into the ways that he had left. In an instant I had resolved to go also, and to pit my influence against MacCoy's. I knew it was a losing fight, but I thought, and my mother thought, that it was my duty. We passed the last night together in prayer for my success, and she gave me her own Testament that my father had given her on the day of their marriage in the Old Country, so that I might always wear it next my heart.

I was a fellow traveller, on the steamship, with Sparrow MacCoy, and at least I had the satisfaction of spoiling his little game for the voyage. The very first night I went into the smoking room, and found him at the head of a card table, with half a dozen young fellows who were carrying their full purses and their empty skulls over to Europe. He was settling down for his harvest, and a rich one it would have been. But I soon changed all that.

"Gentleman," said I, "are you aware whom you are playing with?"

"What's that to you? You mind your own business!" said he, with an oath.

"Who is it, anyway?" asked one of the dudes.

"He's Sparrow MacCoy, the most notorious card-sharper in the States."

Up he jumped with a bottle in his hand, but he remembered that he was under the flag of the effete Old Country, where law and order run, and Tammany has no pull. Jail and the gallows wait for violence and murder, and there's no slipping out by the back door on board an ocean liner.

"Prove your words, you —!" said he.

"I will!" said I. "If you will turn up your right shirtsleeve to the shoulder, I will either prove my words or I will eat them."

He turned white and said not a word. You see, I knew something of his ways, and I was aware that part of the mechanism which he and all such sharpers use consists of an elastic down the arm with a clip just above the wrist. It is by means of this clip that they withdraw from their hands the cards which they do not want, while they substitute other cards from another hiding place. I reckoned on it being there, and it was. He cursed me, slunk out of the saloon and was hardly seen again during the voyage. For once, at any rate, I got level with Mr Sparrow MacCoy.

But he soon had his revenge upon me, for when it came to influencing my brother he outweighed me every time. Edward had kept himself straight in London for the first few weeks, and had done some business with his American watches, until this villain came across his path once more. I did my best, but the best was little enough. The next thing I heard there had been a scandal at one of the Northumberland Avenue hotels: a traveller had been fleeced of a large sum by two confederate card-sharpers, and the matter was in the hands of Scotland Yard. The first I learnt of it was in the evening paper, and I was at once certain that my brother and MacCoy were back at their old games. I hurried at once to Edward's lodgings. They told me that he and a tall gentleman (whom I recognized as MacCoy) had gone off together, and that he had left the lodgings and taken his things with him. The landlady had heard them give several directions to the cabman, ending with Euston Station, and she had accidentally overheard the tall gentleman saying something about Manchester. She believed that that was their destination.

A glance at the timetable showed me that the most likely train was at five, though there was another at 4.35 which they might have caught. I had only time to get the later one, but found no sign of them either at the depot or in the train. They must have gone on by the earlier one, so I determined to follow them to Manchester and search for them in the hotels there. One last appeal to my brother by all that he owed to my mother might even now be the salvation of him. My nerves were overstrung, and I lit a cigar to steady them. At that moment, just as the train was moving off, the door of my compartment was flung open, and there were MacCoy and my brother on the platform.

They were both disguised, and with good reason, for they knew that the London police were after them. MacCoy had a great astrakhan collar drawn up, so that only his eyes and nose were showing. My brother was dressed like a woman, with a black veil half down his face, but of course it did not deceive me for an instant, nor would it have done so even if I had not known that he had often used such a dress before. I started up, and as I did so MacCoy recognized me. He said something, the conductor slammed the door, and they were shown into the next compartment. I tried to stop the train so as to follow them, but the wheels were already moving, and it was too late.

When we stopped at Willesden, I instantly changed my carriage. It appears that I was not seen to do so, which is not surprising, as the station was crowded with people. MacCoy, of course, was expecting me, and he had spent the time between Euston and Willesden in saying all he could to harden my brother's heart and set him against me. That is what I fancy, for I had never found him so impossible to soften or to move. I tried this way and I tried that; I pictured his future in an English jail; I described the sorrow of his mother when I came back with the news; I said everything to touch his heart, but all to no purpose. He sat there with a fixed sneer upon his handsome face, while every now and then Sparrow MacCoy would throw in a taunt at me, or some word of encouragement to hold my brother to his resolutions.

"Why don't you run a Sunday school?" he would say to me, and then, in the same breath: "He thinks you have no will of your own. He thinks you are just the baby brother and that he can lead you where he likes. He's only just finding out that you are a man as well as he."

It was those words of his which set me talking bitterly. We had left Willesden, you understand, for all this took some time. My temper got the better of me, and for the first time in my life I let my brother see the rough side of me. Perhaps it would have been better had I done so earlier and more often.

"A man!" said I. "Well, I'm glad to have your friend's assurance of it, for no one would suspect it to see you like a boarding-school missy. I don't suppose in all this country there is a more contemptible-looking creature than you are as you sit there with that dolly pinafore upon you." He coloured up at that, for he was a vain man, and he winced from ridicule.

"It's only a dust cloak," said he, and he slipped it off. "One has to throw the coppers off one's scent, and I had no other way to do it." He took his toque off with the veil attached, and he put both it and the cloak into his brown bag. "Anyway, I don't need to wear it until the conductor comes round," said he.

"Nor then, either," said I, and taking the bag I slung it with all my force out of the window. "Now," said I, "you'll never make a Mary Jane of yourself while I can help it. If nothing but that disguise stands between you and a jail, then to jail you shall go."

That was the way to manage him. I felt my advantage at once. His supple nature was one which yielded to roughness far more readily than to entreaty. He flushed with shame, and his eyes filled with tears. But MacCoy saw my advantage also, and was determined that I should not pursue it.

"He's my pard,* and you shall not bully him," he cried.

"He's my brother, and you shall not ruin him," said I. "I believe a spell of prison is the very best way of keeping you apart, and you shall have it, or it will be no fault of mine."

"Oh, you would squeal, would you?" he cried, and in an instant he whipped out his revolver. I sprang for his hand, but saw that I was too late, and jumped aside. At the same instant he fired, and the bullet which would have struck me passed through the heart of my unfortunate brother.

He dropped without a groan upon the floor of the compartment, and MacCoy and I, equally horrified, knelt at each side of him, trying to bring back some signs of life. MacCoy still held the loaded revolver in his hand, but his anger against me and my resentment towards him had both for the moment been swallowed up in this sudden tragedy. It was he who first realized the situation. The train was for some reason going very slowly at the moment, and he saw his opportunity for escape. In an instant he had the door open, but I was as quick as he, and jumping upon him the two of us fell off the footboard and rolled in each other's arms down a steep embankment. At the bottom I struck my head against a stone, and I remembered nothing more. When I came to myself I was lying among some low bushes, not far from the railroad track, and somebody was bathing my head with a wet handkerchief. It was Sparrow MacCoy.

"I guess I couldn't leave you," said he. "I didn't want to have the blood of two of you on my hands in one day. You loved your brother, I've no doubt; but you didn't love him a cent more than I loved him, though you'll say that I took a queer way to show it. Anyhow, it seems a mighty empty world now that he is gone, and I don't care a continental* whether you give me over to the hangman or not."

He had turned his ankle in the fall, and there we sat, he with his useless foot and I with my throbbing head, and we talked and talked until gradually my bitterness began to soften and to turn into something like sympathy. What was the use of revenging his death upon a man who was as much stricken by that death as I was? And then, as my wits gradually returned, I began to realize also that I could do nothing against MacCoy which would not recoil upon my mother and myself. How could we convict him without a full account of my brother's career being made public – the very thing which of all others we wished to avoid? It was really as much our interest as his to cover the matter up, and from being an avenger of crime I found myself changed to a conspirator against

Justice. The place in which we found ourselves was one of those pheasant preserves which are so common in the Old Country, and as we groped our way through it I found myself consulting the slayer of my brother as to how far it would be possible to hush it up.

I soon realized from what he said that unless there were some papers of which we knew nothing in my brother's pockets, there was really no possible means by which the police could identify him or learn how he had got there. His ticket was in MacCoy's pocket, and so was the ticket for some baggage which they had left at the depot. Like most Americans, he had found it cheaper and easier to buy an outfit in London than to bring one from New York, so that all his linen and clothes were new and unmarked. The bag, containing the dust cloak, which I had thrown out of the window, may have fallen among some bramble patch where it is still concealed, or may have been carried off by some tramp, or may have come into the possession of the police, who kept the incident to themselves. Anyhow, I have seen nothing about it in the London papers. As to the watches, they were a selection from those which had been entrusted to him for business purposes. It may have been for the same business purposes that he was taking them to Manchester, but – well, it's too late to enter into that.

I don't blame the police for being at fault. I don't see how it could have been otherwise. There was just one little clue that they might have followed up, but it was a small one. I mean that small, circular mirror which was found in my brother's pocket. It isn't a very common thing for a young man to carry about with him, is it? But a gambler might have told you what such a mirror may mean to a card-sharper. If you sit back a little from the table, and lay the mirror, face upwards, upon your lap, you can see, as you deal, every card that you give to your adversary. It is not hard to say whether you see a man or raise him when you know his cards as well as your own. It was as much a part of a sharper's outfit as the elastic clip upon Sparrow MacCoy's arm. Taking that, in connection with the recent frauds at the hotels, the police might have got hold of one end of the string.

I don't think there is much more for me to explain. We got to a village called Amersham that night in the character of two gentlemen upon a walking tour, and afterwards we made our way quietly to London, whence MacCoy went on to Cairo and I returned to New York. My mother died six months afterwards, and I am glad to say that to the day of her death she never knew what happened. She was always under the delusion that Edward was earning an honest living in London, and I never had the heart to tell her the truth. He never wrote; but, then, he never did write at any time, so that made no difference. His name was the last upon her lips.

There's just one other thing that I have to ask you, sir, and I should take it as a kind return for all this explanation, if you could do it for me. You remember that Testament that was picked up. I always carried it in my inside pocket, and it must have come out in my fall. I value it very highly, for it was the family book with my birth and my brother's marked by my father in the beginning of it. I wish you would apply at the proper place and have it sent to me. It can be of no possible value to anyone else. If you address it to X, Bassano's Library, Broadway, New York, it is sure to come to hand.

The Japanned Box

It *was* a curious thing, said the private tutor; one of those grotesque and whimsical incidents which occur to one as one goes through life. I lost the best situation which I am ever likely to have through it. But I am glad that I went to Thorpe Place, for I gained – well, as I tell you the story you will learn what I gained.

I don't know whether you are familiar with that part of the Midlands which is drained by the Avon. It is the most English part of England. Shakespeare, the flower of the whole race, was born right in the middle of it. It is a land of rolling pastures, rising in higher folds to the westward, until they swell into the Malvern Hills. There are no towns, but numerous villages, each with its grey Norman church. You have left the brick of the southern and eastern counties behind you, and everything is stone – stone for the walls, and lichened slabs of stone for the roofs. It is all grim and solid and massive, as befits the heart of a great nation.

It was in the middle of this country, not very far from Evesham, that Sir John Bollamore lived in the old ancestral home of Thorpe Place, and thither it was that I came to teach his two little sons. Sir John was a widower – his wife had died three years before – and he had been left with these two lads aged eight and ten, and one dear little girl of seven. Miss Witherton, who is now my wife, was governess to this little girl. I was tutor to the two boys. Could there be a more obvious prelude to an engagement? She governs me now, and I tutor two little boys of our own. But, there – I have already revealed what it was which I gained in Thorpe Place!

It was a very, very old house, incredibly old – pre-Norman, some of it – and the Bollamores claimed to have lived in that situation since long before the Conquest. It struck a chill to my heart when first I came there, those enormously thick grey walls, the rude crumbling stones, the smell as from a sick animal which exhaled from the rotting plaster of the aged building. But the modern wing was bright and the garden was well kept. No house could be dismal which had a pretty girl inside it and such a show of roses in front.

Apart from a very complete staff of servants there were only four of us in the household. These were Miss Witherton, who was at that time four-and-twenty and as pretty – well, as pretty as Mrs Colmore is now – myself, Frank Colmore, aged thirty, Mrs Stevens, the housekeeper, a dry, silent woman, and Mr Richards, a tall military-looking man who acted as steward to the Bollamore estates. We four always had our meals together, but Sir John had his usually alone in the library. Sometimes he joined us at dinner, but on the whole we were just as glad when he did not.

For he was a very formidable person. Imagine a man six feet three inches in height, majestically built, with a high-nosed, aristocratic face, brindled hair, shaggy eyebrows, a small, pointed Mephistophelian beard and lines upon his brow and round his eyes as deep as if they had been carved with a penknife. He had grey eyes, weary, hopeless-looking eyes, proud and yet pathetic, eyes which claimed your pity and yet dared you to show it. His back was rounded with study, but otherwise he was as fine a looking man of his age – five-and-fifty perhaps – as any woman would wish to look upon.

But his presence was not a cheerful one. He was always courteous, always refined, but singularly silent and retiring. I have never lived so long with any man and known so little of him. If he were indoors he spent his time either in his own small study in the Eastern Tower, or in the library in the modern wing. So regular was his routine that one could always say at any hour exactly where he would be. Twice in the day he would visit his study, once after breakfast, and once about ten at night. You might set your watch by the slam of the heavy door. For the rest of the day he would be in his library – save that for an hour or two in the afternoon he would take a walk or a ride, which was solitary like the rest of his existence. He loved his children, and was keenly interested in the progress of their studies, but they were a little awed by the silent, shaggy-browed figure, and they avoided him as much as they could. Indeed, we all did that.

It was some time before I came to know anything about the circumstances of Sir John Bollamore's life, for Mrs Stevens, the housekeeper, and Mr Richards, the land steward, were too loyal to talk easily of their employer's affairs. As to the governess, she knew no more than I did, and our common interest was one of the causes which drew us together. At last, however, an incident occurred which led to a closer acquaintance with Mr Richards and a fuller knowledge of the life of the man whom I served.

The immediate cause of this was no less than the falling of Master Percy, the youngest of my pupils, into the millrace, with imminent danger both to his life and to mine, since I had to risk myself in order to save him. Dripping and exhausted – for I was far more spent than the child – I was making for my room when Sir John, who had heard the hubbub, opened the door of his little study and asked me what was the matter. I told him of the accident, but assured him that his child was in no danger, while he listened with a rugged, immobile face, which expressed in its intense eyes and tightened lips all the emotion which he tried to conceal.

"One moment! Step in here! Let me have the details!" said he, turning back through the open door.

And so I found myself within that little sanctum, inside which, as I afterwards learnt, no other foot had for three years been set save that of the old servant who cleaned it out. It was a round room, conforming to the shape of the tower in which it was situated, with a low ceiling, a single narrow, ivy-wreathed window and the simplest of furniture. An old carpet, a single chair, a deal table and a small shelf of books made up the whole contents. On the table stood a full-length photograph of a woman – I took no particular notice of the features, but I remember that a certain gracious gentleness was the prevailing impression. Beside it were a large black japanned box and one or two bundles of letters or papers fastened together with elastic bands.

Our interview was a short one, for Sir John Bollamore perceived that I was soaked, and that I should change without delay. The incident led, however, to an instructive talk with Richards, the agent, who had never penetrated into the chamber which chance had opened to me. That very afternoon he came to me, all curiosity, and walked up and down the garden path with me, while my two charges played tennis upon the lawn beside us.

"You hardly realize the exception which has been made in your favour," said he. "That room has been kept such a mystery, and Sir John's visits to it have been so regular and consistent that an almost superstitious feeling has arisen about it in the household. I assure you that if I were to repeat to you the tales which are flying about, tales of mysterious visitors there, and of voices overheard by the servants, you might suspect that Sir John had relapsed into his old ways."

"Why do you say relapsed?" I asked.

He looked at me in surprise.

"Is it possible," said he, "that Sir John Bollamore's previous history is unknown to you?"

"Absolutely."

"You astound me. I thought that every man in England knew something of his antecedents. I should not mention the matter if it were not that you are now one of ourselves, and that the facts might come to your ears in some harsher form if I were silent upon them. I always took it for granted that you knew that you were in the service of 'Devil' Bollamore."

"But why 'Devil'?" I asked.

"Ah, you are young and the world moves fast, but twenty years ago the name of 'Devil' Bollamore was one of the best known in London. He was the leader of the fastest set, bruiser, driver, gambler, drunkard – a survival of the old type, and as bad as the worst of them."

I stared at him in amazement.

"What!" I cried. "That quiet, studious, sad-faced man?"

"The greatest rip and debauchee in England! All between ourselves, Colmore. But you understand now what I mean when I say that a woman's voice in his room might even now give rise to suspicions."

"But what can have changed him so?"

"Little Beryl Clare, when she took the risk of becoming his wife. That was the turning point. He had got so far that his own fast set had thrown him over. There is a world of difference, you know, between a man who drinks and a drunkard. They all drink, but they taboo a drunkard. He had become a slave to it – hopeless and helpless. Then she stepped in, saw the possibilities of a fine man in the wreck, took her chance in marrying him, though she might have had the pick of a dozen and, by devoting her life to it, brought him back to manhood and decency. You have observed that no liquor is ever kept in the house. There never has been any since her foot crossed its threshold. A drop of it would be like blood to a tiger even now."

"Then her influence still holds him?"

"That is the wonder of it. When she died three years ago, we all expected and feared that he would fall back into his old ways. She feared it herself, and the thought gave a terror to death, for she was like a guardian angel to that man, and lived only for the one purpose. By the way, did you see a black japanned box in his room?"

"Yes."

"I fancy it contains her letters. If ever he has occasion to be away, if only for a single night, he invariably takes his black japanned box with him. Well, well, Colmore, perhaps I have told you rather more than I should, but I shall expect you to reciprocate if anything of interest should come to your knowledge." I could see that the worthy man was consumed with curiosity and just a little piqued that I, the newcomer, should have been the first to penetrate into the untrodden chamber. But the fact raised me in his esteem, and from that time onwards I found myself upon more confidential terms with him.

And now the silent and majestic figure of my employer became an object of greater interest to me. I began to understand that strangely human look in his eyes, those deep lines upon his careworn face. He was a man who was fighting a ceaseless battle, holding at arm's length, from morning till night, a horrible adversary, who was forever trying to close with him – an adversary which would destroy him body and soul could it but fix its claws once more upon him. As I watched the grim, round-backed figure pacing the corridor or walking in the garden, this imminent danger seemed to take bodily shape, and I could almost fancy that I saw this most loathsome and dangerous of all the fiends crouching closely in his very shadow, like a half-cowed beast which slinks beside its keeper, ready at any unguarded moment to spring at his throat. And the dead woman, the woman who had spent her life in warding off this danger, took shape also to my imagination, and I saw her as a shadowy but beautiful presence which intervened forever with arms uplifted to screen the man whom she loved.

In some subtle way he divined the sympathy which I had for him, and he showed in his own silent fashion that he appreciated it. He even invited me once to share his afternoon walk, and although no word passed between us on this occasion, it was a mark of confidence which he had never shown to anyone before. He asked me also to index his library (it was one of the best private libraries in England), and I spent many hours in the evening in his presence, if not in his society, he reading at his desk and I sitting in a recess by the window reducing to order the chaos which existed among his books. In spite of these close relations I was never again asked to enter the chamber in the turret.

And then came my revulsion of feeling. A single incident changed all my sympathy to loathing, and made me realize that my employer still remained all that he had ever been, with the additional vice of hypocrisy. What happened was as follows.

One evening Miss Witherton had gone down to Broadway, the neighbouring village, to sing at a concert for some charity, and I, according to my promise, had walked over to escort her back. The drive sweeps round under the eastern turret, and I observed as I passed that the light was lit in the circular room. It was a summer evening, and the window, which was a little higher than our heads, was open. We were, as it happened, engrossed in our own conversation at the moment, and we had paused upon the lawn which skirts the old turret, when suddenly something broke in upon our talk and turned our thoughts away from our own affairs.

It was a voice – the voice undoubtedly of a woman. It was low – so low that it was only in that still night air that we could have heard it, but, hushed as it was, there was no mistaking its feminine timbre. It spoke hurriedly, gaspingly for a few sentences, and then was silent – a piteous, breathless, imploring sort of voice. Miss Witherton and I stood for an instant staring at each other. Then we walked quickly in the direction of the hall door.

"It came through the window," I said.

"We must not play the part of eavesdroppers," she answered. "We must forget that we have ever heard it."

There was an absence of surprise in her manner which suggested a new idea to me.

"You have heard it before," I cried.

"I could not help it. My own room is higher up on the same turret. It has happened frequently."

"Who can the woman be?"

"I have no idea. I had rather not discuss it."

Her voice was enough to show me what she thought. But granting that our employer led a double and dubious life, who could she be, this mysterious woman who kept him company in the old tower? I knew from my own inspection how bleak and bare a room it was. She certainly did not live there. But in that case where did she come from? It could not be anyone of the household. They were all under the vigilant eyes of Mrs Stevens. The visitor must come from without. But how?

And then suddenly I remembered how ancient this building was, and how probable that some medieval passage existed in it. There is hardly an old castle without one. The mysterious room was the basement of the turret, so that if there were anything of the sort it would open through the floor. There were numerous cottages in the immediate vicinity. The other end of the secret passage might lie among some tangle of bramble in the neighbouring copse. I said nothing to anyone, but I felt that the secret of my employer lay within my power.

And the more convinced I was of this the more I marvelled at the manner in which he concealed his true nature. Often as I watched his austere figure, I asked myself if it were indeed possible that such a man should be living this double life, and I tried to persuade myself that my suspicions might after all prove to be ill-founded. But there was the female voice, there was the secret nightly rendezvous in the turret chamber – how could such facts admit of an innocent interpretation? I conceived a horror of the man. I was filled with loathing at his deep, consistent hypocrisy.

Only once during all those months did I ever see him without that sad but impassive mask which he usually presented towards his fellow man. For an instant I caught a glimpse of those volcanic fires which he had damped down so long. The occasion was an unworthy one, for the object of his wrath was none other than the aged charwoman whom I have already mentioned as being the one person who was allowed within his mysterious chamber. I was passing the corridor which led to the turret – for my own room lay in that direction – when I heard a sudden, startled scream, and merged in it the husky, growling note of a man who is inarticulate with passion. It was the snarl of a furious wild beast. Then I heard his voice thrilling with anger. "You would dare!" he cried. "You would dare to disobey my directions!" An instant later the charwoman passed me, flying down the passage, white-faced and tremulous, while the terrible voice thundered behind her. "Go to Mrs Stevens for your money! Never set foot in Thorpe Place again!" Consumed with curiosity, I could not help following the woman, and found her round the corner leaning against the wall and palpitating like a frightened rabbit.

"What is the matter, Mrs Brown?" I asked.

"It's Master!" she gasped. "Oh, 'ow 'e frightened me! If you had seen 'is eyes, Mr Colmore, sir. I thought 'e would 'ave been the death of me."

"But what had you done?"

"Done, sir! Nothing. At least nothing to make so much of. Just laid my 'and on that black box of 'is – 'adn't even opened it, when in 'e came and you 'eard the way 'e went on. I've lost my place, and glad I am of it, for I would never trust myself within reach of 'im again."

So it was the japanned box which was the cause of this outburst – the box from which he would never permit himself to be separated. What was the connection, or was there any connection between this and the secret visits of the lady whose voice I had overheard? Sir John Bollamore's wrath was enduring as well as fiery, for from that day Mrs Brown, the charwoman, vanished from our ken, and Thorpe Place knew her no more.

And now I wish to tell you the singular chance which solved all these strange questions and put my employer's secret in my possession. The story may leave you with some lingering doubt as to whether my curiosity did not get the better of my honour, and whether I did not condescend to play the spy. If you choose to think so I cannot help it, but can only assure you that, improbable as it may appear, the matter came about exactly as I describe it.

The first stage in this denouement was that the small room in the turret became uninhabitable. This occurred through the fall of the worm-eaten oaken beam which supported the ceiling. Rotten with age, it snapped in the middle one morning, and brought down a quantity of plaster with it. Fortunately Sir John was not in the room at the time. His precious box was rescued from amongst the debris and brought into the library, where, henceforward, it was locked within his bureau. Sir John took no steps to repair the damage, and I never had an opportunity of searching for that secret passage, the existence of which I had surmised. As to the lady, I had thought that this would have brought her visits to an end, had I not one evening heard Mr Richards asking Mrs Stevens who the woman was whom he had overheard talking to Sir John in the library. I could not catch her reply, but I saw from her manner that it was not the first time that she had had to answer or avoid the same question.

"You've heard the voice, Colmore?" said the agent.

I confessed that I had.

"And what do *you* think of it?"

I shrugged my shoulders, and remarked that it was no business of mine.

"Come, come, you are just as curious as any of us. Is it a woman or not?"

"It is certainly a woman."

"Which room did you hear it from?"

"From the turret room, before the ceiling fell."

"But I heard it from the library only last night. I passed the doors as I was going to bed, and I heard something wailing and praying just as plainly as I heard you. It may be a woman—"

"Why, what else *could* it be?"

He looked at me hard.

"There are more things in heaven and earth," said he. "If it is a woman, how does she get there?"

"I don't know."

"No, nor I. But if it is the other thing – but there, for a practical businessman at the end of the nineteenth century this is rather a ridiculous line of conversation." He turned away, but I saw that he felt even more than he had said. To all the old ghost stories of Thorpe Place a new one was being added before our very eyes. It may by this time have taken its permanent place, for though an explanation came to me, it never reached the others.

And my explanation came in this way. I had suffered a sleepless night from neuralgia, and about midday I had taken a heavy dose of chlorodyne to alleviate the pain. At that time I was finishing the indexing of Sir John Bollamore's library, and it was my custom to work there from five till seven. On this particular day I struggled against the double effect of my bad night and the narcotic. I have already mentioned that there was a recess in the library, and in this it was my habit to work. I settled down steadily to my task, but my weariness overcame me and, falling back upon the settee, I dropped into a heavy sleep.

How long I slept I do not know, but it was quite dark when I awoke. Confused by the chlorodyne which I had taken, I lay motionless in a semi-conscious state. The great room with its high walls covered with books loomed darkly all round me. A dim radiance from the moonlight came through the farther window, and against this lighter background I saw that Sir John Bollamore was sitting at his study table. His well-set head and clearly cut profile were sharply outlined against the glimmering square behind him. He bent as I watched him, and I heard the sharp turning of a key and the rasping of metal upon metal. As if in a dream I was vaguely conscious that this was the japanned box which stood in front of him, and that he had drawn something out of it, something squat and uncouth, which now lay before him upon the table. I never realized – it never occurred to my bemuddled and torpid brain that I was intruding upon his privacy, that he imagined himself to be alone in the room. And then, just as it rushed upon my horrified perceptions, and I had half-risen to announce my presence, I heard a strange, crisp, metallic clicking, and then the voice.

Yes, it was a woman's voice; there could not be a doubt of it. But a voice so charged with entreaty and with yearning love that it will ring for ever in my ears. It came with a curious faraway tinkle, but every word was clear, though faint – very faint, for they were the last words of a dying woman.

"I am not really gone, John," said the thin, gasping voice. "I am here at your very elbow, and shall be until we meet once more. I die happy to think that morning and night you will hear my voice. Oh, John, be strong, be strong, until we meet again."

I say that I had risen in order to announce my presence, but I could not do so while the voice was sounding. I could only remain half lying, half sitting, paralysed, astounded, listening to those yearning distant musical words. And he – he was so absorbed that even if I had spoken he might not have heard me. But with the silence of the voice came my half-articulated apologies and explanations. He sprang across the room, switched on the electric light, and in its white glare I saw him, his eyes gleaming with anger, his face twisted with passion, as the hapless charwoman may have seen him weeks before.

"Mr Colmore!" he cried. "You here! What is the meaning of this, sir?"

With halting words I explained it all, my neuralgia, the narcotic, my luckless sleep and singular awakening. As he listened the glow of anger faded from his face, and the sad, impassive mask closed once more over his features.

"My secret is yours, Mr Colmore," said he. "I have only myself to blame for relaxing my precautions. Half-confidences are worse than no confidences, and so you may know all since you know so much. The story may go where you will when I have passed away, but until then I rely upon your sense of honour that no human soul shall hear it from your lips. I am proud still – God help me! – or, at least, I am proud enough to resent that pity which this story would draw upon me. I have smiled at envy, and disregarded hatred, but pity is more than I can tolerate.

"You have heard the source from which the voice comes – that voice which has, as I understand, excited so much curiosity in my household. I am aware of the rumours to which it has given rise. These speculations, whether scandalous or superstitious, are such as I can disregard and forgive. What I should never forgive would be a disloyal spying and eavesdropping in order to satisfy an illicit curiosity. But of that, Mr Colmore, I acquit you.

"When I was a young man, sir, many years younger than you are now, I was launched upon town without a friend or adviser, and with a purse which brought only too many false friends and false advisers to my side. I drank deeply of the wine of life – if there is a man living who has drunk more deeply he is not a man whom I envy. My purse suffered, my character suffered, my constitution suffered, stimulants became a necessity to me, I was a creature from whom my memory recoils. And it was at that time, the time of my blackest degradation, that God sent into my life the gentlest, sweetest spirit that ever descended as a ministering angel from above. She loved me, broken as I was, loved me, and spent her life in making a man once more of that which had degraded itself to the level of the beasts.

"But a fell disease struck her, and she withered away before my eyes. In the hour of her agony it was never of herself, of her own sufferings and her own death that she thought. It was all of me. The one pang which her fate brought to her was the fear that when her influence was removed I should revert to that which I had been. It was in vain that I made oath to her that no drop of wine would ever cross my lips. She knew only too well the hold that the Devil had upon me – she who had striven so to loosen it – and it haunted her night and day the thought that my soul might again be within his grip.

"It was from some friend's gossip of the sickroom that she heard of this invention – this phonograph – and with the quick insight of a loving woman she saw how she might use it for her ends. She sent me to London to procure the best which money could buy. With her dying breath she gasped into it the words which have held me straight ever since. Lonely and broken, what else have I in all the world to uphold me? But it is enough. Please God, I shall face her without shame when He is pleased to reunite us! That is my secret, Mr Colmore, and whilst I live I leave it in your keeping."

The Black Doctor

Bishop's Crossing is a small village lying ten miles in a south-westerly direction from Liverpool. Here in the early Seventies there settled a doctor named Aloysius Lana. Nothing was known locally either of his antecedents or of the reasons which had prompted him to come to this Lancashire hamlet. Two facts only were certain about him: the one that he had gained his medical qualification with some distinction at Glasgow; the other that he came undoubtedly of a tropical race, and was so dark that he might almost have had a strain of the Indian in his composition.

His predominant features were, however, European, and he possessed a stately courtesy and carriage which suggested a Spanish extraction. A swarthy skin, raven-black hair and dark, sparkling eyes under a pair of heavily tufted brows made a strange contrast to the flaxen or chestnut rustics of England, and the newcomer was soon known as "the Black Doctor of Bishop's Crossing". At first it was a term of ridicule and reproach; as the years went on it became a title of honour which was familiar to the whole countryside, and extended far beyond the narrow confines of the village.

For the newcomer proved himself to be a capable surgeon and an accomplished physician. The practice of that district had been in the hands of Edward Rowe, the son of Sir William Rowe, the Liverpool consultant, but he had not inherited the talents of his father, and Dr Lana, with his advantages of presence and of manner, soon beat him out of the field. Dr Lana's social success was as rapid as his professional. A remarkable surgical cure in the case of the Hon. James Lowry, the second son of Lord Belton, was the means of introducing him to county society, where he became a favourite through the charm of his conversation and the elegance of his manners. An absence of antecedents and of relatives is sometimes an aid rather than an impediment to social advancement, and the distinguished individuality of the handsome doctor was its own recommendation.

His patients had one fault – and one fault only – to find with him. He appeared to be a confirmed bachelor. This was the more remarkable since the house which he occupied was a large one, and it was known that his success in practice had enabled him to save considerable sums. At first the local matchmakers were continually coupling his name with one or other of the eligible ladies, but as years passed and Dr Lana remained unmarried, it came to be generally understood that for some reason he must remain a bachelor. Some even went so far as to assert that he was already married, and that it was in order to escape the consequence of an early misalliance that he had buried himself at Bishop's Crossing. And, then, just as the matchmakers had finally given him up in despair, his engagement was suddenly announced to Miss Frances Morton, of Leigh Hall.

Miss Morton was a young lady who was well known upon the countryside, her father, James Haldane Morton, having been the squire of Bishop's Crossing. Both her parents were, however, dead, and she lived with her only brother, Arthur Morton, who had inherited the family estate. In person Miss Morton was tall and stately, and she was famous for her quick, impetuous nature and for her strength of character. She met Dr Lana at a garden party, and a friendship, which quickly ripened into love, sprang up between them. Nothing could exceed their devotion to each other. There was some discrepancy in age, he being thirty-seven and she twenty-four; but, save in that one respect, there was no possible objection to be found with the match. The engagement was in February, and it was arranged that the marriage should take place in August.

Upon 3rd June Dr Lana received a letter from abroad. In a small village the postmaster is also in a position to be the gossip master, and Mr Bankley, of Bishop's Crossing, had many of the secrets of his neighbours in his possession. Of this particular letter he remarked only that it was in a curious envelope, that it was in a man's handwriting, that the postscript was Buenos Aires and the stamp of the Argentine Republic. It was the first letter which he had ever known Dr Lana to have from abroad, and this was the reason why his attention was particularly called to it before he handed it to the local postman. It was delivered by the evening delivery of that date.

Next morning – that is, upon 4th June – Dr Lana called upon Miss Morton, and a long interview followed, from which he was observed to return in a state of great agitation. Miss Morton remained in her room all that day, and her maid found her several times in tears. In the course of a week it was an open secret to the whole village that the engagement was at an end, that Dr Lana had behaved shamefully to the young lady, and that Arthur Morton, her brother, was talking of horsewhipping him. In what particular respect the doctor had behaved badly was unknown – some surmised one thing and some another; but it was observed, and taken as the obvious sign of a guilty conscience, that he would go for miles round rather than pass the windows of Leigh Hall, and that he gave up attending morning service upon Sundays where he might have met the young lady. There was an advertisement also in the *Lancet* as to the sale of a practice which mentioned no names, but which was thought by some to refer to Bishop's Crossing, and to mean that Dr Lana was thinking of abandoning the scene of his success. Such was the position of affairs when, upon the evening of Monday, 21st June, there came a fresh development which changed what had been a mere village scandal into a tragedy which arrested the attention of the whole nation. Some detail is necessary to cause the facts of that evening to present their full significance.

The sole occupants of the doctor's house were his housekeeper, an elderly and most respectable woman, named Martha Woods, and a young servant – Mary Pilling. The coachman and the surgery boy slept out. It was the custom of the doctor to sit at night in his study, which was next the surgery in the wing of the house which was farthest from the servants' quarters. This side of the house had a door of its own for the convenience of patients, so that it was possible for the doctor to admit and receive a visitor there without the knowledge of anyone. As a matter of fact, when patients came late it was quite usual for him to let them in and out by the surgery entrance, for the maid and the housekeeper were in the habit of retiring early.

On this particular night Martha Woods went into the doctor's study at half-past nine, and found him writing at his desk. She bade him goodnight, sent the maid to bed and then occupied herself until a quarter to eleven in household matters. It was striking eleven upon the hall clock when she went to her own room. She had been there about a quarter of an hour or twenty minutes when she heard a cry or call, which appeared to come from within the house. She waited some time, but it was not repeated. Much alarmed, for the sound was loud and urgent, she put on a dressing gown, and ran at the top of her speed to the doctor's study.

"Who's there?" cried a voice, as she tapped at the door.

"I am here, sir – Mrs Woods."

"I beg that you will leave me in peace. Go back to your room this instant!" cried the voice, which was, to the best of her belief, that of her master. The tone was so harsh and so unlike her master's usual manner that she was surprised and hurt.

"I thought I heard you calling, sir," she explained, but no answer was given to her. Mrs Woods looked at the clock as she returned to her room, and it was then half-past eleven.

At some period between eleven and twelve (she could not be positive as to the exact hour) a patient called upon the doctor and was unable to get any reply from him. This late visitor was Mrs Madding, the wife of the village grocer, who was dangerously ill of typhoid fever. Dr Lana had asked her to look in the last thing and let him know how her husband was progressing. She observed that the light was burning in the study, but having knocked several times at the surgery door without response, she concluded that the doctor had been called out, and so returned home.

There is a short, winding drive with a lamp at the end of it leading down from the house to the road. As Mrs Madding emerged from the gate a man was coming along the footpath. Thinking that it might be Dr Lana returning from some professional visit, she waited for him, and was surprised to see that it was Mr Arthur Morton, the young squire. In the light of the lamp she observed that his manner was excited, and that he carried in his hand a heavy hunting crop. He was turning in at the gate when she addressed him.

"The doctor is not in, sir," said she.

"How do you know that?" he asked harshly.

"I have been to the surgery door, sir."

"I see a light," said the young squire, looking up the drive. "That is in his study, is it not?"

"Yes, sir, but I am sure that he is out."

"Well, he must come in again," said young Morton, and passed through the gate while Mrs Madding went upon her homeward way.

At three o'clock that morning her husband suffered a sharp relapse, and she was so alarmed by his symptoms that she determined to call the doctor without delay. As she passed through the gate she was surprised to see someone lurking among the laurel bushes. It was certainly a man, and to the best of her belief Mr Arthur Morton. Preoccupied with her own troubles, she gave no particular attention to the incident, but hurried on upon her errand.

When she reached the house she perceived to her surprise that the light was still burning in the study. She therefore tapped at the surgery door. There was no answer. She repeated the knocking several times without effect. It appeared to her to be unlikely that the doctor would either go to bed or go out leaving so brilliant a light behind him, and it struck Mrs Madding that it was possible that he might have dropped asleep in his chair. She tapped at the study window, therefore, but without result. Then, finding that there was an opening between the curtain and the woodwork, she looked through.

The small room was brilliantly lit from a large lamp on the central table, which was littered with the doctor's books and instruments. No one was visible, nor did she see anything unusual, except that in the farther shadow thrown by the table a dingy white glove was lying upon the carpet. And then suddenly, as her eyes became more accustomed to the light, a boot emerged from the other end of the shadow, and she realized, with a thrill of horror, that what she had taken to be a glove was the hand of a man, who was prostrate upon the floor. Understanding that something terrible had occurred, she rang at the front door, roused Mrs Woods, the housekeeper, and the two women made their way into the study, having first dispatched the maidservant to the police station.

At the side of the table, away from the window, Dr Lana was discovered stretched upon his back and quite dead. It was evident that he had been subjected to violence, for one of his eyes was blackened and there were marks of bruises about his face and neck. A slight thickening and swelling of his features appeared to suggest that the cause of his death had been strangulation. He was dressed in his usual professional clothes, but wore cloth slippers, the soles of which were perfectly clean. The carpet was marked all over, especially on the side of the door, with traces of dirty boots, which were presumably left by the murderer. It was evident that someone had entered by the surgery door, had killed the doctor, and had then made his escape unseen. That the assailant was a man was certain, from the size of the footprints and from the nature of the injuries. But beyond that point the police found it very difficult to go.

There were no signs of robbery, and the doctor's gold watch was safe in his pocket. He kept a heavy cash box in the room, and this was discovered to be locked but empty. Mrs Woods had an impression that a large sum was usually kept there, but the doctor had paid a heavy corn bill in cash only that very day, and it was conjectured that it was to this and not to a robber that the emptiness of the box was due. One thing in the room was missing – but that one thing was suggestive. The portrait of Miss Morton, which had always stood upon the side table, had been taken from its frame and carried off. Mrs Woods had observed it there when she waited upon her employer that evening, and now it was gone. On the other hand, there was picked up from the floor a green eyepatch, which the housekeeper could not remember to have seen before. Such a patch might, however, be in the possession of a doctor, and there was nothing to indicate that it was in any way connected with the crime.

Suspicion could only turn in one direction, and Arthur Morton, the young squire, was immediately arrested. The evidence against him was circumstantial, but damning. He was devoted to his sister, and it was shown that since the rupture between her and Dr Lana he had been heard again and again to express himself in the most vindictive terms towards her former lover. He had, as stated, been seen somewhere about eleven o'clock entering the doctor's drive with a hunting crop in his hand. He had then, according to the theory of the police, broken in upon the doctor, whose exclamation of fear or of anger had been loud enough to attract the attention of Mrs Woods. When Mrs Woods descended, Dr Lana had made up his mind to talk it over with his visitor, and had, therefore, sent his housekeeper back to her room. This conversation had lasted a long time, had become more and more fiery, and had ended by a personal struggle, in which the doctor lost his life. The fact, revealed by a post-mortem, that his heart was much diseased – an ailment quite unsuspected during his life – would make it possible that death might in his case ensue from injuries which would not be fatal to a healthy man. Arthur Morton had then removed his sister's photograph and had made his way homeward, stepping aside into the laurel bushes to avoid Mrs Madding at the gate. This was the theory of the prosecution, and the case which they presented was a formidable one.

On the other hand, there were some strong points for the defence. Morton was high-spirited and impetuous, like his sister, but he was respected and liked by everyone, and his frank and honest nature seemed to be incapable of such a crime. His own explanation was that he was anxious to have a conversation with Dr Lana about some urgent family matters (from first to last he refused even to mention the name of his sister). He did not attempt to deny that this conversation would probably have been of an unpleasant nature. He had heard from a patient that the doctor was out, and he therefore waited until about three in the morning for his return, but as he had seen nothing of him up to that hour, he had given it up and had returned home. As to his death, he knew no more about it than the constable who arrested him. He had formerly been an intimate friend of the deceased man; but circumstances, which he would prefer not to mention, had brought about a change in his sentiments.

There were several facts which supported his innocence. It was certain that Dr Lana was alive and in his study at half-past eleven o'clock. Mrs Woods was prepared to swear that it was at that hour that she had heard his voice. The friends of the prisoner contended that it was probable that at that time Dr Lana was not alone. The sound which had originally attracted the attention of the housekeeper, and her master's unusual impatience that she should leave him in peace, seemed to point to that. If this were so, then it appeared to be probable that he had met his end between the moment when the housekeeper heard his voice and the time when Mrs Madding made her first call and found it impossible to attract his attention. But if this were the time of his death, then it was certain that Mr Arthur Morton could not be guilty, as it was *after* this that she had met the young squire at the gate.

If this hypothesis were correct, and someone was with Dr Lana before Mrs Madding met Mr Arthur Morton, then who was this someone, and what motives had he for wishing evil to the doctor? It was universally admitted that if the friends of the accused could throw light upon this, they would have gone a long way towards establishing his innocence. But in the meanwhile it was open to the public to say – as they did say – that there was no proof that anyone had been there at all except the young squire; while, on the other hand, there was ample proof that his motives in going were of a sinister kind. When Mrs Madding called, the doctor might have retired to his room, or he might, as she thought at the time, have gone out and returned afterwards to find Mr Arthur Morton waiting for him. Some of the supporters of the accused laid stress upon the fact that the photograph of his sister Frances, which had been removed from the doctor's room, had not been found in her brother's possession. This argument, however, did not count for much, as he had ample time before his arrest to burn it or to destroy it. As to the only positive evidence in the case – the muddy footmarks upon the floor – they were so blurred by the softness of the carpet that it was impossible to make any trustworthy deduction from them. The most that could be said was that their appearance was not inconsistent with the theory that they were made by the accused, and it was further shown that his boots were very muddy upon that night. There had been a heavy shower in the afternoon, and all boots were probably in the same condition.

Such is a bald statement of the singular and romantic series of events which centred public attention upon this Lancashire tragedy. The unknown origin of the doctor, his curious and distinguished personality, the position of the man who was accused of the murder and the love affair which had preceded the crime all combined to make the affair one of those dramas which absorb the whole interest of a nation. Throughout the three kingdoms men discussed the case of the Black Doctor of Bishop's Crossing, and many were the theories put forward to explain the facts; but it may safely be said that among them all there was not one which prepared the minds of the public for the extraordinary sequel, which caused so much excitement upon the first day of the trial, and came to a climax upon the second. The long files of the *Lancaster Weekly* with their report of the case lie before me as I write, but I must content myself with a synopsis of the case up to the point when, upon the evening of the first day, the evidence of Miss Frances Morton threw a singular light upon the case.

Mr Porlock Carr, the counsel for the prosecution, had marshalled his facts with his usual skill, and as the day wore on, it became more and more evident how difficult was the task which Mr Humphrey, who had been retained for the defence, had before him. Several witnesses were put up to swear to the intemperate expressions which the young squire had been heard to utter about the doctor, and the fiery manner in which he resented the alleged ill-treatment of his sister. Mrs Madding repeated her evidence as to the visit which had been paid late at night by the prisoner to the deceased, and it was shown by another witness that the prisoner was aware that the doctor was in the habit of sitting up alone in this isolated wing of the house, and that he had chosen this very late hour to call because he knew that his victim would then be at his mercy. A servant at the squire's house was compelled to admit that he had heard his master return about three that morning, which corroborated Mrs Madding's statement that she had seen him among the laurel bushes near the gate upon the occasion of her second visit. The muddy boots and an alleged similarity in the footprints were duly dwelt upon, and it was felt when the case for the prosecution had been presented that, however circumstantial it might be, it was nonetheless so complete and so convincing that the fate of the prisoner was sealed, unless something quite unexpected should be disclosed by the defence. It was three o'clock when the prosecution closed. At half-past four, when the court rose, a new and unlooked-for development had occurred. I extract the incident, or part of it, from the journal which I have already mentioned, omitting the preliminary observations of the counsel.

Considerable sensation was caused in the crowded court when the first witness called for the defence proved to be Miss Frances Morton, the sister of the prisoner. Our readers will remember that the young lady had been engaged to Dr Lana, and that it was his anger over the sudden termination of this engagement which was thought to have driven her brother to the perpetration of this crime. Miss Morton had not, however, been directly implicated in the case in any way, either at the inquest or at the police-court proceedings, and her appearance as the leading witness for the defence came as a surprise upon the public.

Miss Frances Morton, who was a tall and handsome brunette, gave her evidence in a low but clear voice, though it was evident throughout that she was suffering from extreme emotion. She alluded to her engagement to the doctor, touched briefly upon its termination, which was due, she said, to personal matters connected with his family, and surprised the court by asserting that she had always considered her brother's resentment to be unreasonable and intemperate. In answer to a direct question from her counsel, she replied that she did not feel that she had any grievance whatever against Dr Lana, and that in her opinion he had acted in a perfectly honourable manner. Her brother, on an insufficient knowledge of the facts, had taken another view, and she was compelled to acknowledge that, in spite of her entreaties, he had uttered threats of personal violence against the doctor, and had, upon the evening of the tragedy, announced his intention of "having it out with him". She had done her best to bring him to a more reasonable frame of mind, but he was very headstrong where his emotions or prejudices were concerned.

Up to this point the young lady's evidence had appeared to make against the prisoner rather than in his favour. The questions of her counsel, however, soon put a very different light upon the matter, and disclosed an unexpected line of defence.

Mr Humphrey: Do you believe your brother to be guilty of this crime?

The judge: I cannot permit that question, Mr Humphrey. We are here to decide upon questions of fact – not of belief.

Mr Humphrey: Do you know that your brother is not guilty of the death of Dr Lana?

Miss Morton: Yes.

Mr Humphrey: How do you know it?

Miss Morton: Because Dr Lana is not dead.

There followed a prolonged sensation in court, which interrupted the examination of the witness.

Mr Humphrey: And how do you know, Miss Morton, that Dr Lana is not dead?

Miss Morton: Because I have received a letter from him since the date of his supposed death.

Mr Humphrey: Have you this letter?

Miss Morton: Yes, but I should prefer not to show it.

Mr Humphrey: Have you the envelope?

Miss Morton: Yes, it is here.

Mr Humphrey: What is the postmark?

Miss Morton: Liverpool.

Mr Humphrey: And the date?

Miss Morton: 22nd June.

Mr Humphrey: That being the day after his alleged death. Are you prepared to swear to this handwriting, Miss Morton?

Miss Morton: Certainly.

Mr Humphrey: I am prepared to call six other witnesses, My Lord, to testify that this letter is in the writing of Doctor Lana.

The judge: Then you must call them tomorrow.

Mr Porlock Carr (counsel for the prosecution): In the meantime, My Lord, we claim possession of this document, so that we may obtain expert evidence as to how far it is an imitation of the handwriting of the gentleman whom we still confidently assert to be deceased. I need not point out that the theory so unexpectedly sprung upon us may prove to be a very obvious device adopted by the friends of the prisoner in order to divert this inquiry. I would draw attention to the fact that the young lady must, according to her own account, have possessed this letter during the proceedings at the inquest and at the police court. She desires us to believe that she permitted these to proceed, although she held in her pocket evidence which would at any moment have brought them to an end.

Mr Humphrey: Can you explain this, Miss Morton?

Miss Morton: Dr Lana desired his secret to be preserved.

Mr Porlock Carr: Then why have you made this public?

Miss Morton: To save my brother.

A murmur of sympathy broke out in court, which was instantly suppressed by the judge.

The judge: Admitting this line of defence, it lies with you, Mr Humphrey, to throw a light upon who this man is whose body has been recognized by so many friends and patients of Dr Lana as being that of the doctor himself.

A juryman: Has anyone up to now expressed any doubt about the matter?

Mr Porlock Carr: Not to my knowledge.

Mr Humphrey: We hope to make the matter clear.

The judge: Then the court adjourns until tomorrow.

This new development of the case excited the utmost interest among the general public. Press comment was prevented by the fact that the trial was still undecided, but the question was everywhere argued as to how far there could be truth in Miss Morton's declaration, and how far it might be a daring ruse for the purpose of saving her brother. The obvious dilemma in which the missing doctor stood was that if by any extraordinary chance he was not dead, then he must be held responsible for the death of this unknown man, who resembled him so exactly, and who was found in his study. This letter which Miss Morton refused to produce was possibly a confession of guilt, and she might find herself in the terrible position of only being able to save her brother from the gallows by the sacrifice of her former lover. The court next morning was crammed to overflowing, and a murmur of excitement passed over it when Mr Humphrey was observed to enter in a state of emotion, which even his trained nerves could not conceal, and to confer with the opposing counsel. A few hurried words – words which left a look of amazement upon Mr Porlock Carr's face – passed between them, and then the counsel for the defence, addressing the judge, announced that, with the consent of the prosecution, the young lady who had given evidence upon the sitting before would not be recalled.

The judge: But you appear, Mr Humphrey, to have left matters in a very unsatisfactory state.

Mr Humphrey: Perhaps, My Lord, my next witness may help to clear them up.

The judge: Then call your next witness.

Mr Humphrey: I call Dr Aloysius Lana.

The learned counsel has made many telling remarks in his day, but he has certainly never produced such a sensation with so short a sentence. The court was simply stunned with amazement as the very man whose fate had been the subject of so much contention appeared bodily before them in the witness box. Those among the spectators who had known him at Bishop's Crossing saw him now, gaunt and thin, with deep lines of care upon his face. But in spite of his melancholy bearing and despondent expression, there were few who could say that they had ever seen a man of more distinguished presence. Bowing to the judge, he asked if he might be allowed to make a statement, and having been duly informed that whatever he said might be used against him, he bowed once more, and proceeded:

"My wish," said he, "is to hold nothing back, but to tell with perfect frankness all that occurred upon the night of 21st June. Had I known that the innocent had suffered, and that so much trouble had been brought upon those whom I love best in the world, I should have come forward long ago; but there were reasons which prevented these things from coming to my ears. It was my desire that an unhappy man should vanish from the world which had known him, but I had not foreseen that others would be affected by my actions. Let me to the best of my ability repair the evil which I have done.

"To anyone who is acquainted with the history of the Argentine Republic the name of Lana is well known. My father, who came of the best blood of old Spain, filled all the highest offices of the state, and would have been president but for his death in the riots of San Juan. A brilliant career might have been open to my twin brother Ernest and myself had it not been for financial losses which made it necessary that we should earn our own living. I apologize, sir, if these details appear to be irrelevant, but they are a necessary introduction to that which is to follow.

"I had, as I have said, a twin brother named Ernest, whose resemblance to me was so great that even when we were together people could see no difference between us. Down to the smallest detail we were exactly the same. As we grew older this likeness became less marked because our expression was not the same, but with our features in repose the points of difference were very slight.

"It does not become me to say too much of one who is dead, the more so as he is my only brother, but I leave his character to those who knew him best. I will only say – for I *have* to say it – that in my early manhood I conceived a horror of him, and that I had good reason for the aversion which filled me. My own reputation suffered from his actions, for our close resemblance caused me to be credited with many of them. Eventually, in a peculiarly disgraceful business, he contrived to throw the whole odium upon me in such a way that I was forced to leave the Argentine for ever, and to seek a career in Europe. The freedom from his hated presence more than compensated me for the loss of my native land. I had enough money to defray my medical studies at Glasgow, and I finally settled in practice at Bishop's Crossing, in the firm conviction that in that remote Lancashire hamlet I should never hear of him again.

"For years my hopes were fulfilled, and then at last he discovered me. Some Liverpool man who visited Buenos Aires put him upon my track. He had lost all his money, and he thought that he would come over and share mine. Knowing my horror of him, he rightly thought that I would be willing to buy him off. I received a letter from him saying that he was coming. It was at a crisis in my own affairs, and his arrival might conceivably bring trouble, and even disgrace, upon some whom I was especially bound to shield from anything of the kind. I took steps to ensure that any evil which might come should fall on me only, and that" – here he turned and looked at the prisoner – "was the cause of conduct upon my part which has been too harshly judged. My only motive was to screen those who were dear to me from any possible connection with scandal or disgrace. That scandal and disgrace would come with my brother was only to say that what had been would be again.

"My brother arrived himself one night not very long after my receipt of the letter. I was sitting in my study after the servants had gone to bed, when I heard a footstep upon the gravel outside, and an instant later I saw his face looking in at me through the window. He was a clean-shaven man like myself, and the resemblance between us was still so great that, for an instant, I thought it was my own reflection in the glass. He had a dark patch over his eye, but our features were absolutely the same. Then he smiled in a sardonic way, which had been a trick of his from his boyhood, and I knew that he was the same brother who had driven me from my native land and brought disgrace upon what had been an honourable name. I went to the door and I admitted him. That would be about ten o'clock that night.

"When he came into the glare of the lamp, I saw at once that he had fallen upon very evil days. He had walked from Liverpool, and he was tired and ill. I was quite shocked by the expression upon his face. My medical knowledge told me that there was some serious internal malady. He had been drinking also, and his face was bruised as the result of a scuffle which he had had with some sailors. It was to cover his injured eye that he wore this patch, which he removed when he entered the room. He was himself dressed in a pea jacket and flannel shirt, and his feet were bursting through his boots. But his poverty had only made him more savagely vindictive towards me. His hatred rose to the height of a mania. I had been rolling in money in England, according to his account, while he had been starving in South America. I cannot describe to you the threats which he uttered or the insults which he poured upon me. My impression is that hardships and debauchery had unhinged his reason. He paced about the room like a wild beast, demanding drink, demanding money, and all in the foulest language. I am a hot-tempered man, but I thank God that I am able to say that I remained master of myself, and that I never raised a hand against him. My coolness only irritated him the more. He raved, he cursed, he shook his fists in my face, and then suddenly a horrible spasm passed over his features, he clapped his hand to his side and with a loud cry he fell in a heap at my feet. I raised him up and stretched him upon the sofa, but no answer came to my exclamations, and the hand which I held in mine was cold and clammy. His diseased heart had broken down. His own violence had killed him.

"For a long time I sat as if I were in some dreadful dream, staring at the body of my brother. I was aroused by the knocking of Mrs Woods, who had been disturbed by that dying cry. I sent her away to bed. Shortly afterwards a patient tapped at the surgery door, but as I took no notice, he or she went off again. Slowly and gradually as I sat there a plan was forming itself in my head in the curious automatic way in which plans do form. When I rose from my chair my future movements were finally decided upon without my having been conscious of any process of thought. It was an instinct which irresistibly inclined me towards one course.

"Ever since that change in my affairs to which I have alluded, Bishop's Crossing had become hateful to me. My plans of life had been ruined, and I had met with hasty judgements and unkind treatment where I had expected sympathy. It is true that any danger of scandal from my brother had passed away with his life, but still I was sore about the past and felt that things could never be as they had been. It may be that I was unduly sensitive, and that I had not made sufficient allowance for others, but my feelings were as I describe. Any chance of getting away from Bishop's Crossing and of everyone in it would be most welcome to me. And here was such a chance as I could never have dared to hope for, a chance which would enable me to make a clean break with the past.

"There was this dead man lying upon the sofa, so like me that save for some little thickness and coarseness of the features there was no difference at all. No one had seen him come and no one would miss him. We were both clean-shaven, and his hair was about the same length as my own. If I changed clothes with him, then Dr Aloysius Lana would be found lying dead in his study, and there would be an end of an unfortunate fellow, and of a blighted career. There was plenty of ready money in the room, and this I could carry away with me to help me to start once more in some other land. In my brother's clothes I could walk by night unobserved as far as Liverpool, and in that great seaport I would soon find some means of leaving the country. After my lost hopes, the humblest existence where I was unknown was far preferable, in my estimation, to a practice, however successful, in Bishop's Crossing, where at any moment I might come face to face with those whom I should wish, if it were possible, to forget. I determined to effect the change.

"And I did so. I will not go into particulars, for the recollection is as painful as the experience; but in an hour my brother lay, dressed down to the smallest detail in my clothes, while I slunk out by the surgery door and, taking the back path which led across some fields, I started off to make the best of my way to Liverpool, where I arrived the same night. My bag of money and a certain portrait were all I carried out of the house, and I left behind me in my hurry the shade which my brother had been wearing over his eye. Everything else of his I took with me.

"I give you my word, sir, that never for one instant did the idea occur to me that people might think that I had been murdered, nor did I imagine that anyone might be caused serious danger through this stratagem by which I endeavoured to gain a fresh start in the world. On the contrary, it was the thought of relieving others from the burden of my presence which was always uppermost in my mind. A sailing vessel was leaving Liverpool that very day for Corunna, and in this I took my passage, thinking that the voyage would give me time to recover my balance and to consider the future. But before I left my resolution softened. I bethought me that there was one person in the world to whom I would not cause an hour of sadness. She would mourn me in her heart, however harsh and unsympathetic her relatives might be. She understood and appreciated the motives upon which I had acted, and if the rest of her family condemned me, she, at least, would not forget. And so I sent her a note under the seal of secrecy to save her from a baseless grief. If under the pressure of events she broke that seal, she has my entire sympathy and forgiveness.

"It was only last night that I returned to England, and during all this time I have heard nothing of the sensation which my supposed death had caused, nor of the accusation that Mr Arthur Morton had been concerned in it. It was in a late-evening paper that I read an account of the proceedings of yesterday, and I have come this morning as fast as an express train could bring me to testify to the truth."

Such was the remarkable statement of Dr Aloysius Lana, which brought the trial to a sudden termination. A subsequent investigation corroborated it to the extent of finding out the vessel in which his brother Ernest Lana had come over from South America. The ship's doctor was able to testify that he had complained of a weak heart during the voyage, and that his symptoms were consistent with such a death as was described.

As to Dr Aloysius Lana, he returned to the village from which he had made so dramatic a disappearance, and a complete reconciliation was effected between him and the young squire, the latter having acknowledged that he had entirely misunderstood the other's motives in withdrawing from his engagement. That another reconciliation followed may be judged from a notice extracted from a prominent column in the *Morning Post*:

A marriage was solemnized upon 19th September, by the Revd Stephen Johnson, at the parish church of Bishop's Crossing, between Aloysius Xavier Lana, son of Don Alfredo Lana, formerly foreign minister of the Argentine Republic, and Frances Morton, only daughter of the late James Morton, JP, of Leigh Hall, Bishop's Crossing, Lancashire.

The Jew's Breastplate

My particular friend, Ward Mortimer, was one of the best men of his day at everything connected with oriental archaeology. He had written largely upon the subject, he had lived two years in a tomb at Thebes, while he excavated in the Valley of the Kings, and finally he had created a considerable sensation by his exhumation of the alleged mummy of Cleopatra in the inner room of the Temple of Horus, at Philae. With such a record at the age of thirty-one, it was felt that a considerable career lay before him, and no one was surprised when he was elected to the curatorship of the Belmore Street Museum, which carries with it the lectureship at the Oriental College, and an income which has sunk with the fall in land, but which still remains at that ideal sum which is large enough to encourage an investigator, but not so large as to enervate him.

There was only one reason which made Ward Mortimer's position a little difficult at the Belmore Street Museum, and that was the extreme eminence of the man whom he had to succeed. Professor Andreas was a profound scholar and a man of European reputation. His lectures were frequented by students from every part of the world, and his admirable management of the collection entrusted to his care was a commonplace in all learned societies. There was, therefore, considerable surprise when, at the age of fifty-five, he suddenly resigned his position and retired from those duties which had been both his livelihood and his pleasure. He and his daughter left the comfortable suite of rooms which had formed his official residence in connection with the museum, and my friend, Mortimer, who was a bachelor, took up his quarters there.

On hearing of Mortimer's appointment, Professor Andreas had written him a very kindly and flattering congratulatory letter. I was actually present at their first meeting, and I went with Mortimer round the museum when the professor showed us the admirable collection which he had cherished so long. The professor's beautiful daughter and a young man, Captain Wilson, who was, as I understood, soon to be her husband, accompanied us in our inspection. There were fifteen rooms, but the Babylonian, the Syrian and the central hall, which contained the Jewish and Egyptian collection, were the finest of all. Professor Andreas was a quiet, dry, elderly man, with a clean-shaven face and an impassive manner, but his dark eyes sparkled and his features quickened into enthusiastic life as he pointed out to us the rarity and the beauty of some of his specimens. His hand lingered so fondly over them that one could read his pride in them and the grief in his heart now that they were passing from his care into that of another.

He had shown us in turn his mummies, his papyri, his rare scarabs, his inscriptions, his Jewish relics and his duplication of the famous seven-branched candlestick of the Temple, which was brought to Rome by Titus,* and which is supposed by some to be lying at this instant in the bed of the Tiber. Then he approached a case which stood in the very centre of the hall, and he looked down through the glass with reverence in his attitude and manner.

"This is no novelty to an expert like yourself, Mr Mortimer," said he, "but I dare say that your friend, Mr Jackson, will be interested to see it."

Leaning over the case I saw an object, some five inches square, which consisted of twelve precious stones in a framework of gold, with golden hooks at two of the corners. The stones were all varying in sort and colour, but they were of the same size. Their shapes, arrangement and gradation of tint made me think of a box of watercolour paints. Each stone had some hieroglyphic scratched upon its surface.

"You have heard, Mr Jackson, of the Urim and Thummim?"

I had heard the term, but my idea of its meaning was exceedingly vague.

"The Urim and Thummim was a name given to the jewelled plate which lay upon the breast of the high priest of the Jews. They had a very special feeling of reverence for it – something of the feeling which an ancient Roman might have for the Sibylline books* in the Capitol. There are, as you see, twelve magnificent stones, inscribed with mystical characters. Counting from the left-hand top corner, the stones are carnelian, peridot, emerald, ruby, lapis lazuli, onyx, sapphire, agate, amethyst, topaz, beryl and jasper."

I was amazed at the variety and beauty of the stones.

"Has the breastplate any particular history?" I asked.

"It is of great age and of immense value," said Professor Andreas. "Without being able to make an absolute assertion, we have many reasons to think that it is possible that it may be the original Urim and Thummim of Solomon's Temple.* There is certainly nothing so fine in any collection in Europe. My friend, Captain Wilson, here, is a practical authority upon precious stones, and he would tell you how pure these are."

Captain Wilson, a man with a dark, hard, incisive face, was standing beside his fiancée at the other side of the case.

"Yes," said he curtly, "I have never seen finer stones."

"And the goldwork is also worthy of attention. The ancients excelled in—" He was apparently about to indicate the setting of the stones, when Captain Wilson interrupted him.

"You will see a finer example of their goldwork in this candlestick," said he, turning to another table, and we all joined him in his admiration of its embossed stem and delicately ornamented branches. Altogether it was an interesting and a novel experience to have objects of such rarity explained by so great an expert; and when, finally, Professor Andreas finished our inspection by formally handing over the precious collection to the care of my friend, I could not help pitying him and envying his successor whose life was to pass in so pleasant a duty. Within a week, Ward Mortimer was duly installed in his new set of rooms, and had become the autocrat of the Belmore Street Museum.

About a fortnight afterwards my friend gave a small dinner to half a dozen bachelor friends to celebrate his promotion. When his guests were departing he pulled my sleeve and signalled to me that he wished me to remain.

"You have only a few hundred yards to go," said he – I was living in chambers in the Albany. "You may as well stay and have a quiet cigar with me. I very much want your advice."

I relapsed into an armchair and lit one of his excellent Matronas. When he had returned from seeing the last of his guests out, he drew a letter from his dress jacket and sat down opposite to me.

"This is an anonymous letter which I received this morning," said he. "I want to read it to you and to have your advice."

"You are very welcome to it for what it is worth."

"This is how the note runs: 'Sir, I should strongly advise you to keep a very careful watch over the many valuable things which are committed to your charge. I do not think that the present system of a single watchman is sufficient. Be upon your guard, or an irreparable misfortune may occur.'"

"Is that all?"

"Yes, that is all."

"Well," said I, "it is at least obvious that it was written by one of the limited number of people who are aware that you have only one watchman at night."

Ward Mortimer handed me the note, with a curious smile. "Have you an eye for handwriting?" said he. "Now, look at this!" He put another letter in front of me. "Look at the *c* in 'congratulate' and the *c* in 'committed'. Look at the capital *I*. Look at the trick of putting in a dash instead of a stop!"

"They are undoubtedly from the same hand – with some attempt at disguise in the case of this first one."

"The second," said Ward Mortimer, "is the letter of congratulation which was written to me by Professor Andreas upon my obtaining my appointment."

I stared at him in amazement. Then I turned over the letter in my hand, and there, sure enough, was "Martin Andreas" signed upon the other side. There could be no doubt, in the mind of anyone who had the slightest knowledge of the science of graphology, that the professor had written an anonymous letter, warning his successor against thieves. It was inexplicable, but it was certain.

"Why should he do it?" I asked.

"Precisely what I should wish to ask you. If he had any such misgivings, why could he not come and tell me direct?"

"Will you speak to him about it?"

"There again I am in doubt. He might choose to deny that he wrote it."

"At any rate," said I, "this warning is meant in a friendly spirit, and I should certainly act upon it. Are the present precautions enough to insure you against robbery?"

"I should have thought so. The public are only admitted from ten till five, and there is a guardian to every two rooms. He stands at the door between them, and so commands them both."

"But at night?"

"When the public are gone, we at once put up the great iron shutters, which are absolutely burglar-proof. The watchman is a capable fellow. He sits in the lodge, but he walks round every three hours. We keep one electric light burning in each room all night."

"It is difficult to suggest anything more – short of keeping your day watchers all night."

"We could not afford that."

"At least, I should communicate with the police, and have a special constable put on outside in Belmore Street," said I. "As to the letter, if the writer wishes to be anonymous, I think he has a right to remain so. We must trust to the future to show some reason for the curious course which he has adopted."

So we dismissed the subject, but all that night after my return to my chambers I was puzzling my brain as to what possible motive Professor Andreas could have for writing an anonymous warning letter to his successor – for that the writing was his was as certain to me as if I had seen him actually doing it. He foresaw some danger to the collection. Was it because he foresaw it that he abandoned his charge of it? But if so, why should he hesitate to warn Mortimer in his own name? I puzzled and puzzled until at last I fell into a troubled sleep, which carried me beyond my usual hour of rising.

I was aroused in a singular and effective method, for about nine o'clock my friend Mortimer rushed into my room with an expression of consternation upon his face. He was usually one of the most tidy men of my acquaintance, but now his collar was undone at one end, his tie was flying and his hat at the back of his head. I read his whole story in his frantic eyes.

"The museum has been robbed!" I cried, springing up in bed.

"I fear so! Those jewels! The jewels of the Urim and Thummim!" he gasped, for he was out of breath with running. "I'm going on to the police station. Come to the museum as soon as you can, Jackson! Goodbye!" He rushed distractedly out of the room, and I heard him clatter down the stairs.

I was not long in following his directions, but I found when I arrived that he had already returned with a police inspector, and another elderly gentleman, who proved to be Mr Purvis, one of the partners of Morson & Company, the well-known diamond merchants. As an expert in stones he was always prepared to advise the police. They were grouped round the case in which the breastplate of the Jewish priest had been exposed. The plate had been taken out and laid upon the glass top of the case, and the three heads were bent over it.

"It is obvious that it has been tampered with," said Mortimer. "It caught my eye the moment that I passed through the room this morning. I examined it yesterday evening, so that it is certain that this has happened during the night."

It was, as he had said, obvious that someone had been at work upon it. The settings of the uppermost row of four stones – the carnelian, peridot, emerald and ruby – were rough and jagged as if someone had scraped all round them. The stones were in their places, but the beautiful goldwork which we had admired only a few days before had been very clumsily pulled about.

"It looks to me," said the police inspector, "as if someone had been trying to take out the stones."

"My fear is," said Mortimer, "that he not only tried, but succeeded. I believe these four stones to be skilful imitations which have been put in the place of the originals."

The same suspicion had evidently been in the mind of the expert, for he had been carefully examining the four stones with the aid of a lens. He now submitted them to several tests, and finally turned cheerfully to Mortimer.

"I congratulate you, sir," said he heartily. "I will pledge my reputation that all four of these stones are genuine, and of a most unusual degree of purity."

The colour began to come back to my poor friend's frightened face, and he drew a long breath of relief.

"Thank God!" he cried. "Then what in the world did the thief want?"

"Probably he meant to take the stones, but was interrupted."

"In that case one would expect him to take them out one at a time, but the setting of each of these has been loosened, and yet the stones are all here."

"It is certainly most extraordinary," said the inspector. "I never remember a case like it. Let us see the watchman."

The commissionaire was called – a soldierly, honest-faced man, who seemed as concerned as Ward Mortimer at the incident.

"No, sir, I never heard a sound," he answered, in reply to the questions of the inspector. "I made my rounds four times, as usual, but I saw nothing suspicious. I've been in my position ten years, but nothing of the kind has ever occurred before."

"No thief could have come through the windows?"

"Impossible, sir."

"Or passed you at the door?"

"No, sir; I never left my post except when I walked my rounds."

"What other openings are there in the museum?"

"There is the door into Mr Ward Mortimer's private rooms."

"That is locked at night," my friend explained, "and in order to reach it anyone from the street would have to open the outside door as well."

"Your servants?"

"Their quarters are entirely separate."

"Well, well," said the inspector, "this is certainly very obscure. However, there has been no harm done, according to Mr Purvis."

"I will swear that those stones are genuine."

"So that the case appears to be merely one of malicious damage. But nonetheless, I should be very glad to go carefully round the premises, and to see if we can find any trace to show us who your visitor may have been."

His investigation, which lasted all the morning, was careful and intelligent, but it led in the end to nothing. He pointed out to us that there were two possible entrances to the museum which we had not considered. The one was from the cellars by a trapdoor opening in the passage. The other through a skylight from the lumber room, overlooking that very chamber to which the intruder had penetrated. As neither the cellar nor the lumber room could be entered unless the thief was already within the locked doors, the matter was not of any practical importance, and the dust of cellar and attic assured us that no one had used either one or the other. Finally we ended as we began, without the slightest clue as to how, why or by whom the setting of these four jewels had been tampered with.

There remained one course for Mortimer to take, and he took it. Leaving the police to continue their fruitless researches, he asked me to accompany him that afternoon in a visit to Professor Andreas. He took with him the two letters, and it was his intention to openly tax his predecessor with having written the anonymous warning, and to ask him to explain the fact that he should have anticipated so exactly that which had actually occurred. The professor was living in a small villa in Upper Norwood, but we were informed by the servant that he was away from home. Seeing our disappointment, she asked us if we should like to see Miss Andreas, and showed us into the modest drawing room.

I have mentioned incidentally that the professor's daughter was a very beautiful girl. She was a blonde, tall and graceful, with a skin of that delicate tint which the French call *mat*, the colour of old ivory, or of the lighter petals of the sulphur rose. I was shocked, however, as she entered the room to see how much she had changed in the last fortnight. Her young face was haggard and her bright eyes heavy with trouble.

"Father has gone to Scotland," she said. "He seems to be tired, and has had a good deal to worry him. He only left us yesterday."

"You look a little tired yourself, Miss Andreas," said my friend.

"I have been so anxious about father."

"Can you give me his Scotch address?"

"Yes, he is with his brother, the Revd David Andreas, 1 Arran Villas, Ardrossan."

Ward Mortimer made a note of the address, and we left without saying anything as to the object of our visit. We found ourselves in Belmore Street in the evening in exactly the same position in which we had been in the morning. Our only clue was the professor's letter, and my friend had made up his mind to start for Ardrossan next day, and to get to the bottom of the anonymous letter, when a new development came to alter our plans.

Very early on the following morning I was aroused from my sleep by a tap upon my bedroom door. It was a messenger with a note from Mortimer.

"Do come round," it said. "The matter is becoming more and more extraordinary."

When I obeyed his summons I found him pacing excitedly up and down the central room, while the old soldier who guarded the premises stood with military stiffness in a corner.

"My dear Jackson," he cried, "I am so delighted that you have come, for this is a most inexplicable business."

"What has happened, then?"

He waved his hand towards the case which contained the breastplate.

"Look at it," said he.

I did so, and could not restrain a cry of surprise. The setting of the middle row of precious stones had been profaned in the same manner as the upper ones. Of the twelve jewels eight had been now tampered with in this singular fashion. The setting of the lower four was neat and smooth. The others jagged and irregular.

"Have the stones been altered?" I asked.

"No, I am certain that these upper four are the same which the expert pronounced to be genuine, for I observed yesterday that little discoloration on the edge of the emerald. Since they have not extracted the upper stones, there is no reason to think the lower have been transposed. You say that you heard nothing, Simpson?"

"No, sir," the commissionaire answered. "But when I made my round after daylight I had a special look at these stones, and I saw at once that someone had been meddling with them. Then I called you, sir, and told you. I was backwards and forwards all the night, and I never saw a soul or heard a sound."

"Come up and have some breakfast with me," said Mortimer, and he took me into his own chambers. "Now, what *do* you think of this, Jackson?" he asked.

"It is the most objectless, futile, idiotic business that ever I heard of. It can only be the work of a monomaniac."

"Can you put forward any theory?"

A curious idea came into my head. "This object is a Jewish relic of great antiquity and sanctity," said I. "How about the anti-Semitic movement? Could one conceive that a fanatic of that way of thinking might desecrate—"

"No, no, no!" cried Mortimer. "That will never do! Such a man might push his lunacy to the length of destroying a Jewish relic, but why on earth should he nibble round every stone so carefully that he can only do four stones in a night? We must have a better solution than that, and we must find it for ourselves, for I do not think that our inspector is likely to help us. First of all, what do you think of Simpson, the porter?"

"Have you any reason to suspect him?"

"Only that he is the one person on the premises."

"But why should he indulge in such wanton destruction? Nothing has been taken away. He has no motive."

"Mania?"

"No, I will swear to his sanity."

"Have you any other theory?"

"Well, yourself, for example. You are not a somnambulist, by any chance?"

"Nothing of the sort, I assure you."

"Then I give it up."

"But I don't – and I have a plan by which we will make it all clear."

"To visit Professor Andreas?"

"No, we shall find our solution nearer than Scotland. I will tell you what we shall do. You know that skylight which overlooks the central hall? We will leave the electric lights in the hall, and we will keep watch in the lumber room, you and I, and solve the mystery for ourselves. If our mysterious visitor is doing four stones at a time, he has four still to do, and there is every reason to think that he will return tonight and complete the job."

"Excellent!" I cried.

"We will keep our own secret, and say nothing either to the police or to Simpson. Will you join me?"

"With the utmost pleasure," said I – and so it was agreed.

It was ten o'clock that night when I returned to the Belmore Street Museum. Mortimer was, as I could see, in a state of suppressed nervous excitement, but it was still too early to begin our vigil, so we remained for an hour or so in his chambers, discussing all the possibilities of the singular business which we had met to solve. At last the roaring stream of hansom cabs and the rush of hurrying feet became lower and more intermittent as the pleasure-seekers passed on their way to their stations or their homes. It was nearly twelve when Mortimer led the way to the lumber room which overlooked the central hall of the museum.

He had visited it during the day, and had spread some sacking so that we could lie at our ease, and look straight down into the museum. The skylight was of unfrosted glass, but was so covered with dust that it would be impossible for anyone looking up from below to detect that he was overlooked. We cleared a small piece at each corner, which gave us a complete view of the room beneath us. In the cold white light of the electric lamps everything stood out hard and clear, and I could see the smallest detail of the contents of the various cases.

Such a vigil is an excellent lesson, since one has no choice but to look hard at those objects which we usually pass with such half-hearted interest. Through my little peephole I employed the hours in studying every specimen, from the huge mummy case which leant against the wall to those very jewels which had brought us there, gleaming and sparkling in their glass case immediately beneath us. There was much precious goldwork and many valuable stones scattered through the numerous cases, but those wonderful twelve which made up the Urim and Thummim glowed and burned with a radiance which far eclipsed the others. I studied in turn the tomb pictures of Sicara, the friezes from Karnak,* the statues of Memphis and the inscriptions of Thebes, but my eyes would always come back to that wonderful Jewish relic, and my mind to the singular mystery which surrounded it. I was lost in the thought of it when my companion suddenly drew his breath sharply in, and seized my arm in a convulsive grip. At the same instant I saw what it was which had excited him.

I have said that against the wall – on the right-hand side of the doorway (the right-hand side as we looked at it, but the left as one entered) – there stood a large mummy case. To our unutterable amazement it was slowly opening. Gradually, gradually the lid was swinging back, and the black slit which marked the opening was becoming wider and wider. So gently and carefully was it done that the movement was almost imperceptible. Then, as we breathlessly watched it, a white thin hand appeared at the opening, pushing back the painted lid, then another hand, and finally a face – a face which was familiar to us both, that of Professor Andreas. Stealthily he slunk out of the mummy case, like a fox stealing from its burrow, his head turning incessantly to left and to right, stepping, then pausing, then stepping again, the very image of craft and of caution. Once some sound in the street struck him motionless, and he stood listening, with his ear turned, ready to dart back to the shelter behind him. Then he crept onwards again upon tiptoe, very, very softly and slowly, until he had reached the case in the centre of the room. There he took a bunch of keys from his pocket, unlocked the case, took out the Jewish breastplate, and, laying it upon the glass in front of him, began to work upon it with some sort of small, glistening tool. He was so directly underneath us that his bent head covered his work, but we could guess from the movement of his hand that he was engaged in finishing the strange disfigurement which he had begun.

I could realize from the heavy breathing of my companion, and the twitchings of the hand which still clutched my wrist, the furious indignation which filled his heart as he saw this vandalism in the quarter of all others where he could least have expected it. He, the very man who a fortnight before had reverently bent over this unique relic, and who had impressed its antiquity and its sanctity upon us, was now engaged in this outrageous profanation. It was impossible, unthinkable – and yet there, in the white glare of the electric light beneath us, was that dark figure with the bent grey head, and the twitching elbow. What inhuman hypocrisy, what hateful depth of malice against his successor must underlie these sinister nocturnal labours. It was painful to think of and dreadful to watch. Even I, who had none of the acute feelings of a virtuoso, could not bear to look on and see this deliberate mutilation of so ancient a relic. It was a relief to me when my companion tugged at my sleeve as a signal that I was to follow him as he softly crept out of the room. It was not until we were within his own quarters that he opened his lips, and then I saw by his agitated face how deep was his consternation.

"The abominable Goth!" he cried. "Could you have believed it?"

"It is amazing."

"He is a villain or a lunatic – one or the other. We shall very soon see which. Come with me, Jackson, and we shall get to the bottom of this black business."

A door opened out of the passage which was the private entrance from his rooms into the museum. This he opened softly with his key, having first kicked off his shoes, an example which I followed. We crept together through room after room, until the large hall lay before us, with that dark figure still stooping and working at the central case. With an advance as cautious as his own we closed in upon him, but softly as we went we could not take him entirely unawares. We were still a dozen yards from him when he looked round with a start and, uttering a husky cry of terror, ran frantically down the museum.

"Simpson! Simpson!" roared Mortimer, and far away down the vista of electric-lit doors we saw the stiff figure of the old soldier suddenly appear.

Professor Andreas saw him also, and stopped running, with a gesture of despair. At the same instant we each laid a hand upon his shoulder.

"Yes, yes, gentlemen," he panted, "I will come with you. To your room, Mr Ward Mortimer, if you please! I feel that I owe you an explanation."

My companion's indignation was so great that I could see that he dared not trust himself to reply. We walked on each side of the old professor, the astonished commissionaire bringing up the rear. When we reached the violated case, Mortimer stopped and examined the breastplate. Already one of the stones of the lower row had had its setting turned back in the same manner as the others. My friend held it up and glanced furiously at his prisoner.

"How could you!" he cried. "How could you!"

"It is horrible – horrible!" said the professor. "I don't wonder at your feelings. Take me to your room."

"But this shall not be left exposed!" cried Mortimer. He picked the breastplate up and carried it tenderly in his hand, while I walked beside the professor, like a policeman with a malefactor. We passed into Mortimer's chambers, leaving the amazed old soldier to understand matters as best he could. The professor sat down in Mortimer's armchair, and turned so ghastly a colour that for the instant all our resentment was changed to concern. A stiff glass of brandy brought the life back to him once more.

"There, I am better now!" said he. "These last few days have been too much for me. I am convinced that I could not stand it any longer. It is a nightmare – a horrible nightmare – that I should be arrested as a burglar in what has been for so long my own museum. And yet I cannot blame you. You could not have done otherwise. My hope always was that I should get it all over before I was detected. This would have been my last night's work."

"How did you get in?" asked Mortimer.

"By taking a very great liberty with your private door. But the object justified it. The object justified everything. You will not be angry when you know everything – at least, you will not be angry with me. I had a key to your side door and also to the museum door. I did not give them up when I left. And so you see it was not difficult for me to let myself into the museum. I used to come in early before the crowd had cleared from the street. Then I hid myself in the mummy case, and took refuge there whenever Simpson came round. I could always hear him coming. I used to leave in the same way as I came."

"You ran a risk."

"I had to."

"But why? What on earth was your object? *You* to do a thing like that!" Mortimer pointed reproachfully at the plate which lay before him on the table.

"I could devise no other means. I thought and thought, but there was no alternative except a hideous public scandal, and a private sorrow which would have clouded our lives. I acted for the best, incredible as it may seem to you, and I only ask your attention to enable me to prove it."

"I will hear what you have to say before I take any further steps," said Mortimer grimly.

"I am determined to hold back nothing, and to take you both completely into my confidence. I will leave it to your own generosity how far you will use the facts with which I supply you."

"We have the essential facts already."

"And yet you understand nothing. Let me go back to what passed a few weeks ago, and I will make it all clear to you. Believe me that what I say is the absolute and exact truth.

"You have met the person who calls himself Captain Wilson. I say 'calls himself' because I have reason now to believe that it is not his correct name. It would take me too long if I were to describe all the means by which he obtained an introduction to me and ingratiated himself into my friendship and the affection of my daughter. He brought letters from foreign colleagues which compelled me to show him some attention. And then, by his own attainments, which are considerable, he succeeded in making himself a very welcome visitor at my rooms. When I learnt that my daughter's affections had been gained by him, I may have thought it premature, but I certainly was not surprised, for he had a charm of manner and of conversation which would have made him conspicuous in any society.

"He was much interested in oriental antiquities, and his knowledge of the subject justified his interest. Often when he spent the evening with us he would ask permission to go down into the museum and have an opportunity of privately inspecting the various specimens. You can imagine that I, as an enthusiast, was in sympathy with such a request, and that I felt no surprise at the constancy of his visits. After his actual engagement to Elise, there was hardly an evening which he did not pass with us, and an hour or two were generally devoted to the museum. He had the free run of the place, and when I have been away for the evening I had no objection to his doing whatever he wished here. This state of things was only terminated by the fact of my resignation of my official duties and my retirement to Norwood, where I hoped to have the leisure to write a considerable work which I had planned.

"It was immediately after this – within a week or so – that I first realized the true nature and character of the man whom I had so imprudently introduced into my family. The discovery came to me through letters from my friends abroad, which showed me that his introductions to me had been forgeries. Aghast at the revelation, I asked myself what motive this man could originally have had in practising this elaborate deception upon me. I was too poor a man for any fortune-hunter to have marked me down. Why, then, had he come? I remembered that some of the most precious gems in Europe had been under my charge, and I remembered also the ingenious excuses by which this man had made himself familiar with the cases in which they were kept. He was a rascal who was planning some gigantic robbery. How could I, without striking my own daughter, who was infatuated about him, prevent him from carrying out any plan which he might have formed? My device was a clumsy one, and yet I could think of nothing more effective. If I had written a letter under my own name, you would naturally have turned to me for details which I did not wish to give. I resorted to an anonymous letter, begging you to be upon your guard.

"I may tell you that my change from Belmore Street to Norwood had not affected the visits of this man, who had, I believe, a real and overpowering affection for my daughter. As to her, I could not have believed that any woman could be so completely under the influence of a man as she was. His stronger nature seemed to entirely dominate her. I had not realized how far this was the case, or the extent of the confidence which existed between them, until that very evening when his true character for the first time was made clear to me. I had given orders that when he called he should be shown into my study instead of to the drawing room. There I told him bluntly that I knew all about him, that I had taken steps to defeat his designs, and that neither I nor my daughter desired ever to see him again. I added that I thanked God that I had found him out before he had time to harm those precious objects which it had been the work of my lifetime to protect.

"He was certainly a man of iron nerve. He took my remarks without a sign either of surprise or of defiance, but listened gravely and attentively until I had finished. Then he walked across the room without a word and struck the bell.

"'Ask Miss Andreas to be so kind as to step this way,' said he to the servant.

"My daughter entered, and the man closed the door behind her. Then he took her hand in his.

"'Elise,' said he, 'your father has just discovered that I am a villain. He knows now what you knew before.'

"She stood in silence, listening.

"'He says that we are to part for ever,' said he.

"She did not withdraw her hand.

"'Will you be true to me, or will you remove the last good influence which is ever likely to come into my life?'

"'John,' she cried passionately, 'I will never abandon you! Never, never, not if the whole world were against you.'

"In vain I argued and pleaded with her. It was absolutely useless. Her whole life was bound up in this man before me. My daughter, gentlemen, is all that I have left to love, and it filled me with agony when I saw how powerless I was to save her from her ruin. My helplessness seemed to touch this man who was the cause of my trouble.

"'It may not be as bad as you think, sir,' said he, in his quiet, inflexible way. 'I love Elise with a love which is strong enough to rescue even one who has such a record as I have. It was but yesterday that I promised her that never again in my whole life would I do a thing of which she should be ashamed. I have made up my mind to it, and never yet did I make up my mind to a thing which I did not do.'

"He spoke with an air which carried conviction with it. As he concluded he put his hand into his pocket and he drew out a small cardboard box.

"'I am about to give you a proof of my determination,' said he. 'This, Elise, shall be the first fruits of your redeeming influence over me. You are right, sir, in thinking that I had designs upon the jewels in your possession. Such ventures have had a charm for me, which depended as much upon the risk run as upon the value of the prize. Those famous and antique stones of the Jewish priest were a challenge to my daring and my ingenuity. I determined to get them.'

"'I guessed as much.'

"'There was only one thing that you did not guess.'

"'And what is that?'

"'That I got them. They are in this box.'

"He opened the box, and tilted out the contents upon the corner of my desk. My hair rose and my flesh grew cold as I looked. There were twelve magnificent square stones engraved with mystical characters. There could be no doubt that they were the jewels of the Urim and Thummim.

"'Good God!' I cried. 'How have you escaped discovery?'

"'By the substitution of twelve others, made especially to my order, in which the originals are so carefully imitated that I defy the eye to detect the difference.'

"'Then the present stones are false?' I cried.

"'They have been for some weeks.'

"We all stood in silence, my daughter white with emotion, but still holding this man by the hand.

"'You see what I am capable of, Elise,' said he.

"'I see that you are capable of repentance and restitution,' she answered.

"'Yes, thanks to your influence! I leave the stones in your hands, sir. Do what you like about it. But remember that whatever you do against me, is done against the future husband of your only daughter. You will hear from me soon again, Elise. It is the last time that I will ever cause pain to your tender heart' – and with these words he left both the room and the house.

"My position was a dreadful one. Here I was with these precious relics in my possession, and how could I return them without a scandal and an exposure? I knew the depth of my daughter's nature too well to suppose that I would ever be able to detach her from this man now that she had entirely given him her heart. I was not even sure how far it was right to detach her if she had such an ameliorating influence over him. How could I expose him without injuring her – and how far was I justified in exposing him when he had voluntarily put himself into my power? I thought and thought until at last I formed a resolution which may seem to you to be a foolish one, and yet, if I had to do it again, I believe it would be the best course open to me.

"My idea was to return the stones without anyone being the wiser. With my keys I could get into the museum at any time, and I was confident that I could avoid Simpson, whose hours and methods were familiar to me. I determined to take no one into my confidence – not even my daughter – whom I told that I was about to visit my brother in Scotland. I wanted a free hand for a few nights, without enquiry as to my comings and goings. To this end I took a room in Harding Street that very night, with an intimation that I was a pressman, and that I should keep very late hours.

"That night I made my way into the museum, and I replaced four of the stones. It was hard work, and took me all night. When Simpson came round I always heard his footsteps, and concealed myself in the mummy case. I had some knowledge of goldwork, but was far less skilful than the thief had been. He had replaced the setting so exactly that I defy anyone to see the difference. My work was rude and clumsy. However, I hoped that the plate might not be carefully examined, or the roughness of the setting observed, until my task was done. Next night I replaced four more stones. And tonight I should have finished my task had it not been for the unfortunate circumstance which has caused me to reveal so much which I should have wished to keep concealed. I appeal to you, gentlemen, to your sense of honour and of compassion, whether what I have told you should go any farther or not. My own happiness, my daughter's future, the hopes of this man's regeneration, all depend upon your decision."

"Which is," said my friend, "that all is well that ends well and that the whole matter ends here and at once. Tomorrow the loose settings shall be tightened by an expert goldsmith, and so passes the greatest danger to which, since the destruction of the Temple, the Urim and Thummim has been exposed. Here is my hand, Professor Andreas, and I can only hope that under such difficult circumstances I should have carried myself as unselfishly and as well."

Just one footnote to this narrative. Within a month Elise Andreas was married to a man whose name, had I the indiscretion to mention it, would appeal to my readers as one who is now widely and deservedly honoured. But if the truth were known, that honour is due not to him, but to the gentle girl who plucked him back when he had gone so far down that dark road along which few return.

The Nightmare Room

The sitting room of the Masons was a very singular apartment. At one end it was furnished with considerable luxury. The deep sofas, the low, luxurious chairs, the voluptuous statuettes and the rich curtains hanging from deep and ornamental screens of metalwork made a fitting frame for the lovely woman who was the mistress of the establishment. Mason, a young but wealthy man of affairs, had clearly spared no pains and no expense to meet every want and every whim of his beautiful wife. It was natural that he should do so, for she had given up much for his sake. The most famous dancer in France, the heroine of a dozen extraordinary romances, she had resigned her life of glittering pleasure in order to share the fate of the young American, whose austere ways differed so widely from her own. In all that wealth could buy he tried to make amends for what she had lost. Some might perhaps have thought it in better taste had he not proclaimed this fact – had he not even allowed it to be printed – but save for some personal peculiarities of the sort, his conduct was that of a husband who has never for an instant ceased to be a lover. Even the presence of spectators would not prevent the public exhibition of his overpowering affection.

But the room was singular. At first it seemed familiar, and yet a longer acquaintance made one realize its sinister peculiarities. It was silent – very silent. No footfall could be heard upon those rich carpets and heavy rugs. A struggle – even the fall of a body – would make no sound. It was strangely colourless also, in a light which seemed always subdued. Nor was it all furnished in equal taste. One would have said that when the young banker had lavished thousands upon this boudoir, this inner jewel case for his precious possession, he had failed to count the cost and had suddenly been arrested by a threat to his own solvency. It was luxurious where it looked out upon the busy street below. At the farther side it was bare, spartan, and reflected rather the taste of a most ascetic man than of a pleasure-loving woman. Perhaps that was why she only came there for a few hours, sometimes two, sometimes four, in the day, but while she was there she lived intensely, and within this nightmare room Lucille Mason was a very different and a more dangerous woman than elsewhere.

Dangerous – that was the word. Who could doubt it who saw her delicate figure stretched upon the great bearskin which draped the sofa. She was leaning upon her right elbow, her delicate but determined chin resting upon her hand, while her eyes, large and languishing, adorable but inexorable, stared out in front of her with a fixed intensity which had in it something vaguely terrible. It was a lovely face – a child's face – and yet Nature had placed there some subtle mark, some indefinable expression, which told that a devil lurked within. It had been noticed that dogs shrank from her, and that children screamed and ran from her caresses. There are instincts which are deeper than reason.

Upon this particular afternoon something had greatly moved her. A letter was in her hand, which she read and reread with a tightening of those delicate little eyebrows and a grim setting of those delicious lips. Suddenly she started, and a shadow of fear softened the feline menace of her features. She raised herself upon her arm, and her eyes were fixed eagerly upon the door. She was listening intently – listening for something which she dreaded. For a moment a smile of relief played over her expressive face. Then with a look of horror she stuffed her letter into her dress. She had hardly done so before the door opened, and a young man came briskly into the room. It was Archie Mason, her husband – the man whom she had loved, the man for whom she had sacrificed her European fame, the man whom now she regarded as the one obstacle to a new and wonderful experience.

The American was a man about thirty, clean-shaven, athletic, dressed to perfection in a closely cut suit, which outlined his perfect figure. He stood at the door with his arms folded, looking intently at his wife, with a face which might have been a handsome, sun-tinted mask save for those vivid eyes. She still leant upon her elbow, but her eyes were fixed on his. There was something terrible in the silent exchange. Each interrogated the other, and each conveyed the thought that the answer to their question was vital. He might have been asking, "What have you done?" She in her turn seemed to be saying, "What do you know?" Finally, he walked forward, sat down upon the bearskin beside her and, taking her delicate ear gently between his fingers, turned her face towards his.

"Lucille," he said, "are you poisoning me?"

She sprang back from his touch with horror in her face and protests upon her lips. Too moved to speak, her surprise and her anger showed themselves rather in her darting hands and her convulsed features. She tried to rise, but his grasp tightened upon her wrist. Again he asked a question, but this time it had deepened in its terrible significance.

"Lucille, why are you poisoning me?"

"You are mad, Archie! Mad!" she gasped.

His answer froze her blood. With pale parted lips and blanched cheeks she could only stare at him in helpless silence, whilst he drew a small bottle from his pocket and held it before her eyes.

"It is from your jewel case!" he cried.

Twice she tried to speak and failed. At last the words came slowly one by one from her contorted lips:

"At least I never used it."

Again his hand sought his pocket. From it he drew a sheet of paper, which he unfolded and held before her.

"It is the certificate of Dr Angus. It shows the presence of twelve grains of antimony. I have also the evidence of Du Val, the chemist who sold it."

Her face was terrible to look at. There was nothing to say. She could only lie with that fixed hopeless stare like some fierce creature in a fatal trap.

"Well?" he asked.

There was no answer save a movement of desperation and appeal.

"Why?" he said. "I want to know why." As he spoke his eye caught the edge of the letter which she had thrust into her bosom. In an instant he had snatched it. With a cry of despair she tried to regain it, but he held her off with one hand while his eyes raced over it.

"Campbell!" he gasped. "It was Campbell!"

She had found her courage again. There was nothing more to conceal. Her face set hard and firm. Her eyes were deadly as daggers.

"Yes," she said, "it is Campbell."

"My God! Campbell of all men!"

He rose and walked swiftly about the room. Campbell, the grandest man that he had ever known, a man whose whole life had been one long record of self-denial, of courage, of every quality which marks the chosen man. And yet, he, too, had fallen a victim to this siren, and had been dragged down to such a level that he had betrayed, in intention if not in actual deed, the man whose hand he shook in friendship. It was incredible – and yet here was the passionate, pleading letter imploring his wife to fly and share the fate of a penniless man. Every word of the letter showed that Campbell had at least no thought of Mason's death, which would have removed all difficulties. That devilish solution was the outcome of the deep and wicked brain which brooded within that perfect habitation.

Mason was a man in a million, a philosopher, a thinker, with a broad and tender sympathy for others. For an instant his soul had been submerged in his bitterness. He could for that brief period have slain both his wife and Campbell, and gone to his own death with the serene mind of a man who has done his plain duty. But already, as he paced the room, milder thoughts had begun to prevail. How could he blame Campbell? He knew the absolute witchery of this woman. It was not only her wonderful physical beauty. She had a unique power of seeming to take an interest in a man, in writhing into his inmost conscience, in penetrating those parts of his nature which were too sacred for the world, and in seeming to stimulate him towards ambition and even towards virtue. It was just there that the deadly cleverness of her net was shown. He remembered how it had been in his own case. She was free then – or so he thought – and he had been able to marry her. But suppose she had not been free. Suppose she had been married. And suppose she had taken possession of his soul in the same way. Would he have stopped there? Would he have been able to draw off with his unfulfilled longings? He was bound to admit that with all his New England strength he could not have done so. Why, then, should he feel so bitter with his unfortunate friend who was in the same position? It was pity and sympathy which filled his mind as he thought of Campbell.

And she? There she lay upon the sofa, a poor broken butterfly, her dreams dispersed, her plot detected, her future dark and perilous. Even for her, poisoner as she was, his heart relented. He knew something of her history. He knew her as a spoilt child from birth, untamed, unchecked, sweeping everything easily before her from her cleverness, her beauty and her charm. She had never known an obstacle. And now one had risen across her path, and she had madly and wickedly tried to remove it. But if she had wished to remove it, was not that in itself a sign that he had been found wanting – that he was not the man who could bring her peace of mind and contentment of heart? He was too stern and self-contained for that sunny volatile nature. He was of the North, and she of the South, drawn strongly together for a time by the law of opposites, but impossible for permanent union. He should have seen to this – he should have understood it. It was on him, with his superior brain, that the responsibility for the situation lay. His heart softened towards her as it would to a little child which was in helpless trouble. For a time he had paced the room in silence, his lips compressed, his hands clenched till his nails had marked his palms. Now with a sudden movement he sat beside her and took her cold and inert hand in his. One thought beat in his brain. "Is it chivalry, or is it weakness?" The question sounded in his ears, it framed itself before his eyes, he could almost fancy that it materialized itself and that he saw it in letters which all the world could read.

It had been a hard struggle, but he had conquered.

"You shall choose between us, dear," he said. "If really you are sure – *sure*, you understand – that Campbell could make you happy as a husband, I will not be the obstacle."

"A divorce!" she gasped.

His hand closed upon the bottle of poison. "You can call it that," said he.

A new strange light shone in her eyes as she looked at him. This was a man who had been unknown to her. The hard, practical American had vanished. In his place she seemed to have a glimpse of a hero, and a saint, a man who could rise to an inhuman height of unselfish virtue. Both her hands were round that which held the fatal phial.

"Archie," she cried, "you could forgive me even that!"

He smiled at her. "You are only a little wayward kiddie after all."

Her arms were outstretched to him when there was a tap at the door, and the maid entered in the strange silent fashion in which all things moved in that nightmare room. There was a card on the tray. She glanced at it.

"Captain Campbell! I will not see him."

Mason sprang to his feet.

"On the contrary, he is most welcome. Show him up this instant."

A few minutes later a tall, sunburnt young soldier had been ushered into the room. He came forward with a smile upon his pleasant features, but as the door closed behind him, and the faces before him resumed their natural expressions, he paused irresolutely and glanced from one to the other.

"Well?" he asked.

Mason stepped forward and laid his hand upon his shoulder.

"I bear no ill will," he said.

"Ill will?"

"Yes, I know all. But I might have done the same myself had the position been reversed."

Campbell stepped back and looked a question at the lady. She nodded and shrugged her graceful shoulders. Mason smiled.

"You need not fear that it is a trap for a confession. We have had a frank talk upon the matter. See, Jack, you were always a sportsman. Here's a bottle. Never mind how it came here. If one or other of us drink it, it would clear the situation." His manner was wild, almost delirious. "Lucille, which shall it be?"

There had been a strange force at work in the nightmare room. A third man was there, though not one of the three who had stood in the crisis of their life's drama had time or thought for him. How long he had been there – how much he had heard – none could say. In the corner farthest from the little group he lay crouched against the wall, a sinister snake-like figure, silent and scarcely moving save for a nervous twitching of his clenched right hand. He was concealed from view by a square case and by a dark cloth drawn cunningly above it, so as to screen his features. Intent, watching eagerly every new phase of the drama, the moment had almost come for his intervention. But the three thought little of that. Absorbed in the interplay of their own emotions they had lost sight of a force stronger than themselves – a force which might at any moment dominate the scene.

"Are you game, Jack?" asked Mason.

The soldier nodded.

"No! For God's sake, no!" cried the woman.

Mason had uncorked the bottle, and turning to the side table he drew out a pack of cards. Cards and bottle stood together.

"We can't put the responsibility on her," he said. "Come, Jack, the best of three."

The soldier approached the table. He fingered the fatal cards. The woman, leaning upon her hand, bent her face forward and stared with fascinated eyes.

Then and only then the bolt fell.

The stranger had risen, pale and grave.

All three were suddenly aware of his presence. They faced him with eager enquiry in their eyes. He looked at them coldly, sadly, with something of the master in his bearing.

"How is it?" they asked, all together.

"Rotten!" he answered. "Rotten! We'll take the whole reel once more tomorrow."

Note on the Texts

The texts in the present edition are reproduced from the first editions of *Tales of Twilight and the Unseen* (1922) and *Tales of Terror and Mystery* (1922). The spelling and punctuation have been standardized, modernized and made consistent throughout.

Notes

p. 5, *CB, KCSI*: Companion of the Order of the Bath and Knight Commander of the Order of the Star of India.

p. 9, *the Mutiny*: A reference to the revolt against British rule in India that occurred in 1857–58 and that resulted in the liquidation of the East India Company, which had ruled the subcontinent for a century, and the imposition of direct rule by the British Crown.

p. 12, *Peshawur*: City in the Punjab near the eastern end of the Khyber Pass, today located in north-western Pakistan, near the Afghan border. Usually spelt "Peshawar".

p. 12, *Kaffiristan*: A historic region of Afghanistan. Usually spelt "Kafiristan".

p. 12, *Pushtoo*: The native language of the Pashtun people of a region comprising parts of modern-day Afghanistan and Pakistan.

p. 21, *Selwyn*: Selwyn College, Cambridge.

p. 23, *Humanum est errare*: "To err is human" (Latin).

p. 25, *euchre*: A card game.

p. 45, *September the 13th*: Changed from "September the 14th" for consistency with the date given at the beginning of the story.

p. 48, *mauvais sujet*: "Bad person" (French).

p. 49, *Keinplatz wöchentliche Medicalschrift*: A fictional journal whose name translates as "Keinplatz weekly medical paper" (German).

p. 50, *Potztausend!*: "Upon my soul!" (German).

p. 51, *a Swedenborgian minister*: That is, a follower of the Swedish scientist and Christian mystic Emanuel Swedenborg (1688–1772).

p. 51, *the doctrines of the Rosy Cross*: That is, the teachings of Rosicrucianism, a seventeenth- and eighteenth-century occult sect said to have been founded by a fifteenth-century knight named Christian Rosenkreuz.

p. 52, *Tausend Teufel!*: "A thousand devils!" (German).

p. 52, *Where the Henker am I then*: "*Henker*" is the German for "hangman", but is also the equivalent of "hell" in expressions like "*Wo zum Henker…*" ("Where the hell…").

p. 53, *Grüner Mann*: "Green man" (German), here the name of an inn.

p. 54, *Donner und Blitzen!*: "Thunder and lightning!" (German).

p. 54, *Kellner*: "Waiter" (German).

p. 55, *Sie soll leben – hoch!*: Literally, "She should live – high!" (German), a toast.

p. 55, *Donnerwetter!*: "Thunderstorm!" (German), here the equivalent of "Damn!"

p. 56, *Gott in Himmel!*: "God in heaven!" (German).

p. 56, *Schinken*: "Ham" (German).

p. 60, *Gott sei gedanket!*: "Thank God!" (German).

p. 60, *pas de joie*: Literally, "step of joy" (French).

p. 60, *Uhlans*: Cavalrymen.

p. 61, *the nebular hypothesis*: The theory that the sun and the planets were formed from a vast cloud of dust and gas.

p. 62, *like the great Silas Wegg, I would drop into poetry*: In Charles Dickens's *Our Mutual Friend* (1865), Silas Wegg is a street vendor who is hired to read to the illiterate Mr Boffin after the latter has overheard Wegg reciting a ballad.

p. 62, *Calabar*: A port in West Africa, part of present-day Nigeria.

p. 62, *Bonny and Fernando Po*: The Kingdom of Bonny was a region of West Africa, part of present-day Nigeria. Fernando Póo is the former name of the island of Bioko off the West African coast, part of present-day Equatorial Guinea.

p. 63, *peruke wigs*: Periwigs, long wigs that became popular in England during the Restoration and remained an indicator of social rank during the seventeenth and eighteenth centuries.

p. 64, *Rory Random*: A reference to *The Adventures of Roderick Random* (1748), a picaresque novel by the Scottish writer Tobias Smollett (1721–71).

p. 64, *poor Robin on his island*: That is, Robinson Crusoe, identifying the speaker as pioneering novelist Daniel Defoe (1660–1731).

p. 64, *my Lord of Rochester*: John Wilmot, 2nd Earl of Rochester (1647–80), English poet and notorious libertine of the Restoration period, remembered for his satirical and often sexually explicit verse. Daniel Defoe held Rochester in great esteem, making several references to him and his poetry in his own works, notably in *Moll Flanders* (1722).

p. 64, *The Dickens it is!*: The remark qualifies as a pun (as it is subsequently identified) since the term "dickens" (usually lower case) is a euphemism for "devil", used in expressions such as "What the dickens" since at least the late sixteenth century.

p. 64, *Charley Lamb*: The English writer Charles Lamb (1775–1834), best known for *Tales from Shakespeare* (1807), written with his sister Mary (1764–1847).

p. 65, *the famous author of Gulliver*: Jonathan Swift (1667–1745), Irish author best known for the satirical and fantastical novel *Gulliver's Travels* (1726).

p. 65, *Fielding and Richardson... Laurence Sterne*: The English novelists Henry Fielding (1707–54), famous for the picaresque adventures *Joseph Andrews* (1742) and *Tom Jones* (1749), and Samuel Richardson (1689–1761), pioneer of the epistolary novel in *Pamela* (1740–41) and *Clarissa* (1747–48), and the Anglo-Irish writer Laurence Sterne (1713–68), best known for the humorous and experimental novel *The Life and Opinions of Tristram Shandy* (1759–67).

p. 65, *Sir Walter Scott... Thackeray*: The novelists Sir Walter Scott (1771–1832), who virtually invented historical fiction in books such as *Waverley* (1814), *Rob Roy* (1817) and *Ivanhoe* (1819), George Eliot (1819–80), whose real name was Mary Ann Evans and whose works – notably *Adam Bede* (1859) and *Middlemarch* (1871–72) – broke new ground in terms of psychological insight, and William Makepeace Thackeray (1811–63), best known for his satirical social panorama *Vanity Fair* (1847–48).

p. 65, *James Payn... Robert Louis Stevenson*: James Payn (1830–98) was an English journalist and novelist, famous during his lifetime as the author of novels such as *Lost Sir Massingberd* (1864) and *By Proxy* (1878). Sir Walter Besant (1836–1901) was an English historian and novelist best known for two works of social realism, *All Sorts and Conditions of Men* (1882) and *Children of Gibeon* (1886). In 1884 he was one of the founders of the Society of Authors. "Ouida" was the pen name of Marie Louise de la Ramée (1839–1908), the English author of popular, melodramatic novels such as *Under Two Flags* (1867). Robert Louis Stevenson (1850–94) was a Scottish writer, remembered for novels such as *Treasure Island* (1883), *The Strange Case of Dr Jekyll and Mr Hyde* (1886) and *Kidnapped* (1886).

p. 66, *the Dean*: Jonathan Swift, known as "Dean Swift" due to his position as dean of St Patrick's Cathedral, Dublin.

p. 66, *Barbary rover*: A pirate ship.

p. 67, *Captain Marryat*: Captain Frederick Marryat (1792–1848), officer in the Royal Navy and novelist. He is remembered for his sea stories, including *Mr Midshipman Easy* (1836), and his children's novel *The Children of the New Forest* (1847).

p. 68, *a Sentimental Journey... a dead donkey*: A reference to an episode in Laurence Sterne's novel *A Sentimental Journey through France and Italy* (1768) in which the narrator, Yorick, encounters a man mourning the death of his beloved donkey, which he believes died as a result of his own mistreatment of it.

p. 68, *Yahooland*: A reference to the Yahoos, a race of unpleasant and brutish beings in Swift's *Gulliver's Travels*.

p. 68, *Admiral Benbow*: John Benbow (1653–1702), officer in the Royal Navy.

p. 69, *a deadlight mounted on one side... of the Hard*: A deadlight is a protective cover for a porthole on a ship, the point being that the woman the sailor claims to have seen is wearing an eyepatch. The Hard is a street in Portsmouth.

p. 71, *stopping*: Changed from "sopping" for consistency with earlier printed versions of the story.

p. 71, *the Wizard of the North*: Sir Walter Scott became known as "the Wizard of the North" on account of the typically Scottish settings of his historical novels.

p. 71, *St Ursula of Alpuxerra*: Evidently Conan Doyle's invention. St Ursula (*fl.* fourth century) is a figure from British legend, who is said to have been martyred along with 11,000 virgins by the Huns near Cologne while on a pilgrimage to Rome. She has no connection with the region of Alpujarras in Andalusia, Spain.

p. 72, *caitiffly*: Contemptible, wretched.

p. 72, *glaive... curtel axe... morion*: A "glaive" is a sword. A "curtel axe" is a cutlass (not an axe). A "morion" was a helmet worn by soldiers in the sixteenth and seventeenth centuries.

p. 72, *Jack Cade*: The leader of a rebellion against Henry VI in 1450.
p. 72, *chine*: Backbone.
p. 72, *countering in carte, I returned in tierce*: Carte (or quarte) and tierce are two of the eight standard parries in fencing.
p. 73, *when the learned Alfred reigned in the land*: Alfred the Great (849–99), King of Wessex (an Anglo-Saxon kingdom in southern England) from 871 to 899, was remembered for his learning and promotion of literacy.
p. 73, *The impost and the anpost... hundred tax*: The terms "impost" and "anpost" are both anglicizations of the French "*impôt*" ("tax"), reflecting the fact that, in the England of the Middle Ages, administrative affairs were conducted in Norman French. The tithe was the ten per cent of earnings that traditionally were given to the Church. A "hundred" was a subdivision of a county or shire; the "hundred tax" was therefore a tax on landownership.
p. 74, *The Lady of Lyons*: A play by English novelist and dramatist Edward Bulwer-Lytton (1803–73).
p. 74, *when I was in India... speeches in the House*: During his life Bulwer-Lytton sat in both the House of Commons and the House of Lords, and was Secretary of State for the Colonies in the Earl of Derby's government between 1858 and 1859.
p. 74, *Rienzi, and Harold, and The Last of the Barons*: The novels *Rienzi, Last of the Roman Tribunes* (1835), *Harold, the Last of the Saxons* (1848) and *The Last of the Barons* (1843).
p. 74, *Macaulay*: The English historian Thomas Babington Macaulay (1800–59).
p. 74, *a brown bill*: A medieval weapon similar to a halberd.
p. 75, *the divine Ananke*: In Greek mythology, Ananke is one of the primordial deities, a group of ancient beings who are as old as the cosmos itself and from whom all other gods (including the Titans and the Olympians) are descended. She is the personification of fate and destiny, and the mate of Kronos, the god of time.
p. 77, *animal-magnetic force*: A reference to the mysterious emanation to which the German doctor Franz Anton Mesmer (1734–1815) attributed hypnosis.
p. 79, *I never saw a unicorn except beside the Royal Arms*: The Royal Coat of Arms of the United Kingdom features a unicorn, representing Scotland, as its "sinister supporter" (that is, a unicorn appears on the shield's left-hand side).

p. 79, *the Rosy Cross*: See second note to p. 51.

p. 80, *Hein?*: "Hey?" (French).

p. 89, *Thoth*: An Egyptian god of the moon, as well as of learning and writing.

p. 89, *FRS*: Fellow of the Royal Society.

p. 89, *El-Kab*: Site of ancient remains on the east bank of the Nile in Egypt.

p. 89, *Lepsius... Champollion*: Karl Richard Lepsius (1810–84) was a German Egyptologist, a follower of Jean-François Champollion (1790–1832), a French orientalist who was, in 1822, the first translator of the Rosetta Stone hieroglyphs.

p. 91, *Où est la collection de Memphis?*: "Where is the Memphis collection?" (French).

p. 91, *C'est là*: "It's over there" (French).

p. 91, *Vous êtes un Égyptien, n'est-ce pas?*: "You're an Egyptian, aren't you?" (French).

p. 91, *Non, monsieur: je suis français*: "No, sir: I am French" (French).

p. 92, *membrana nictitans*: The third eyelid present in birds and reptiles that protects the eye from dust and keeps it moist.

p. 94, *cerecloths*: Waxed cloths used for wrapping dead bodies.

p. 94, *Ma petite!... Ma pauvre petite!*: "My little one!... My poor little one!" (French).

p. 97, *Tuthmosis*: The name of the third, fourth, sixth and eighth pharaohs of the eighteenth dynasty, whose reigns spanned the period from 1493 BC to 1390 BC.

p. 97, *temple of Abaris... Bubastic branch of the Nile*: Abaris, usually "Avaris", was a city in the north-eastern Nile delta that was the capital of ancient Egypt during the Hyksos period (see next note). It was located on the easternmost branch of the Nile, referred to as "Bubastic" or "Bubastite" due to its proximity to the city of Bubastis.

p. 98, *the Hyksos*: A Semitic-Asiatic people who invaded Egypt during the eighteenth century BC, forming the fifteenth and sixteenth dynasties and ruling Lower Egypt from the city of Avaris. They were finally expelled when Avaris fell to Ahmose, the first pharaoh of the eighteenth dynasty, in 1521 BC. If, as the events in his account suggest, Sosra lived during the time of the invasion of the Hyksos, his earlier reference to the reign of a pharaoh named Tuthmosis, who came much later, is anachronistic.

p. 102, *the Boulak Museum at Cairo*: The Egyptian Museum of Antiquities was located in the Cairo district of Bulaq between 1858 and 1878. Today it is located on Tahrir Square.

p. 102, *Mariette Bey*: Auguste Mariette (1821–81), a French Egyptologist who became the Egyptian government's official conservator of monuments, thereby gaining a monopoly on archaeological excavation in the country. He was responsible for setting up the museum in Bulaq (see previous note). "Bey" is a courtesy title used in Egypt.

p. 103, *ouvriers*: "Workmen" (French).

p. 110, *the shell*: A rudimentary coffin.

p. 110, *euchred*: Outwitted.

p. 113, *Robur*: Likely an allusion to the science-fiction novel *Robur-le-Conquérant* (*Robur the Conqueror*) by Jules Verne (1828–1905), published in 1886, about the inventor of a world-beating flying machine.

p. 115, *Bloemfontein in the Boer War*: The failure of a conference in Bloemfontein, a city in present-day South Africa, led to the outbreak of the Second Boer War (1899–1902), fought between the British Empire and the independent Boer republics of the Transvaal and the Orange Free State. The Boers were Dutch and Huguenot colonists who settled in southern Africa in the seventeenth century.

p. 117, *Plantagenet days*: That is, the period from the accession of Henry II in 1154 to the death of Richard III in 1485.

p. 118, *single-sticks*: Wooden, sword-length sticks used in fencing.

p. 118, *the sculls*: A rowing race.

p. 119, *second cataract last long*: He is talking about the second cataract of the Nile, in the Nubia region, located in northern Sudan and southern Egypt. "Long" refers to the long vacation, the university's summer break.

p. 125, *natron*: A naturally occurring mineral salt harvested from dried lakebeds in ancient Egypt and used in mummification, among other things.

p. 129, *bird's-eye*: A variety of tobacco in which sections of the ribs of the leaf are visible, resembling birds' eyes.

p. 132, *pulling a steady thirty-six… with a jerky forty*: The numbers here refer to strokes per minute.

p. 137, *a blue pill*: The word "a" has been restored here, following earlier printed versions of the story. The term "blue pill" refers to a mercury-based medicine once used as a remedy for syphilis and constipation, among other ailments.

p. 147, *"De Profundis"*: "From the depths" (Latin), the first words of Psalm 130.

p. 147, *Peshawur, and Umballah, and Korti, and Fort Pearson*: For Peshawur, see first note to p. 12. Umballah, or Ambala, is a city in north-western India. Korti is a town in Sudan, the site of a British fort during the Anglo-Sudan War (1881–99). Fort Pearson in South Africa was built by the British officer Colonel Charles Pearson (1834–1909) during the Anglo-Zulu War (1879).

p. 148, *The learned... even labelled it with a name*: Presumably "telepathy", coined in 1882 by the English classical scholar Frederic W.H. Myers (1843–1901), one of the founders of the Society for Psychical Research (SPR).

p. 148, *before a single season... ingenuity ever won*: A reference to the outbreak of the fungus known as *Hemileia vastatrix* in British Ceylon (now Sri Lanka), which destroyed entirely the island's coffee plantations in just over a decade. In fact the disease first appeared in 1869, three years before the events of this story.

p. 152, *storm wrack*: Storm clouds.

p. 154, *Los Desertos*: The Desertas Islands, an archipelago fifteen miles off the eastern tip of Madeira.

p. 158, *the great latticed Tower*: Although later called "Northam", the location of the story is clearly Blackpool, a seaside resort in the north-west of England, whose famous tower was opened in 1894 and stands 158 metres tall.

p. 162, *Dixmude*: A city in Flanders that was the site of the Battle of the Yser in October 1914. Usually known in English as Diksmuide.

p. 166, *shambles*: A slaughterhouse.

p. 171, *RN*: Royal Navy.

p. 172, *the Aero Club*: Founded in 1901, the Aero Club of Great Britain, later the Royal Aero Club, was (and still is) the national coordinating body for competitive aviation.

p. 173, *Gnome or Green*: Early aircraft engines, produced respectively by the French company the Société des Moteurs Gnome and the British manufacturer the Green Engine Co.

p. 173, *Garros*: Roland Garros (1888–1918), a French aviator.

p. 174, *vol plané*: A steep dive.

p. 175, *Paul Veroner machine and its 175 Robur*: See note to p. 113.

p. 175, *Beaumont*: The pseudonym used by the French aviator Jean Louis Conneau (1880–1937).

p. 175, *talc goggles*: That is, goggles made from a translucent mineral such as talc.

p. 178, *tourbillon*: "Whirlwind" (French).

p. 179, *Glaisher... Coxwell*: James Glaisher (1809–1903) and Henry Tracey Coxwell (1819–1900), pioneering balloonists.

p. 180, *Mannheim glass*: Another detail apparently made up by the author.

p. 182, *vol piqué*: "Nosedive" (French).

p. 187, *Albertus Magnus*: St Albertus Magnus (*c.*1200–80) was a Dominican bishop as well as a philosopher and scientist. He was known as *doctor universalis* due to the breadth of his learning.

p. 188, *Nicolas de la Reynie*: Gabriel Nicolas de la Reynie (1625–1709), the first lieutenant general of the Paris police.

p. 188, *the draconic laws of that epoch*: A reference to the eradication of feudalism and the centralization of state power in the capital and the monarchy that took place during the reign of Louis XIV (1643–1715), a ruler who believed in royal absolutism and the divine right of kings.

p. 189, *the wars of the Frondists*: A reference to a rebellion by the French nobles in the period 1648–53, during the minority of Louis XIV, against the chief minister, Jules Mazarin (1602–61), and the court, which resulted in a series of civil wars. The rebels were referred to as "Frondists" or "the Fronde" in reference to a children's game in which stones were projected at the nobility using a slingshot (*fronde*).

p. 192, *le Roi-Soleil*: "The Sun King" (French), the nickname of Louis XIV.

p. 194, *Marie-Madeleine... Brinvilliers*: A historical figure, Marie-Madeleine-Marguerite d'Aubray, Marquise de Brinvilliers (*c.*1630–76), poisoned her father and two brothers in order to inherit their estates, and was tried and executed in the manner described in this story.

p. 197, *Baths of Caracalla*: Large public baths in ancient Rome, built between ad 212 and 216.

p. 199, *the Castle of St Angelo*: Castel Sant'Angelo, a cylindrical tower in Parco Adriano, Rome, built by the Emperor Hadrian (76–138 AD) as his personal mausoleum.

p. 200, *the Temple of the Vestals*: A circular temple in the Roman Forum dedicated to Vesta, the goddess of the hearth, in which a sacred fire was kept constantly alight and was attended to by the Vestal Virgins.

p. 201, *St John's clock*: A reference to the Papal Archbasilica of St John Lateran, Rome's cathedral church.

p. 204, *Catacombs of St Callixtus*: Named after Pope Callixtus I (d. 223) and famous for containing the Cappella dei Papi, the tombs of several early popes.
p. 204, *Cecilia Metella*: The Mausoleo di Cecilia Metella was built during the first century BC for Cecilia (or Caecilia) Metella, the daughter of a consul.
p. 210, *spud*: A small spade.
p. 212, *the Almohades*: A Berber Muslim dynasty that conquered the Almoravid empire in North Africa and Spain in the twelfth century.
p. 212, *Smyrna*: An ancient city in Asia Minor.
p. 213, *bistouries*: Surgical knives.
p. 215, *yashmak*: A veil worn by some Muslim women that covers the whole face.
p. 220, *Blue John Gap*: The real-life Blue John Cavern, near the village of Castleton in Derbyshire.
p. 236, *intoed*: That is, with toes pointing inwards.
p. 236, *Palladio pillars*: Designed in the manner of the Paduan architect Andrea Palladio (1508–80), who led a revival of classical architectural styles.
p. 239, *the Rio Negro*: A river in South America, a tributary of the Amazon, that flows through north-western Brazil.
p. 241, *the turf*: Horse racing.
p. 250, *Pernambuco*: A state in north-eastern Brazil.
p. 258, *parliamentary*: A railway service for which passengers were charged no more than one penny per mile, per the terms of the Railway Regulation Act of 1844.
p. 262, *when the impossible has been eliminated… the truth*: A dictum closely associated with Arthur Conan Doyle's most famous creation, Sherlock Holmes.
p. 262, *Camorra*: A criminal organization originating in Naples and resembling the Mafia.
p. 267, *fishplates*: Flat metal plates used to attach rails together on a railway line.
p. 271, *the Metropolitan station*: The Metropolitan Railway, which opened in 1863, was the forerunner of the London Underground.
p. 278, *scarabaei*: Beetles belonging to the genus *Scarabaeus*; dung beetles.
p. 278, *elytra*: The wing cases of a beetle.
p. 289, *Nihilistic propaganda*: A reference to the Russian Nihilist movement that developed in the second half of the nineteenth century, which

advocated the violent overthrow of the established order. Knowledge of its existence spread throughout Europe following the assassination of Tsar Alexander II in 1881.

p. 293, *bunco-steerer, green-goods man*: "Bunco-steerer" is an American slang term for a confidence trickster. A green-goods man was a swindler who would claim to be selling good-quality, "authentic" counterfeit money ("green goods"); he would then present his victim with a quantity of real cash, claiming it to be the forged variety, and sell it to him at what appeared to be a very low price. In reality, however, the real money would be switched for something worthless such as ordinary paper.

p. 293, *Tammany*: A notoriously corrupt organization within the US Democratic Party that dominated New York City politics in the nineteenth and early twentieth centuries. A "Tammany" became a byword for a corrupt political organization.

p. 293, *Lexow Commission*: An inquiry into police corruption in New York City led by the state senate in 1894–95. It was named after its chairman, Clarence Lexow (1852–1910).

p. 296, *pard*: Partner.

p. 297, *I don't care a continental*: That is, "I don't give a damn". A "continental" was a banknote issued by the Continental Congress during the American War of Independence. Its subsequent depreciation in value made it a byword for valuelessness.

p. 330, *seven-branched candlestick of the Temple... by Titus*: Before he became Roman Emperor, Titus (39–81 AD) led the campaign to suppress a rebellion against Roman rule in Judea known as the Great Jewish Revolt. In 70 AD, he captured Jerusalem and destroyed the Second Temple, the centre of Jewish worship, which stood on Temple Mount in the city and which had been built as a replacement for the original Temple after the release of the Israelites from the Babylonian Captivity in 538 BC. The holy candelabrum known as the Menorah, which was kept in the Temple, represented that built for the Tabernacle, the tent used to house the Ark of the Covenant by the Israelites during their wanderings in the wilderness and until the building of the First Temple. See Exodus 37.

p. 330, *Sibylline books*: A collection of prophecies supposedly made by the sibyls, women in the ancient world who were believed to have oracular powers. The last of the seven kings of Rome, Tarquinius Superbus (d. 495 BC), purchased the books from one of the sibyls, and thereafter they were kept in the temple of Jupiter on the Capitoline Hill in Rome, to be consulted only in times of crisis.

p. 330, *Solomon's Temple*: The first of the Jewish temples to have stood on Temple Mount in Jerusalem. It was built in the mid tenth century BC by Solomon, king of Israel (*c.*970–*c.*930 BC), and destroyed by the Babylonian king Nebuchadnezzar when he laid siege to Jerusalem in 586 BC.

p. 338, *Sicara... Karnak*: Saqqara was a burial ground in Memphis, the capital of ancient Egypt, containing numerous pyramids. Karnak is the site of extensive ruins of the ancient city of Thebes.